LAST SACRIFICE

LAST SACRIFICE

RICHELLE MEAD

razOr bill

Last Sacrifice

RAZORBILL

Published by the Penguin Group
Penguin Young Readers Group
345 Hudson Street, New York, New York 10014, U.S.A.
Penguin Group (USA) Inc., 375 Hudson Street, New York, New York 10014, U.S.A.
Penguin Group (Canada), 90 Eglinton Avenue East, Suite 700, Toronto, Ontario, Canada M4P 2Y3 (a division of Pearson Penguin Canada Inc.)
Penguin Books Ltd, 80 Strand, London WC2R 0RL, England
Penguin Ireland, 25 St Stephen's Green, Dublin 2, Ireland (a division of Penguin Books Ltd)
Penguin Group (Australia), 250 Camberwell Road, Camberwell, Victoria 3124, Australia (a division of Pearson Australia Group Pty Ltd)
Penguin Books India Pvt Ltd, 11 Community Centre, Panchsheel Park, New Delhi – 110 017, India
Penguin Group (NZ), 67 Apollo Drive, Mairangi Bay, Auckland 1311, New Zealand (a division of Pearson New Zealand Ltd)
Penguin Books (South Africa) (Pty) Ltd, 24 Sturdee Avenue, Rosebank, Johannesburg 2196, South Africa

Penguin Books Ltd, Registered Offices: 80 Strand, London WC2R 0RL, England

10 9 8 7 6 5 4 3 2 1

Razorbill hardcover ISBN: 9781595143068
Library of Congress Cataloging-in-Publication Data is available

Printed in the United States of America

Vampire Academy novels
by Richelle Mead:

Vampire Academy
Frostbite
Shadow Kiss
Blood Promise
Spirit Bound
Last Sacrifice

This is dedicated to Rich Bailey and Alan Doty, the teachers who had the greatest influence on my writing, and to all my teacher friends out there helping young writers now. Keep fighting the good fight, all of you.

ONE

I DON'T LIKE CAGES.

I don't even like going to zoos. The first time I went to one, I almost had a claustrophobic attack looking at those poor animals. I couldn't imagine any creature living that way. Sometimes I even felt a little bad for criminals, condemned to life in a cell. I'd certainly never expected to spend *my* life in one.

But lately, life seemed to be throwing me a lot of things I'd never expected, because here I was, locked away.

"Hey!" I yelled, gripping the steel bars that isolated me from the world. "How long am I going to be here? When's my trial? You can't keep me in this dungeon forever!"

Okay, it wasn't exactly a dungeon, not in the dark, rusty-chain sense. I was inside a small cell with plain walls, a plain floor, and well . . . plain everything. Spotless. Sterile. Cold. It was actually more depressing than any musty dungeon could have managed. The bars in the doorway felt cool against my skin, hard and unyielding. Fluorescent lighting made the metal gleam in a way that felt harsh and irritating to my eyes. I could see the shoulder of a man standing rigidly to the side of the cell's entrance and knew there were probably four more guardians in the hallway out of my sight. I also knew none of them were going to answer me back, but that hadn't stopped me from constantly demanding answers from them for the last two days.

When the usual silence came, I sighed and slumped back on the cot in the cell's corner. Like everything else in my new home, the cot was colorless and stark. Yeah. I really was starting to wish I had a real dungeon. Rats and cobwebs would have at least given me something to watch. I stared upward and immediately had the disorienting feeling I always did in here: that the ceiling and walls were closing in around me. Like I couldn't breathe. Like the sides of the cell would keep coming toward me until no space remained, pushing out all the air . . .

I sat up abruptly, gasping. *Don't stare at the walls and ceiling, Rose,* I chastised myself. Instead, I looked down at my clasped hands and tried to figure out how I'd gotten into this mess.

The initial answer was obvious: someone had framed me for a crime I didn't commit. And it wasn't petty crime either. It was murder. They'd had the audacity to accuse me of the highest crime a Moroi or dhampir could commit. Now, that isn't to say I haven't killed before. I have. I've also done my fair share of rule (and even law) breaking. Cold-blooded murder, however, was not in my repertoire. Especially not the murder of a queen.

It was true Queen Tatiana hadn't been a friend of mine. She'd been the coolly calculating ruler of the Moroi—a race of living, magic-using vampires who didn't kill their victims for blood. Tatiana and I had had a rocky relationship for a number of reasons. One was me dating her great-nephew, Adrian. The other was my disapproval of her policies on how to fight off

Strigoi—the evil, undead vampires who stalked us all. Tatiana had tricked me a number of times, but I'd never wanted her dead. Someone apparently had, however, and they'd left a trail of evidence leading right to me, the worst of which were my fingerprints all over the silver stake that had killed Tatiana. Of course, it was *my* stake, so naturally it'd have my fingerprints. No one seemed to think that was relevant.

I sighed again and pulled out a tiny crumpled piece of paper from my pocket. My only reading material. I squeezed it in my hand, having no need to look at the words. I'd long since memorized them. The note's contents made me question what I'd known about Tatiana. It had made me question a lot of things.

Frustrated with my own surroundings, I slipped out of them and into someone else's: my best friend Lissa's. Lissa was a Moroi, and we shared a psychic link, one that let me go to her mind and see the world through her eyes. All Moroi wielded some type of elemental magic. Lissa's was spirit, an element tied to psychic and healing powers. It was rare among Moroi, who usually used more physical elements, and we barely understood its abilities—which were incredible. She'd used spirit to bring me back from the dead a few years ago, and that's what had forged our bond.

Being in her mind freed me from my cage but offered little help for my problem. Lissa had been working hard to prove my innocence, ever since the hearing that had laid out all the evidence against me. My stake being used in the murder had only been the beginning. My opponents had been quick to remind everyone about my antagonism toward the queen and had also found a witness to testify about my whereabouts during the murder. That testimony had left me without an alibi. The Council had decided there was enough evidence to send me to a full-fledged trial—where I would receive my verdict.

Lissa had been trying desperately to get people's attention and convince them I'd been framed. She was having trouble finding anyone who would listen, however, because the entire Moroi Royal Court was consumed with preparations for Tatiana's elaborate funeral. A monarch's death was a big deal. Moroi and dhampirs—half-vampires like me—were coming from all over the world to see the spectacle. Food, flowers, decorations, even musicians . . . The full deal. If Tatiana had gotten married, I doubted the event would have been this elaborate. With so much activity and buzz, no one cared about me now. As far as most people were concerned, I was safely stashed away and unable to kill again. Tatiana's murderer had been found. Justice was served. Case closed.

Before I could get a clear picture of Lissa's surroundings, a commotion at the jail jerked me back into my own head. Someone had entered the area and was speaking to the guards, asking to see me. It was my first visitor in days. My heart pounded, and I leapt up to the bars, hoping it was someone who would tell me this had all been a horrible mistake.

My visitor wasn't *quite* who I'd expected.

"Old man," I said wearily. "What are you doing here?"

Abe Mazur stood before me. As always, he was a sight to behold. It was the middle of summer—hot and humid, seeing as we were right in the middle of rural Pennsylvania—but that didn't stop him from wearing a full suit. It was a flashy one, perfectly tailored and adorned with a brilliant purple silk tie and matching scarf that just seemed like overkill. Gold jewelry flashed against the dusky hue of his skin, and he looked like he'd recently trimmed his short black beard. Abe was a Moroi, and although he wasn't royal, he wielded enough influence to be.

He also happened to be my father.

"I'm your lawyer," he said cheerfully. "Here to give you legal counsel, of course."

"You aren't a lawyer," I reminded him. "And your last bit of advice didn't work out so well." That was mean of me. Abe—despite having no legal training whatsoever—had defended me at my hearing. Obviously, since I was locked up and headed for trial, the outcome of that hadn't been so great. But, in all my solitude, I'd come to realize that he'd been right about something. No lawyer, no matter how good, could have saved me at the hearing. I had to give him credit for stepping up to a lost cause, though considering our sketchy relationship, I still wasn't sure why he had. My biggest theories were that he didn't trust royals and that he felt paternal obligation. In that order.

"My performance was perfect," he argued. "Whereas your compelling speech in which you said 'if I was the murderer' didn't do us any favors. Putting that image in the judge's head wasn't the smartest thing you could have done."

I ignored the barb and crossed my arms. "So what are you

doing here? I know it's not just a fatherly visit. You never do anything without a reason."

"Of course not. Why do anything without a reason?"

"Don't start up with your circular logic."

He winked. "No need to be jealous. If you work hard and put your mind to it, you might just inherit my brilliant logic skills someday."

"Abe," I warned. "Get on with it."

"Fine, fine," he said. "I've come to tell you that your trial might be moved up."

"W-what? That's great news!" At least, I thought it was. His expression said otherwise. Last I'd heard, my trial might be months away. The mere thought of that—of being in this cell so long—made me feel claustrophobic again.

"Rose, you do realize that your trial will be nearly identical to your hearing. Same evidence and a guilty verdict."

"Yeah, but there must be something we can do before that, right? Find proof to clear me?" Suddenly, I had a good idea of what the problem was. "When you say 'moved up,' how soon are we talking?"

"Ideally, they'd like to do it after a new king or queen is crowned. You know, part of the post-coronation festivities."

His tone was flippant, but as I held his dark gaze, I caught the full meaning. Numbers rattled in my head. "The funeral's this week, and the elections are right after . . . You're saying I could go to trial and be convicted in, what, practically two weeks?"

Abe nodded.

I flew toward the bars again, my heart pounding in my chest. "*Two weeks*? Are you serious?"

When he'd said the trial had been moved up, I'd figured maybe it was a month away. Enough time to find new evidence. How would I have pulled that off? Unclear. Now, time was rushing away from me. Two weeks wasn't enough, especially with so much activity at Court. Moments ago, I'd resented the long stretch of time I might face. Now, I had too little of it, and the answer to my next question could make things worse.

"How long?" I asked, trying to control the trembling in my voice. "How long after the verdict until they . . . carry out the sentence?"

I still didn't entirely know what all I'd inherited from Abe, but we seemed to clearly share one trait: an unflinching ability to deliver bad news.

"Probably immediately."

"Immediately." I backed up, nearly sat on the bed, and then felt a new surge of adrenaline. "Immediately? So. Two weeks. In two weeks, I could be . . . dead."

Because that was the thing—the thing that had been hanging over my head the moment it became clear someone had planted enough evidence to frame me. People who killed queens didn't get sent to prison. They were *executed*. Few crimes among Moroi and dhampirs got that kind of punishment. We tried to be civilized in our justice, showing we were better than the bloodthirsty Strigoi. But certain crimes, in the eyes of the law, deserved death. Certain people deserved it, too—say, like, treasonous murderers. As the full impact of the future fell upon me, I felt myself shake and tears come dangerously close to spilling out of my eyes.

"That's not right!" I told Abe. "That's not right, and you know it!"

"Doesn't matter what I think," he said calmly. "I'm simply delivering the facts."

"Two weeks," I repeated. "What can we do in two weeks? I mean . . . you've got some lead, right? Or . . . or . . . you can find something by then? That's your specialty." I was rambling and knew I sounded hysterical and desperate. Of course, that was because I felt hysterical and desperate.

"It's going to be difficult to accomplish much," he explained. "The Court's preoccupied with the funeral and elections. Things are disorderly—which is both good and bad."

I knew about all the preparations from watching Lissa. I'd seen the chaos already brewing. Finding any sort of evidence in this mess wouldn't just be difficult. It could very well be impossible.

Two weeks. Two weeks, and I could be dead.

"I can't," I told Abe, my voice breaking. "I'm not . . . meant to die that way."

"Oh?" He arched an eyebrow. "You know how you're supposed to die?"

"In battle." One tear managed to escape, and I hastily wiped it away. I'd always lived my life with a tough image. I didn't want that shattering, not now when it mattered most of all. "In fighting. Defending those I love. Not . . . not through some planned execution."

"This is a fight of sorts," he mused. "Just not a physical one. Two weeks is still two weeks. Is it bad? Yes. But it's better than one week. And nothing's impossible. Maybe new evidence will turn up. You simply have to wait and see."

"I hate waiting. This room . . . it's so small. I can't breathe. It'll kill me before any executioner does."

"I highly doubt it." Abe's expression was still cool, with no sign of sympathy. Tough love. "You've fearlessly fought groups of Strigoi, yet you can't handle a small room?"

"It's more than that! Now I have to wait each day in this hole, knowing there's a clock ticking down to my death and almost no way to stop it."

"Sometimes the greatest tests of our strength are situations that don't seem so obviously dangerous. Sometimes surviving is the hardest thing of all."

"Oh. No. *No.*" I stalked away, pacing in small circles. "Do not start with all that noble crap. You sound like Dimitri when he used to give me his deep life lessons."

"He survived this very situation. He's surviving other things too."

Dimitri.

I took a deep breath, calming myself before I answered. Until this murder mess, Dimitri had been the biggest complication in my life. A year ago—though it seemed like eternity—he'd been my instructor in high school, training me to be one of the dhampir guardians who protect Moroi. He'd accomplished that—and a lot more. We'd fallen in love, something that wasn't allowed. We'd managed it as best we could, even finally coming up with a way for us to be together. That hope had disappeared when he'd been bitten and turned Strigoi. It had been a living nightmare for me. Then, through a miracle no one had believed possible, Lissa had used spirit to transform him back to a dhampir. But things unfortunately hadn't quite returned to how they'd been before the Strigoi attack.

I glared at Abe. "Dimitri survived this, but he was horribly depressed about it! He still is. About everything."

The full weight of the atrocities he'd committed as a Strigoi haunted Dimitri. He couldn't forgive himself and swore he could never love anyone now. The fact that I had begun dating Adrian didn't help matters. After a number of futile efforts, I'd accepted that Dimitri and I were through. I'd moved on, hoping I could have something real with Adrian now.

"Right," Abe said dryly. "He's depressed, but you're the picture of happiness and joy."

I sighed. "Sometimes talking to you is like talking to myself: pretty damned annoying. Is there any other reason you're here? Other than to deliver the terrible news? I would have been happier living in ignorance."

I'm not supposed to die this way. I'm not supposed to see it coming. My death is not some appointment penciled in on a calendar.

He shrugged. "I just wanted to see you. And your arrangements."

Yes, he had indeed, I realized. Abe's eyes had always come back to me as we spoke; there'd been no question I held his attention. There was nothing in our banter to concern my guards. But every so often, I'd see Abe's gaze flick around, taking in the hall, my cell, and whatever other details he found interesting. Abe had not earned his reputation as *zmey*—the serpent—for nothing. He was always calculating, always looking for an advantage. It seemed my tendency toward crazy plots ran in the family.

"I also wanted to help you pass the time." He smiled and from under his arm, he handed me a couple of magazines and a book through the bars. "Maybe this will improve things."

I doubted any entertainment was going to make my two-week death countdown more manageable. The magazines were fashion and hair oriented. The book was *The Count of Monte Cristo*. I held it up, needing to make a joke, needing to do anything to make this less real.

"I saw the movie. Your subtle symbolism isn't really all that subtle. Unless you've hidden a file inside it."

"The book's always better than the movie." He started to turn away. "Maybe we'll have a literary discussion next time."

"Wait." I tossed the reading material onto the bed. "Before you go . . . in this whole mess, no one's ever brought up who actually did kill her." When Abe didn't answer right away, I gave him a sharp look. "You *do* believe I didn't do it, right?" For all I knew, he did think I was guilty and was just trying to help anyway. It wouldn't have been out of character.

"I believe my sweet daughter is capable of murder," he said at last. "But not this one."

"Then who did it?"

"That," he said before walking away, "is something I'm working on."

"But you just said we're running out of time! Abe!" I didn't want him to leave. I didn't want to be alone with my fear. "There's no way to fix this!"

"Just remember what I said in the courtroom," he called back.

He left my sight, and I sat back on the bed, thinking back to that day in court. At the end of the hearing, he'd told me—quite adamantly—that I wouldn't be executed. Or even go to trial. Abe Mazur wasn't one to make idle promises, but I was starting to think that even he had limits, especially since our timetable had just been adjusted.

I again took out the crumpled piece of paper and opened it. It too had come from the courtroom, covertly handed to me by Ambrose—Tatiana's servant and boy-toy.

Rose,

If you're reading this, then something terrible has happened. You probably hate me, and I don't blame you. I can only ask that you trust that what I did with the age decree was better for your people than what others had planned. There are some Moroi who want to force all *dhampirs into service, whether they want it or not, by using compulsion. The age decree has slowed that faction down.*

However, I write to you with a secret you must put right, and it is a secret you must share with as few as possible. Vasilisa needs her spot on the Council, and it can be done. She is not the last Dragomir. Another lives, the illegitimate child of Eric Dragomir. I know nothing else, but if you can find this son or daughter, you will give Vasilisa the power she deserves. No matter your faults and dangerous temperament, you are the only one I feel can take on this task. Waste no time in fulfilling it.

—Tatiana Ivashkov

The words hadn't changed since the other hundred times I'd read them, nor had the questions they always triggered. Was the note true? Had Tatiana really written it? Had she—in spite of her outwardly hostile attitude—trusted me with this dangerous knowledge? There were twelve royal families who made decisions for the Moroi, but for all intents and purposes, there might as well have only been eleven. Lissa was the last of her line, and without another member of the Dragomir family, Moroi law said she had no power to sit on and vote with the Council that made our decisions. Some pretty bad laws had already been made, and if the note was true, more would come. Lissa could fight those laws—and some people wouldn't like that, people who had already demonstrated their willingness to kill.

Another Dragomir.

Another Dragomir meant Lissa could vote. One more Council vote could change so much. It could change the Moroi world. It could change my world—say, like, whether I was found guilty or not. And certainly, it could change Lissa's world. All this time she'd believed she was alone. Yet . . . I uneasily wondered if she'd welcome a half-sibling. I accepted that my father was a scoundrel, but Lissa had always held hers up on a pedestal, believing the best of him. This news would come as a shock, and although I'd trained my entire life to keep her safe from physical threats, I was starting to think there were other things she needed to be protected from as well.

But first, *I* needed the truth. I had to know if this note had really come from Tatiana. I was pretty sure I could find out, but it involved something I hated doing.

Well, why not? It wasn't like I had anything else to do right now.

Rising from the bed, I turned my back to the bars and stared at the blank wall, using it as a focus point. Bracing myself, remembering that I was strong enough to keep control, I released the mental barriers I always subconsciously kept around my mind. A great pressure lifted from me, like air escaping a balloon.

And suddenly, I was surrounded by ghosts.

TWO

AS ALWAYS, IT WAS DISORIENTING. Faces and skulls, translucent and luminescent, all hovered around me. They were drawn to me, swarming in a cloud as though they all desperately needed to say something. And really, they probably did. The ghosts that lingered in this world were restless, souls who had reasons that kept them from moving on. When Lissa had brought me back from the dead, I'd kept a connection to their world. It had taken a lot of work and self-control to learn to block out the phantoms that followed me. The magical wards that protected the Moroi Court actually kept most ghosts away from me, but this time, I wanted them here. Giving them that access, drawing them in . . . well, it was a dangerous thing.

Something told me that if ever there was a restless spirit, it would be a queen who had been murdered in her own bed. I saw no familiar faces among this group but didn't give up hope.

"Tatiana," I murmured, focusing my thoughts on the dead queen's face. "Tatiana, come to me."

I had once been able to summon one ghost easily: my friend Mason, who'd been killed by Strigoi. While Tatiana and I weren't as close as Mason and I had been, we certainly had a connection. For a while, nothing happened. The same blur of faces swirled before me in the cell, and I began to despair. Then, all of a sudden, she was there.

She stood in the clothes she'd been murdered in, a long nightgown and robe covered in blood. Her colors were muted, flickering like a malfunctioning TV screen. Nonetheless, the crown on her head and regal stance gave her the same queenly air I remembered. Once she materialized, she said and did nothing. She simply stared at me, her dark gaze practically piercing my soul. A tangle of emotions tightened in my chest. That gut reaction I always got around Tatiana—anger and resentment—flared up. Then, it was muddled by a surprising wave of sympathy. No one's life should end the way hers had.

I hesitated, afraid the guards would hear me. Somehow, I had a feeling the volume of my voice didn't matter, and none of them could see what I saw. I held up the note.

"Did you write this?" I breathed. "Is it true?"

She continued to stare. Mason's ghost had behaved similarly. Summoning the dead was one thing; communicating with them was a whole other matter.

"I have to know. If there is another Dragomir, I'll find them." No point in drawing attention to the fact that I was in no position to find anything or anyone. "But you have to tell me. Did you write this letter? Is it true?"

Only that maddening gaze answered me. My frustration grew, and the pressure of all those spirits began to give me a headache. Apparently, Tatiana was as annoying in death as she had been in life.

I was about to bring my walls back and push the ghosts away when Tatiana made the smallest of movements. It was a tiny nod, barely noticeable. Her hard eyes then shifted down to the note in my hand, and just like that—she was gone.

I slammed my barriers back up, using all my will to close myself off from the dead. The headache didn't disappear, but those faces did. I sank back on the bed and stared at the note without seeing it. There was my answer. The note was real. Tatiana had written it. Somehow, I doubted her ghost had any reason to lie.

Stretching out, I rested my head on the pillow and waited for that terrible throbbing to go away. I closed my eyes and used the spirit bond to return and see what Lissa had been doing. Since my arrest, she'd been busy pleading and arguing on my behalf, so I expected to find more of the same. Instead she was . . . dress shopping.

I was almost offended at my best friend's frivolity until I realized she was looking for a funeral dress. She was in one of the Court's tucked away stores, one that catered to royal families. To my surprise, Adrian was with her. Seeing his familiar, handsome face eased some of the fear in me. A quick probe of her mind told me why he was here: she'd talked him into coming because she didn't want him left alone.

I could understand why. He was completely drunk. It was a wonder he could stand, and in fact, I strongly suspected the wall he leaned against was all that held him up. His brown hair was a mess—and not in the purposeful way he usually styled it. His deep green eyes were bloodshot. Like Lissa, Adrian was a spirit user. He had an ability she didn't yet: he could visit people's dreams. I'd expected him to come to me since my imprisonment, and now it made sense why he hadn't. Alcohol stunted spirit. In some ways, that was a good thing. Excessive spirit created a darkness that drove its users insane. But spending life perpetually drunk wasn't all that healthy either.

Seeing him through Lissa's eyes triggered emotional confusion nearly as intense as what I'd experienced with Tatiana. I felt bad for him. He was obviously worried and upset about me, and the startling events this last week had blindsided him as much as the rest of us. He'd also lost his aunt whom, despite her brusque attitude, he'd cared for.

Yet, in spite of all this, I felt . . . scorn. That was unfair, perhaps, but I couldn't help it. I cared about him so much and understood him being upset, but there were better ways of dealing with his loss. His behavior was almost cowardly. He was hiding from his problems in a bottle, something that went against every piece of my nature. Me? I couldn't let my problems win without a fight.

"Velvet," the shopkeeper told Lissa with certainty. The wizened Moroi woman held up a voluminous, long-sleeved gown. "Velvet is traditional in the royal escort."

Along with the rest of the fanfare, Tatiana's funeral would have a ceremonial escort walking alongside the coffin, with a representative from each family there. Apparently, no one minded that Lissa fill that role for her family. But voting? That was another matter.

Lissa eyed the dress. It looked more like a Halloween costume than a funeral gown. "It's ninety degrees out," said Lissa. "And humid."

"Tradition demands sacrifice," the woman said melodramatically. "As does tragedy."

Adrian opened his mouth, undoubtedly ready with some inappropriate and mocking comment. Lissa gave him a sharp headshake that kept him quiet. "Aren't there any, I don't know, sleeveless options?"

The saleswoman's eyes widened. "No one has ever worn straps to a royal funeral. It wouldn't be right."

"What about shorts?" asked Adrian. "Are they okay if they're with a tie? Because that's what I was gonna go with."

The woman looked horrified. Lissa shot Adrian a look of disdain, not so much because of the remark—which she found mildly amusing—but because she too was disgusted by his constant state of intoxication.

"Well, no one treats me like a full-fledged royal," said Lissa, turning back to the dresses. "No reason to act like one now. Show me your straps and short-sleeves."

The saleswoman grimaced but complied. She had no problem advising royals on fashion but wouldn't dare order them to do or wear anything. It was part of the class stratification of our world. The woman walked across the store to find the requested dresses, just as Lissa's boyfriend and his aunt entered the shop.

Christian Ozera, I thought, was who Adrian should have been acting like. The fact that I could even think like that was startling. Times had certainly changed from when I held Christian up as a role model. But it was true. I'd watched him with Lissa this last week, and Christian had been determined and steadfast, doing whatever he could to help her in the wake of Tatiana's death and my arrest. From the look on his face now, it was obvious he had something important to relay.

His outspoken aunt, Tasha Ozera, was another study in strength and grace under pressure. She'd raised him after his parents had turned Strigoi—and had attacked her, leaving Tasha with scarring on one side of her face. Moroi had always relied on guardians for defense, but after that attack, Tasha had decided to take matters into her own hands. She'd learned to fight, training with all sorts of hand-to-hand methods and weapons. She was really quite a badass and constantly pushed for other Moroi to learn combat too.

Lissa let go of a dress she'd been examining and turned to Christian eagerly. After me, there was no one else she trusted more in the world. He'd been her rock throughout all of this.

He looked around the store, not appearing overly thrilled to be surrounded by dresses. "You guys are shopping?" he asked, glancing from Lissa to Adrian. "Getting in a little girl time?"

"Hey, you'd benefit from a wardrobe change," said Adrian. "Besides, I bet you'd look great in a halter top."

Lissa ignored the guys' banter and focused on the Ozeras. "What did you find out?"

"They've decided not to take action," said Christian. His lips curled in disdain. "Well, not any punishment kind of action."

Tasha nodded. "We're trying to push the idea that he just

thought Rose was in danger and jumped in before he realized what was actually happening."

My heart stopped. Dimitri. They were talking about Dimitri.

For a moment, I was no longer with Lissa. I was no longer in my cell. Instead, I was back to the day of my arrest. I'd been arguing with Dimitri in a café, scolding him for his continued refusal to talk to me, let alone continue our former relationship. I'd decided then that I was done with him, that things were truly over and that I wouldn't let him keep tearing my heart apart. That was when the guardians had come for me, and no matter what Dimitri claimed about his Strigoi-time making him unable to love, he had reacted with lightning speed in my defense. We'd been hopelessly outnumbered, but he hadn't cared. The look on his face—and my own uncanny understanding of him—had told me all I needed to know. I was facing a threat. He had to defend me.

And defend me he had. He'd fought like the god he'd been back at St. Vladimir's Academy, when he'd taught me how to battle Strigoi. He incapacitated more guardians in that café than one man should have been able to. The only thing that had ended it—and I truly believe he would have fought until his last breath—had been my intervention. I hadn't known at the time what was going on or why a legion of guardians would want to arrest me. But I had realized that Dimitri was in serious danger of harming his already fragile status around Court. A Strigoi being restored was unheard of, and many still didn't trust him. I'd begged Dimitri to stop, more afraid of what would happen to him than me.

Little had I known what was in store for me.

He'd come to my hearing—under guard—but neither Lissa nor I had seen him since. Lissa had been working hard to clear him of any wrongdoing, fearing they'd lock him up again. And me? I'd been trying to tell myself not to overthink what he had done. My arrest and potential execution took precedence. Yet . . . I still wondered. Why had he done it? Why had he risked his life for mine? Was it an instinctive reaction to a threat? Had he done it as a favor to Lissa, whom he'd sworn to help in return for freeing him? Or had he truly done it because he still had feelings for me?

I still didn't know the answer, but seeing him like that, like the fierce Dimitri from my past, had stirred up the feelings I was so desperately trying to get over. I kept trying to assure myself that recovering from a relationship took time. Lingering feelings were natural. Unfortunately, it took longer to get over a guy when he threw himself into danger for you.

Regardless, Christian and Tasha's words gave me hope about Dimitri's fate. After all, I wasn't the only one walking a tenuous line between life and death. Those convinced Dimitri was still Strigoi wanted to see a stake through his heart.

"They're keeping him confined again," said Christian. "But not in a cell. Just in his room, with a couple of guards. They don't want him out around Court until things settle down."

"That's better than jail," admitted Lissa.

"It's still absurd," snapped Tasha, more to herself than the others. She and Dimitri had been close over the years, and she'd once wanted to take that relationship to another level.

She'd settled for friendship, and her outrage over the injustice done to him was as strong as ours. "They should have let him go as soon as he became a dhampir again. Once the elections are settled, I'm going to make sure he's free."

"And that's what's weird . . ." Christian's pale blue eyes narrowed thoughtfully. "We heard that Tatiana had told others before she—before she—" Christian hesitated and glanced uneasily at Adrian. The pause was uncharacteristic for Christian, who usually spoke his mind abruptly.

"Before she was murdered," said Adrian flatly, not looking at any of them. "Go on."

Christian swallowed. "Um, yeah. I guess—not in public—she'd announced that she believed Dimitri really was a dhampir again. Her plan was to help him get more acceptance once the other stuff settled down." The "other stuff" was the age law mentioned in Tatiana's note, the one saying dhampirs turning sixteen would be forced to graduate and start defending Moroi. It had infuriated me, but like so many other things now . . . well, it was kind of on hold.

Adrian made a strange sound, like he was clearing his throat. "She did not."

Christian shrugged. "Lots of her advisors said she did. That's the rumor."

"I have a hard time believing it too," Tasha told Adrian. She'd never approved of Tatiana's policies and had vehemently spoken out against them on more than one occasion. Adrian's disbelief wasn't political, though. His was simply coming from ideas he'd always had about his aunt. She'd never given any indication that she wanted to help Dimitri regain his old status.

Adrian made no further comment, but I knew this topic was kindling sparks of jealousy within him. I'd told him Dimitri was in the past and that I was ready to move on, but Adrian—like me—must have undoubtedly wondered about the motivations behind Dimitri's gallant defense.

Lissa began to speculate on how they might get Dimitri out of house arrest when the saleswoman returned with an armful of dresses she clearly disapproved of. Biting her lip, Lissa fell silent. She filed away Dimitri's situation as something to deal with later. Instead, she wearily prepared to try on clothes and play the part of a good little royal girl.

Adrian perked up at the sight of the dresses. "Any halters in there?"

I returned to my cell, mulling over the problems that just seemed to keep piling up. I was worried about both Adrian and Dimitri. I was worried about myself. I was also worried about this so-called lost Dragomir. I was starting to believe the story could be real, but there was nothing I could do about it, which frustrated me. I needed to take action when it came to helping Lissa. Tatiana had told me in her letter to be careful whom I spoke to about the matter. Should I pass this mission on to someone else? I wanted to take charge of it, but the bars and suffocating walls around me said I might not be able to take charge of anything for a while, not even my own life.

Two weeks.

Needing further distraction, I gave in and began reading

Abe's book, which was exactly the tale of wrongful imprisonment I'd expected it to be. It *was* pretty good and taught me that faking my own death apparently wouldn't work as an escape method. The book unexpectedly stirred up old memories. A chill went down my spine as I recalled a Tarot reading that a Moroi named Rhonda had given to me. She was Ambrose's aunt, and one of the cards she'd drawn for me had shown a woman tied to swords. *Wrongful imprisonment. Accusations. Slander*. Damn. I was really starting to hate those cards. I always insisted they were a scam, yet they had an annoying tendency to come true. The end of her reading had shown a journey, but to where? A real prison? My execution?

Questions with no answers. Welcome to my world. Out of options for now, I figured I might as well try to get some rest. Stretching out on the pallet, I tried to push away those constant worries. Not easy. Every time I closed my eyes, I saw a judge banging a gavel, condemning me to death. I saw my name in the history books, not as a hero, but as a traitor.

Lying there, choking on my own fear, I thought of Dimitri. I pictured his steady gaze and could practically hear him lecturing me. *Don't worry now about what you can't change. Rest when you can so you'll be ready for tomorrow's battles.* The imaginary advice calmed me. Sleep came at last, heavy and deep. I'd tossed and turned a lot this week, so true rest was welcome.

Then—I woke up.

I sat upright in bed, my heart pounding. Peering around, I looked for danger—any threat that might have startled me out of that sleep. There was nothing. Darkness. Silence. The faint squeak of a chair down the hall told me my guards were still around.

The bond, I realized. The bond had woken me up. I'd felt a sharp, intense flare of . . . what? Intensity. Anxiety. A rush of adrenaline. Panic raced through me, and I dove deeper into Lissa, trying to find what had caused that surge of emotion from her.

What I found was . . . nothing.

The bond was gone.

THREE

WELL, NOT GONE EXACTLY.

Muted. Kind of like how it had felt immediately after she'd restored Dimitri back to a dhampir. The magic had been so strong then that it had "burned out" our link. There was no blast of magic now. It was almost as though the blankness was intentional on her part. Like always, I still had a sense of Lissa: she was alive; she was well. So what was keeping me from feeling more of her? She wasn't asleep, because I could feel a sense of alert consciousness on the other side of this wall. Spirit was there, hiding her from me . . . and she was making it happen.

What the hell? It was an accepted fact that our bond worked only one way. I could sense her; she couldn't sense me. Likewise, I could control when I went into her mind. Often, I tried to keep myself out (jail captivity time excluded), in an attempt to protect her privacy. Lissa had no such control, and her vulnerability infuriated her sometimes. Every once in a while, she could use her power to shield herself from me, but it was rare, difficult, and required considerable effort on her part. Today, she was pulling it off, and as the condition persisted, I could feel her strain. Keeping me out wasn't easy, but she was managing it. Of course, I didn't care about the how of it. I wanted to know the *why*.

It was probably my worst day of imprisonment. Fear for myself was one thing. But for her? That was agonizing. If it was my life or hers, I would have walked into execution without hesitation. I had to know what was going on. Had she learned something? Had the Council decided to skip right over a trial and execute me? Was Lissa trying to protect me from that news? The more spirit she wielded, the more she endangered her life. This mental wall required a lot of magic. But why? Why was she taking this risk?

It was astonishing in that moment to realize just how much I relied on the bond to keep track of her. True: I didn't always welcome someone else's thoughts in my head. Despite the control I'd learned, her mind still sometimes poured into mine in moments I'd rather not experience. None of that was a concern now—only her safety was. Being blocked off was like having a limb removed.

All day I tried to get inside her head. Every time, I was kept out. It was maddening. No visitors came to me either, and the book and magazines had long since lost their appeal. The caged animal feeling was getting to me again, and I spent a fair amount of time yelling at my guards—with no results. Tatiana's funeral was tomorrow, and the clock to my trial was ticking loudly.

Bedtime came, and the wall in the bond dropped at last—because Lissa went to sleep. The link between us was firm, but her mind was closed off in unconsciousness. I'd find no answers there. Left with nothing else, I went to bed as well, wondering if I'd be cut off again in the morning.

I wasn't. She and I were linked again, and I was able to see the world through her eyes once more. Lissa was up and around early, preparing for the funeral. I neither saw nor felt any sign of why I'd been blocked the day before. She was letting me back into her mind, just like normal. I almost wondered if I'd imagined being cut off from her.

No . . . there it was. Barely. Within her mind, I sensed thoughts she was still hiding from me. They were slippery. Each time I tried to grasp them, they fell out of my hands. I was amazed she could still use enough magic to pull it off, and it was also a clear indication that she'd blocked me out intentionally yesterday. What was going on? Why on earth would she need to hide something from me? What could I do about anything, locked in this hellhole? Again, my unease grew. What awful thing didn't I know about?

I watched Lissa get ready, seeing no ostensible sign of anything unusual. The dress she'd ended up selecting had cap sleeves and went to the knee. Black, of course. It was hardly a clubbing dress, but she knew it would raise some eyebrows. Under different circumstances, this would have delighted me. She chose to wear her hair down and unbound, its pale blond color showing brightly against the dress's black when she surveyed herself in a mirror.

Christian met Lissa outside. He cleaned up well, I had to admit, uncharacteristically wearing a dress shirt and tie. He'd drawn the line at a jacket, and his expression was an odd mix of nervousness, secrecy, and typical snark. When he saw Lissa, though, his face momentarily transformed, turning radiant and awestruck as he gazed at her. He gave her a small smile and took her into his arms for a brief embrace. His touch brought her contentment and comfort, easing her anxiety. They'd gotten back together recently after a breakup, and that time apart had been agonizing for both of them.

"It's going to be okay," he murmured, his look of worry returning. "This'll work. We can do this."

She said nothing but tightened her hold on him before stepping back. Neither of them spoke as they walked to the beginning of the funeral procession. I decided this was suspicious. She caught hold of his hand and felt strengthened by it.

The funeral procedures for Moroi monarchs had been the same for centuries, no matter if the Court was in Romania or its new home in Pennsylvania. That was the Moroi way. They mixed the traditional with the modern, magic with technology.

The queen's coffin would be carried by pallbearers out of the palace and taken with great ceremony all through the Court's grounds, until it reached the Court's imposing cathedral. There, a select group would enter for mass. After the service, Tatiana would be buried in the church's graveyard, taking her place beside other monarchs and important royals.

The coffin's route was easy to spot. Poles strung with red and black silk banners marked each side. Rose petals had been strewn on the ground the coffin would pass over. Along the sides, people crammed together, hoping to catch a glimpse of their former queen. Many Moroi had come from far off places, some to see the funeral and some to see the monarch elections that would soon follow over the next couple of weeks.

The royal family escort—most of whom wore saleswoman-approved black velvet—were already heading into the palace building. Lissa stopped outside to part ways with Christian since he certainly had never been in the running to represent his family for such an honored event. She gave him another fierce hug and a light kiss. As they stepped away, there was a knowing glint in his blue eyes—that secret that was hidden from me.

Lissa pushed through the gathering crowds, trying to get to the entrance and find the procession's starting point. The building didn't look like the palaces or castles of ancient Europe. Its grand stone façade and tall windows matched the Court's other structures, but a few features—its height, wide marble steps—subtly distinguished it from other buildings. A tug at Lissa's arm stopped her progress, nearly causing her to run into an ancient Moroi man.

"Vasilisa?" It was Daniella Ivashkov, Adrian's mother. Daniella wasn't so bad as royals went, and she was actually okay with Adrian and me dating—or at least, she had been before I became an accused murderer. Most of Daniella's acceptance had come from the fact that she believed Adrian and I would split up anyways once I received my guardian assignment. Daniella had also convinced one of her cousins, Damon Tarus, to be my lawyer—an offer I'd rejected when I chose Abe to represent me instead. I still wasn't entirely sure if I'd made the best decision there, but it probably tarnished Daniella's view of me, which I regretted.

Lissa offered up a nervous smile. She was anxious to join the procession and get all of this over with. "Hi," she said.

Daniella was dressed in full black velvet and even had small diamond barrettes shining in her dark hair. Worry and agitation lined her pretty face. "Have you seen Adrian? I haven't been able to find him anywhere. We checked his room."

"Oh." Lissa averted her eyes.

"What?" Daniella nearly shook her. "What do you know?"

Lissa sighed. "I'm not sure where he is, but I saw him last night when he was coming back from some party." Lissa hesitated, like she was too embarrassed to tell the rest. "He was . . . really drunk. More than I've ever seen him. He was going off with some girls, and I don't know. I'm sorry, Lady Ivashkov. He's probably . . . well, passed out somewhere."

Daniella wrung her hands, and I shared her dismay. "I hope nobody notices. Maybe we can say . . . he was overcome with grief. There's so much going on. Surely no one will notice. You'll tell them, right? You'll say how upset he was?"

I liked Daniella, but this royal obsession with image was really starting to bug me. I knew she loved her son, but her main concern here seemed to be less about Tatiana's final rest than it was about what others would think about a breach of protocol. "Of course," said Lissa. "I wouldn't want anyone to . . . well, I'd hate for that to get out."

"Thank you. Now go." Daniella gestured to the doors, still looking anxious. "You need to take your place." To Lissa's surprise, Daniella gave her a gentle pat on the arm. "And don't be nervous. You'll do fine. Just keep your head up."

Guardians stationed at the door recognized Lissa as someone with access and allowed her in. There, in the foyer, was Tatiana's coffin. Lissa froze, suddenly overwhelmed, and nearly forgot what she was doing there.

The coffin alone was a work of art. It was made of gleaming black wood, polished to brilliance. Paintings of elaborate garden scenes in shining metallic colors of every hue adorned each side. Gold glittered everywhere, including the poles that the pallbearers would hold. Those poles were draped with strings of mauve roses. It seemed like the thorns and leaves would make it difficult for the pallbearers to get a good grip, but that was their problem to deal with.

Inside, uncovered and lying on a bed of more mauve roses, was Tatiana herself. It was strange. I saw dead bodies all the time. Hell, I created them. But seeing a body that had been preserved, lying peacefully and ornamentally . . . well, it was creepy. It was strange for Lissa, too, particularly since she didn't have to deal with death as often as I did.

Tatiana wore a gleaming silk gown that was a rich shade of purple—the traditional color for royal burial. The dress's long sleeves were decorated with an elaborate design of small pearls. I'd often seen Tatiana in red—a color associated with the Ivashkov family—and I was glad for the purple burial tradition. A red dress would have been too strong a reminder of the bloody pictures of her that I'd seen at my hearing, pictures I kept trying to block out. Strings of gemstones and more pearls hung around her neck, and a gold crown set with diamonds and amethysts rested upon her graying hair. Someone had done a good job with Tatiana's makeup, but even they couldn't hide the whiteness of her skin. Moroi were naturally pale. In death, they were like chalk—like Strigoi. The image struck Lissa so vividly that she swayed on her feet a little and had to look away. The roses' scent filled the air, but there was a hint of decay mixed in with that sweetness.

The funeral coordinator spotted Lissa and ordered her into position—after first bemoaning Lissa's fashion choice. The sharp words snapped Lissa back to reality, and she fell in line with five other royals on the right side of the coffin. She tried not to look too closely at the queen's body and directed her gaze elsewhere. The pallbearers soon showed up and lifted their burden, using the rose-draped poles to rest the coffin on their shoulders and slowly carry it out to the waiting crowd. The pallbearers were all dhampirs. They wore formal suits, which confused me at first, but then I realized they were all Court guardians—except one. Ambrose. He looked as gorgeous as always and stared straight ahead as he did his job, face blank and expressionless.

I wondered if Ambrose mourned Tatiana. I was so fixated on my own problems that I kept forgetting a life had been lost here, a life that many had loved. Ambrose had defended Tatiana when I'd been angry about the age law. Watching him through Lissa's eyes, I wished I was there to speak to him in person. He had to know something more about the letter he'd slipped me in the courtroom. Surely he wasn't just the delivery boy.

The procession moved forward, ending my musings about Ambrose. Before and ahead of the coffin were other ceremonial people. Royals in elaborate clothing, making a glittering display. Uniformed guardians carrying banners. Musicians with flutes walked at the very back, playing a mournful tune. For her part, Lissa was very good at public appearances and managed the slow, stately pace with elegance and grace, her gaze level and confident. I couldn't see outside her body, of course, but it was easy to imagine what the spectators saw. She was beautiful and regal, worthy to inherit the Dragomir legacy, and hopefully more and more would realize that. It would save us a lot of trouble if someone would change the voting law through standard procedures, so we didn't have to rely on a quest for a lost sibling.

Walking the funeral route took a long time. Even when the sun started sinking down toward the horizon, the day's heat still hung in the air. Lissa began to sweat but knew her discomfort was nothing compared to the pallbearers'. If the watching crowd felt the heat, they didn't show it. They craned their necks to get their one glimpse of the spectacle passing before them. Lissa didn't process the onlookers so much, but in their faces, I saw that the coffin wasn't their only focus. They were also watching Lissa. Word of what she'd done for Dimitri had blazed around the Moroi world, and while many were skeptical of her ability to heal, there were just as many who believed. I saw expressions of wonder and awe in the crowd, and for a second, I wondered who they'd *really* come to see: Lissa or Tatiana?

Finally, the cathedral came into view, which was good news for Lissa. The sun didn't kill Moroi like it did Strigoi, but the heat and sunlight were still uncomfortable for any vampire. The procession was nearly finished, and she, being one of those allowed into the church service, would soon get to enjoy air conditioning.

As I studied the surroundings, I couldn't help but think what a circle of irony my life was. Off to the sides of the church's extensive grounds were two giant statues showing ancient Moroi monarchs of legend, a king and queen who had helped the Moroi prosper. Even though they were a fair distance from the church, the statues loomed ominously, like they were scrutinizing everything. Near the queen's statue was a garden that I knew well. I'd been forced to landscape it as punishment for running off to Las Vegas. My true purpose on that trip—which no one knew—had been to free Victor Dashkov from prison. Victor had been a longtime enemy of ours, but he and his brother Robert, a spirit user, had held the knowledge we needed to save Dimitri. If any guardians had found out that I'd freed Victor—then later lost him—my punishment would have been a lot worse than filing and landscaping. At least I'd done a good job with the garden, I thought bitterly. If I was executed, I'd leave a lasting mark at Court.

Lissa's eyes lingered on one of the statues for a long time before she turned back to the church. She was sweating heavily now, and I realized some of it wasn't just the heat. She was anxious too. But why? Why was she so nervous? This was just ceremony. All she had to do was go through the motions here.

Yet . . . there it was again. Something else was bothering her. She was still keeping a cluster of thoughts from me, but a few leaked out as she worried.

Too close, too close. We're moving too fast.

Fast? Not by my estimation. I could have never handled this slow, stately pace. I felt especially bad for the pallbearers. If I were one, I would've said to hell with propriety and started jogging toward my final destination. Of course, that might jostle the body. If the funeral coordinator had been upset over Lissa's dress, there was no telling how she'd react if Tatiana fell out of the coffin.

Our view of the cathedral was getting clearer, its domes shining amber and orange in the setting sun. Lissa was still several yards away, but the priest standing out front was clearly visible. His robes were almost blinding. They were made of heavy, glittering gold brocade, long and full. A rounded hat with a cross, also gold, sat on his head. I thought it was in poor taste for him to outshine the queen's clothing, but maybe that was just what priests did on formal occasions. Maybe it got God's attention. He lifted his arms in welcome, showing off more of that rich fabric. The rest of the crowd and I couldn't help but stare at the dazzling display.

So, you can imagine our surprise when the statues blew up.

FOUR

AND WHEN I SAY THEY blew up, I mean *they blew up*.

Flames and smoke unfurled like petals from a newly opened flower as those poor monarchs exploded into pieces of rock. For a moment, I was stunned. It was like watching an action movie, the explosion cracking the air and shaking the ground. Then, guardian training kicked in. Critical observation and calculation took over. I immediately noticed that the bulk of the statue's material blew toward the outer sides of the garden. Small stone pieces and dust rained down on the funeral procession, but no large chunks of rock hit Lissa or anyone standing nearby. Assuming the statues had not spontaneously combusted, whoever had blown them up had done so in a precise way.

The logistics aside, huge billowing pillars of flame are still pretty scary. Chaos broke loose as everyone tried to get away. Only, they all took different routes, so collisions and entanglements occurred. Even the pallbearers set down their precious burden and took off. Ambrose was the last to do so, his mouth agape and eyes wide as he stared at Tatiana, but another look at the statues sent him off into the mob. A few guardians tried to keep order, herding people back down the funeral path, but it didn't do a lot of good. Everyone was out for themselves, too terrified and panicked to think reasonably.

Well, everyone except for Lissa.

To my surprise, she *wasn't* surprised.

She had been expecting the explosion.

She didn't run right away, despite people pushing past and shoving her aside. She stood rooted where she'd been when the statues blew up, studying them and the wreckage they'd caused. In particular, she seemed concerned about anyone in the crowd who might have been hurt by the blasts. But, no. As I'd already observed, there seemed to be no injuries. And if there were, it was going to be because of the stampede.

Satisfied, Lissa turned and began walking away with the others. (Well, she was walking; they were running). She'd only gone a little distance when she saw a huge group of guardians hurrying *toward* the church, faces grim. Some of them stopped to aid those escaping the destruction, but most of the guardians were on their way to the blast site to see what had happened.

Lissa paused again, causing the guy behind her to slam into her back, but she barely felt the impact. She intently watched the guardians, taking note of how many there were, and then moved on once more. Her hidden thoughts were starting to unravel. Finally, I began to see pieces of the plan she'd kept hidden from me. She was pleased. Nervous, too. But overall, she felt—

A commotion back at the jail snapped me into my own mind. The usual quiet of the holding area had shattered and was now filled with grunts and exclamations. I leapt up from where I'd been sitting and pressed against the bars, straining to see what was happening. Was this building about to explode too? My cell only faced a wall in the hallway, with no view of the rest of the corridor or its entrance. I did, however, see the guardians who usually stood at the hall's far end come tearing past me, toward whatever altercation was occurring.

I didn't know what this meant for me and braced for anything, friend or foe. For all I knew, there could be some political fringe group launching attacks on the Court to make a statement against the Moroi government. Peering around the cell, I swore silently, wishing I had anything to defend myself. The closest I had was Abe's book, which was no good at all. If he was the badass he pretended to be, he really would have slipped a file into it. Or gotten me something bigger, like *War and Peace*.

The scuffling died down and footsteps thundered toward me. Clenching my fists, I took a few steps back, ready to defend myself against anyone.

"Anyone" turned out to be Eddie Castile. And Mikhail Tanner.

Friendly faces were *not* what I had expected. Eddie was a longtime friend from St. Vladimir's, another new guardian like me and someone who'd stuck by me through a lot of misadventures, including the Victor Dashkov prison break. Mikhail was older than us, mid-twenties, and had helped us restore Dimitri in the hopes that Sonya Karp—a woman Mikhail had loved who had turned Strigoi—might be saved as well. I glanced back and forth between the two guys' faces.

"What's going on?" I demanded.

"Nice to see you too," said Eddie. He was sweating and keyed up with battle fervor, a few purple marks on his face showing he'd met someone's fist tonight. In his hand was a weapon I'd seen in the guardians' arsenal: a baton-type thing used to incapacitate people without killing them. But Mikhail held something much more valuable: the keycard and mechanical key to open my cell.

My friends were staging a prison break. Unbelievable. Crazy was usually *my* specialty.

"Did you guys . . ." I frowned. The thought of escape filled me with joy, but the logistics were sobering. Clearly, they'd been responsible for the fight with my guards that I'd just heard. Getting down here in the first place wasn't that easy either. "Did you two just take on every guardian in this building?"

Mikhail finished unlocking the door, and I didn't waste any time in hurrying out. After feeling so oppressed and smothered for days, it was like stepping onto a mountain ledge, wind and space all around me.

"Rose, there are no guardians in this building. Well, maybe one. And these guys." Eddie gestured in the direction of the earlier fight, where I assumed my guards lay unconscious. Surely my friends hadn't killed anyone.

"The rest of the guardians are all checking out the explosion," I realized. Pieces began coming together—including

Lissa's lack of surprise over the commotion. "Oh no. You had Christian blow up ancient Moroi artifacts."

"Of course not," said Eddie. He seemed shocked that I would have suggested such an atrocity. "Other fire users would be able to tell if he did."

"Well, that's something," I said. I should have had more faith in their sanity.

Or maybe not.

"We used C4," explained Mikhail.

"Where on earth did you—"

My tongue locked up when I saw who was standing at the end of the hallway. Dimitri.

Not knowing how he was during my imprisonment had been frustrating. Christian and Tasha's report had been only a tease. Well, here was the answer. Dimitri stood near the hall's entrance in all his six-foot-seven glory, as imperious and intimidating as any god. His sharp brown eyes assessed everything in an instant, and his strong, lean body was tensed and ready for any threat. The look on his face was so focused, so filled with passion, that I couldn't believe anyone ever could have thought he was a Strigoi. Dimitri burned with life and energy. In fact, looking at him now, I was again reminded of how he'd stood up for me at my arrest. He wore that same expression. Really, it was the same one I'd seen countless times. It was the one people feared and admired. It was the one I had loved.

"You're here too?" I tried reminding myself that my muddled romantic history wasn't the most important thing in the world for a change. "Aren't you under house arrest?"

"He escaped," said Eddie slyly. I caught the real meaning: he and Mikhail had *helped* Dimitri escape. "It's what people would expect some violent probably-still-a-Strigoi guy to do, right?"

"You'd also expect him to come bust you out," added Mikhail, playing along with the game. "Especially considering how he fought for you last week. Really, everyone is going to think he busted you out *alone*. Not with us."

Dimitri said nothing. His eyes, while still carefully watching our surroundings, were also assessing me. He was making sure I was okay and uninjured. He looked relieved that I was.

"Come on," Dimitri finally said. "We don't have much time." That was an understatement, but there was one thing bugging me about my friends' "brilliant" plan.

"There's no way they'll think *he* did it alone!" I exclaimed, realizing what Mikhail was getting at. They were setting Dimitri up as the culprit in this escape. I gestured to the unconscious guardians at our feet. "They saw your faces."

"Not really," a new voice said. "Not after a little spirit-induced amnesia. By the time they wake up, the only person they'll remember seeing will be that unstable Russian guy. No offense."

"None taken," said Dimitri, as Adrian stepped through the doorway.

I stared, trying not to gape. There they were together, the two men in my life. Adrian hardly looked like he could jump into a fistfight, but he was as alert and serious as the other fighters here. His lovely eyes were clear and full of the cunning I knew they could possess when he really tried. That's when it hit me: he showed no sign of intoxication whatsoever. Had what I'd seen the other day been a ruse? Or had he forced himself to take control? Either way, I felt a slow grin creeping over my face.

"Lissa lied to your mom earlier," I said. "You're supposed to be passed out drunk somewhere."

He rewarded me with one of his cynical smiles. "Well, yes, that would probably be the smarter—and more enjoyable—thing to be doing right now. And hopefully, that's what everyone thinks I'm doing."

"We need to go," said Dimitri, growing agitated.

We turned toward him. Our jokes vanished. That attitude I'd noticed about Dimitri, the one that said he could do anything and would always lead you to victory, made people want to follow him unconditionally. The expressions on Mikhail and Eddie's faces—as they grew serious—showed that was exactly how they felt. It seemed natural to me too. Even Adrian looked like he believed in Dimitri, and in that moment, I admired Adrian for putting aside any jealousy—and also for risking himself like this. Especially since Adrian had made it clear on more than one occasion he didn't want to be involved with any dangerous adventures or use his spirit in a covert way. In Las Vegas, for example, he'd simply accompanied us in an observer's role. Of course, he'd also been drunk most of the time, but that probably made no difference.

I took a few steps forward, but Adrian suddenly held out a hand to stop me. "Wait—before you go with us, you need to know something." Dimitri started to protest, eyes glinting with impatience. "She *does*," argued Adrian, meeting Dimitri's gaze squarely. "Rose, if you escape . . . you're more or less confirming your guilt. You'll be a fugitive. If the guardians find you, they aren't going to need a trial or sentence to kill you on sight."

Four sets of eyes rested on me as the full meaning sank in. If I ran now and was caught, I was dead for sure. If I stayed, I had the slim chance that in my short time before trial, we might find evidence to save me. It wasn't impossible. But if nothing turned up, I was also most certainly dead. Either option was a gamble. Either one had the strong possibility of me not surviving.

Adrian looked as conflicted as I felt. We both knew I didn't have any good choices. He was simply worried and wanted me to know what I was risking. Dimitri, however . . . for him, there was no debate. I could see it all over his face. He was an advocate of rules and doing the proper thing. But in this case? With such bad odds? It was better to risk living as a fugitive, and if death came, better to face it fighting.

My death will not be penciled in on someone's calendar.

"Let's go," I said.

We hurried out of the building, anxious to get moving with the plan. I couldn't help but comment to Adrian, "You've got to be using a lot of spirit to pull off all those illusions on the guards."

"I am," he agreed. "And I don't really have the power to do it for very long. Lissa could probably make a dozen guardians think they'd seen ghosts. Me? I can barely make a few forget Eddie and Mikhail. That's why there had to be someone they remembered to attract the attention, and Dimitri's the ideal scapegoat."

"Well, thank you." I gave his hand a gentle squeeze. As warmth flowed between us, I didn't bother telling him I was a long way from being free yet. It would diminish his heroics. We had a lot of obstacles ahead, but I still appreciated him stepping up like this and respecting my decision to go along with the escape plan.

Adrian shot me a sidelong glance. "Yeah, well, I'm supposed to be crazy, right?" A flash of affection shone in his eyes. "And there isn't much I wouldn't do for you. The stupider, the better."

We emerged to the main floor, and I saw that Eddie had been right about guardian security. The halls and rooms were virtually deserted. Without a second glance, we hurried outdoors, and the fresh air seemed to renew my energy.

"Now what?" I asked my rescuers.

"Now we take you to the getaway car," said Eddie.

The garages weren't far, but they weren't close either. "That's a lot of open ground to cover," I said. I didn't bring up the obvious problem: me being killed if spotted.

"I'm using spirit to keep us all vague and nondescript," said Adrian. More testing of his magic. He couldn't handle much more. "People won't recognize us unless they stop and stare directly at us."

"Which they probably won't," said Mikhail. "If anyone

even notices us at all. Everyone's too worried about themselves to pay much attention to others in all this chaos."

Looking around outside, I could see he was right. The jail building was far from the church, but by now, people who'd been near the blast had made their way to this part of Court. Some were running into their residences. Some were seeking guardians, hoping for protection. And some . . . some were going the same direction we were, toward the garages.

"People are freaked out enough to actually try to leave Court," I realized. Our group was moving as fast as we could with Adrian, who wasn't in the shame shape as dhampirs. "The garages will be crowded." Both official Court vehicles and visiting guests parked in the same area.

"That could help us," said Mikhail. "More chaos."

With so many distractions in my own reality, I couldn't plunge completely into Lissa's. A light brush of the bond found her safe, over in the palace.

"What's Lissa doing during all of this?" I asked.

Believe me, I was glad she wasn't involved with this busting-me-out-of-jail madness. But, as Adrian had noted, her ability with spirit could have gone much farther than his here. And now, looking back on it all, it was obvious she had known about this plan. That had been her secret.

"Lissa needs to stay innocent. She can't be linked to any part of the escape or explosion," replied Dimitri, eyes fixed ahead on his goal. His tone was firm. He still regarded her as his savior. "She has to keep herself visible with the other royals. So does Christian." He almost smiled. Almost. "Those two would certainly be my first suspects if something exploded."

"But the guardians won't suspect them once they realize the blast wasn't caused by magic," I mused. Mikhail's earlier words returned to me. "And hey, where *did* you guys get a hold of C4? Military grade explosives are kind of extreme, even for you."

No one answered me because three guardians suddenly leapt out into our path. Apparently, they weren't all out at the church. Dimitri and I surged ahead of our group, moving as one, just as we always had in battle together. Adrian had said the illusion he'd stretched over our group wouldn't hold if anyone was facing us directly. I wanted to make sure Dimitri and I were the first line of contact with these guardians, in the hopes they wouldn't recognize the others behind us. I threw myself into the fight without hesitation, defensive instincts kicking in. But in those milliseconds, the reality of what I was doing truly sank in.

I'd fought guardians before and always felt guilty about it. I'd taken on the ones at Tarasov Prison, as well as the queen's guard during my arrest. I hadn't really known any of them, though. Just realizing they were my colleagues had been bad enough . . . but now? Now I was facing one of the most difficult challenges in my life, as small as it seemed. After all, three guardians were an easy match for me and Dimitri. The problem was—I *knew* these guardians. Two of them I'd run into quite a bit after graduation. They worked at Court and had always been kind to me.

The third guardian wasn't just someone I knew—she was a friend. Meredith, one of the few girls in my class at St. Vladimir's. I saw the flash of uneasiness in her eyes, a sentiment mirroring my own. This felt wrong to her too. But, she was a guardian now, and like me, she had had duty drilled into her throughout her life. She believed I was a criminal. She could see I was free and in attack mode. Procedure dictated she take me down, and honestly, I wouldn't have expected anything less. It's what I would have done had our roles been reversed. This was life and death.

Dimitri was on the other two guys, as fast and badass as ever. Meredith and I went for each other. At first, she tried to knock me down by virtue of her weight, probably in the hopes of pinning me down until backup could help grab me. Only, I was stronger. She should have known that. How many times had we sparred in the school's gym? I'd almost always won. And this was no game, no practice drill. I pushed back at her attack, punching her on the side of her jaw and desperately praying I didn't break anything. She kept moving through the pain, but—again—I was superior. I caught a hold of her shoulders and threw her down. Her head hit hard, but she remained conscious. I didn't know whether to be grateful or not. Maintaining my grip, I put her in a chokehold, waiting until her eyes closed. I released as soon as I was sure she was out, my heart twisting in my chest.

Glancing over, I saw Dimitri had also taken down his opponents. Our group kept moving as though nothing had happened, but I glanced at Eddie, knowing there was grief on my face. He looked pained too but sought to reassure me as we hurried along.

"You did what you had to," he said. "She'll be okay. Banged up, but okay."

"I hit her hard."

"The medics can deal with concussions. Hell, how many did we get in practice?"

I hoped he was right. The lines between right and wrong were getting confusing. The one good thing, I supposed, was that Meredith had been so occupied by the sight of me that she probably hadn't noticed Eddie and the others. They'd held back from the fight, hopefully keeping on Adrian's veil of spirit while Dimitri and I took the attention.

We finally reached the garages, which were indeed more crowded than usual. Some Moroi had already driven off. One royal was hysterical because her driver had her car's keys, and she didn't know where he was. She was shouting to passers-by to see if anyone could hotwire the car for her.

Dimitri led us purposefully forward, never wavering. He knew exactly where we were going. There had been a lot of planning, I realized. Most of which had probably happened yesterday. Why had Lissa obscured it from me? Wouldn't it have been better for me to have a heads-up on the plan?

We scurried through the people, heading toward the garage on the very farthest side. There, sitting just outside of it and seemingly ready to go, was a drab gray Honda Civic. A man stood near it, arms crossed as he examined the windshield.

Hearing our approach, he turned around.

"Abe!" I exclaimed.

My illustrious father turned and gave me one of those charming smiles that could lure the unwary to their doom.

"What are you doing here?" demanded Dimitri. "You'll be on the list of suspects too! You were supposed to stay back with the others."

Abe shrugged. He looked remarkably unconcerned at Dimitri's angry expression. I wouldn't have wanted that fury directed at me. "Vasilisa will make sure a few people at the palace swear they saw me there during suspicious times." He turned his dark eyes toward me. "Besides, I couldn't leave without telling you goodbye, could I?"

I shook my head in exasperation. "Was this all part of your plan as my lawyer? I don't recall explosive escapes being part of legal training."

"Well, I'm sure it wasn't part of Damon Tarus's legal training." Abe's smile never wavered. "I told you, Rose. You will never face execution—or even a trial, if I can help it." He paused. "Which, of course, I can."

I hesitated, glancing toward the car. Dimitri stood by it with a set of keys, looking impatient. Adrian's words echoed in my memory.

"If I run, it's just going to make me seem that much more guilty."

"They already think you're guilty," said Abe. "You wasting away in that cell won't change that. This just ensures we now have more time to do what we need to without your execution looming over us."

"And what are you going to do exactly?"

"Prove you're innocent," said Adrian. "Or, well, that you didn't kill my aunt. I've known for a while you aren't all that innocent."

"What, are you guys going to destroy the evidence?" I asked, ignoring the dig.

"No," said Eddie. "We have to find who really did kill her."

"You guys shouldn't be involved with that, now that I'm free. It's my problem. Isn't that why you got me out?"

"It's a problem you can't solve while you're at Court," said Abe. "We need you gone and safe."

"Yeah, but I—"

"We're wasting time arguing," said Dimitri. His gaze fell on the other garages. The crowds were still chaotic, too busy with their own fears to notice us yet. That didn't affect Dimitri's concern. He handed me a silver stake, and I didn't question the reasons. It was a weapon, something I couldn't turn down. "I know everything looks disorganized, but you'll be amazed at how quickly the guardians will restore order. And when they do, they're going to lock this place down."

"They don't need to," I said slowly, my mind spinning. "We're already going to have trouble going out of Court. We'll be stopped—if we can even get to the gate. There are going to be cars lined up for miles!"

"Ah, well," said Abe, idly studying his fingertips. "I have it on good authority there's going to be a new 'gate' opening up soon over on the south side of the wall."

The truth dawned on me. "Oh lord. You're the one who's been doling out C4."

"You make it sound so easy," he said with a frown. "That stuff's hard to get a hold of."

Dimitri's patience was at an end. "All of you: Rose needs to leave *now*. She's in danger. I'll drag her out if I have to."

"You don't have to go with me," I shot back, kind of offended at the presumption. Memories of our recent arguments emerged, of Dimitri saying he couldn't love me and didn't even want to be friends. "I'll take care of myself. No one else needs to get in trouble. Give me the keys."

Instead, Dimitri gave me one of those rueful looks that said he thought I was being utterly ridiculous. We could have been back in class at St. Vladimir's Academy.

"Rose, I can't really get in any more trouble. Someone has to be responsible for helping you, and I'm the best choice." I wasn't so sure of that. If Tatiana really had made progress in convincing people Dimitri wasn't a threat, this escapade would ruin it all.

"Go," said Eddie, surprising me with a quick hug. "We'll be in touch through Lissa." I realized then that I was fighting a losing battle with this group. It really was time to leave.

I hugged Mikhail too, murmuring in his ear, "Thank you. Thank you so much for your help. I swear, we'll find her. We'll find Sonya." He gave me that sad smile of his and didn't reply.

Adrian was the hardest to leave behind. I could tell it was difficult for him too, no matter how relaxed his grin seemed. He couldn't be happy about me going off with Dimitri. Our hug lasted a little bit longer than the others, and he gave me a soft, brief kiss on the lips. I almost felt like crying after how brave he'd been tonight. I wished he could go with me but knew he'd be safer here.

"Adrian, thank you for—"

He held up his hand. "It's not goodbye, little dhampir. I'll see you in your dreams."

"If you stay sober enough."

He winked. "For you I just might."

A loud booming noise interrupted us, and we saw a flash of light off to my right. People near the other garages screamed.

"There, you see?" asked Abe, quite pleased with himself. "A new gate. Perfect timing."

I gave him a reluctant hug too and was surprised when he didn't pull back right away. He smiled at me . . . fondly. "Ah, my daughter," he said. "Eighteen, and already you've been accused of murder, aided felons, and acquired a death count higher than most guardians will ever see." He paused. "I couldn't be prouder."

I rolled my eyes. "Goodbye, old man. And thanks." I didn't bother asking him about the "felons" part. Abe wasn't stupid. After I'd asked him about a prison that had later been breeched, he'd probably figured out who was behind Victor Dashkov's escape.

And like that, Dimitri and I were in the car, speeding off toward Abe's "new gate." I regretted not being able to say goodbye to Lissa. We were never truly apart with the bond, but it couldn't take the place of face-to-face communication.

Still, it was worth it to know she would be safe and free of any connection to my escape. I hoped.

Like always, Dimitri drove, which I still thought was totally unfair. It had been one thing when I was his student, but now? Wouldn't he *ever* give up that wheel? This didn't seem like the time to discuss it, though—particularly since I didn't plan on us staying together much longer.

A few people had come out to see where the wall had blown up, but no one official had surfaced yet. Dimitri raced through the gap as impressively as Eddie had when he'd driven through Tarasov Prison's gate, only the Civic didn't handle the bumpy, grassy terrain as well as the SUV in Alaska. The problem with making your own exit was that it didn't come with an actual road. Even that was beyond Abe.

"Why is our getaway car a Civic?" I asked. "It's not really great for off-roading."

Dimitri didn't look at me but continued navigating over the rough ground toward a more drivable area. "Because Civics are one of the most common cars out there and don't attract attention. And this should be the only off-roading we do. Once we hit a freeway, we're putting as much distance between us and Court as we can—before abandoning the car, of course."

"Abandon—" I shook my head, letting it go. We reached a dirt road that felt like the smoothest surface on earth after that jolting start. "Look, now that we're out of there, I want you to know that I mean it: you don't have to come with me. I appreciate your help in the escape. Really. But hanging out with me won't do you any favors. They'll be hunting for me more than you. If you take off, you can live somewhere around humans and not be treated like a lab animal. You might even be able to slink back to Court. Tasha would put up a fight for you."

Dimitri didn't answer for a long time. It drove me crazy. I wasn't the kind of person who handled silence well. It made me want to chatter and fill the void. Plus, the longer I sat there, the more it hit me that *I was alone with Dimitri*. Like, really and truly alone for the first time since he'd become a dhampir. I felt like a fool, but in spite of the dangers we still risked . . . well, I was still overwhelmed by him. There was something so powerful about his presence. Even when he made me angry, I still found him attractive. Maybe the adrenaline pounding through me was addling my brain.

Whatever it was, I was consumed by more than just his physical aspects—though they were certainly distracting. The hair, the face, his closeness to me, his scent . . . I felt it all, and it made my blood burn. But the inner Dimitri—the Dimitri who'd just led a small army through a prison break—captivated me just as much. It took me a moment to realize why this was so powerful: I was seeing the old Dimitri again, the one I'd worried was gone forever. He wasn't. He was back.

At long last, Dimitri replied, "I'm not leaving you. None of your Rose-logic arguments are going to work. And if you try to get away from me, I'll just find you."

I didn't doubt he could, which just made the situation more confusing. "But why? I don't want you with me." I still felt a lingering attraction for him, yes, but that didn't change the fact that he had hurt me in breaking things off between us. He had rejected me, and I needed to harden my heart, particularly if I wanted to move on with Adrian. Clearing my name and leading a normal life seemed far away right now, but if it happened, I wanted to be able to return to Adrian with open arms.

"It doesn't matter what you want," he said. "Or what I want." Ouch. "Lissa asked me to protect you."

"Hey, I don't need anyone to—"

"And," he continued, "I meant what I said to her. I swore I'd serve her and help her for the rest of my life, anything she asks. If she wants me to be your bodyguard, then that's what I'll be." He gave me a dangerous look. "There's no way you're getting rid of me anytime soon."

Five

GETTING AWAY FROM DIMITRI WASN'T just about our rocky romantic past. I'd meant it when I said I didn't want him getting in trouble because of me. If the guardians found me, my fate wouldn't be that much different from what I'd already been facing. But Dimitri? He'd been making baby steps toward acceptance. Sure, that was pretty much destroyed now, but his chance for a life wasn't over. If he didn't want to live at Court or with humans, he could go back to Siberia and return to his family. Out there in the middle of nowhere, he'd be hard to find. And with how close that community was, they'd go to a lot of trouble to hide him if someone ever did try to hunt him down. Staying with me was definitely the wrong option. I just needed to convince him.

"I know what you're thinking," Dimitri said, after we'd been on the road for about an hour.

We hadn't spoken much, both of us lost in our own thoughts. After a few more country roads, we'd finally made it to an interstate and were making good time toward . . . well, I had no idea. I'd been staring out the window, pondering all the disasters around me and how I alone could fix them.

"Huh?" I glanced over at him.

I thought there might be the smallest hint of a smile on his lips, which seemed absurd considering this was probably the worst situation he'd been in since being restored from his Strigoi state.

"And it won't work," he added. "You're planning how to get away from me, probably when we eventually stop for gas. You're thinking maybe you'll have a chance to run off then."

The crazy thing was, I *had* been thinking very much along those lines. The old Dimitri was a good partner on the road, but I wasn't so sure I liked having his old ability to guess my thoughts back as well.

"This is a waste of time," I said, gesturing around the car.

"Oh? You have better things to do than flee the people who want to lock you up and execute you? Please don't tell me again that this is too dangerous for me."

I glared. "It's about more than just you. Running away shouldn't be my only concern. I should be helping clear my name, not hiding in whatever remote place you're undoubtedly taking me to. The answers are at Court."

"And you have lots of friends at Court who will be working on that. It'll be easier on them if they know you're safe."

"What I want to know is why no one told me about this—or, I mean, why Lissa didn't. Why'd she hide it? Don't you think I'd have been more helpful if I'd been ready?"

"We did the fighting, not you," Dimitri said. "We were afraid if you knew, you might give away that something was up."

"I would have never told!"

"Not intentionally, no. But if you were tense or anxious . . .

well, your guards can pick up on those kinds of things."

"Well, now that we're out, can you tell me where we're going? Was I right? Is it some crazy, remote place?"

No answer.

I narrowed my eyes at him. "I hate not being in the loop."

That tiny smile on his lips grew a little bigger. "Well, I have my own personal theory that the more you don't know, the more your curiosity is likely to make sure you stick around with me."

"That's ridiculous," I replied, though really, it wasn't all that unreasonable of a theory. I sighed. "When the hell did things get so out of control? When did you guys start being the masterminds? I'm the one who comes up with the wacky, impossible plans. I'm supposed to be the general here. Now I'm barely a lieutenant."

He started to say something else but then froze for a few seconds, his face instantly taking on that wary, lethal guardian look. He swore in Russian.

"What's wrong?" I asked. His attitude was contagious, and I immediately forgot all thoughts of crazy plans.

In the erratic flash of headlights from oncoming traffic, I could see his eyes dart up to the rearview mirror. "We have a tail. I didn't think it would happen this soon."

"Are you sure?" It had grown dark, and the number of cars on the highway had increased. I didn't know how anyone could spot one suspicious car among that many, but well . . . he was Dimitri.

He swore again and suddenly, in a maneuver that made

me grab the dashboard, he cut sharply across two lanes, barely missing a minivan that expressed its annoyance with a lot of honking. There was an exit right there, and he just barely made it without clipping the exit ramp's rail. I heard more honking, and when I looked back, I saw the headlights of a car that had made just as crazy a move to follow us onto the exit.

"The Court must have gotten the word out pretty fast," he said. "They had someone watching the interstates."

"Maybe we should have taken back roads."

He shook his head. "Too slow. None of it would have been an issue once we switched cars, but they found us too soon. We'll have to get a new one here. This is the biggest city we'll hit before the Maryland border."

A sign said we were in Harrisburg, Pennsylvania, and as Dimitri skillfully drove us down a busy, commerce-filled road, I could see the tail mirroring everything we did. "What exactly is your plan to get a new car?" I asked warily.

"Listen carefully," he said, ignoring my question. "It is very, *very* important that you do exactly as I say. No improvising. No arguing. There are guardians in that car, and by now, they've alerted every other guardian around here—possibly even the human police."

"Wouldn't the police catching us create a few problems?"

"The Alchemists would sort it out and make sure we ended up back with the Moroi."

The Alchemists. I should have known they'd get involved. They were a secret society of humans who helped protect Moroi and dhampir interests, keeping us out of the mainstream human public. Of course, the Alchemists didn't do it out of kindness. They thought we were evil and unnatural and mostly wanted to make sure we stayed on the fringes of their society. An escaped "criminal" like me would certainly be a problem they would want to help the Moroi with.

Dimitri's voice was hard and commanding when he spoke again, though his eyes weren't on me. They were busy scanning the sides of the road. "No matter what you think of the choices everyone's been making for you, no matter how unhappy you are with this situation, you know—I know you do—that I've never failed you when our lives were at stake. You trusted me in the past. Trust me now."

I wanted to tell him that what he said wasn't entirely true. He *had* failed me. When he'd been taken down by Strigoi, when he'd shown that he wasn't perfect, he had failed me by shattering the impossible, godly image I had of him. But my life? No, he had always kept mine safe. Even as a Strigoi, I'd never entirely been convinced he could kill me. The night the Academy had been attacked, when he'd been turned, he'd told me to obey him without question too. It had meant leaving him to fight Strigoi, but I'd done it.

"Okay," I said quietly. "I'll do whatever you say. Just remember not to talk down to me. I'm not your student anymore. I'm your equal now."

He glanced away from the side of the road just long enough to give me a surprised look. "You've always been my equal, Roza."

The use of the affectionate Russian nickname made me too

stupid to respond, but it didn't matter. Moments later, he was all business again. "There. Do you see that movie theater sign?"

I gazed down the road. There were so many restaurants and stores that their signs made a glittering haze in the night. At last, I saw what he meant. WESTLAND CINEMA.

"Yes."

"That's where we're going to meet."

We were splitting up? I'd wanted to part ways but not like this. In the face of danger, separating suddenly seemed like an awful idea. I'd promised not to argue, though, and kept listening.

"If I'm not there in a half hour, you call this number and go without me." Dimitri handed me a small piece of paper from his duster pocket. It had a phone number scrawled on it, not one I recognized.

If I'm not there in a half hour. The words were so shocking that I couldn't help my protest this time. "What do you mean if you're not—ah!"

Dimitri made another abrupt turn, one that caused him to run a red light and only narrowly miss a number of cars. More honking ensued, but the move had been too sudden for our tail to keep up. I saw our pursuers whiz past on the main road, brake lights flashing as they searched for a place to turn around.

Dimitri had taken us into a mall parking lot. It was packed with cars, and I glanced at the clock to get a grasp for human time. Almost eight o'clock at night. Early in the Moroi day, prime entertainment time for humans. He drove past a few entrances to the mall and finally selected one, pulling into a handicap spot. He was out of the car in one fluid motion, with me following just as quickly.

"Here's where we split up," he said jogging toward a set of doors. "Move fast, but don't run when we're inside. Don't attract attention. Blend in. Wind through it for a little bit; then get out through any exit but this one. Walk out near a group of humans and then head for the theater." We stepped into the mall. "Go!"

As though afraid I might not move, he gave me a small push toward an escalator while he took off on the main floor. There was a part of me that wanted to just freeze and stand there, that felt dumbfounded by the sudden onslaught of people, light, and activity. I soon pushed that startled part aside and began heading up the escalator. Fast reflexes and instinctual reactions were part of my training. I'd honed them in school, in my travels, and with him.

Everything I'd been taught about eluding someone came rushing back to my head. What I wanted to do more than anything was look around and see if I had a follower, but that would have definitely attracted attention. I had to imagine that, at most, we had a couple minutes' lead on our pursuers. They would have had to turn around to get back to the mall and then circle to spot our car, presuming they figured out we'd gone into the mall. I didn't think Harrisburg had enough of a Moroi presence to summon very many guardians on short notice. The ones they had would likely split up, some searching the mall and some guarding the entrances. This place had too many doors for the guardians to watch them all; my escape choice would be pure luck.

I walked as fast as I reasonably could, weaving through couples, families with strollers, and giggling teens. I envied that last group. Their lives seemed so easy compared to mine. I also passed the usual mall stores, their names registering but not much more: Ann Taylor, Abercrombie, Forever 21 . . . Ahead of me, I could see the center of the mall where several corridors branched out. I'd have a choice to make soon.

Passing an accessories store, I ducked inside and pretended to look at headbands. As I did, I covertly glanced back out to the mall's main section. I saw nothing obvious. No one had stopped; no one had followed me into the store. Beside the headbands section was a clearance bin filled with items that obviously deserved to be on clearance. One item was a "girly" baseball cap, hot pink with a star done in rainbow rhinestones on the front. It was god-awful.

I bought it, grateful the guardians hadn't taken away the meager cash I'd had on me when arrested. They probably figured it wasn't enough to bribe anyone. I also bought a ponytail holder, all the while still keeping an eye on the store's doorway. Before leaving, I bound my hair up as much as I could with the holder and then put on the hat. There was something silly about being reduced to disguises, but my hair was an easy way to ID me. It was a deep, almost-black brown, and my lack of any recent haircut had it hanging to my mid-back. In fact, between that and Dimitri's height, we would have made a very conspicuous pair walking through here.

I merged back into the shoppers and soon reached the mall's center. Not wanting to show any hesitation, I took a left toward Macy's. As I walked, I felt slightly embarrassed at the hat and wished I'd at least had time to find a more stylish one. Minutes later, when I spotted a guardian, I was glad I'd made such a quick fashion choice.

He was near one of those carts you always see in the center of malls, pretending to be interested in cell phone covers. I recognized him first because of his stance and the way he was managing to act interested in a zebra print phone cover while simultaneously searching around him. Plus, dhampirs could always distinguish each other from humans with close enough examination. For the most part, our two races appeared pretty identical, but I could spot one of my own.

I made sure not to look right at him and felt his eyes pass over me. I didn't know him, which meant he probably didn't know me either. He was likely going off a photo he'd seen once and expected my hair to be a big giveaway. Keeping as casual an air as I could, I moved past him at a leisurely pace, glancing in windows that kept my back to him but sent no obvious messages that I was on the run. All the while, my heart pounded in my chest. Guardians could kill me on sight. Did that apply to the middle of a mall? I didn't want to find out.

When I was clear of the cart, I picked up my pace a little. Macy's would have its own outside door, and now it was just a gamble to see whether or not I'd made a good call coming in this direction. I entered the store, went down its escalator, and headed toward the main floor exit—passing a very nice selection of cute berets and fedoras. I paused near them, not because I planned on upgrading my hat, but because it allowed me to fall in step just behind a group of girls who were also exiting.

We left the store together, and my eyes quickly adjusted to the change in light. There were lots of people around, but I again saw nothing threatening. My girls stopped to chat, giving me an opportunity to get my bearings without appearing totally lost. To my right, I spotted the busy road Dimitri and I had come in on, and from there, I knew how to get to the movie theater. I exhaled in relief and cut across the parking lot, still watching my surroundings.

The farther I walked from the mall, the less crowded the parking lot became. Lampposts kept it from being totally dark, but there was still an eerie feel as things grew quieter and quieter. My initial impulse was to head right for the road and take the sidewalk directly to the theater. It was well lit and had people. But a moment later, I decided it was too conspicuous. I was pretty sure I could cut across parking lots much more quickly to get to the theater.

It proved true—kind of. I had the theater in sight when I realized I had been followed after all. Not far ahead of me, the shadow of a parking lamp's post didn't cast correctly. The shadow was too broad. Someone was behind the pole. I doubted a guardian had coincidentally picked this spot in the hopes Dimitri or I would come by. Most likely it was a scout who'd seen me and circled ahead for an ambush.

I kept walking, trying not to obviously slow down, though every muscle in my body was tensing for attack. *I* had to be the one who attacked first. I had to be in control.

My moment came, seconds before I suspected my ambusher would have made his move. I leapt out, throwing him—it turned out to be a dhampir I didn't recognize—against a nearby car. Yup. I'd surprised him. Of course, the surprise was mutual when the car's alarm went off, blaring into the night. I winced, trying to ignore the shrieking as I punched my captive on the left side of his jaw. I had to make the most of having him pinned.

The force of my fist knocked his head against the car, but he took it admirably, promptly pushing back in an effort to free himself. He was stronger, and I did stumble a little, but not enough to lose my balance. What I lacked in strength, I made up for in speed. I dodged each attempt at me, but it brought me little satisfaction. That stupid car alarm was still going strong, and it was eventually going to attract the attention of other guardians or human authorities.

I dashed around the side of the car, and he gave chase, stopping when we were on opposite sides. It was like two kids playing keep-away. We mirrored each other as he tried to anticipate which direction I'd go. In the dim lighting, I saw something surprising tucked into his belt: a gun. My blood ran cold. Guardians were trained to use guns but rarely carried them. Stakes were our weapon of choice. We were in the business of killing Strigoi, after all, and guns were ineffective. But against me? Yeah. A gun simplified his job, but I had a feeling he'd hesitate to use it. A car alarm could be blamed on someone accidentally getting too close, but a gunshot? That would elicit a call to the police. This guy wouldn't fire if he could help it—but he *would* if he ran out of options. This needed to end soon.

At last I made a move toward the front of the car. He tried to intercept me, but then I surprised him by springing onto the car's hood (because honestly, at this point, it wasn't like the alarm could get any louder). In my split second of advantage, I threw myself off the car and onto him, knocking him flat to the ground. I landed on top of his stomach and held him down with all my weight while my hands went around his neck. He struggled, trying to throw me off, and nearly succeeded. At last, the lack of air won out. He stopped moving and fell into unconsciousness. I let go.

For a brief moment, I had a flashback to our escape from Court, when I'd used the same technique on Meredith. I saw her lying on the ground all over again and felt that same pang of guilt. Then, I shook it off. Meredith was okay. Meredith wasn't even here. None of that mattered. All that mattered was that this guy was out of commission, and I had to get out of here. Now.

Without looking to see if others were coming, I tore off across the parking lot toward the theater. I stopped once I had some distance between me and the wailing car, using another car as cover. I saw no one near the guy yet, but over by the parking lot's front, close to the mall, there seemed to be some activity. I didn't stick around to get a closer look. Whatever it was, it couldn't be good for me.

I reached the theater a couple minutes later, breathless

more from fear than exhaustion. Running endurance was something I had built up a lot of, thanks to Dimitri. But where *was* Dimitri? Theatergoers mingled around, some giving my disheveled state an odd look, as they either waited for tickets or discussed what movie they'd just seen. I saw no sign of Dimitri anywhere.

I had no watch. How long had passed since we'd parted? Surely not a half hour. I walked around the theater, staying obscured in the crowd, searching for any indication of Dimitri or more pursuers. Nothing. Minutes ticked by. Uneasily, I reached into my pocket and touched the piece of paper with the phone number. Leave, he'd told me. Leave and call the number. Of course, I had no cell phone, but that was the least of my problems right now—

"Rose!"

A car pulled up at the curb where others were dropping people off. Dimitri was leaning out the driver's side window, and I nearly fell over in relief. Well, okay, not nearly. In reality, I didn't waste a moment in hurrying over to him and hopping into the passenger seat. Without a word, he hit the gas and got us away from the theater and back to the main road.

We said nothing at first. He was so wound up and on edge, it seemed the slightest provocation would make him snap in half. He drove as fast as he could without attracting police attention, all the while glancing into the rearview mirror.

"Is there anyone behind us?" I asked at last, as he drove back onto the highway.

"It doesn't look like it. It'll take them a while to figure out what car we're in."

I hadn't paid much attention when I'd entered, but we were in a Honda Accord—another ordinary-looking car. I also noticed that there was no key in the ignition.

"Did you hotwire this car?" I then rephrased my question. "Did you *steal* this car?"

"You have an interesting set of morals," he observed. "Breaking out of jail is okay. But steal a car, and you sound totally outraged."

"I'm just more surprised than outraged," I said, leaning back against the seat. I sighed. "I was afraid . . . well, for a moment there, I was afraid you weren't coming. That they'd caught you or something."

"No. Most of my time was spent sneaking out and finding a suitable car."

A few minutes of silence fell. "You didn't ask what happened to me," I pointed out, a little miffed.

"Don't need to. You're here. That's what counts."

"I got in a fight."

"I can tell. Your sleeve is ripped."

I glanced down. Yup, ripped. I'd also lost the hat in my mad dash. No big loss. "Don't you want to know anything about the fight?"

His eyes stayed on the road ahead of us. "I already know. You took down your enemy. You did it fast, and you did it well. Because you're just that good."

I pondered his words for a moment. They were matter-of-fact, all business . . . and yet, his statement brought a tiny smile to my lips. "Okay. So what now, General? Don't you think they'll scan reports of stolen cars and get our license plate number?"

"Likely. But by then, we'll have a new car—one they won't have any clue about."

I frowned. "How are you pulling that off?"

"We're meeting someone in a few hours."

"Damn it. I *really* hate being the last one to know about everything."

'A few hours' put us in Roanoke, Virginia. Most of our drive had passed uneventfully up until that point. But as the city came into view, I noticed Dimitri watching the exit signs until he found the one he wanted. Turning off the interstate, he continued checking for a tail and found none. We reached another commerce-filled road, and he drove to a McDonald's that stood out clearly from the rest of the businesses.

"I don't suppose," I said, "that this is a food break?"

"This," he responded, "is where we catch our next ride."

He drove around the restaurant's parking lot, his eyes scanning for something, though I didn't initially know what. I spotted it a fraction of a second before he did. In the far corner of the lot, I saw a woman leaning against a tan SUV, her back to us. I couldn't see much of her except that she wore a dark shirt and had tousled blond hair that almost touched her shoulders.

Dimitri pulled into the spot next to her vehicle, and I was out of ours the second he hit the brake. I recognized her before she even turned around.

"Sydney?" The name came out as a question, though I knew for sure it was her.

Her head turned, and I saw a familiar face—a human face—with brown eyes that could turn amber in the sun and a faint gold tattoo on her cheek.

"Hey, Rose," she said, a rueful smile playing on her lips. She held up a McDonald's bag. "Figured you'd be hungry."

SIX

REALLY, WHEN YOU THOUGHT ABOUT it, Sydney showing up wasn't much weirder than half the other stuff that seemed to happen to me on a regular basis. Sydney was an Alchemist, one I'd met in Russia when trying to find and kill Dimitri. She was my age and had hated being assigned over there, though I'd certainly appreciated her aid. As Dimitri had noted earlier, the Alchemists would want to help the Moroi find and capture me. Yet, judging from the tension radiating off both her and Dimitri in the car, it became obvious that she was assisting in this escape.

With great effort, I pushed my questions to the side for the time being. We were still fugitives, still undoubtedly being pursued. Sydney's car was a brand new Honda CR-V with Louisiana plates and a rental sticker.

"What the hell?" I asked. "Is this daring escape being sponsored by Honda?" When this got no response, I went to the next obvious question. "Are we going to New Orleans?" That was Sydney's new post. Sightseeing was the last thing on my mind at the moment, but if you had to run away, you might as well run somewhere good.

"No," she said, backing out of the spot. "We're going to West Virginia."

I looked sharply at Dimitri, who sat in the backseat, in the hopes that he would deny this. He didn't.

"I assume by 'West Virginia,' you actually mean 'Hawaii,'" I said. "Or some place equally exciting."

"Honestly, I think you're better off avoiding excitement right now," Sydney pointed out. The car's GPS device directed her to her next turn, leading us back toward I-81. She frowned slightly. "And West Virginia's actually really pretty."

I remembered that she was from Utah and probably didn't know any better. Having long since given up on any control in this escape plot, I moved on to the next obvious set of questions.

"Why are you helping us?"

I had a feeling Sydney was grimacing in the dark. "Why do you think?"

"Abe."

She sighed. "I'm really starting to wonder if New Orleans was worth it."

I'd recently learned that Abe—with that inexplicable, far-reaching influence of his—had been responsible for getting her out of Russia. How he'd done it, I didn't know. What I did know was that it had left Sydney in open-ended debt to him, one he kept using to get favors. Sometimes, I wondered if there was more to the deal than just a job transfer, like maybe he'd done something else that neither had told me about. Regardless, I started to chastise her again that she should have expected this for making a deal with the devil, but I soon reconsidered. With a bunch of guardians in pursuit, it probably wasn't a smart idea to tease someone helping me. I asked a different question.

"Okay. So why are we going to West Virginia?"

Sydney opened her mouth to respond, but Dimitri interrupted her. "Not yet."

I turned around again and shot him a glare. "I am so sick of this! We've been on the run for six hours now, and I still don't know all the details. I get that we're staying away from the guardians, but are we seriously going to West Virginia? Are we going to make some cabin our base of operation? Like, one on the side of a mountain that doesn't have plumbing?"

Sydney gave me one of her trademark exasperated sighs. "Do you actually know anything *about* West Virginia?"

I didn't like her and Dimitri teaming up to keep me in the dark. Of course, with Sydney, her reticence could be from any number of things. It could still be Abe's orders. Or maybe she just didn't want to talk to me. Since most Alchemists considered dhampirs and vampires the spawn of hell, they didn't usually get too friendly with us. Spending time with me in Siberia had altered her views a little. I hoped. Sometimes I got the vibe she just wasn't that social of a person to begin with.

"You know we've been set up, right?" I asked her. "We didn't really do anything. They say I killed the queen, but—"

"I know," Sydney interrupted. "I've heard all about it. All the Alchemists know about it. You two are at the top of our most wanted list." She attempted a businesslike tone but couldn't entirely hide her uneasiness. I had a feeling Dimitri made her more nervous than I did, which was understandable since he made some of our own people nervous too.

"I didn't do it," I insisted. Somehow, it was important that she know that.

Sydney didn't acknowledge my comment. Instead, she said, "You should eat. Your food's getting cold. We've got a little over three hours to go and won't be stopping except for gas."

I recognized the finality in her voice, as well as the logic. She didn't want to talk anymore. Inside the bag, I found two giant orders of fries, and three cheeseburgers. She apparently still knew me pretty well. It took all of my restraint to keep from stuffing fries into my mouth then and there. Instead, I offered a cheeseburger to Dimitri.

"You want one? Gotta keep up your strength."

He hesitated several seconds before taking it. He seemed to regard it with a kind of wonder, and it hit me that eating food was still a new thing for him after these last few months. Strigoi only subsisted on blood. I handed him a couple of fries too and then turned back around to devour the rest. I didn't bother offering any to Sydney. She was notorious for her lack of appetite, and besides, I figured she would have eaten already if she'd wanted to while waiting for us.

"I think this is for you," Dimitri said, handing me a small backpack. I opened it and found a few changes of clothes, as well as some basic toiletries. I double-checked the outfits.

"Shorts, shirts, and a dress. I can't fight in these. I need jeans." The dress was cute, admittedly: a long gauzy sundress in a watercolor print of black, white, and gray. But very impractical.

"That's gratitude for you," said Sydney. "This happened kind of fast. There was only so much I could put together."

Glancing behind me, I saw Dimitri unpacking his own bag. It had basic clothing like mine and also—

"A duster?" I exclaimed, watching him pull out the long, leather coat. How it even fit in there defied physics. "You managed to get him a duster, but you couldn't find me a pair of jeans?"

Sydney seemed unconcerned by my outrage. "Abe said it was essential. Besides, if all goes like it's supposed to, you won't be doing any fighting." I didn't like the sound of that. *Safe and remote.*

Seeing as I had what were potentially the quietest car companions in the world, I knew better than to expect any real conversation for the next three hours. I supposed it was just as well because it let me check in on Lissa. I was still too on edge about my own escape to spend much time in her head, so it was just a quick assessment of life at Court.

Just as Dimitri had predicted, the guardians had restored order pretty soon. The Court was under lockdown, and everyone with any connection to me was being questioned extensively. The thing was, they all had alibis. Everyone had seen my allies at the funeral—or, in Abe's case, *thought* they'd seen them. A couple girls swore they'd been with Adrian, which I could only imagine was the result of more compulsion. I could feel Lissa's satisfaction through the bond as the guardians' frustration grew and grew.

Although she had no idea when I might be checking in on

her, she sent me a message through the bond: *Don't worry, Rose. I'll take care of everything. We're going to clear your name.*

I slumped back in the car seat, unsure how to feel about this situation. All my life, I'd taken care of her. I'd protected her from danger and gone out of my way to keep her away from any threats. Now, the roles were reversed. She'd come through for me in saving Dimitri, and I was in her—and apparently everyone else's—hands as far as this escape was concerned. It went against every instinct I had and troubled me. I wasn't used to being protected by others, let alone her.

The interrogations were still going on, and Lissa hadn't had hers yet, but something told me my friends were going to get off the hook for this. They wouldn't be punished for my escape, and for the moment, I was really the only one in danger—which was what I preferred.

West Virginia might have been as beautiful as Sydney claimed, but I couldn't really tell since it was the middle of the night when we arrived. Mostly I had the sense of driving through mountains, feeling the ups and downs as we went through switchbacks and tunnels. After almost exactly three hours, we rolled into a small hole of a town that had one traffic light and a restaurant simply marked DINER. There hadn't been any traffic on the road for over an hour, though, which was really the most important thing. We hadn't been followed.

Sydney drove us to a building with a sign that read MOTEL. Apparently, this town liked to stick to the basics when it came to names. I wouldn't be surprised if it was actually just called TOWN. As we walked across the motel's parking lot, I was surprised to feel how sore my legs were. Every part of me ached, and sleep sounded fantastic. It had been more than half a day since this adventure began.

Sydney checked us in under fake names, and the sleepy desk clerk didn't ask any questions. We walked down a hall that wasn't dirty exactly but also wasn't anything a royal would have gone near. A cleaning cart leaned against one wall, as though someone had given up and abandoned it. Sydney suddenly came to a halt in front of a room and handed us a key. I realized she was heading off to a different room.

"We're not all staying together?" I asked.

"Hey, if you guys get caught, I don't want to be anywhere near you," she said, with a smile. I had a feeling she also didn't want to sleep in the same room as "evil creatures of the night." "I'll still be nearby, though. We'll talk in the morning."

This made me realize something else. I eyed Dimitri. "We're sharing a room?"

Sydney shrugged. "All the better to defend yourselves."

She left us in that abrupt way of hers, and Dimitri and I glanced at each other briefly before heading into the room. Like the rest of the motel, it wasn't fancy, but it would do. The carpet was worn but intact, and I appreciated the weak attempt at decorating with a very bad painting of some pears. A small window looked sad. There was one bed.

Dimitri locked the bolt and chain on the door and then sat back in the room's lone chair. It was wooden with a straight back, but he seemed to regard it as the most comfortable thing in the world. He still wore that perpetually vigilant look of his, but I could see exhaustion around the edges. This had been a long night for him too.

I sat down on the edge of the bed. "What now?"

"Now we wait," he said.

"For what?"

"For Lissa and the others to clear your name and find out who killed the queen."

I expected more explanation, but all I got was silence. Disbelief began to build up in me. I'd remained as patient as I could tonight, always assuming Dimitri was leading me toward some mysterious mission to help solve the murder. When he said we were going to wait, surely he didn't mean we were just going to . . . well, wait?

"What are *we* going to do?" I demanded. "How are we going to help them?"

"We told you earlier: You can hardly go looking for clues at Court. You need to stay away. You need to stay safe."

My jaw dropped as I gestured around the drab room. "What, and this is it? This is where you're stashing me? I thought . . . I thought there was something here. Something to help."

"It *is* helping," he said, in that damnably calm way of his. "Sydney and Abe researched this place and decided it was out of the way enough to avoid detection."

I shot up from the bed. "Okay, comrade. There's one serious problem here with your logic. You guys keep acting like me staying out of the way is *helping*."

"What's a serious problem is us repeating this conversation over and over. The answers to who murdered Tatiana are at Court, and that's where your friends are. They'll figure this out."

"I didn't just get in a high-speed chase and jump state lines to hole up in some crappy motel! How long are you planning on 'staying out of the way' here?"

Dimitri crossed his arms over his chest. "As long as it takes. We have the funds to stay here indefinitely."

"I probably have enough spare change in my pocket to stay here indefinitely! But it's not happening. I have to do something. I won't just take the easy way out and sit around."

"Surviving isn't as easy as you think."

"Oh God," I groaned. "You've been hanging out with Abe, haven't you? You know, when you were a Strigoi, you told me to stay away from him. Maybe you should take your own advice."

I regretted the words as soon as they left my lips and saw in his eyes that I'd inflicted serious damage. He might have been acting like the old Dimitri in this escape, but his time as a Strigoi still tormented him.

"I'm sorry," I said. "I didn't mean—"

"We're done discussing this," he said harshly. "Lissa says we're staying here, so we're staying here."

Anger shoved aside my guilt. "*That's* why you're doing this? Because Lissa told you to?"

"Of course. I swore I'd serve and help her."

That was when I snapped. It had been bad enough that when Lissa restored him to a dhampir, Dimitri had thought it was okay to stick around Lissa while spurning me. Despite the fact that *I'd* been the one who went to Siberia and that *I* was the one who learned about how Victor's brother Robert knew how to restore Strigoi . . . well, apparently those things didn't matter. Only Lissa wielding the stake had seemed to matter, and Dimitri now held her up as some kind of angelic goddess, one he'd made an archaic, knight-like vow to serve.

"Forget it," I said. "I am *not* staying here."

I made it to the door in three steps and managed to undo the chain, but in seconds, Dimitri was out of his chair and had thrown me against the wall. Really, that was pretty slow reaction time. I would have expected him to stop me before I'd taken two steps.

"You *are* staying here," he said evenly, hands gripping my wrists. "Whether you like it or not."

Now, I had a few options. I *could* stay, of course. I could hang out for days—months, even—in this motel until Lissa cleared my name. That was presuming Lissa could clear my name and that I didn't get food poisoning from the DINER diner. This was the safest option. Also the most boring for me.

Another option was to fight my way through Dimitri. That was neither safe nor easy. It would also be particularly challenging because I'd have to try to fight in such a way that would allow me to escape but wouldn't kill him or cause either of us serious injury.

Or, I could just throw caution away and not hold back. Hell, the guy had battled Strigoi and half the Court's guardians. He could handle me giving everything I had. We'd certainly shared some pretty rough encounters back at St. Vladimir's.

Would my best be enough for me to escape? Time to find out.

I kneed him in the stomach, which he clearly hadn't expected. His eyes widened in shock—and a little pain—providing me with an opening to break free of his grip. That opening was only long enough for me to yank out the door's bolt. Before I could reach for the knob, Dimitri had a hold of me again. He gripped me hard and threw me onto the bed stomach first, both pinning me with his weight and preventing my limbs from doing any more surprise kicking. This was always my biggest problem in fights: opponents—usually men—with more strength and weight. My speed was my greatest asset in those situations, but being held down made dodging and evasion a non-option. Still, every part of me struggled, making it difficult for him to keep me down.

"Stop this," he said in my ear, his lips nearly touching it. "Be reasonable for once. You can't get past me."

His body was warm and strong against mine, and I promised my own body a stern scolding later. *Quit it*, I thought. *Focus on getting out of here, not how he feels.*

"I'm not the one being unreasonable," I growled, trying to turn my face toward him. "You're the one caught up in some noble promise that makes no sense. And I know you don't like to sit out of the action any more than I do. Help me. Help me find the murderer and do something useful." I stopped struggling and pretended our argument had distracted me.

"I don't like sitting around, but I also don't like rushing into an impossible situation!"

"Impossible situations are our specialty," I pointed out.

Meanwhile, I tried to assess his hold on me. He hadn't relaxed his grip, but I hoped maybe the conversation was distracting him. Normally, Dimitri was too good to lose his focus. But I knew he was tired. And maybe, just maybe, he might be a little careless since it was me and not a Strigoi.

Nope.

I lashed out abruptly, trying to break away and scramble out from under him. The best I managed to do was roll myself over before he had a hold of me again, now leaving me back-down on the bed. Being so close to him . . . his face, his lips . . . the warmth of his skin on mine. Well. It appeared that all I'd accomplished was putting myself at a greater disadvantage. He certainly didn't seem to be affected by our bodies' closeness. He wore that typical steel resolve of his, and even though it was stupid of me, even though I knew I shouldn't care anymore that he was over me . . . well, I did care.

"One day," he said. "You can't even wait one day?"

"Maybe if we'd gone to a nicer hotel. With cable."

"This is no time for jokes, Rose."

"Then let me do something. Anything."

"I. Can't."

Saying the words obviously pained him, and I realized something. I was so mad at him, so furious that he'd try to make me sit around and play it safe. But he didn't like any of this either. How could I have forgotten how alike we were? We both craved action. We both wanted to be useful, to help those we cared about. It was only his self-resolve to help Lissa that was keeping him here with this babysitting job. He claimed me rushing back to Court was reckless, but I had a feeling that if he hadn't been the one in charge of me—or, well, *thought* he was—he would have run right back there too.

I studied him, the determined dark eyes and expression softened by the brown hair that had escaped its ponytail holder. It hung around his face now, just barely touching mine. I could try to break free again but was losing hope of that working. He was too fierce and too set on keeping me safe. I suspected pointing out my suspicion that he wanted to go back to Court too wouldn't do any good. True or not, he would be expecting me to argue with Rose-logic. He was Dimitri, after all. He would be expecting *everything*.

Well, almost.

An idea hit me so fast that I didn't pause to analyze it. I just acted. My body might be constrained, but my head and neck had just enough freedom to shift up—and kiss him.

My lips met his, and I learned a few things. One was that it was possible to catch him totally by surprise. His body froze and locked up, shocked at the sudden turn of events. I also realized that he was just as good a kisser as I recalled. The last time we'd kissed had been when he was Strigoi. There had been an eerie sexiness to that, but it didn't compare to the heat and energy of being alive. His lips were just like I remembered from our time at St. Vladimir's, both soft and hungry at the same time. Electricity spread through the rest of my body as he kissed me back. It was both comforting and exhilarating.

And that was the third thing I discovered. *He was kissing me back.* Maybe, just maybe, Dimitri wasn't as resolved as he claimed to be. Maybe under all that guilt and certainty that he couldn't love again, he still wanted me. I would have liked to have found out. But I didn't have the time.

Instead, I punched him.

It's true: I've punched lots of guys who were kissing me but never one I actually *wanted* to keep kissing. Dimitri still had a solid hold on me, but the shock of the kiss had dropped his guard. My fist broke out and connected with the side of his face. Without missing a beat, I shoved him off me as hard as I could and leapt away from the bed and toward the door. I heard him scramble to his feet as I threw it open. I shot out of the room and slammed the door shut before I could see what he did next. Not that I needed to. He was coming after me.

Without a moment's hesitation, I shoved the abandoned cleaning cart in front of the room's door and sprinted off down the hall. A couple seconds later, the door opened, and I heard a cry of annoyance—as well as a very, very bad word in Russian—as he ran into the cart. It would only take him a few moments to push it aside, but that was all I needed. I was down the flight of stairs in a flash and into the meager lobby where a bored desk clerk was reading a book. He nearly jumped out of his chair when I came tearing through.

"There's a guy chasing me!" I called as I headed out the door.

The clerk didn't really look like anyone who would try to stop Dimitri, and I had a feeling Dimitri wouldn't stop anyway if the guy asked him to. In the most extreme case, the man would call the police. In this town, the POLICE probably consisted of one guy and a dog.

Regardless, it was no longer my concern. I had escaped the motel and was now in the middle of a sleepy mountain town, its streets cast in shadows. Dimitri might be right behind me, but as I plunged into some woods nearby, I knew it was going to be easy for me to lose him in the darkness.

SEVEN

THE PROBLEM WAS, OF COURSE, that I soon lost myself in the darkness.

After living in the wilds of Montana, I was used to how completely the night could swallow you once you stepped away from even the tiniest hint of civilization. I was even used to wandering the twists and turns of dark forests. But the St. Vladimir's terrain had been familiar. The woods of West Virginia were new and foreign, and I had completely lost my bearings.

Once I was pretty sure I'd put enough distance between me and the motel, I paused and looked around. Night insects hummed and sang, and the oppressive summer humidity hung around me. Peering up through the leafy canopy of trees, I could see a brilliant sky of stars, totally untouched by city lights. Feeling like a true wilderness survivor, I studied the stars until I spotted the Big Dipper and figured out which direction was north. The mountains Sydney had driven us through had been to the east, so I certainly didn't want to go in that direction. It seemed reasonable that if I hiked north, I'd eventually hit an interstate and either hitchhike or walk my way back to civilization. It wasn't an airtight plan, but it wasn't the worst one I'd ever had, not by a long shot.

I wasn't really dressed for hiking, but as my eyes adjusted to the darkness, I managed to avoid most trees and other obstacles. Following the tiny road out of town would have been easier—but was also what Dimitri would expect me to do.

I fell into a steady, subconscious rhythm as I made my way north. I decided it was a good time to check in on Lissa, now that I had time on my hands and no guardians trying to arrest me. I slipped into her mind and found her within the depths of the guardians' headquarters, sitting in a hallway lined with chairs. Other Moroi sat nearby, including Christian and Tasha.

"They'll question you hard," Tasha murmured. "Especially *you.*" That was to Christian. "You'd be my first choice if something illicitly blew up." That seemed to be everyone's opinion. From the troubled look on her face, I could see Tasha had been as surprised by my escape as I had. Even if my friends hadn't filled her in on the whole story yet, she had probably pieced most things together—at the very least, who was behind it.

Christian gave her as charming a smile as he could manage, like a kid trying to dodge being grounded. "They'll know by now that it wasn't caused by magic," he said. "The guardians will have scoured every inch of those statues." He didn't elaborate, not in public, but Lissa's mind was working along the same lines as his. The guardians would know now the explosion hadn't been elemental. And even if my friends were the primary suspects, the authorities would have to wonder—just as I had—how teenagers would get a hold of C4.

Lissa nodded her agreement and rested her hand on Christian's. "We'll be okay."

Her thoughts turned to both Dimitri and me, wondering if we'd made it out according to the plan. She couldn't focus on finding Tatiana's killer until she knew we were safe. Like me, the breakout had been a hard choice: freeing me put me in more danger than keeping me locked up. Her emotions were keyed up, prickly and a bit wilder than I would have liked. *So much spirit*, I realized. *She's using too much.* Back at school, she'd managed it with prescription medication and later through self-control. But somewhere, as our situations grew increasingly complicated, she'd allowed herself to wield more and more. Recently, she'd used astonishing amounts, and we'd come to take it for granted. Sooner or later, Lissa's reliance on spirit would catch up with her. With us.

"Princess?" A door across from Lissa opened, and a guardian peered out. "We're ready for you."

The guardian stepped aside, and inside the room, Lissa heard a familiar voice say, "Always a pleasure speaking with you, Hans. We should do it again sometime." Abe then appeared, strutting out with his usual swagger. He stepped past the guardian in the doorway and gave Lissa and the Ozeras a winning, all-is-right-in-the-world grin. Without a word, he strode past them toward the hall's exit.

Lissa almost smiled but reined it in, putting on a sober look as she and her companions entered. The door shut behind them, and she found herself facing three guardians seated at a table. One of them I'd seen around but had never met. I think his last name was Steele. The other two I knew well. One was Hans Croft, who ran the guardians' operations at Court. Beside him—to my astonishment—was Alberta, who was in charge of St. Vladimir's guardians and novices.

"Lovely," growled Hans. "A whole entourage." Christian had insisted on being present when Lissa was questioned, and Tasha had insisted on being present with Christian. If Abe had known the interrogation time, he probably would have joined the group too, undoubtedly followed by my mother . . . Hans didn't realize he'd dodged a house party.

Lissa, Christian, and Tasha sat down opposite the guardians. "Guardian Petrov," said Lissa, ignoring Hans's disapproval. "What are you doing here?"

Alberta gave Lissa a small smile but otherwise kept in professional guardian mode. "I was here for the funeral, and Guardian Croft decided he'd like an outside opinion for the investigation."

"As well as someone familiar with Hathaway and her, uh, associates," added Hans. Hans was the kind of guy who got straight to the point. Usually, his attitude bothered me—that was my normal reaction to most authority figures—but I did respect the way he ran operations here. "This meeting was intended just for *you*, princess."

"We won't say a word," said Christian.

Lissa nodded and kept her face smooth and polite, even though there was a trembling in her voice. "I want to help . . . I've been so, I don't know. I'm so stunned about everything that's happened."

"I'm sure," said Hans, voice dry. "Where were you when the statues exploded?"

"With the funeral procession," she said. "I was part of the escort."

Steele had a pile of papers in front of him. "That's true. There are plenty of witnesses."

"Very convenient. What about *afterward*?" asked Hans. "Where did you go when the crowd panicked?"

"Back to the Council's building. That's where all the others were meeting up, and I thought it'd be safest." I couldn't see her face but could feel her trying to look cowed. "I was afraid when things started going crazy."

"We also have witnesses to support that," said Steele.

Hans drummed his fingers on the table. "Did you have any prior knowledge about any of this? The explosions? Hathaway's breakout?"

Lissa shook her head. "No! I had no clue. I didn't even know it was possible to get out of the cells. I thought there was too much security."

Hans ignored the dig on his operations. "You've got that bond thing, right? You didn't pick up anything through that?"

"I don't read her," explained Lissa. "She sees my thoughts but not the other way around."

"That," said Alberta, speaking up at last, "is true."

Hans didn't contradict her but still wasn't buying my friends' innocence. "You realize, if you're caught concealing information—or aiding her—you'll face consequences almost as serious as hers. *All* of you. Royalty doesn't exempt you from treason."

Lissa lowered her gaze, as though his threat had frightened

her. "I just can't believe . . . I just can't believe she'd do this. She was my friend. I thought I knew her. I didn't think she could do any of these things . . . I never thought she'd murder anyone." If not for the feelings in the bond, I might have taken offense. I knew the truth, though. She was acting, trying to distance herself from me. It was smart.

"Really? Because not long ago, you were swearing up and down that she was innocent," pointed out Hans.

Lissa looked back up and widened her eyes. "I thought she was! But then . . . then I heard about what she did to those guardians in the escape . . ." Her distress wasn't entirely faked this time. She still needed to act like she thought I was guilty, but the news of Meredith's condition had reached her—which truly had shocked her. That made two of us, but at least I now knew Meredith was okay.

Hans still looked skeptical at Lissa's change of heart but let it go. "What about Belikov? You swore he wasn't a Strigoi anymore, but obviously something went wrong there as well."

Christian stirred beside Lissa. As an advocate for Dimitri, Christian grew as irritated as us at the suspicions and accusations. Lissa spoke before Christian could say anything.

"He's not Strigoi!" Lissa's remorse over me vanished, her old, fierce defense of Dimitri kicking in. She hadn't expected this line of questioning about him. She'd been preparing herself to defend me and her alibi. Hans seemed pleased at the reaction and watched her closely.

"Then how do you explain his involvement?"

"It wasn't because he was Strigoi," said Lissa, forcing her

control back. Her heart was pounding rapidly. "He changed back. There's no Strigoi left."

"But he attacked a number of guardians—on more than one occasion."

It looked like Tasha wanted to interrupt now and defend Dimitri as well, but she visibly bit her lip. It was remarkable. The Ozeras liked to speak their minds, not always tactfully.

"It wasn't because he was Strigoi," Lissa repeated. "And he didn't kill any of those guardians. Not one. Rose did what she did . . . well, I don't know why. She hated Tatiana, I guess. Everyone knew that. But Dimitri . . . I'm telling you, being Strigoi had nothing to do with this. He helped her because he used to be her teacher. He thought she was in trouble."

"That was pretty extreme for a teacher, particularly one who—before turning Strigoi—was known for being level-headed and rational."

"Yeah, but he wasn't thinking rationally because—"

Lissa cut herself off, suddenly caught in a bad situation. Hans seemed to have realized quickly in this conversation that if Lissa was involved with recent events—and I don't think he was certain yet—she would have an airtight alibi. Talking to her, however, had given him the chance to pursue another puzzle in my escape: Dimitri's involvement. Dimitri had sacrificed himself to take the fall, even if it meant others not trusting him again. Lissa thought she'd made people think his actions were a former teacher's protective instinct, but apparently, not everyone was buying that.

"He wasn't thinking rationally because?" prompted Hans,

eyes sharp. Before the murder, Hans had believed Dimitri truly had become a dhampir again. Something told me he still believed that but sensed there was something big dangling before him.

Lissa stayed silent. She didn't want people thinking Dimitri was Strigoi. She wanted people to believe in her powers to restore the undead. But if Dimitri helping a student didn't seem convincing enough to others, all that mistrust might surface again.

Glancing at her interrogators, Lissa suddenly met Alberta's eyes. The older guardian said nothing. She wore that neutral, scrutinizing expression that guardians excelled at. She also had an air of wisdom about her, and Lissa briefly allowed spirit to show her Alberta's aura. It had good, steady colors and energy, and in Alberta's eyes, Lissa swore she could see a message, a knowing glint.

Tell them, the message seemed to say. *It'll create problems—but they won't be as bad as your current ones.* Lissa held that gaze, wondering if she was just projecting her own thoughts onto Alberta. It didn't matter who'd come up with the idea. Lissa knew it was right.

"Dimitri helped Rose because . . . because they were involved."

As I'd guessed, Alberta wasn't surprised, and she seemed relieved to have the truth out there. Hans and Steele, however, were very surprised. I had only seen Hans shocked a few times.

"When you say 'involved,' do you mean . . ." He paused to structure his words. "Do you mean romantically involved?"

Lissa nodded, feeling horrible. She'd revealed a big secret here, one she'd sworn she'd keep for me, but I didn't blame her. Not in this situation. Love—I hoped—would defend Dimitri's actions.

"He loved her," said Lissa. "She loved him. If he helped her escape—"

"He *did* help her escape," interrupted Hans. "He attacked guardians and blew up priceless, centuries-old statues brought over from Europe!"

Lissa shrugged. "Well, like I said. He wasn't acting rationally. He wanted to help her and probably thought she was innocent. He would have done anything for her—and it had nothing to do with Strigoi."

"Love only justifies so much." Hans clearly wasn't a romantic.

"She's underage!" exclaimed Steele. That part hadn't escaped him.

"She's eighteen," corrected Lissa.

Hans cut her a look. "I can do the math, princess. Unless they managed some beautiful, touching romance in the last few weeks—while he was mostly in isolation—then there were things going on at your school that someone should have reported."

Lissa said nothing, but from the corner of her eye, she could see Tasha and Christian. They were trying to keep their expressions neutral, but it was obvious this news wasn't a surprise to them, no doubt confirming Hans's suspicions that illicit things had been going on. I actually hadn't realized Tasha knew about Dimitri and me and felt a little bad. Had she known that part of his rejection of her had been because of me? And if she knew, how many others did? Christian had probably tipped her off, but something told me more people were probably starting to find out as well. After the school's attack, my reaction had likely been a big clue about my feelings for Dimitri. Maybe telling Hans now wasn't so big a deal after all. The secret wouldn't be a secret much longer.

Alberta cleared her throat, speaking up at last. "I think we have more important things to worry about right now than some romance that may or may not have happened."

Steele gave her an incredulous look and slammed his hand against the table. "This is pretty serious. Did *you* know about it?"

"All I know is that we're getting distracted from the point here," she replied, neatly dodging the question. Alberta was about twenty years older than Steele, and the tough look she gave him said that he was a child wasting her time. "I thought we were here to figure out if Miss Hathaway had any accomplices, not dredge up the past. So far, the only person we can say for sure that helped her is Belikov, and he did it out of irrational affection. That makes him a fugitive and a fool, not a Strigoi."

I'd never thought of my relationship with Dimitri as "irrational affection," but Alberta's point was taken. Something in Hans's and Steele's faces made me think soon the whole world would know about us, but that was nothing compared to murder. And if it cleared Dimitri of being a Strigoi, then it meant he'd be imprisoned instead of staked if ever captured. Small blessings.

Lissa's questioning continued a bit longer before the guardians decided she was free and clear of any part in my escape (that they could prove). She did a good job playing surprised and confused the whole time, even mustering a few tears over how she could have so misjudged me. She spun a little bit of compulsion into her act too—not enough to brainwash anyone, but enough that Steele's earlier outrage transformed to sympathy. Hans was harder to read, but as my group left, he reminded Tasha and Christian that he would be speaking with each of them later, preferably without an entourage.

For now, the next person in the hot seat was waiting in the hall: Eddie. Lissa gave him the same smile she'd give any friend. There was no indication that they were both part of a conspiracy. Eddie nodded in return as he was called to the room for his interrogation. Lissa was anxious for him, but I knew his guardian self-control would make sure he stuck to the story. He probably wouldn't pull the tears Lissa had, but he'd likely act just as shocked by my "treason" as she had.

Tasha left Christian and Lissa once they were outside, first warning them to be careful. "You've gotten out of this so far, but I don't think the guardians have completely cleared you. Especially Hans."

"Hey, I can take care of myself," said Christian.

Tasha rolled her eyes. "Yes. I see what happens when you're left to your own devices."

"Hey, don't get all pissy because we didn't tell you," he

exclaimed. "We didn't have time, and there were only so many people we could get involved. Besides, you've done your share of crazy plans before."

"True," Tasha admitted. She was hardly a role model for playing by the rules. "It's just that everything's gotten that much more complicated. Rose is on the run. And now Dimitri . . ." She sighed, and I didn't need her to finish to guess her thoughts. There was a profound look of sadness in her eyes, one that made me feel guilty. Just like the rest of us, Tasha had wanted Dimitri's reputation restored. By freeing the queen's accused assassin, he'd seriously damaged any chance at acceptance. I *really* wished he hadn't gotten involved and hoped my current escape plan paid off.

"This'll all work out," said Christian. "You'll see." He didn't look so confident as he spoke, and Tasha gave him a small, amused smile.

"Just be careful. Please. I don't want to see you in a cell, too. I don't have time for jail visits with everything else going on." Her amusement faded, and her outspoken activist mode kicked in. "Our family's being ridiculous, you know. Can you believe they're actually talking about running Esmond for us? Good God. We've already had one tragedy after another around here. At the very least, we should try to salvage something out of this mess."

"I don't think I know Esmond," said Christian.

"Moron," she said matter-of-factly. "Him, I mean. Not you. Someone's got to talk sense into our family before they embarrass themselves."

Christian grinned. "And let me guess: you're just the one to do it?"

"Of course," she said, a mischievous gleam in her eye. "I've already drawn up a list of ideal candidates. Our family just needs some persuasion to see how ideal they are."

"I'd feel bad for them if they weren't still being assholes to us," Christian remarked, watching his aunt walk away. The stigma of his parents turning Strigoi still lingered after all these years. Tasha accepted it more gracefully—despite her complaining—if only to be able to participate in the Ozera family's larger decisions. Christian made no such attempts at civility. It was terrible enough to be treated as less than other Moroi, to be denied guardians and other things royals were entitled to. But from his own family? It was especially harsh. He refused to pretend it was acceptable.

"They'll come around eventually," said Lissa, sounding more optimistic than she felt.

Any response of Christian's was swallowed when a new companion fell into step with them: my father. His abrupt appearance startled both of my friends, but I wasn't surprised. He probably knew about Lissa's interrogation and had been skulking outside the building, waiting to talk to her.

"It's nice out," said Abe amiably, looking around at the trees and flowers as though the three of them were on a nature walk through Court. "But it's going to be scorching when the sun comes up."

The darkness that was giving me so much trouble in the woods of West Virginia made for pleasant, "midday" conditions for those on a vampiric schedule. Lissa gave Abe a sidelong glance. With eyes well-tuned to low light, she had no difficulty taking in the brilliant teal dress shirt under his beige sports jacket. A blind person could have probably seen him in that color.

Lissa scoffed at Abe's faked casualness. It was a habit of his, opening with small talk before moving on to more sinister topics. "You're not here to talk about the weather."

"Trying to be civilized, that's all." He fell silent as a couple of Moroi girls passed them. Once they were well out of earshot, he asked in a low voice, "I assume everything went well at your little meeting?"

"Fine," she said, not bothering to fill him in about "irrational affection." She knew all he'd care about was that none of their associates had been implicated.

"The guardians have Eddie now," said Christian. "And want me later, but I think that'll be it for all of us."

Lissa sighed. "Honestly, I have a feeling the interrogation was the easy part, compared to what's coming." She meant figuring out who had really killed Tatiana.

"One step at a time," murmured Abe. "No point in letting the larger picture overwhelm us. We'll just start at the beginning."

"That's the problem," said Lissa, kicking irritably at a branch lying across the cobblestone path in front of her. "I have no idea *where* to start. Whoever killed Tatiana did a good job covering their tracks and shifting it all to Rose."

"One step at a time," repeated Abe.

He spoke in that sly tone of his that annoyed me sometimes, but to Lissa today, it was grating. Until now, all of her energy had been focused on getting me out of jail and somewhere safe. That was the goal that had driven her and kept her going in my escape's aftermath.

Now, after some of the intensity had faded, the pressure of it all was beginning to crash down on her. Christian put an arm around her shoulders, sensing her dismay. He turned to Abe, unusually serious.

"Do you have any ideas?" Christian asked Abe. "We certainly don't have any real evidence."

"We have reasonable assumptions," Abe replied. "Like that whoever killed Tatiana would have had access to her private rooms. That's not a long list."

"It's not short either." Lissa ticked off people on her fingers. "The royal guards, her friends and family . . . and that's assuming no one altered the guardians' records of her visitors. And for all we know, some visits were never logged at all. She probably had secret business meetings all the time."

"Unlikely she'd have business meetings in her bedroom, in her nightgown," mused Abe. "Of course, it depends on the type of business, I suppose."

Lissa stumbled, realization stunning her. "Ambrose."

"Who?"

"He's a dhampir . . . really good-looking . . . He and Tatiana were, um . . ."

"Involved?" said Christian with a smile, echoing the interrogation.

Now Abe came to a stop. Lissa did the same, and his dark eyes met hers. "I've seen him. Sort of a pool boy type."

"He'd have access to her bedroom," said Lissa. "But I just can't—I don't know. I can't see him doing this."

"Appearances are deceiving," said Abe. "He was terribly interested in Rose back in the courtroom."

More surprise for Lissa. "What are you talking about?"

Abe stroked his chin in an evil-villain sort of way. "He spoke to her . . . or gave her some signal. I'm not really sure, but there was some kind of interaction between them."

Clever, watchful Abe. He'd noticed Ambrose giving me the note but hadn't fully realized what had happened.

"We should talk to him then," said Christian.

Lissa nodded. Conflicting feelings churned inside of her. She was excited by a lead—but upset that it meant kind, gentle Ambrose might be a suspect.

"I'll take care of it," said Abe breezily.

I felt her gaze fall heavily on him. I couldn't see her expression, but I did see Abe take an involuntary step back, the faintest glimmer of surprise in his eyes. Even Christian flinched. "And I'm going to be there when you do," she said, steel in her voice. "Do *not* attempt some crazy torture-style interrogation without me."

"You want to be there for the torture?" asked Abe, recovering.

"There won't be any. We'll talk to Ambrose like civilized people, understand?" She stared hard at him again, and Abe finally shrugged in acquiescence, as though being overpowered by a woman half his age was no big deal.

"Fine. We'll do it together."

Lissa was a little suspicious at his willingness, and he must have picked up on that.

"We *will*," he said, continuing walking. "This is a good time—well, as good as any time—for an investigation. Court's going to get chaotic as the monarch elections get under way. Everyone here will be busy, and new people will start pouring in."

A breeze, heavy with humidity, ruffled Lissa's hair. The promise of heat was on it, and she knew Abe would be right about sunrise. It would be worth going to bed early.

"When will the elections happen?" she asked.

"As soon as they put dear Tatiana to rest. These things move fast. We need our government restored. She'll be buried tomorrow at the church with a ceremony and service, but there'll be no repeat of the procession. They're still too uneasy."

I felt kind of bad that she hadn't received a full queenly funeral in the end, but then, if it meant her true murderer was found, maybe she would have preferred it that way.

"Once the burial happens and elections begin," Abe continued, "any family who wants to put out a candidate for the crown will do so—and of course they'll want to. You've never seen a monarchial election, have you? It's quite a spectacle. Of course, before the voting occurs, all the candidates will have to be tested."

There was something ominous in the way he said "tested," but Lissa's thoughts were elsewhere. Tatiana had been the only queen she'd ever known, and the full impact of a regime change was staggering. "A new king or queen can affect everything—for better or worse. I hope it's someone good. One of the Ozeras, maybe. One of Tasha's people." She glanced hopefully at Christian, who could only shrug. "Or Ariana Szelsky. I like her. Not that it matters who I want," she added bitterly. "Seeing as I can't vote." The Council's votes determined the election's winner, so again, she was locked out of the Moroi legal process.

"A lot of work will go into the nominations," Abe explained, avoiding her last comment. "Each family will want someone to further their interests but who also has a chance of getting votes from—"

"Oomph!"

I was thrust harshly out of the calculating world of Moroi politics and back into the wilds of West Virginia—very painfully so. Something solid and fierce slammed me against the hard-packed earth, leaves and branches cutting my face and hands. Strong hands held me down, and Dimitri's voice spoke in my ear.

"You should have just hidden in town," he said, a little amused. His weight and position allowed me no room to move. "It would have been the last place I looked. Instead, I knew exactly where you'd go."

"Whatever. Don't act so smart," I said through gritted teeth, trying to break out of his hold. Goddamn it. He *was* smart. And once again, the closeness of him was disorienting. Earlier, it had seemed to affect him too, but he'd apparently learned his lesson. "You made a lucky guess, that's all."

"I don't need luck, Roza. I'll always find you. So, really it's up to you how difficult you want this situation to be." There was an almost conversational tone to his voice, made all the more ridiculous by the situation we were in. "We can do this over and over, or you can do the reasonable thing and just stay put with Sydney and me."

"It's not reasonable! It's wasteful."

He was sweating, from the heat and undoubtedly because he'd had to run pretty hard to catch up with me. Adrian wore a cologne that always made me heady, but the natural scent of Dimitri's warm skin was intoxicating too. It was amazing to me that I could keep noticing these little things—and be attracted to them—even when I was legitimately mad at him for keeping me captive. Maybe anger was a turn-on for me.

"How many times do I have to explain the logic behind what we're doing?" he asked in exasperation.

"Until you give up." I pushed back against him, trying again to get loose, but all it did was put us closer together. I had a feeling the kissing trick wouldn't work this time.

He jerked me to my feet, keeping my arms and hands pinned behind my back. I had a little more room to maneuver than I had on the ground, but not quite enough to break free. Slowly, he began trying to make me walk back toward the direction I'd come from.

"I am *not* letting you and Sydney risk getting in trouble with me. I'll take care of myself, so just let me go!" I said, literally dragging my feet. Seeing a tall, skinny tree, I stuck one leg out and hooked myself onto the trunk, completely bringing us to a halt.

Dimitri groaned and shifted his grip to get me away from the tree. It almost gave me an escape opportunity, but I didn't even manage two steps before he had a hold of me again.

"Rose," he said wearily. "You can't win."

"How's your face feeling?" I asked. I couldn't see any marks in the poor lighting but knew the punch I'd given him would leave a mark tomorrow. It was a shame to damage his face like that, but he'd heal, and maybe it would teach him a lesson about messing with Rose Hathaway.

Or not. He began dragging me again. "I'm seconds away from just tossing you over my shoulder," he warned.

"I'd like to see you try."

"How do you think Lissa would feel if you got killed?" His grip tightened, and while I had a feeling he'd make good on his over-the-shoulder threat, I also suspected he wanted to shake me. He was that upset. "Can you imagine what it would do to her if she lost you?"

For a moment, I was out of snappy retorts. I didn't want to die, but risking my life was exactly that: risking *my* life. No one else's. Still, I knew he was right. Lissa would be devastated if anything happened to me. And yet . . . it was a risk I had to take.

"Have a little faith, comrade. I won't get killed," I said stubbornly. "I'll stay alive."

Not the answer he'd wanted. He shifted his hold. "There

are other ways to help her than whatever insanity you're thinking of."

I suddenly went limp. Dimitri stumbled, caught by surprise at my sudden lack of resistance. "What's wrong?" he asked, both puzzled and suspicious.

I stared off into the night, my eyes not really focused on anything. Instead, I was seeing Lissa and Abe back at Court, remembering Lissa's feeling of powerlessness and longing for her vote. Tatiana's note came back to me, and for a moment, I could hear her voice in my head. *She is not the last Dragomir. Another lives.*

"You're right," I said at last.

"Right about . . . ?" Dimitri was at a total loss. It was a common reaction for people when I agreed to something reasonable.

"Rushing back to Court won't help Lissa."

Silence. I couldn't fully make out his expression, but it was probably filled with shock.

"I'll go back to the motel with you, and I won't go running off to Court." Another Dragomir. Another Dragomir needing to be found. I took a deep breath. "But I'm not going to sit around and do nothing. I *am* going to do something for Lissa—and you and Sydney are going to help me."

EIGHT

IT TURNED OUT I WAS wrong about the local police department comprising of one guy and a dog. When Dimitri and I walked back to the motel, we saw flashing red and blue lights in the parking lot and a few bystanders trying to see what was happening.

"The whole town turned out," I said.

Dimitri sighed. "You just had to say something to the desk clerk, didn't you?"

We'd stopped some distance away, hidden in the shadow of a run-down building. "I thought it would slow you down."

"It's going to slow us down now." His eyes did a sweep of the scene, taking in all the details in the flickering light. "Sydney's car is gone. That's something, at least."

My earlier cockiness faded. "Is it? We just lost our ride!"

"She wouldn't leave us, but she was smart enough to get out before the police came knocking on her door." He turned and surveyed the town's one main road. "Come on. She has to be close, and there's a good chance the police might actually start searching around if they thought some defenseless girl was being chased down." The tone he used for "defenseless" spoke legions.

Dimitri made an executive decision to walk back toward

the road that had led us into town, assuming Sydney would want to get out of there now that I'd blown our cover. Getting the police involved had created complications, but I felt little regret over what I'd done. I was excited about the plan that had occurred to me in the woods and wanted, as usual, to get moving on it right away. If I'd helped get us out of this hole of a town, so much the better.

Dimitri's instincts about Sydney were right. About a half-mile outside of town, we spotted a CR-V pulled off on the road's shoulder. The engine was off, the lights dark, but I could see well enough to identify the Louisiana plates. I walked over to the driver side window and knocked on the glass. Inside, Sydney flinched. She rolled down the window, face incredulous.

"What did you do? Never mind. Don't bother. Just get in."

Dimitri and I complied. I felt like a naughty child under her disapproving glare. She started the car without a word and began driving in the direction we'd originally come from, eventually merging with the small state highway that led back to the interstate. That was promising. Only, once we'd driven a few miles, she pulled off again, this time at a dark exit that didn't seem to have anything at it.

She turned off the car and turned to peer at me in the backseat. "You ran, didn't you?"

"Yeah, but I got this—"

Sydney held up a hand to silence me. "No, don't. Not yet. I wish you could have pulled off your daring escape without attracting the authorities."

"Me too," said Dimitri.

I scowled at them both. "Hey, I came back, didn't I?" Dimitri arched an eyebrow at that, apparently questioning just how voluntary that had been. "And now I know what we have to do to help Lissa."

"What we have to do," said Sydney, "is find a safe place to stay."

"Just go back to civilization and pick a hotel. One with room service. We can make that our base of operation while we work on the next plan."

"We researched that town specifically!" she said. "We can't go to some random place—at least not nearby. I doubt they took down my plates, but they could put out a call to look for this kind of car. If they've got that and our descriptions, and it gets to the state police, it'll get to the Alchemists and then it'll—"

"Calm down," said Dimitri, touching her arm. There was nothing intimate about that, but I still felt a spark of envy, particularly after the tough love I'd just had being nearly dragged through the woods. "We don't know that any of that's going to happen. Why don't you just call Abe?"

"Yeah," she said glumly. "That's exactly what I want. To tell him I messed up the plan in less than twenty-four hours."

"Well," I said, "if it makes you feel better, the plan's about to change anyway—"

"Be quiet," she snapped. "Both of you. I need to think."

Dimitri and I exchanged glances, but stayed silent. When I'd told him I knew a way to seriously help Lissa, he'd been intrigued. I knew he wanted details now, but we both had to wait for Sydney.

She flipped on the dome light and produced a paper map of the state. After studying it for a minute, she folded it back up and simply stared ahead. I couldn't see her face but suspected she was frowning. Finally, she sighed in that woeful way of hers, turned off the light, and started the car. I watched as she punched in *Altswood, West Virginia* into her GPS.

"What's in Altswood?" I asked, disappointed she hadn't entered something like *Atlantic City*.

"Nothing," she said, pulling back onto the road. "But it's the closest place to where we're going that the GPS can find."

A passing car's headlights briefly illuminated Dimitri's profile, and I saw curiosity on his face too. So. I wasn't the only one out of the loop anymore. The GPS read almost an hour and a half to our destination. He didn't question her choice, though, and turned back to me.

"So what's going on with Lissa? What's this great plan of yours?" He glanced at Sydney. "Rose says there's something important we have to do."

"So I gathered," said Sydney dryly. Dimitri looked back at me expectantly.

I took a deep breath. It was time to reveal the secret I'd been holding since my hearing. "So, it, um, turns out Lissa has a brother or sister. And I think we should find them."

I managed to sound cool and casual as I spoke. Inside me, my heart lurched. Even though I'd had plenty of time to process Tatiana's note, saying the words out loud made them *real* in a way they hadn't been before. It shocked me, hitting me with the full impact of what this information truly meant and how it changed everything we'd all come to believe.

Of course, my shock was nothing compared to the others'. Score one for Rose and the element of surprise. Sydney made no attempt to hide her astonishment and gasped. Even Dimitri seemed a little taken aback.

Once they recovered, I could see them preparing their protests. They would either demand evidence or simply dismiss the idea as ridiculous. I immediately jumped into action before the arguments could start. I produced Tatiana's note, reading it aloud and then letting Dimitri look at it. I told them about my ghostly encounter, where the queen's troubled spirit made me believe there was truth to this. Nonetheless, my companions were skeptical.

"You have no proof Tatiana wrote the note," said Dimitri.

"The Alchemists have no records of another Dragomir," said Sydney.

They each said exactly what I thought they would. Dimitri was the kind of guy always ready for a trick or trap. He suspected anything without hard proof. Sydney lived in a world of facts and data and had total faith in the Alchemists and their information. If the Alchemists didn't believe it, neither did she. Ghostly evidence didn't convince either of them.

"I don't really see why Tatiana's spirit would want to deceive me," I argued. "And the Alchemists aren't all-knowing. The note says this is a pretty heavily guarded secret from

Moroi—it makes sense it would be secret from the Alchemists too."

Sydney scoffed, not liking my "all-knowing" comment, but otherwise remained silent. It was Dimitri who pushed forward, refusing to take anything on faith without more evidence.

"You've said before that it's not always clear what the ghosts are trying to say," he pointed out. "Maybe you misread her."

"I don't know . . ." I thought again about her solemn, translucent face. "I think she did write this note. My gut says she did." I narrowed my eyes. "You know it's been right before. Can you trust me on this?"

He stared at me for several moments, and I held that gaze steadily. In that uncanny way of ours, I could guess what was going on. The whole situation was far-fetched, but he knew I was right about my instincts. They'd proven true in the past. No matter what he'd been through, no matter the current antagonism between us, he still knew me enough to trust in this.

Slowly, almost reluctantly, he nodded. "But if we decided to search for this alleged sibling, we'd be going against Lissa's instructions to stay put."

"You believe that note?" exclaimed Sydney. "You're *considering* listening to it?"

A flash of anger lit up within me, one I worked to hide. Of course. Of course this would be the next obstacle: Dimitri's inability to disobey Lissa. Sydney feared Abe, which I could kind of understand, but Dimitri's concern was still the lofty vow of chivalry he'd made to Lissa. I took a deep breath. Telling him how ridiculous I thought he was behaving wouldn't accomplish what I needed.

"Technically, yes. But if we could actually prove she wasn't the last in her family, it would help her a lot. We can't ignore the chance, and if you manage to keep me out of trouble while we do it"—I tried not to grimace at that—"then there shouldn't be a problem."

Dimitri considered this. He knew me. He also knew I would use roundabout logic if need be to get my way.

"Okay," he said at last. I saw the shift in his features. The decision was made, and he'd stick to it now. "But where do we start? You have no other clues, aside from a mysterious note."

It was déjà vu and reminded me of Lissa and Christian's earlier conversation with Abe when they were figuring out where to start their investigation. She and I lived parallel lives, it seemed, both pursuing an impossible puzzle with a sketchy trail. As I replayed their discussion, I attempted the same reasoning Abe had used: without clues, start working through obvious conclusions.

"Obviously, this is a secret," I said. "A big one. One people have apparently wanted to cover up—enough that they'd try to steal records about it and keep the Dragomirs out of power." Someone had broken into an Alchemist building and taken papers indicating Eric Dragomir had indeed been funding a mystery woman. I pointed out to my companions that it seemed very likely to me this woman was the mother of his love child. "You could look into that case some more." Those last words were spoken toward Sydney. Maybe she didn't care about another Dragomir, but the Alchemists still wanted to know who had stolen from them.

"Whoa, hey. How was I not even part of this decision process?" She still hadn't recovered from our conversation suddenly running away without her. After the way our night had gone so far, she didn't look too pleased about being sucked into another of my rogue schemes. "Maybe breaking Lissa's orders is no big deal for you two, but *I'd* be going against Abe. He might not be so lenient."

It was a fair point. "I'll pull in a daughterly favor," I assured her. "Besides, the old man *loves* secrets. He'd be into this, believe me. And you've already found the biggest clue of all. I mean, if Eric was giving money to some anonymous woman, then why wouldn't it be for his secret mistress and child?"

"Anonymous is the key word," Sydney said, still clearly skeptical of *Zmey*'s "leniency." "If your theory's right—and it's kind of a leap—we still have no idea who this mistress is. The stolen documents didn't say."

"Are there other records that tie into the stolen ones? Or could you investigate the bank he was sending money to?" The Alchemists' initial concern had simply been that someone had stolen hard copies of their records. Her colleagues had discovered which items were taken but hadn't given much thought to the content. I was willing to bet they hadn't searched for any other documents related to the same topic. She affirmed as much.

"You really have no idea how 'researching records' works, do you? It's not that easy," she said. "It could take a while."

"Well . . . I guess that's why it's good we're going somewhere, um, secure, right?" I asked. Struck with the realization that we might need time to put our next step together, I could kind of see the disadvantage of having lost our out-of-the-way hideout.

"Secure . . ." She shook her head. "Well, we'll see. I hope I'm not doing something stupid."

With those ominous words, silence fell. I wanted to know more about where we were going but felt I shouldn't push the small victory I'd made. The victory I thought I'd made, at least. I wasn't entirely sure Sydney was 100 percent on board but felt certain Dimitri had been convinced. Best not to agitate her right now. I looked at the GPS. Almost an hour. Enough time to check back on Lissa.

It took me a minute to recognize where Lissa was, probably because I'd been expecting her to return to her room. But no, she was in a location I'd only been once: Adrian's parents' home. Surprising. In a few moments, though, I read the reasoning from her mind. Her current suite was in guest housing, and in the ensuing panic over my escape, her building was swarming with visitors now trying to leave. The Ivashkov townhouse, situated in a permanent residential area, was a bit quieter—not that there weren't a few fleeing neighbors there too.

Adrian sat back in an armchair, feet carelessly resting on an expensive coffee table that some interior designer had probably helped his mother choose. Lissa and Christian had just arrived, and she caught a whiff of smoke in the air that made her think Adrian had been sneaking in some bad behavior beforehand.

"If we're lucky," he was telling Lissa and Christian, "the parental units will be tied up for a while and give us some peace and quiet. How rough was your questioning?"

Lissa and Christian sat on a couch that was prettier than it was comfortable. She leaned into him and sighed. "Not so bad. I don't know if they're fully convinced we had nothing to do with Rose's escape . . . but they definitely don't have any proof."

"I think we got in more trouble with Aunt Tasha," said Christian. "She was kind of pissed off that we didn't tell her what was going on. I think she probably wanted to blow up the statues herself."

"I think she's more upset that we got Dimitri involved," pointed out Lissa. "She thinks we screwed up his chances of ever being accepted again."

"She's right," said Adrian. He picked up a remote control and turned on a large, plasma screen TV. He muted the sound and flipped randomly through channels. "But no one forced him."

Lissa nodded but secretly wondered if she had forced Dimitri inadvertently. His dedicated vow to protect her was no secret. Christian seemed to pick up on her worry.

"Hey, for all we know, he never would have—"

A knock interrupted him.

"Damn," said Adrian, standing up. "So much for peace and quiet."

"Your parents wouldn't knock," said Christian.

"True, but it's probably one of their friends wanting to sip port and gossip about the terrible state of today's murderous youth," Adrian called back.

Lissa heard the door open and a muffled conversation. A few moments later, Adrian returned with a young Moroi guy that Lissa didn't recognize.

"Look," the guy was saying, glancing around uneasily, "I can come back." He caught sight of Lissa and Christian and froze.

"No, no," said Adrian. His transformation from grumpy to cordial had happened as quickly as a light switch being flipped. "I'm sure she'll be back any minute. Do you guys all know each other?"

The guy nodded, eyes darting from face to face. "Of course."

Lissa frowned. "I don't know you."

The smile never left Adrian's face, but Lissa picked up quickly that something important was going on. "This is Joe. Joe's the janitor who helped me out by testifying that I wasn't with Rose when Aunt Tatiana was murdered. The one who was working in Rose's building."

Both Lissa and Christian straightened up. "It was a lucky thing you turned up before the hearing," said Christian carefully. For a while, there'd been panic that Adrian might be implicated with me, but Joe had come forward just in time to testify about when he'd seen both me and Adrian in my building.

Joe took a few steps back toward the foyer. "I really should go. Just tell Lady Ivashkov that I came by—and that I'm leaving Court. But that everything's set."

"What's set?" asked Lissa, slowly standing up.

"She—she'll know." Lissa, I knew, didn't look intimidating. She was cute and slim and pretty, but from the fear on Joe's face—well. She must have been giving him a scary look. It reminded me of the earlier encounter with Abe. "Really," he added. "I need to go."

He started to move again, but suddenly, I felt a surge of spirit burn through Lissa. Joe came to a halt, and she strode toward him.

"What did you need to talk to Lady Ivashkov about?" demanded Lissa.

"Easy, cousin," murmured Adrian. "You don't need that much spirit to get answers."

Lissa was using compulsion on Joe, so much that he might as well have been a puppet on strings.

"The money," Joe gasped, eyes wide. "The money's set."

"What money?" she asked.

Joe hesitated, as though he might resist, but soon gave in. He couldn't fight that much compulsion, not from a spirit user. "The money . . . the money to testify . . . about where *he* was." Joe jerked his head toward Adrian.

Adrian's cool expression faltered a little. "What do you mean where I was? The night my aunt died? Are you saying . . ."

Christian picked up where Adrian couldn't. "Is Lady

Ivashkov paying you off to say you saw Adrian?"

"I *did* see him," cried Joe. He was visibly sweating. Adrian had been right: Lissa was using too much spirit. It was physically hurting Joe. "I just . . . I just . . . I don't remember the time . . . I don't remember any of the times. That's what I told the other guy, too. She paid me to put a time on when you were there."

Adrian didn't like that, not at all. To his credit, he remained calm. "What do you mean you told 'the other guy'?"

"Who else?" repeated Lissa. "Who else was with her?"

"No one! Lady Ivashkov just wanted to make sure her son was clear. I fudged the details for her. It was the guy . . . the other guy who came later . . . who wanted to know when Hathaway was around."

There was a click from the foyer, the sound of the front door opening. Lissa leaned forward, cranking up the compulsion. "Who? Who was he? What did he want?"

Joe looked like he was in serious pain now. He swallowed. "I don't know who he was! No one I'd seen. Some Moroi. Just wanted me to testify about when I'd seen Hathaway. Paid me more than Lady Ivashkov. No harm . . ." He looked at Lissa desperately. "No harm in helping them both . . . especially since Hathaway did it . . ."

"Adrian?" Daniella's voice rang down the hall. "Are you here?"

"Back off," Adrian warned Lissa in a low voice. There was no joking in it.

Her voice was just as soft, her attention still on Joe. "What did he look like? The Moroi? Describe him."

The sound of high heels clicked on the hall's wooden floor.

"Like no one!" said Joe. "I swear! Plain. Ordinary. Except the hand . . . please let me go . . ."

Adrian shoved Lissa aside, breaking the contact between her and Joe. Joe nearly sagged to the ground and then went rigid as he locked gazes with Adrian. More compulsion—but much less than Lissa had used.

"Forget this," hissed Adrian. "We never had this conversation."

"Adrian, what are you—"

Daniella stopped in the living room's doorway, taking in the strange sights. Christian was still on the couch, but Adrian and Lissa were inches from Joe, whose shirt was soaked with sweat.

"What's going on?" Daniella exclaimed.

Adrian stepped back and gave his mother one of those charming smiles that captivated so many women. "This guy came by to see you, Mom. We told him we'd wait until you got back. We're going to head out now."

Daniella glanced between her son and Joe. She was clearly uneasy about the scenario and also confused. Lissa was surprised at the "heading out" comment but followed Adrian's lead. Christian did too.

"It was nice seeing you," said Lissa, attempting a smile to match Adrian's. Joe looked totally dazed. After Adrian's last command, the poor janitor had also probably forgotten how he'd ended up at the Ivashkov home.

Lissa and Christian hastily followed Adrian out before

Daniella could say much more. "What the hell was that?" asked Christian, once they were outside. I wasn't sure if he meant Lissa's scary compulsion or what Joe had revealed.

"Not sure," said Adrian, expression dark. No more cheery smile. "But we should talk to Mikhail."

"Rose."

Dimitri's voice was gentle, bringing me back to him, Sydney, and the car. He'd undoubtedly recognized the expression on my face and knew where I'd been.

"Everything okay back there?" he asked.

I knew "back there" meant Court and not the backseat. I nodded, though "okay" wasn't quite the right word for what I'd just witnessed. What *had* I just witnessed? An admission of false testimony. An admission that contradicted some of the evidence against me. I didn't care so much that Joe had lied to keep Adrian safe. Adrian hadn't been involved with Tatiana's murder. I wanted him free and clear. But what about the other part? Some "ordinary" Moroi who'd paid Joe to lie about when I'd been around, leaving me without an alibi during the murder window?

Before I could fully process the implications, I noticed the car had stopped. Forcing the Joe-info to the back of my mind, I tried to take stock of our new situation. Sydney's laptop glowed in the front seat as she scrolled through something.

"Where are we?" I peered out the window. In the headlights, I saw a sad, closed gas station.

"Altswood," said Dimitri.

By my estimation, there was nothing else but the gas

station. "Makes our last town look like New York."

Sydney shut her laptop. She handed it back, and I set it on the seat beside me, near the backpacks she'd miraculously grabbed when leaving the motel. She shifted the car into drive and pulled out of the parking lot. Not too far away, I could see the highway and expected her to turn toward it. Instead, she drove past the gas station, deeper into darkness. Like the last place, we were surrounded by mountains and forests. We crept along at a snail's pace until Sydney spotted a tiny gravel road disappearing into the woods. It was only big enough for one car to go down, but somehow, I didn't expect we'd run into much traffic out here. A similar road took us in deeper and deeper, and although I couldn't see her face, Sydney's anxiety was palpable in the car.

Minutes felt like hours until our narrow path opened up into a large, dirt-packed clearing. Other vehicles—pretty old-looking—were parked there. It was a strange place for a parking lot, considering all I could see around us was dark forest. Sydney shut off the car.

"Are we at a campground?" I asked.

She didn't answer. Instead, she looked at Dimitri. "Are you as good as they say you are?"

"What?" he asked, startled.

"Fighting. Everyone keeps talking about how dangerous you are. Is it true? Are you that good?"

Dimitri considered. "Pretty good."

I scoffed. "*Very* good."

"I hope it's enough," said Sydney, reaching for the door's handle.

I opened my door as well. "Aren't you going to ask about me?"

"I already know you're dangerous," she said. "I've seen it."

Her compliment offered little comfort as we walked out across the rural parking lot. "Why'd we stop?"

"Because we have to go on foot now." She turned on a flashlight and shone it along the lot's perimeter. At last, it flickered across a footpath snaking through the trees. The path was small and easy to miss because weeds and other plants were encroaching on it. "There." She began to move toward it.

"Wait," said Dimitri. He moved in front of her, leading the way, and I immediately took up the back position in our group. It was a standard guardian formation. We were flanking her the way we would a Moroi. All earlier thoughts of Lissa flitted from my mind. My attention was totally on the situation at hand, all my senses alert to the potential danger. I could see Dimitri was in the same mode, both of us holding our stakes.

"Where are we going?" I asked as we carefully avoided roots and holes along the path. Branches scraped along my arms.

"To people I guarantee won't turn you in," she said, voice grim.

More questions were on my lips when brilliant light suddenly blinded me. My eyes had grown attuned to the darkness, and the unexpected brightness was too abrupt a change. There was a rustling in the trees, a sense of many bodies around us, and as my vision returned, I saw vampire faces everywhere.

NINE

FORTUNATELY, THEY WERE MOROI FACES.

That didn't stop me from raising my stake and moving closer to Sydney. No one was attacking us, so I held my position—not that it probably mattered. As I took in more and more of the setting, I saw that we were completely surrounded by about ten people. We'd told Sydney we were good, and it was true: Dimitri and I could probably take out a group like this, though the poor fighting quarters would make it difficult. I also realized the group wasn't entirely Moroi. The ones closest to us were, but around them were dhampirs. And the light I'd thought had come from torches or flashlights was actually coming from a ball of flame held in one of the Moroi's hands.

One Moroi man stepped forward, about Abe's age, with a bushy brown beard and a silver stake in his hand. Some part of me noted the stake was crudely made compared to mine, but the point held the same threat. The man's gaze passed over me and Dimitri, and the stake lowered. Sydney became the object of the guy's scrutiny, and he suddenly reached out for her. Dimitri and I moved to stop him, but other hands reached out to stop *us*. I could have fought them but froze when Sydney let out a strangled, "Wait."

The bearded Moroi gripped her chin and turned her head

so that the light fell on her cheek, lighting up the golden tattoo. He released his hold and stepped back.

"Lily-girl," he grunted.

The others relaxed very slightly, though they kept their stakes poised and still looked ready to attack if provoked. The Moroi leader turned his attention from Sydney to Dimitri and me.

"You're here to join us?" he asked warily.

"We need shelter," said Sydney, lightly touching her throat. "They're being chased by—by the Tainted."

The woman holding the flame looked skeptical. "More like spies for the Tainted."

"The Tainted Queen is dead," said Sydney. She nodded toward me. "They think she did it."

The inquisitive part of me started to speak but promptly shut up, wise enough to know this bizarre turn of events was best left in Sydney's hands. I didn't understand what she was saying. When she'd said Tainted were pursuing us, I thought she was trying to make this group think we had Strigoi after us. Now, after she'd mentioned the queen, I wasn't so sure. I also wasn't so sure identifying me as a potential murderer was that smart. For all I knew, Brown Beard would turn me in and try to score a reward. From the looks of his clothes, he could have used one.

To my surprise, this brought a smile to his face. "And so, another usurper passes on. Is there a new one yet?"

"No," said Sydney. "They'll have elections soon and choose."

The group's smiles were replaced by looks of disdain and disapproving mutters about elections. I couldn't help myself. "How else would they choose a new king or queen?"

"In the true way," said a nearby dhampir. "The way it used to be, long ago. In a battle to the death."

I waited for the punch line, but the guy was clearly serious. I wanted to ask Sydney what she'd gotten us into, but by this point, we'd apparently passed inspection. Their leader turned and began walking down the path. The group followed, moving us along as they did. Listening to their conversation, I couldn't help a small frown—and not just because our lives might be on the line. I was intrigued by their accents. The motel's desk clerk had had a thick southern accent, exactly like you'd expect in this part of the country. These guys, while sounding similar, had a few other pronunciations mixed in. It almost reminded me a little of Dimitri's accent.

I was so tense and anxious that I could hardly focus on how long we walked. Eventually, the path led us to what seemed like a well-hidden campground. A huge bonfire blazed in a clearing with people sitting around. Yet, there were structures scattered off to one side, stretching into the woods along the now widened path. It wasn't quite a road yet, but it gave the illusion of a town, or at least a village. The buildings were small and shabby but appeared permanent. On the other side of the fire, the land rose sharply into the Appalachians, blocking out the stars. In the flickering light, I could see a mountain's face that was textured with rough stone and scattered trees, dotted here and there with dark holes.

My attention moved back to the living. The crowd gathered around the fire—a couple dozen or so—fell silent as our escort led us in. At first, all I saw were numbers. That was the warrior in me, counting opponents and planning for attack. Then, just like I had earlier, I truly took in the faces. More Moroi mixed with dhampirs. And—I was shocked to discover—humans.

These weren't feeders either. Well, not in the sense that I knew feeders. Even in the dark, I could see glimpses of bite marks along some of the humans' necks, but judging by their curious expressions, I could tell these people didn't give blood regularly. They weren't high. They were mixed in among the Moroi and dhampirs, sitting, standing, talking, engaging—the whole group clearly unified in some kind of community. I wondered if these humans were like the Alchemists. Maybe they had some sort of a business relationship with my kind.

The tight formation around us began to spread out, and I moved closer to Sydney. "What in God's name is all this?"

"The Keepers," she said in a low voice.

"Keepers? What does that mean?"

"It means," said the bearded Moroi, "that unlike your people, we still keep the old ways, the way we truly should."

I eyed these "Keepers" in their worn clothes and the dirty, barefoot children. Reflecting upon how far we were from civilization—and based on how dark it was away from the fire—I was willing to bet they didn't have electricity. I was on the verge of saying that I didn't think this was how anyone should truly be living. Then, remembering the casual way these people had spoken about fights to the death, I decided to keep my views to myself.

"Why are they here, Raymond?" asked a woman sitting by the fire. She was human but spoke to the bearded Moroi in a perfectly ordinary and familiar way. It wasn't the dreamy manner a feeder usually used with a Moroi. It wasn't even like the stilted conversations my kind had with the Alchemists. "Are they joining us?"

Raymond shook his head. "No. The Tainted are after them for killing their queen."

Sydney elbowed me before I could deny the claim. I clenched my teeth, waiting to be mobbed. Instead, I was surprised to find the crowd looking at me with a mix of awe and admiration, just as our welcoming party had.

"We're giving them refuge," explained Raymond. He beamed at us, though I didn't know if his approval came from us being murderers or if he simply liked the attention he was getting. "Although, you *are* welcome to join us and live here. We have room in the caves."

Caves? I jerked my head toward the cliffs beyond the fire, realizing now what those black holes were. Even as I watched, a few people retiring for the night crawled off and disappeared into the dark depths of the mountain.

Sydney answered while I worked to keep a look of horror off my face. "We only need to stay here . . ." She faltered, not surprising considering how sketchy our plans had become. "A couple days, probably."

"You can stay with my family," said Raymond. "Even you."

That was directed toward Sydney, and he made it sound like quite the favor.

"Thank you," she said. "We'd be grateful to spend the night at your *house*." The emphasis on the last word was for me, I realized. The wooden structures along the dusty path didn't look luxurious by any stretch of the imagination, but I'd take one over a cave any day.

The village or commune or whatever was getting increasingly excited as our novelty sank in. They bombarded us with a flurry of questions, starting with ordinary things like our names but moving quickly on to specific details about how exactly I'd killed Tatiana.

I was saved from having to answer when the human woman who had spoken to Raymond earlier jumped up and steered my threesome away. "Enough," she said, chastising the others. "It's getting late, and I'm sure our guests are hungry."

I was starving, actually, but didn't know if I was in dire enough straits to eat opossum stew or whatever passed as food around here. The woman's proclamation was met with some disappointment, but she assured the others they could talk to us tomorrow. Glancing around, I saw a faint purpling of what must have been the eastern sky. Sunrise. A group of Moroi clinging to "traditional" ways would most certainly run on a nocturnal schedule, meaning these people probably only had a few more hours before bedtime.

The woman said her name was Sarah and led us down the dusty path. Raymond called that he'd see us soon. As we walked, we saw other people wandering near scattered, ramshackle homes, on their way to bed or possibly woken up with all the commotion. Sarah glanced over at Sydney.

"Did you bring us anything?"

"No," said Sydney. "I'm just here to escort them."

Sarah looked disappointed but nodded. "An important task."

Sydney frowned and appeared even more uneasy. "How long has it been since my people brought you anything?"

"A few months," said Sarah after a moment's thought.

Sydney's expression darkened at this, but she said no more.

Sarah finally took us inside one of the larger and nicer looking of the houses, though it was still plain and made of unpainted wooden boards. The inside was pitch black, and we waited as Sarah lit old-fashioned lanterns. I'd been right. No electricity. This suddenly made me wonder about plumbing.

The floors were hardwood like the walls and covered in large, brightly patterned rugs. We appeared to be in some hybrid kitchen-living-dining room. There was a large fireplace in the center, a wooden table and chairs on one side, and large cushions on the other that I presumed served as sofas. Racks of drying herbs hung near the fireplace, filling the room with a spicy scent that mingled with the smell of burnt wood. There were three doors in the back wall, and Sarah nodded to one.

"You can sleep in the girls' room," she said.

"Thanks," I said, not sure I really wanted to see what our guest accommodations were like. I was already missing the MOTEL. I studied Sarah curiously. She looked to be about Raymond's age and wore a plain, knee-length blue dress.

Her blond hair was pulled back and tied at her neck, and she seemed short to me the way all humans did. "Are you Raymond's housekeeper?" It was the only role I could deduce for her. She had a few bite marks but obviously wasn't a feeder. At least not a full-time one. Maybe around here, feeders doubled as household help.

She smiled. "I'm his wife."

It was a mark of my self-control that I managed any sort of response. "Oh."

Sydney's sharp eyes fell on me, a warning in them: *Let it go.* I again clenched my jaw shut and gave her a brief nod to let her know I understood.

Except, I didn't understand. Dhampirs and Moroi hooked up all the time. Dhampirs had to. More permanent liaisons were scandalous—but not completely out of the realm of possibility.

But Moroi and humans? That was beyond comprehension. Those races hadn't gotten together in centuries. They'd produced dhampirs long ago, but as the modern world progressed, Moroi had completely withdrawn from intermingling (in an intimate way) with humans. We lived among them, sure. Moroi and dhampirs worked alongside humans out in the world, bought houses in their neighborhoods, and apparently had bizarre arrangements with secret societies like the Alchemists. And, of course, Moroi fed from humans—and that was the thing. If you kept a human close to you, it was because they were a feeder. That was your level of intimacy. Feeders were food, pure and simple. Well-treated food, yes, but not food you became friends with. A Moroi having sex with a dhampir? Racy. A Moroi having sex with a dhampir *and* drinking blood? Dirty and humiliating. A Moroi having sex with a human—with or without blood drinking? Incomprehensible.

There were few things that shocked me or gave me offense. I was pretty liberal in my views when it came to romance, but the idea of human and Moroi marriage blew me away. It didn't matter if the human was a type of feeder—as Sarah appeared to be—or someone "above" that like Sydney. Humans and Moroi didn't get together. It was primitive and wrong, which was why it was no longer done. Well, at least not where I came from.

Unlike your people, we still follow the old ways.

The funny thing was that no matter how wrong I thought all this was, Sydney had to feel even more strongly about it with her vampire hang-ups. I supposed she'd been prepared, however, which is why she could manage that cool expression of hers. She hadn't been blindsided like Dimitri and me, because I felt with some certainty that he shared my feelings. He was just better at hiding surprise.

A commotion at the door startled me out of my shock. Raymond had arrived and wasn't alone. A dhampir boy of about eight or so sat on his shoulders, and a Moroi girl about the same age scurried alongside them. A pretty Moroi woman who looked to be in her twenties followed, and behind her was a cute dhampir guy who couldn't have been more than a couple years older than me, if not exactly my age.

Introductions followed. The children were Phil and Molly,

and the Moroi woman was named Paulette. They all appeared to live there, but I couldn't exactly figure out the relationships, except for the guy my age. He was Raymond and Sarah's son, Joshua. He had a ready smile for all of us—especially me and Sydney—and eyes that reminded me of the piercing, crystalline blue of the Ozeras. Only, whereas Christian's family tended to have dark hair, Joshua's was a sandy blond with lighter gold highlights. I had to admit, it was an attractive combination, but that stunned part of my brain reminded me again that he'd been born from a human-Moroi hookup, not a dhampir and Moroi like me. The end product was the same, but the means were bizarre.

"I'm putting them in your room," Sarah told Paulette. "The rest of you can share the loft."

It took me a moment to realize "the rest of you" meant Paulette, Joshua, Molly, and Phil. Glancing up, I saw there was indeed what looked like a loft space covering half the house's width. It didn't look big enough for four people.

"We don't want to inconvenience you," said Dimitri, sharing my thoughts. He'd been silent for almost all of this woodland adventure, saving his energy for actions, not words. "We'll be fine out here."

"Don't worry about it," said Joshua, again giving me that pretty smile. "We don't mind. Angeline won't either."

"Who?" I asked.

"My sister."

I repressed a grimace. Five of them crammed up there so that we could have a room. "Thank you," said Sydney. "We appreciate it. And we really won't be staying long." Their dislike of the vampire world aside, Alchemists could be polite and charming when they chose.

"Too bad," said Joshua.

"Stop flirting, Josh," said Sarah. "Do you three want something to eat before bed? I could warm up some stew. We had it earlier with some of Paulette's bread."

At the word *stew*, all my opossum fears came racing back. "No need," I said hastily. "I'd just be fine with bread."

"Me too," said Dimitri. I wondered if he was trying to reduce their work or if he shared my food fears. Probably not the latter. Dimitri seemed like the kind of guy you could throw into the wilderness and he would survive off anything.

Paulette had apparently baked a lot of bread, and they let us have a picnic in our small little room with a full loaf and a bowl of butter that Sarah had probably churned herself. The room was about the size of my dorm room at St. Vladimir's, with two down stuffed mattresses on the floor. Quilts neatly covered them, quilts that probably hadn't been used in months with these temperatures. Munching on a piece of bread that was surprisingly good, I ran my hand over one of the quilts.

"It reminds me of some of the designs I saw in Russia," I said.

Dimitri studied the pattern too. "Similar. But not quite the same."

"It's the evolution of the culture," said Sydney. She was tired but not enough to abandon textbook mode. "Traditional Russian patterns brought over and eventually fused with a typical Americana patchwork quilt form."

Whoa. "Um, good to know." The family had left us alone while they got ready for bed, and I eyed our cracked door warily. With the noise and activity out there, it seemed unlikely we'd be overheard, but I lowered my voice anyway. "Are you ready to explain who the hell these people are?"

She shrugged. "The Keepers."

"Yeah, I got that. And we're the Tainted. Sounds like a better name for Strigoi."

"No." Sydney leaned back against the wooden wall. "Strigoi are the Lost. You're Tainted because you joined the modern world and left behind their backward ways for your own messed up customs."

"Hey," I retorted. "We're not the ones with overalls and banjos."

"Rose," chastised Dimitri, with a pointed look at the door. "Be careful. And besides, we only saw one person in overalls."

"If it makes you feel better," said Sydney, "I think your ways are better. Seeing humans mixing with all this . . ." The pleasant and professional face she had shown to the Keepers was gone. Her blunt nature was back. "It's disgusting. No offense."

"None taken," I said with a shiver. "Trust me, I feel the same way. I can't believe . . . I can't believe they live like that."

She nodded, seeming grateful I shared her view. "I like you guys sticking with your own kind better. Except . . ."

"Except what?" I prodded.

She looked sheepish. "Even if the people you come from don't marry humans, you do still interact with them and live in their cities. These guys don't."

"Which Alchemists prefer," guessed Dimitri. "You don't approve of this group's customs, but you do like having them conveniently stashed out of mainstream society."

Sydney nodded. "The more vampires who stay off on their own in the woods, the better—even if their lifestyle is crazy. These guys keep to themselves—and keep others out."

"Through hostile means?" I asked. We'd been met by a war party, and she'd expected it. All of them had been ready to fight: Moroi, dhampir, and human.

"Hopefully not too hostile," she said evasively.

"They let you through," said Dimitri. "They know the Alchemists. Why did Sarah ask about you bringing them things?"

"Because that's what we do," she said. "Every so often for groups like these, we drop off supplies—food for everyone, medicine for the humans." Again, I heard that derision in her voice, but then she turned uneasy. "The thing is, if Sarah's right, they could be due for an Alchemist visit. That would just be our luck to be here when that happens."

I was going to reassure her that we only needed to lie low a couple days when an earlier phrase tugged at me. "Wait. You said 'groups like these.' How many of these commune things are out there?" I turned to Dimitri. "This isn't like the Alchemists, is it? Something only some of you know about that you're keeping from the rest of us?"

He shook his head. "I'm as astonished by all of this as you are."

"Some of your leaders probably know about the Keepers in a vague way," said Sydney. "But no details. No locations. These guys hide themselves pretty well and can move on a moment's notice. They stay away from your people. They don't like your people."

I sighed. "Which is why they won't turn us in. And why they're so excited I might have killed Tatiana. Thanks for that, by the way."

Sydney wasn't apologetic in the least. "It gets us protection. Such as it is." She stifled a yawn. "But for now? I'm exhausted. I'm not going to be able to follow anyone's crazy plans—yours or Abe's—if I don't get some sleep."

I'd known she was tired, but only now did the extent of it hit me. Sydney wasn't like us. We needed sleep but had the endurance to put it off if needed. She'd been up all night and forced into some situations that were definitely outside of her comfort zone. She looked like she could fall asleep against the wall then and there. I turned to Dimitri. He was already looking at me.

"Shifts?" I asked. I knew neither one of us would allow our group to stay unguarded in this place, even if we were allegedly queen-killing heroes.

He nodded. "You go first, and I'll—"

The door was flung open, and both Dimitri and I nearly leapt up to attack. A dhampir girl stood there, glaring at all of us. She was a couple years younger than me, about the age of my friend Jill Mastrano, a student back at St. Vladimir's who wanted to be a Moroi fighter. This girl looked like she did too, just by her stance alone. She possessed the strong, lean build most dhampirs had, her whole body braced like it might tackle any one of us. Her hair was stick-straight to her waist, a dark auburn that had picked up gold and copper highlights from the sun. She had the same blue eyes as Joshua.

"So," she said. "You're the big heroes taking my room."

"Angeline?" I guessed, remembering Joshua mentioning his sister.

She narrowed her eyes, not liking that I knew who she was. "Yes." She studied me unflinchingly and didn't seem to approve of what she found. That sharp gaze flicked to Dimitri next. I expected a softening, expected her to fall prey to his good looks the way most women did. But, no. He received suspicion as well. Her attention turned back to me.

"I don't believe it," she declared. "You're too soft. Too prim."

Prim? Really? I didn't feel that way, not in my battle-scarred jeans and T-shirt. Looking at her attire, I could maybe understand the attitude, though. Her clothes were clean, but her jeans had been around a while, both knees worn to threads. The shirt was a plain, off-white tank top that had a homemade feel. I didn't know if it had originally been white. Maybe I was prim by comparison. Of course, if anyone deserved the title of prim, it would be Sydney. Her clothes would've passed at a business meeting, and she hadn't been in any fights or jailbreaks recently.

Angeline hadn't even given her a second glance, though. I was getting the feeling Alchemists were in a strange category around here, a different type of human from the ones who intermarried with the Keepers. Alchemists brought supplies and left. They were almost a type of feeder to these people, really, which boggled the mind. The Keepers had more respect for the types of humans my culture looked down on.

Regardless, I didn't know what to say to Angeline. I didn't like being called soft or having my battle prowess called into question. A spark of my temper flared, but I refused to cause trouble by getting in a fight with our host's daughter, nor was I going to start making up details about Tatiana's murder. I simply shrugged.

"Looks are deceiving," I said.

"Yes," Angeline said coolly. "They are."

She stalked over to a small chest in the corner and pulled out what looked like a nightgown. "You better not mess up my bed," she warned me. She glanced over at Sydney, sitting on the other mattress. "I don't care what you do to Paulette's."

"Is Paulette your sister?" I asked, still trying to put this family together.

There didn't seem to be anything I could say that wouldn't offend this girl. "Of course not," Angeline snapped, slamming the door as she left. I stared at it in astonishment.

Sydney yawned and stretched out on her bed. "Paulette is probably Raymond's . . . eh, I don't know. Mistress. Concubine."

"What?" I exclaimed. A Moroi married to a human and having an affair with a Moroi. I wasn't sure how much more I could take. "Living with his family?"

"Don't ask me to explain it. I don't want to know any more about your twisted ways than I have to."

"It's not *my* way," I retorted.

Sarah came shortly thereafter to apologize for Angeline and see if we needed anything else. We assured her we were fine and thanked her profusely for her hospitality. Once she was gone, Dimitri and I set up sleeping shifts. I would have rather we both stayed on alert, particularly since I felt pretty sure Angeline would slit someone's throat in their sleep. But, we needed rest and knew we'd both react promptly if anyone came busting down our door.

So, I let Dimitri take the first watch while I snuggled into Angeline's bed and tried not to "mess it up." It was surprisingly comfortable. Or, maybe I was just that tired. I was able to let go of my worries about execution, lost siblings, and vampire hillbillies. Deep sleep wrapped around me, and I began to dream . . . but not just any dream. It was a shifting of my inner world, the sense of being both in and out of reality. I was being pulled into a spirit-induced dream.

Adrian!

The thought excited me. I'd missed him and was eager to talk to someone directly after all that had happened at Court. There hadn't been much time to talk during my escape, and after this bizarre backwoods world I'd stumbled into, I really needed some piece of normality and civilization around me.

The dream's world began to form around me, growing clearer and clearer. It was a location I'd never seen, a formal parlor with chairs and couches covered in lavender paisley cushions. Oil paintings lined the walls, and there was a large harp in the corner. I'd learned long ago that there was no predicting where Adrian would send me—or what he'd make me wear. Fortunately, I was in jeans and a T-shirt, my blue *nazar* hanging around my neck.

I turned around anxiously, looking for him so that I could give him a giant hug. Yet, as my eyes searched the room, it wasn't Adrian's face I suddenly found myself looking into.

It was Robert Doru's.

And Victor Dashkov was with him.

TEN

WHEN YOUR BOYFRIEND IS A dream-walker, you pick up a few lessons. One of the most important is that doing physical things in dreams feels exactly like doing them in the real world. Say, like kissing someone. Adrian and I had shared a number of dream-kisses intense enough to spark my body wanting to try a whole lot more. Although I'd never actually attacked someone in a dream, I was willing to bet a punch here would feel just as painful as a real one.

Without hesitation, I lunged toward Victor, uncertain as to whether I should sock him or choke him. Both seemed like good ideas. Turned out, I did neither. Before I could reach him, I slammed into an invisible wall—hard. It both blocked me from him and bounced me back at the impact. I stumbled, tried to regain my footing, but instead landed painfully on the ground. Yup—dreams felt just like real life.

I glared at Robert, feeling a mix of both anger and uneasiness. I tried to hide that last emotion. "You're a spirit user with telekinesis?"

We'd known that was possible, but it was a skill neither Lissa nor Adrian had mastered yet. I really didn't like the idea that Robert might have the power to throw objects around and create invisible barriers. It was a disadvantage we didn't need.

Robert remained enigmatic. "I control the dream."

Victor was looking down at me with that smug, calculating expression he excelled at. Realizing what an undignified position I was in, I leapt to my feet. I kept a hard stance, my body tense and ready as I wondered if Robert would keep the wall up continuously.

"Are you done with your tantrum?" asked Victor. "Behaving like a civilized person will make our talk so much more pleasant."

"I have no interest in talking to you," I snapped. "The only thing I'm going to do is hunt you down in the real world and drag you back to the authorities."

"Charming," said Victor. "We can share a cell."

I winced.

"Yes," he continued. "I know all about what happened. Poor Tatiana. Such a tragedy. Such a loss."

His mocking, melodramatic tone sparked an alarming idea. "You . . . you didn't have anything to do with it, did you?" Victor's escape from prison had triggered a lot of fear and paranoia amongst the Moroi. They'd been convinced he was coming for them all. Knowing the truth about the escape, I'd dismissed such talk and figured he'd simply lie low. Now, remembering how he'd once wanted to start a revolution among the Moroi, I wondered if the queen's murderer actually *was* the most evil villain we knew.

Victor snorted. "Hardly." He put his hands behind his back as he paced the room and pretended to study the art. I again wondered how far Robert's shield extended. "I have much more sophisticated methods to accomplish my goals. I wouldn't stoop to something like that—and neither would you."

I was about to point out that messing with Lissa's mind was hardly sophisticated, but his last words caught my attention. "You don't think I did it?"

He glanced back from where he'd been studying a man with a top hat and cane. "Of course not. You'd never do anything that required that much foresight. And, if what I've heard about the crime scene is true, you'd never leave that much evidence behind."

There was both an insult and a compliment there. "Well, thanks for the vote of confidence. I've been worrying about what you'd think." This earned me a smile, and I crossed my arms over my chest. "How do you guys even know what's happening at Court? Do you have spies?"

"This sort of thing spreads throughout the Moroi world quickly," said Victor. "I'm not that out of touch. I knew about her murder almost as soon as it happened. And about your most impressive escape."

My attention mostly stayed on Victor, but I did cast a quick glance at Robert. He remained silent, and from the blank, distracted look in his eyes, I wondered if he was even aware of what was being said around him. Seeing him always sent a chill down my spine. He was a prominent example of spirit at its worst.

"Why do you care?" I demanded. "And why the hell are you bothering me in my dreams?"

Victor continued his pacing, pausing to run his fingertips along the harp's smooth, wooden surface. "Because I have a great interest in Moroi politics. And I'd like to know who's responsible for the murder and what their game is."

I smirked. "Sounds like you're just jealous someone else is pulling the strings besides you for a change. No pun intended."

His hand dropped from the harp, back to his side, and he fixed his sharp eyes on me, eyes the same pale green as Lissa's. "Your witty commentary isn't going to get you anywhere. You can either let us help you or not."

"You are the *last* person I want help from. I don't need it."

"Yes. Things seem to be going quite well for you, now that you're a hunted fugitive and on the run with a man that many still believe is Strigoi." Victor gave a calculated pause. "Of course, I'm sure you don't mind that last part so much. You know, if I found you two, *I* could probably shoot you and be welcomed back as a hero."

"Don't bet on it." Rage burned through me, both at his insinuation and because he'd caused so much trouble for Dimitri and me in the past. With great force of will, I replied in a low, deadly voice: "I am going to find *you*. And you probably won't live to see the authorities."

"We already established murder isn't in your skill set." Victor sat down in one of the cushioned chairs, making himself comfortable. Robert continued standing, that out-of-it expression still on his face. "Now, the first thing we need to do is determine why someone would want to kill our late queen. Her abrasive personality is hardly motivation, though I'm sure it didn't hurt. People do things like this for power and advantage, to push their agendas through. From what I hear, Tatiana's most controversial action recently was that age law—yes, that's the one. The one making you scowl at me like that. It stands to reason that her murderer opposed that."

I didn't want to comply with Victor at all. I didn't want a reasonable discussion with him. What I wanted was some indication of where he was in real life, and then, I wanted to take a chance on slamming into that invisible wall again. It'd be worth the risk if I could do some damage. So, I was a bit surprised when I found myself saying, "Or, whoever did it wanted to push something worse through—something harsher on dhampirs. They thought her decree was too soft."

I admit, catching Victor Dashkov off guard was one of the greatest joys of my life. I had that satisfaction now, seeing his eyebrows rise in astonishment. It wasn't easy proposing something a master schemer like him hadn't already considered. "Interesting," he said at last. "I may have underestimated you, Rose. That's a brilliant deduction on your part."

"Well, um . . . it wasn't exactly my deduction."

Victor waited expectantly. Even Robert snapped out of his daze and focused on me. It was creepy.

"It was Tatiana's. I mean, not her deduction. She said it directly—well, that is, the note she left for me did." Why was I rambling in front of these guys? At least I surprised Victor again.

"Tatiana Ivashkov left *you* a note with clandestine information? Whatever for?"

I bit my lip and turned my attention over to one of the paintings. It showed an elegant Moroi woman with those same jade green eyes most Dashkovs and Dragomirs shared. I suddenly wondered if perhaps Robert had formed this dream in some Dashkov mansion from their childhood. Movement in my periphery made me instantly turn back to the brothers.

Victor rose and took a few steps toward me, curiosity and cunning all over him. "There's more. What else did she tell you? She knew she was in danger. She knew this law was part of it . . . but it wasn't the only thing, was it?"

I remained silent, but a crazy idea began forming in my mind. I was actually considering seeing if Victor could help me. Of course, in retrospect, that wasn't such a crazy notion, considering I'd already busted him out of prison to get his help.

"Tatiana said . . ." Should I say it? Should I give up the secret even Lissa didn't know? If Victor knew there was another Dragomir, he might use that knowledge for one of his schemes. How? I wasn't sure but had long learned to expect the unexpected from him. Yet . . . Victor knew a lot of Moroi secrets. I would have enjoyed watching him and Abe match wits. And I didn't doubt that a lot of Victor's inside knowledge involved the Dragomirs and Dashkovs. I swallowed. "Tatiana said that there was another Dragomir. That Lissa's dad had an affair and that if I could find whoever this is, it'll give Lissa her power back on the Council."

When Victor and Robert exchanged shocked looks, I knew my plan had backfired. Victor wasn't going to give me insight.

Instead, I'd been the one to just yield valuable information. Damn, damn, damn.

He turned his attention back to me, his expression speculative. "So. Eric Dragomir wasn't the saint he so often played."

I balled my fists. "Don't slam her dad."

"Wouldn't dream of it. I liked Eric immensely. But yes . . . if this is true, then Tatiana is right. Vasilisa technically has family backing, and her liberal views would certainly cause friction on a Council that never seems to change their ways." He chuckled. "Yes, I can definitely see that upsetting many people—including a murderer who wants to oppress dhampirs. I imagine he or she wouldn't want this knowledge to get out."

"Someone already tried to get rid of records linking Lissa's dad to a mistress." I again spoke without thinking and hated myself for it. I didn't want to give the brothers any more info. I didn't want to play like we were all working together here.

"And let me guess," said Victor. "That's what you're trying to do, isn't it? Find this Dragomir bastard."

"Hey, don't—"

"It's just an expression," he interrupted. "If I know you two—and I feel confident I do—Vasilisa is desperately trying to clear your name back at Court while you and Belikov are off on a sexually charged adventure to find her brother or sister."

"You don't know anything about us," I growled. Sexually charged indeed.

He shrugged. "Your face says it all. And really, it's not a bad idea. Not a great one either, but not bad. Give the Dragomir family a quorum, and you'll have a voice speaking on your behalf on the Council. I don't suppose you have any leads?"

"We're working on it," I replied evasively.

Victor looked at Robert. I knew the two didn't have any psychic communication, but as they exchanged glances, I had a feeling they were both thinking the same thing and confirming with each other. At last, Victor nodded and turned back to me.

"Very well then. We'll help you." He made it sound like he was reluctantly agreeing to do me a big favor.

"We don't need your help!"

"Of course you do. You're out of your league, Rose. You're wandering into a nest of ugly, complex politics—something you have no experience with. There's no shame in acknowledging that, just as I'm not ashamed to admit that in an irrational, ill-planned fist fight, you would certainly prove superior."

Another backhanded compliment. "We're doing just fine. We have an Alchemist helping us." There. That would show him who was out of whose league. And, to my credit, he did look slightly impressed. Slightly.

"Better than I expected. Has your Alchemist come up with a location or any lead yet?"

"She's working on it," I repeated.

He sighed in frustration. "We're going to need time then, aren't we? Both for Vasilisa to investigate Court and you to start tracking this child."

"You're the one who acts like you know everything,"

I pointed out. "I figured you'd know something about this."

"To my chagrin, no." Victor didn't really sound all that put out. "But as soon as we get a thread, I assure you, I'll be essential in unraveling it." He walked over to his brother and patted Robert's arm comfortingly. Robert stared back adoringly. "We'll visit you again. Let us know when you have something useful, and then we'll meet up with you."

My eyes widened. "You'll do no such—" I hesitated. I'd let Victor escape in Las Vegas. Now he was offering to come to me. Maybe I could repair that mistake and make good on my earlier threat to him. Quickly, I tried to cover my lapse of speech. "How do I know I can trust you?"

"You can't," he said bluntly. "You've got to take it on faith that the enemy of your enemy is your friend."

"I've always hated that saying. You'll always be my enemy."

I was a bit surprised when Robert suddenly came to life. He glared and stepped forward. "My brother is a good man, shadow-girl! If you hurt him . . . if you hurt him, you'll pay. And next time you won't come back. The world of the dead won't give you up a second time."

I knew better than to take the threats of a crazy man seriously, but his last words sent a chill through me. "Your brother is a psycho—"

"Enough, enough." Victor again gave Robert a reassuring pat on the arm. Still scowling at me, the younger Dashkov brother backed off, but I was willing to bet that invisible wall was back in place. "This does us no good. We're wasting time—which is something we don't have enough of. We need more. The monarch elections will start any day now, and Tatiana's murderer could have a hand in those if there really was some agenda going on. We need to slow down the elections—not just to thwart the assassin, but also to give all of us time to accomplish our tasks."

I was getting tired of all this. "Yeah? And how do you propose we do that?"

Victor smiled. "By running Vasilisa as a candidate for queen."

Seeing as this was Victor Dashkov we were dealing with, I really shouldn't have been surprised by anything he said. It was a testament to his level of craziness that he continually caught me unprepared.

"That," I declared, "is impossible."

"Not really," he replied.

I threw my hands up in exasperation. "Haven't you been paying attention to what we've been talking about? The whole point is to get Lissa full family rights with the Moroi. She can't even vote! How could she run for queen?"

"Actually, the law says she can. According to the way the nomination policy is written, one person from each royal line may run for the monarch position. That's all it says. One person from each line may run. There is no mention of how many people need to be in her family, as there is for her to vote on the Council. She simply needs three nominations—and the law doesn't specify which family they come from."

Victor spoke in such a precise, crisp way that he might as well have been reciting from a legal book. I wondered if he had all the laws memorized. I supposed if you were going to make a career of breaking laws, you might as well know them.

"Whoever wrote that law probably assumed the candidates would have family members. They just didn't bother spelling it out. That's what people will say if Lissa runs. They'll fight it."

"They can fight it all they want. Those who are denying her a Council spot base it on one line in the law books that mentions another family member. If that's their argument, that every detail *must* count, then they'll have to do the same for the election laws—which, as I have said, do not mention family backing. That's the beauty of this loophole. Her opponents can't have it both ways." A smile twisted at Victor's lips, supremely confident. "I assure you, there is absolutely nothing in the wording that prevents her from doing this."

"How about her age?" I pointed out. "The princes and princesses who run are always old." The title of prince or princess went to a family's oldest member, and traditionally, that was the person who ran for king or queen. The family could decide to nominate someone else more fitting, but even then—to my knowledge—it was always someone older and experienced.

"The only age restriction is full adulthood," said Victor. "She's eighteen. She qualifies. The other families have much larger pools to draw from, so naturally, they'd select someone who seemed more experienced. In the Dragomir case? Well, that's not an option, now is it? Besides, young monarchs aren't without precedence. There was a very famous queen—Alexandra—who wasn't much older than Vasilisa. Very well loved, very extraordinary. Her statue is by the Court's church."

I shifted uncomfortably. "Actually . . . it's, um, not there anymore. It kind of blew up."

Victor just stared. He'd apparently heard about my escape but not all of the details.

"It's not important," I said hastily, feeling guilty that I'd been indirectly responsible for blowing up a renowned queen. "This whole idea about using Lissa is ridiculous."

"You won't be the only one who thinks so," Victor said. "They'll argue. They'll fight. In the end, the law will prevail. They'll have to let her run. She'll go through the tests and probably pass. Then, when voting comes, the laws that govern those procedures reference a family member assisting with the vote."

My head was spinning by now. I felt mentally exhausted listening to all these legal loopholes and technicalities.

"Just come right out and put it in simple language," I ordered.

"When voting comes, she won't be eligible. She has no family to fulfill the role required at the actual election. In other words, the law says she can run and take the tests. Yet, people can't actually vote for her because she has no family."

"That's . . . idiotic."

"Agreed." He paused. I don't think either of us ever expected to concur on something.

"Lissa would hate this. She would never, ever want to be queen."

"Are you not following this?" exclaimed Victor. "She won't

be queen. She *can't*. It's a badly written law for a situation no one foresaw. It's a mess. And it will bog down the elections so badly that we'll have extra time to find Vasilisa's sibling and find out who really killed Tatiana."

"Hey! I told you: There's no 'we' here. I'm not going to—"

Victor and Robert exchanged looks.

"Get Vasilisa nominated," said Victor abruptly. "We'll be in touch soon on where to meet you for the Dragomir search."

"That's not—"

I woke up.

My immediate reaction was to swear, but then, remembering where I was, I kept my expletives inside my own head. I could make out Dimitri's silhouette in the corner, alert and watchful, and didn't want him to know I was awake. Closing my eyes, I shifted into a more comfortable position, hoping for true sleep that would block out the Dashkov brothers and their ridiculous schemes. Lissa running for queen? It was crazy. And yet . . . it really wasn't much crazier than most of the things I did.

Putting that aside, I let my body relax and felt the tug of true sleep start to take me down. Emphasis on *start*. Because suddenly, I felt another spirit dream materializing around me.

Apparently, this was going to be a busy night.

ELEVEN

I BRACED MYSELF, EXPECTING TO see the Dashkov brothers appear again with some last minute "advice." Instead I saw—

"Adrian!"

I ran across the garden I'd appeared in and threw my arms around him. He hugged me back just as tightly and lifted me off the ground.

"Little dhampir," he said, once he put me down again. His arms stayed around my waist. "I've missed you."

"I've missed you too." And I meant it. The last couple days and their bizarre events had completely unhinged my life, and being with him—even in a dream—was comforting. I stood on my tiptoes and kissed him, enjoying a small moment of warmth and peace as our lips met.

"Are you okay?" he asked when I broke away. "No one'll tell me much about you. Your old man says you're safe and that the Alchemist would let him know if anything went wrong."

I didn't bother telling Adrian that that probably wasn't true, seeing as Abe didn't know we'd gone freelancing with some backwoods vampires.

"I'm fine," I assured Adrian. "Mostly bored. We're holed up in this dive of a town. I don't think anyone will come looking for us. I don't think they'd want to."

A look of relief spread over his handsome face, and it occurred to me just how worried he was. "I'm glad. Rose, you can't imagine what it's like. They aren't just questioning people who might have been involved. The guardians are making all sorts of plans to hunt you down. There's all this talk about 'deadly force.'"

"Well, they won't find me. I'm somewhere pretty remote." *Very* remote.

"I wish I could have gone with you."

He still looked concerned, and I pressed a finger to his lips. "No. Don't say that. You're better off where you are—and better not to be associated with me any more than you already are. Have you been questioned?"

"Yeah, they didn't get anything useful out of me. Too tight an alibi. They brought me in when I went to find Mikhail because we talked to—"

"I know. Joe."

Adrian's surprise was brief. "Little dhampir, you've been spying."

"It's hard not to."

"You know, as much as I like the idea of having someone always know when you're in trouble, I'm still kind of glad I don't have anyone bound to me. Not sure I'd want them looking in my head."

"I don't think anyone would want to look in your head either. One person living Adrian Ivashkov's life is hard enough." Amusement flickered in his eyes, but it faded when

I switched back to business. "Anyway, yeah. I overheard Lissa's . . . um, interrogation of Joe. That's serious stuff. What did Mikhail say? If Joe lied, that clears half the evidence against me." It also theoretically killed Adrian's alibi.

"Well, not quite half. It would have been better if Joe said you were in your room during the murder instead of admitting he's a flake who doesn't remember anything. It also would have been better if he hadn't said all this under Lissa's compulsion. Mikhail can't report that."

I sighed. Hanging out with spirit users, I'd started to take compulsion for granted. It was easy to forget that among Moroi, it was taboo, the kind of thing you'd get in serious trouble for. In fact, Lissa wouldn't just get in trouble for illicitly using it. She could also be accused of simply making Joe say whatever she wanted. Anything he said in my favor would be suspect. No one would believe it.

"Also," added Adrian, looking dismayed, "if what Joe said gets out, the world would learn about my mother's misguided acts of love."

"I'm sorry," I said, putting my arms around him. He complained about his parents all the time but really did care about his mother. Finding out about her bribery had to be tough for him, and I knew Tatiana's death still pained him. It seemed I was around a lot of men in anguish lately. "Although, I really am glad she cleared you of any connection."

"It was stupid of her. If anyone finds out, she'll be in serious trouble."

"What's Mikhail's advice then?"

"He's going to find Joe and question him privately. Go from there. For now, there's not much more we can do with the info. It's useful for us . . . but not for the legal system."

"Yeah," I said, trying not to feel disheartened. "I guess it's better than nothing."

Adrian nodded and then brushed away his dark mood in that easy way of his. Still keeping his arms around me, he pulled back slightly, smiling as he looked down at me. "Nice dress, by the way."

The topic change caught me by surprise, though I should have been used to it with him by now. Following his gaze, I noticed I was wearing an old dress of mine, the sexy black dress I'd had on when Victor had unleashed a lust charm on Dimitri and me. Since Adrian hadn't dressed me for the dream, my subconscious had dictated my appearance. I was kind of astonished it had chosen this.

"Oh . . ." I suddenly felt embarrassed but didn't know why. "My own clothes are kind of beat up. I guess I wanted something to counteract that."

"Well, it looks good on you." Adrian's fingers slid along the strap. "*Really* good."

Even in a dream, the touch of his finger made my skin tingle. "Watch it, Ivashkov. We've got no time for this."

"We're asleep. What else are we going to do?"

My protests were muffled in a kiss. I sank into it. One of his hands slid down the side of my thigh, near the dress's edge, and it took a lot of mental energy to convince myself that him pulling the dress up was probably not going to clear my name.

I reluctantly moved back.

"We're going to figure out who killed Tatiana," I said, trying to catch my breath.

"There's no 'we,'" he said, echoing the line I'd just used on Victor. "There's me. And Lissa. And Christian. And the rest of our misfit friends." He stroked my hair and then drew me close again, brushing a kiss against my cheek. "Don't worry, little dhampir. You take care of yourself. Just stay where you are."

"I can't," I said. "Don't you get it? I can't just do nothing." The words were out of my mouth before I could stop them. It was one thing to protest my inactivity with Dimitri, but with Adrian, I needed to make him and everyone else at Court think I was doing the "right thing."

"You have to. We'll take care of you." He didn't get it, I realized. He didn't understand how badly I needed to do something to help. To his credit, his intentions were good. He thought taking care of me was a big deal. He wanted to keep me safe. But he didn't truly get how agonizing inaction was for me. "We'll find this person and stop them from doing whatever it is . . . they want to do. It might take a long time, but we'll fix it."

"Time . . ." I murmured against his chest, letting the argument go. I'd get nowhere convincing him I needed to help my friends, and anyway, I had my own quest now. So much to do, so little time. I stared off into the landscape he'd created. I'd noticed trees and flowers earlier but only now realized we were in the Church's courtyard—the way it had been before

Abe's assault. The statue of Queen Alexandra stood intact, her long hair and kind eyes immortalized in stone. The murder investigation really was in my friends' hands for now, but Adrian had been right: it might take a while. I sighed. "Time. We need more time."

Adrian pulled away slightly. "Hmm? What'd you say?"

I stared up at him, biting my lower lip as a million thoughts spun through my mind. I looked again at Alexandra and made my decision, wondering if I was about to set new records in foolishness. I turned back to Adrian and squeezed his hand.

"I said we need more time. And I know how we can get it . . . but . . . well, there's something you have to do for me. And you, uh, probably shouldn't mention it to Lissa yet . . ."

I had just enough time to deliver my instructions to Adrian—who was as shocked as I'd expected—before Dimitri woke me up for my shift. We switched off with little conversation. He had his usual tough face on, but I could see the lines of fatigue etched upon his features. I didn't want to bother him—yet—with my Victor and Robert encounter. Not to mention what I'd just told Adrian to do. There'd be plenty of time for a recap later. Dimitri fell asleep in that easy way of his, and Sydney never stirred the entire time. I envied her for a full night's sleep but couldn't help a smile as the room grew lighter and lighter. She'd been inadvertently put on a vampire schedule after our all-night adventures.

Of course, Lissa was on the same schedule, which meant I couldn't visit her during my watch. Just as well. I needed to keep an eye on this creepy collective we'd stumbled into.

These Keepers might not want to turn us in, but that didn't make them harmless either. I also hadn't forgotten Sydney's fears about surprise Alchemist visits.

When late afternoon came for the rest of the world, I heard stirring inside the house. I gently touched Dimitri's shoulder, and he jerked awake instantly.

"Easy," I said, unable to hide a smile. "Just a wakeup call. Sounds like our redneck friends are getting up."

This time, our voices woke Sydney. She rolled over toward us, her eyes squinting at the light coming through the badly screened window. "What time is it?" she asked, stretching her limbs.

"Not sure." I had no watch. "Probably past midday. Three? Four?"

She sat up almost as quickly as Dimitri had. "In the afternoon?" The sunlight gave her the answer. "Damn you guys and your unholy schedule."

"Did you just say 'damn'? Isn't that against Alchemist rules?" I teased.

"Sometimes it's necessary." She rubbed her eyes and glanced toward the door. The faint noises I'd heard in the rest of the house were louder now, audible even to her ears. "I guess we need a plan."

"We have one," I said. "Find Lissa's sibling."

"I never entirely agreed to that," she reminded me. "And you guys keep thinking I can just magically type away like some movie hacker to find all your answers."

"Well, at least it's a place to—" A thought occurred to me,

one that could seriously mess things up. "Crap. Your laptop won't even work out here."

"It's got a satellite modem, but it's the battery we have to worry about." Sydney sighed and stood up, smoothing her rumpled clothes with dismay. "I need a coffee shop or something."

"I think I saw one in a cave down the road," I said.

That almost got a smile from her. "There's got to be some town close by where I could use my laptop."

"But it's probably not a good idea to take the car out anywhere in this state," said Dimitri. "Just in case someone at the motel got your license plate number."

"I know," she said grimly. "I was thinking about that too."

Our brilliant scheming was interrupted by a knock at the door. Without waiting for an answer, Sarah stuck her head inside and smiled. "Oh, good. You're all awake. We're getting breakfast ready if you want to join us."

Through the doorway, scents of what seemed like a normal breakfast drifted in: bacon, eggs . . . The bread had gotten me through the night, but I was ready for real food and willing to roll the dice on whatever Raymond's family had to offer.

In the house's main section, we found a flurry of domestic activity. Raymond appeared to be cooking something over the fireplace while Paulette set the long table. It already had a platter of perfectly ordinary scrambled eggs and more slices of yesterday's bread. Raymond rose from the fireplace, holding a large metal sheet covered in crisp bacon. A smile split his bearded face when he spotted us. The more of these Keepers I saw, the more I kept noticing something. They made no attempts to hide their fangs. From childhood, my Moroi were taught to smile and speak in a way that minimized fang exposure, in case they were out in human cities. There was nothing like that here.

"Good morning," said Raymond, carefully pushing the bacon onto another platter on the table. "I hope you're all hungry."

"Do you think that's, like, *real* bacon?" I whispered to Sydney and Dimitri. "And not like squirrel or something?"

"Looks real to me," said Dimitri.

"I'd say so too," said Sydney. "Though, I guarantee it's from their own pigs and not a grocery store."

Dimitri laughed at whatever expression crossed my face. "I always love seeing what worries you. Strigoi? No. Questionable food? Yes."

"What about Strigoi?"

Joshua and Angeline entered the house. He had a bowl of blackberries, and she was pushing the little kids along. From their squirming and dirty faces, they clearly wanted to go back outside. It was Angeline who had asked the question.

Dimitri covered for my squeamishness. "Just talking about some of Rose's Strigoi kills."

Joshua came to a standstill and stared at me, those pretty blue eyes wide with amazement. "You've killed the Lost? Er—Strigoi?" I admired his attempt to use "our" term. "How many?"

I shrugged. "I don't really know anymore."

"Don't you use the marks?" Raymond scolded. "I didn't think the Tainted had abandoned those."

"The marks—oh. Yeah. Our tattoos? We do." I turned around and lifted up my hair. I heard a scuffling of feet and then felt a finger touching my skin. I flinched and whipped back around, just in time to see Joshua lowering his hand sheepishly.

"Sorry," he said. "I've just never seen some of these. Only the *molnija* marks. That's how we count our Strigoi kills. You've got . . . a lot."

"The S-shaped mark is unique to *them*," said Raymond disapprovingly. That look was quickly replaced by admiration. "The other's the *zvezda*."

This earned gasps from Joshua and Angeline and a "What?" from me.

"The battle mark," said Dimitri. "Not many people call it *zvezda* anymore. It means 'star.'"

"Huh. Makes sense," I said. The tattoo was, in fact, kind of shaped like a star and was given when someone had fought in a big enough battle to lose count of Strigoi kills. After all, there were only so many *molnija* marks you could cram on your neck.

Joshua smiled at me in a way that made my stomach flutter just a little. Maybe he was part of a pseudo-Amish cult, but that didn't change the fact that he was still good-looking. "Now I understand how you could have killed the Tainted queen."

"It's probably fake," said Angeline.

I'd been about to protest the queen-killing part, but her

comment derailed me. "It is not! I earned it when Strigoi attacked our school. And then there were plenty more I took down after that."

"The mark can't be that uncommon," said Dimitri. "Your people must have big Strigoi fights every once in a while."

"Not really," said Joshua, his eyes still on me. "Most of us have never fought or even seen the Lost. They don't really bother us."

That was surprising. If ever there was a Strigoi target, a group of Moroi, dhampirs, and humans out in the middle of nowhere would be it. "Why not?" I asked.

Raymond winked at me. "Because we fight back."

I pondered his enigmatic statement as the family sat down to eat. Again, I thought about the entire community's willingness to fight when we'd first arrived. Was it really enough to scare off Strigoi? Not much scared them, but maybe certain things were too much of an inconvenience to deal with. I wondered what Dimitri's opinion would be on that. His own family had come from a community that separated itself somewhat from mainstream Moroi life, but it was nothing like this.

All of this spun in my mind while we ate and talked. The Keepers still had a lot more questions about us and Tatiana. The only one not participating was Angeline. She ate as little as Sydney and kept watching me with a scowl.

"We need some supplies," said Sydney abruptly, interrupting me in the middle of a gruesome story. I didn't mind, but the others looked disappointed. "Where's the nearest town that would have a coffee shop . . . or any restaurant?"

"Well," said Paulette. "Rubysville is a little over an hour north. But we have plenty of food here for you."

"It's not about food," I said quickly. "Yours has been great." I glanced at Sydney. "An hour's not so bad, right?"

She nodded and then glanced hesitantly at Raymond. "Is there any way . . . is there any way we could borrow a car? I'll . . ." The next words clearly caused her pain. "I'll leave the keys to mine until we get back."

He arched an eyebrow. "You've got a nice car."

Sydney shrugged. "The less we drive it around here, the better."

He told us we could take his truck and that he "probably" wouldn't even need to use the CR-V. Sydney gave him a tight smile of thanks, but I knew images of vampires joyriding in her car were dancing through her head.

We set out soon after that, wanting to be back before the sun went down. People were out and about in the commune, doing chores or whatever else it was they did with their lives. A group of children sat around a dhampir reading a book to them, making me wonder what sort of education process they had here.

All of the Keepers stopped whatever they were doing as we passed, giving us either curious looks or outright smiles. I smiled back occasionally but mostly kept my eyes ahead. Joshua was escorting us back to the "parking lot" and managed to walk beside me when we reached the narrow path.

"I hope you won't be gone long," he said. "I'd wanted us to talk more."

"Sure," I said. "That'd be fun."

He brightened and chivalrously pushed aside a low-hanging branch. "Maybe I can show you my cave."

"Your—wait. What? Don't you live with your dad?"

"For now. But I'm getting my own place." There was pride in his voice. "It's not as big as his, of course, but it's a good start. It's almost cleaned out."

"That's really, um, great. Definitely show me when we're back." The words came easily to my lips, but my mind was pondering the fact that Raymond's house was apparently "big."

Joshua parted ways from us when we reached Raymond's truck, a big red pickup with a seat that could just barely hold the three of us. Considering the Keepers didn't leave the woods much, the truck seemed like it had seen a lot of miles. Or maybe just a lot of years of disuse.

"You shouldn't lead him on like that," Dimitri said, when we'd been on the road for about ten minutes. Surprisingly, Sydney had let him drive. I guessed she figured a manly truck deserved a manly driver.

Now that we were moving, my mind had focused back on the task at hand: finding the other Dragomir. "Huh?"

"Joshua. You were flirting with him."

"I was not! We were just talking."

"Aren't you with Adrian?"

"Yes!" I exclaimed, glaring at Dimitri. His eyes were fixed on the road. "And that's why I wasn't flirting. How can you read so much into that? Joshua doesn't even like me that way."

"Actually," said Sydney, sitting between us, "he does."

I turned my incredulity on her. "How do you know? Did he pass you a note in class or something?"

She rolled her eyes. "No. But you and Dimitri are like gods back at camp."

"We're outsiders," I reminded her. "Tainted."

"No. You're renegade Strigoi- and queen-killers. It might have all been southern charm and hospitality back there, but those people can be savage. They put a big premium on being able to beat people up. And, considering how scruffy most of them are, you guys are . . . well . . . let's just say you two are the hottest things to walk through there in a while."

"You're not hot?" I asked.

"It's irrelevant," she said, flustered by the comment. "Alchemists aren't even on their radar. We don't fight. They think we're weak."

I thought back to the enraptured faces and had to admit that a lot of the people there did have a weathered, worn-out look. Almost. "Raymond's family was pretty good-looking," I pointed out. I heard a grunt from Dimitri who no doubt read this as evidence of me flirting with Joshua.

"Yeah," she said. "Because they're probably the most important family in town. They eat better, probably don't have to work in the sun as much. That kind of stuff makes a difference."

There was no more talk of flirting as we continued the drive. We made good time to Rubysville, which looked eerily similar to the first town we'd stayed in. When we stopped at what appeared to be the Rubysville's only gas station, Sydney ran inside to ask a few questions. She came back, reporting that there was indeed a café of sorts where she could plug in her laptop and try to look up what we needed.

She ordered coffee, and we sat there with her, too full from breakfast to order anything substantial. After a couple dirty looks from a waitress who seemed to regard us as loiterers, Dimitri and I decided to take a walk around town. Sydney looked almost as pleased as the waitress about this. I don't think she liked having us hover around.

I'd given Sydney a hard time about West Virginia, but I had to admit the scenery was beautiful. Soaring trees, full of summer leaves, surrounded the town like an embrace. Beyond them, mountains loomed, very different from the ones I'd grown up with near St. Vladimir's. These were rolling and green, covered in more trees. Most of the mountains surrounding St. Vladimir's had been stony and jagged, often with snowy peaks. A strange sense of nostalgia came over me, thinking back to Montana. There was a good possibility I'd never see it again. If I spent the rest of my life on the run, St. Vladimir's was the last place I could go. If I was caught, well . . . then I'd definitely never get to see Montana again.

"Or any place," I murmured, speaking out loud before I could catch myself.

"Hmm?" asked Dimitri.

"I was just thinking about if the guardians find us. I never realized how much there was I wanted to do and see. Suddenly, that's all at stake, you know?" We moved off to the side of the road as an orange pickup came driving by. Children out of school for the summer screeched and laughed in the back of it. "Okay, suppose my name isn't cleared and we never find the real murderer. What's the next-best-case scenario? Me: always running, always hiding. That'll be my life. For all I know, I *will* have to go live with the Keepers."

"I don't think it'll come to that," said Dimitri. "Abe and Sydney would help you find some place safe."

"Is there a safe place? For real? Adrian said the guardians are increasing their efforts to find us. They've got the Alchemists and probably human authorities looking for us too. No matter where we go, we'll run the risk of being spotted. Then we'll have to move on. It'll be like that forever."

"You'll be alive," he pointed out. "That's what matters. Enjoy what you have, every little detail of wherever you are. Don't focus on where you *aren't*."

"Yeah," I admitted, trying to follow his advice. The sky seemed a little bluer, the birds a little louder. "I suppose I shouldn't whine over the dream places I won't get to see. I should be grateful I get to see anything at all. And that I'm not living in a cave."

He glanced over at me and smiled, something unreadable in his eyes. "Where do you want to go?"

"What, right now?" I glanced around, sizing up our options. There was a bait and tackle store, a drugstore, and an ice cream parlor. I had a feeling that last one would be a necessary trip before leaving town.

"No, in the world."

I eyed him warily. "Sydney's going to be pissed if we take off for Istanbul or something."

This got me full-fledged laughter. "Not what I had in mind. Come on."

I followed him toward what looked like the bait and tackle store and then noticed a small building tucked behind it. Naturally, his sharp eyes had seen what I missed—probably because I'd been fixated on the ice cream. RUBYSVILLE PUBLIC LIBRARY.

"Whoa, hey," I said. "One of the few perks of graduating was avoiding places like this."

"It's probably air conditioned," he pointed out.

I looked down at my sweat-soaked tank top and noticed a faint pink tinge to my skin. With my tanned complexion, I rarely burned, but this was some serious sun—even so late in the day. "Lead on," I told him.

The library was mercifully cool, though even smaller than the one at St. Vladimir's. With some uncanny sense (or maybe just a knowledge of the Dewey Decimal System), Dimitri led us over to the travel section—which consisted of about ten books, three of which were about West Virginia. He frowned.

"Not quite what I expected." He scanned the shelf twice and then pulled out a large, bright-colored one entitled *100 Best Places to Visit in the World*.

We sat down cross-legged on the floor, and he handed me the book. "No way, comrade," I said. "I know books are a journey of the imagination, but I don't think I'm up for that today."

"Just take it," he said. "Close your eyes, and flip randomly to a page."

It seemed silly, considering everything else going on in our life, but his face said he was serious. Indulging him, I closed my eyes and selected a page in the middle. I opened to it.

"Mitchell, South Dakota?" I exclaimed. Remembering I was in a library, I lowered my voice. "Out of all the places in the world, that makes the top hundred?"

He was smiling again, and I'd forgotten how much I'd missed that. "Read it."

"'Located ninety minutes outside of Sioux Falls, Mitchell is home to the Corn Palace.'" I looked up at him in disbelief. *"Corn Palace?"*

He scooted over next to me, leaning close to look at the pictures. "I figured it'd be made of corn husks," he noted. The pictures actually showed what looked like a Middle Eastern—or even Russian—style building, with turrets and onion domes.

"Me too." Reluctantly, I added, "I'd visit it. I bet they have great T-shirts."

"And," he said, a sly look in his eyes, "I bet no guardians would look for us there."

I made no attempts to conceal my laughter, imagining us living as fugitives in the Corn Palace for the rest of our lives. My amusement brought us a scolding from a librarian, and we quieted as Dimitri took his turn. Sao Paolo, Brazil. Then my turn: Honolulu, Hawaii. Back and forth we passed the book, and before long, we were both lying on the floor, side by side, sharing mixed reactions as we continued our "global tour of the imagination." Our arms and legs just barely touched.

If anyone had told me forty-eight hours ago that I'd be lying in a library with Dimitri, reading a travel book, I would have said they were crazy. Almost as crazy was the realization that I was doing something perfectly ordinary and casual with him. Since the moment we'd met, our lives had been about secrecy and danger. And really, those *were* still the dominant themes in our lives. But in those quiet couple of hours, time seemed to stand still. We were at peace. We were friends.

"Florence, Italy," I read. Pictures of elaborate churches and galleries filled the page. "Sydney wants to go there. She wanted to study there, actually. If Abe could have managed that, I think she would have served him for life."

"She's still pretty obedient," Dimitri remarked. "I don't know her well, but I'm pretty sure Abe's got something on her."

"He got her out of Russia, back to the U.S."

He shook his head. "It's got to be more than that. Alchemists are loyal to their order. They don't like us. She hides it—they're trained to—but every minute with the Keepers is agony. For her to help us and betray her superiors, she owes him for some serious reason." We both paused a moment, wondering what mysterious arrangement my father had with her. "It's irrelevant, though. She's helping us, which is what matters . . . and we should probably get back to her."

I knew he was right but hated to go. I wanted to stay here, in this illusion of tranquility and safety, letting myself believe I might really make it to the Parthenon or even the Corn Palace someday. I handed the book back to him. "One more."

He picked his random page and opened the book. His

smile fell. "Saint Petersburg."

A weird mix of feelings entangled themselves in my chest. Nostalgia—because the city was beautiful. Sorrow—because my visit had been tainted by the awful task I'd gone there to do.

Dimitri stared at the page for a long time, wistfulness on his face. It occurred to me then that, despite his earlier pep talk, he had to be experiencing what I did for Montana: our old, favorite places were lost to us now.

I nudged him gently. "Hey, enjoy where you're at, remember? Not where you can't go."

He reluctantly shut the book and dragged his eyes away from it. "How'd you get so wise?" he teased.

"I had a good teacher." We smiled at each other. Something occurred to me. All this time, I'd figured he'd helped break me out because of Lissa's orders. Maybe there was more to it. "Is that why you escaped with me?" I asked. "To see what parts of the world you could?"

His surprise was brief. "You don't need me to be wise, Rose. You're doing fine on your own. Yes, that was part of it. Maybe I would have been welcomed back eventually, but there was the risk I wouldn't. After . . . after being Strigoi . . ." He stumbled over the words a little. "I gained a new appreciation for life. It took a while. I'm still not there. We're talking about focusing on the present, not the future—but it's my past that haunts me. Faces. Nightmares. But the farther I get from that world of death, the more I want to embrace life. The smell of these books and the perfume you wear. The way the light bends through that window. Even the taste of breakfast with the Keepers."

"You're a poet now."

"No, just starting to realize the truth. I respect the law and the way our society runs, but there was no way I could risk losing life in some cell after only just finding it again. I wanted to run too. That's why I helped you. That and—"

"What?" I studied him, desperately wishing he wasn't so good at keeping emotions off his face. I knew him well; I understood him. But he could still hide things from me.

He sat up, not meeting my eyes. "It doesn't matter. Let's go back to Sydney and see if she found out anything . . . although, as much as I hate to say it, I think it's unlikely."

"I know." I stood with him, still wondering what else he would have said. "She probably gave up and started playing *Minesweeper*."

We headed back toward the café, stopping briefly for ice cream. Eating it while we walked proved quite the challenge. The sun was nearing the horizon, painting everything orange and red, but the heat lingered. *Enjoy it, Rose,* I told myself. *The colors. The taste of chocolate.* Of course, I'd always loved chocolate. My life didn't need to be on the line for me to enjoy dessert.

We reached the café and found Sydney bent over her laptop, with a barely eaten Danish and what was probably her fourth cup of coffee. We slid into seats beside her.

"How's it—hey! You *are* playing *Minesweeper*!" I tried to peer closer at her screen, but she turned it from me. "You're supposed to be finding a connection to Eric's mistress."

"I already did," she said simply.

Dimitri and I exchanged astonished looks.

"But I don't know how useful it'll be."

"Anything'll be useful," I proclaimed. "What did you find?"

"After trying to track down all those bank records and transactions—and let me tell you, that is *not* fun at all—I finally found a small piece of info. The bank account we have now is a newer one. It was moved from another bank about five years ago. The old account was still a Jane Doe, *but* it did have a next-of-kin reference in the event something happened to the account holder."

I could hardly breathe. Financial transactions were lost on me, but we were about to get something solid. "A real name?"

Sydney nodded. "Sonya Karp."

TWELVE

DIMITRI AND I BOTH FROZE as the shock of that name hit us. Sydney, glancing between our faces, gave us a dry smile.

"I take it you know who that is?"

"Of course," I exclaimed. "She was my teacher. She went crazy and turned Strigoi."

Sydney nodded. "I know."

My eyes widened further. "She's not . . . she's not the one who had an affair with Lissa's dad, is she?" Oh dear God. That would be one of the most unexpected developments in the rollercoaster that was my life. I couldn't even begin to process the effects of that.

"Not likely," she said. "The account was opened several years before she was added as the beneficiary—which was right when she turned eighteen. So, if we're assuming the account was created around the time the baby was born, then she would have been way too young. Sonya's probably a relative."

My earlier astonishment was giving way to excitement, and I could see the same thing happening to Dimitri. "You must have records about her family," he said. "Or if not, some Moroi probably does. Who's close to Sonya? Does she have a sister?"

Sydney shook her head. "No. That'd be an obvious choice, though. Unfortunately, she has other family—*tons* of it. Her parents both came from giant families, so she has lots of cousins. Even some of her aunts are the right age."

"We can look them up, right?" I asked. A thrill of anticipation was running through me. I honestly hadn't expected this much information. True, it was small, but it was something. If Sonya Karp was related to Eric's mistress, that had to be something we could track.

"There's a lot of them." Sydney shrugged. "I mean, yeah, we could. It'd take a long time to find everyone's life history, and even then—especially if this was covered up enough—we'd have a hard time finding out if any of them is the woman we're looking for. Or even if any of them know who she is."

Dimitri's voice was low and thoughtful when he spoke. "One person knows who Jane Doe is."

Sydney and I both looked at him expectantly.

"Sonya Karp," he replied.

I threw up my hands. "Yeah, but we can't talk to her. She's a lost cause. Mikhail Tanner spent over a year hunting her and couldn't find her. If he can't, then we're not going to be able to."

Dimitri turned away from me and stared out the window. His brown eyes filled with sorrow, his thoughts momentarily far away from us. I didn't entirely understand what was happening, but that peaceful moment in the library—where Dimitri had smiled and shared in the daydream of an ordinary life—had vanished. And not just the moment. That Dimitri had vanished. He was back in his fierce mode, carrying the weight of the world on his shoulders again. At last, he sighed and looked back at me. "That's because Mikhail didn't have the right connections."

"Mikhail was her boyfriend," I pointed out. "He had more connections than anyone else."

Dimitri didn't acknowledge my comment. Instead, he grew pensive again. I could see turmoil behind his eyes, some inner war. At last, it must have been decided.

"Does your phone have reception out here?" he asked her.

She nodded, reaching into her purse and handing him her phone. He held it a moment, looking like it caused him total agony to touch it. At last, with another sigh, he stood up and headed for the door. Sydney and I exchanged questioning looks and then both followed him. She lagged behind me, having to toss cash on the table and grab her laptop. I emerged outside just as Dimitri finished dialing a number and put the phone to his ear. Sydney joined us, and a moment later, the person on the other end of the line must have answered.

"Boris?" asked Dimitri.

That was all I understood because the rest was a string of rapid Russian. A strange sensation spread over me as he spoke. I was confused, lost because of the language . . . but there was more than that. I felt chilled. My pulse raced with fear. That voice . . . I knew that voice. It was his voice and yet not his voice. It was the voice of my nightmares, a voice of coldness and cruelty.

Dimitri was playing Strigoi.

Well, "playing" was really too gentle of a word. Pretending was a better way to describe it. Whatever it was, it was pretty damned convincing.

Beside me, Sydney frowned, but I didn't think she was experiencing what I was. She had never known him as Strigoi. She didn't have those horrible memories. His change in demeanor had to be obvious, but as I glanced at her face, I realized she was focused on following the conversation. I'd forgotten she knew Russian.

"What's he saying?" I whispered.

Her frowned deepened, either from the conversation or me distracting her. "He . . . he sounds like he's talking to someone he hasn't spoken to in a while. Dimitri's accusing this person of slacking off while he's been away." She fell silent, continuing her own mental translation. At one point, Dimitri's voice rose in anger, and both Sydney and I flinched. I turned to her questioningly. "He's mad about having his authority questioned. I can't tell, but now . . . it sounds like the other person's groveling."

I wanted to know every word, but it had to be hard for her to translate to me and listen at the same time. Dimitri's voice returned to normal levels—though still filled with that terrible menace—and among the flurry of words, I heard "Sonya Karp" and "Montana."

"He's asking about Ms. Kar—Sonya?" I murmured. She hadn't been my teacher for a long time. I might as well call her Sonya now.

"Yeah," said Sydney, eyes still on Dimitri. "He's asking—er, telling—this person to locate someone else and see if he can find Sonya. This person . . ." She paused to listen again. "This person he's asking about sounds like he knows a lot of people in the area she was last seen in."

I knew "people" in this context meant "Strigoi." Dimitri had risen quickly in their ranks, asserting his will and power over others. Most Strigoi operated solo, rarely working in groups, but even the lone ones recognized threats and more dominant Strigoi. Dimitri was working his contacts, just as he'd said earlier. If any Strigoi had heard about his transformation—and believed it—they wouldn't have been able to pass the news quickly, not with their disorganization. As it was, Dimitri was already having to play leapfrog to find sources who knew other sources who might know Sonya's location.

Dimitri grew loud and angry again, his voice becoming—if possible—more sinister. I suddenly felt trapped, and even Sydney looked scared now. She swallowed.

"He's telling this guy that if he doesn't get answers by tomorrow night, Dimitri's going to find him and rip him apart and . . ." Sydney didn't bother finishing. Her eyes were wide. "Use your imagination. It's pretty terrible." I decided then that I was kind of glad I hadn't heard all of the conversation in English.

When Dimitri finished the call and returned Sydney's phone, that mask of malice melted from his face. Once again, he was my Dimitri, Dimitri the dhampir. Dejection and despair radiated off him, and he slumped against the café's wall, staring upward into the sky. I knew what he was doing. He was trying to calm himself, seize control of the emotions that had to be warring within him. He'd just done something that might give us clues we needed . . . but it had been at a terrible cost to himself. My fingers twitched. I wanted to put a comforting arm around him or at least pat his shoulder so he'd know he wasn't alone. But, I held back, suspecting he wouldn't like it.

At last, he turned his gaze back to us. He'd regained his control—at least on the outside. "I've sent someone to ask about her," he said wearily. "It might not work out. Strigoi are hardly the type to keep a database. But they do occasionally keep an eye on one another, if only for their own self-preservation. We'll find out soon if there are any hits."

"I . . . wow. Thank you," I said, fumbling at the words. I knew he needed no thanks, but it felt necessary to me.

He nodded. "We should get back to the Keepers . . . unless you think this is a safe place to stay?"

"I'd rather stay off civilized radar," said Sydney, moving toward the truck. "Besides, I want my car keys back."

The ride back felt ten times longer. Dimitri's mood filled up the whole cabin, almost suffocating us with its despair. Even Sydney could feel it. She'd let him drive again, and I couldn't decide if that was a good or bad thing. Would the road distract him from his Strigoi torment? Or would his agony distract him from the road and put us off in a ditch?

Fortunately, we made it back safe and sound and found two of the Keepers waiting for us in the lot, a Moroi woman and a human guy who both looked fierce. I still couldn't shake the strangeness of both races being battle-ready. I wondered if these two were a couple.

Back in the camp, we found the communal bonfire ablaze and people sitting out around it, some eating and some just socializing. I'd learned at breakfast that the fire was always there for those who wanted to bond but that plenty of families kept to their own households as well.

We went back to Raymond's house, but only Sarah and Joshua were there. She was cleaning up dishes, and he sat restlessly in a chair. As soon as he caught sight of me at the door, he sprang up, radiant smile on high-beam again.

"Rose! You're back. We were starting to worry . . . I mean, not that anything had happened to you—not with your skills—but that maybe you'd just left us."

"Not without our car," said Sydney, placing the truck keys on the table. The CR-V's were sitting there already, and relief flooded her face as she snatched them up.

Sarah offered us leftovers, which we declined, having stocked up on snack food at Rubysville's gas station. "Well," she said, "if you're not going to eat, you might as well join the others out at the fire. Jess McHale might sing tonight if they can get her to drink enough, and drunk or sober, that woman has the finest voice I've ever heard."

I briefly met Dimitri and Sydney's eyes. I admit, I was a little curious to see how this wilderness group partied it up, even though moonshine and folk songs weren't really my first choice of entertainment. Dimitri still wore that haunted look from the phone call.

I had a suspicion he would have been content to isolate

himself in our room, but when Sydney said she'd go to the fire, his response came automatically: "I'll go too." I knew instantly what he was doing. His Strigoi days tormented him. Talking to Strigoi tormented him. And maybe—no, certainly—he wanted to hide away and try to block it all out, but he was Dimitri. Dimitri protected those who needed it, and even if listening to fireside songs wasn't exactly life-threatening, it was still a semi-dangerous situation for a civilian like Sydney. He couldn't allow that. Plus, he knew Sydney would feel safer with both of us nearby.

I started to say I'd join them, but Joshua spoke before I could. "Do you still want to see my cave? There's a little light left outside. You'll get a better view that way than if we have to use a torch."

I'd forgotten about my last conversation with Joshua and started to decline his offer. But then, something flashed in Dimitri's eyes, something disapproving. So. He didn't want me going off with some young, good-looking guy. Was it legitimate concern about the Keepers? Was it jealousy? No, surely not the latter. We'd established—many, many times—that Dimitri wanted no romantic connection with me. He'd even stood up for Adrian earlier. Was this some kind of ex-boyfriend thing? Back in Rubysville, I'd believed Dimitri and I could be friends, but that wouldn't happen if he thought he could control me and my love life. I'd known girls with exes like that. I wouldn't be one. I could hang out with whomever I wanted.

"Sure," I said. Dimitri's expression darkened. "I'd love to."

Joshua and I headed off, leaving the others behind. I knew

part of my decision was to prove my independence. Dimitri had said we were equals, yet he'd made an awful lot of decisions in this escape plan without me. It was nice to feel like I had the upper hand for a change, and besides, I liked Joshua and was kind of curious to learn more about how his people lived. I don't think Sydney wanted me to leave, but Dimitri would look after her.

As Joshua and I walked, we passed plenty of Keepers out and about. Just like earlier, I received a fair amount of stares. Rather than lead us down the road to where his father lived, Joshua took me around the small mountain. It was still good-sized, but after living near the Rockies, everything in the Appalachians seemed "small" to me. I guess I was a mountain snob.

Still, the mountain extended quite a ways, and we moved farther and farther from the Keepers' main settlement. The forest grew thicker, the light growing scarce as the sun finally began sinking into the horizon.

"I'm kind of on the outskirts," Joshua said apologetically. "We keep growing and growing, and there's not much room in the town's center." I thought "town" was an optimistic term but didn't say so. Yeah. I was definitely a snob. "But the caves keep going, so there's still space."

"Are they natural?" I asked.

"Some are. Some are abandoned mining caves."

"It's pretty out here," I said. I liked all the deciduous trees. I might be homesick for Montana, but the wide leaves here were a neat contrast to pine needles. "And hey, at least you get lots of privacy, right?"

"True." He smiled. "I figured you'd think it was . . . I don't know. Too rustic. Or savage. You probably think we all are."

His observation startled me. Most of the Keepers had been so fiercely defensive of their way of life that I hadn't thought anyone would even think an outsider would question it—or that any Keeper would care if we did.

"It's just different," I said diplomatically. "A lot different from what I'm used to." I felt a flash of homesickness for all the people and places I was now cut off from. Lissa. Adrian. Our other friends. Court. St. Vladimir's. I shook the feeling off quickly. I had no time to mope and could at least check on Lissa later.

"I've been to human towns," continued Joshua. "And other places the Tainted live. I can see why you'd like them." He turned a bit sheepish. "I wouldn't mind electricity."

"Why don't you guys use it?"

"We would if we could. We're just too far out, and no one really knows we're here anyway. The lily-people say it's better for hiding us."

It hadn't occurred to me that they simply endured these conditions because they were forced to in order to conceal themselves. I wondered how many of their choices came from clinging to the so-called old ways . . . and how much was influenced by the Alchemists.

"Here we are," said Joshua, pulling me from my musings.

He gestured to a dark hole at ground level. The opening was big enough for an adult to enter.

"Nice," I said. I'd noticed earlier that some of the caves were set higher into the mountains and had watched their residents either climb the rock bare-handed or use homemade ladders. An easy-access doorway seemed luxurious.

Joshua looked surprised at my praise. "Really?"

"Really."

We'd ended up losing too much daylight. He paused to light a torch, and then I followed him inside. We had to duck a little at first, but as we went deeper into the cave, the ceiling slowly expanded and opened up into a wide, rounded space. The floor was hard-packed dirt, the stone walls rough and jagged. This was a natural cave, but I could pick out the efforts made to civilize it. The floor had been cleaned and leveled, and I saw some stones and rocks in a corner that looked like they'd been gathered up to clear space. A couple pieces of furniture had already been moved in: a narrow wooden chair and a mattress that looked like it could barely hold one person.

"You probably think it's small," said Joshua.

It was true, but it was actually bigger than my dorm room at St. Vladimir's. "Well . . . yeah, but I mean, how old are you?"

"Eighteen."

"Same as me," I said. This seemed to make him pretty happy. "Having your own, um, cave at eighteen is pretty cool." It would have been cooler still with electricity, Internet, and plumbing, but there was no need to bring that up.

His blue eyes practically shone. I couldn't help but notice what a pretty contrast they made against his tanned skin. I dismissed the thought immediately. I wasn't here for a boyfriend. But apparently, I was the only one who believed that.

Joshua suddenly took a step forward.

"You can stay if you want," he said. "The other Tainted would never find you here. We could get married, and then when we had kids, we could build a loft like my parents' and—"

The word *married* had me moving toward the entrance as shocked and panicked as I would be by a Strigoi attack. Except, I usually had fair warning before those.

"Whoa, whoa, slow down." No. I hadn't seen a proposal coming. "We just met!"

Thankfully, he didn't come closer. "I know, but sometimes that's how it is."

"What, marriages between people who hardly know each other?" I asked incredulously.

"Sure. Happens all the time. And seriously, just in this short of time, I already know I like you. You're amazing. You're beautiful and obviously a good fighter. And the way you carry yourself . . ." He shook his head, awe on his face. "I've never seen anything like it."

I wished he wasn't so cute and nice. Having creepy guys profess their adoration was a lot easier to deal with than one you liked. I remembered Sydney saying I was a hot commodity here. Scorching was more like it, apparently.

"Joshua, I really like you, but," I added hastily, seeing hope fill his features, "I'm too young to get married."

He frowned. "Didn't you say you were eighteen?"

Okay. Age was probably not a good argument around here. I'd seen how young people had kids back in Dimitri's hometown. In a place like this, they probably had child marriages. I tried another angle.

"I don't even know if I want to get married."

This didn't faze him. He nodded in understanding. "That's smart. We could live together first, see how we get along." His serious expression turned back into a smile. "But I'm pretty easygoing. I'd let you win every argument."

I couldn't help it. I laughed. "Well, then, I'm going to have to win this one and tell you I'm just not ready for . . . any of it. Besides, I'm already involved with someone."

"Dimitri?"

"No. Another guy. He's back at the Tainted Court." I couldn't even believe I was saying that.

Joshua frowned. "Why isn't he here protecting you then?"

"Because . . . that's not how he is. And I can take care of myself." I'd never liked the assumption that I needed rescuing. "And look, even if he wasn't in the picture, I'm leaving soon anyway. It would never work out between you and me."

"I understand." Joshua looked disappointed but seemed to be taking the rejection okay. "Maybe when you've got everything sorted out, you'll come back."

I started to tell him not to wait for me and that he should just marry someone else (despite how ridiculous it was at his age), but then I realized that was a pointless comment. In Joshua's fantasies, he could probably marry someone else now and then add me on to his harem later, like Sarah and Paulette. So, I just simply said, "Maybe." Groping for a change in subject, I searched for anything to distract us. My eyes fell on the chair and a leafy pattern carved into it. "That's really neat."

"Thanks," he said, walking over. To my relief, he didn't pursue the earlier topic. He ran his hand lovingly over the ornately carved wood. The design looked like braided leaves. "I did it myself."

"Really?" I asked in true surprise. "That . . . that's amazing."

"If you like it . . ." His hand moved, and I feared there was a kiss or embrace coming. Instead, he reached into his shirt pocket and produced a finely carved wooden bracelet. It was a simple, sinuous design, the true marvel being how narrow and delicate it was to all be one piece. The wood had been polished to brilliance. "Here." He handed me the bracelet.

"This is for me?" I ran my finger along the smooth edge.

"If you want it. I made it while you were out today. So you'll remember me after you leave."

I hesitated, wondering if accepting this would be encouraging him. No, I decided. I'd made my views on teenage marriage clear, and anyway, he looked so nervous, I couldn't stand the thought of hurting his feelings. I slipped it onto my wrist. "Of course I'll remember. Thank you."

From the happy look on his face, taking the bracelet made up for my earlier refusal. He showed me a few more details around the cave and then followed my suggestion to join the others at the fire. We could hear the music echoing through the trees long before we made it back, and while it was hardly my style, there was something warm and friendly about this community's way of life. I'd never been to summer camp, but I imagined this was what it'd be like.

Sydney and Dimitri sat near the group's edge. They were quiet and watchful, but everyone else sang, clapped, and talked. Again, I was stunned at how easily dhampirs, humans, and Moroi could all be involved with one another. Mixed couples were everywhere, and one—a human and Moroi—were openly making out. Every so often, when he kissed her neck, he'd also bite and take some blood. I had to glance away.

I turned back toward my friends. Sydney noticed me and looked relieved. Dimitri's expression was unreadable. Like always, the others' eyes followed my movement, and to my surprise, I saw open jealousy on some of the guys' faces. I hoped they didn't think Joshua and I had been off getting naked in the cave. That was hardly the reputation I wanted to leave behind.

"I have to talk to Sydney," I told him over the noise. I decided it'd be best to keep my distance before any rumors started, and truthfully, Sydney looked like she wanted me by her side. Joshua nodded, and I turned away. I'd taken two steps when a fist suddenly came right toward my face.

I'd had no defenses up and just barely had the presence of mind to turn my head and catch the blow on my cheek, rather than end up with a broken nose. After the initial surprise, all my training kicked in. I quickly sidestepped out of the line of attack and put my body into a fighter's stance. The music and singing stopped, and I turned to face my attacker.

Angeline.

She stood in a way similar to my own, fists clenched and eyes completely honed in on me. "Okay," she said. "It's time to find out how tough you really are."

What it was time for was someone—say, like, a parent—to come and drag her off and punish her for punching guests. Amazingly, no one moved or tried to stop her. No—that wasn't quite true. One person stood up. Dimitri had sprung to action the instant he saw me in danger. I expected him to come pull Angeline away, but a group of Keepers hastily moved to his side, saying something to him that I couldn't hear. They didn't try to physically restrain him, but whatever they said, it kept him where he stood. I would have demanded to know what they'd told him, but Angeline was coming at me again. It looked like I was on my own.

Angeline was short, even for a dhampir, but her whole body was packed with strength. She was pretty fast too, though not fast enough to get that second hit in on me. I neatly dodged it and kept my distance, not wanting to go on the offensive with this girl. She could probably do a fair amount of damage in a fight, but there was a sloppy—no, more like rough—edge to it. She was a scrapper, someone who'd done a lot of brawling but without any formal training.

"Are you insane?" I exclaimed, moving out of the way of another assault. "Stop this. I don't want to hurt you."

"Sure," she said. "That's what you want everyone to think, right? If you don't actually have to fight, then they'll all go on believing those marks are real."

"They *are* real!" The insinuation that I'd faked my tattoos sparked my temper, but I refused to get drawn into this ridiculous scuffle.

"Prove it," she said, coming at me again. "Prove you're who you say you are."

It was like a dance, keeping away from her. I could have done it all night, and a few dismayed cries from the crowd demanded we "get on with it."

"I don't have to prove anything," I told her.

"It's a lie then." Her breathing was heavy now. She was working a lot harder than me. "Everything you Tainted do is a lie."

"Not true," I said. Why was Dimitri letting this go on? Out of the corner of my eye, I caught sight of him, and so help me, he was *smiling*.

Meanwhile, Angeline was still continuing her tirade as she tried to hit me. "You all lie. You're all weak. Especially your 'royals.' They're the worst of all."

"You don't know them at all. You don't know anything about them."

She might be able to carry on a conversation, but I could see her growing increasingly frustrated. If not for the fact I was pretty sure she'd hit me in the back, I would have taken the noble approach and simply walked away. "I know enough," she said. "I know they're selfish and spoiled and don't do anything for themselves. They don't care about anyone else. They're all the same."

I actually agreed with Angeline about some royals but didn't like the generalization. "Don't talk about things you don't understand," I snapped. "They're not all like that."

"They *are*," she said, pleased to see me angry. "I wish they were all dead."

It was hardly enough to push me into offense mode, but the comment did cloud my thoughts enough that I let her get through my guard, just a little. I never would have let that happen with a Strigoi, but I'd underestimated this wild girl. Her leg snaked out just enough to hit my knee, and it was like tossing a spark into gasoline. Everything exploded.

With that hit, I stumbled slightly, and she pushed her advantage. My battle instincts took over, and I had no choice but to strike back before she could hit me. People began cheering now that the fight was "really going." I was on offense, trying to subdue her, meaning the physical contact had jumped up exponentially. I was still better than her, no doubt, but in trying to get to her, I put myself in her range. She landed a few blows on me, nothing serious, before I was able to tackle her to the ground. I expected that to be the end, but she pushed back against me before I could fully restrain her. We rolled over, and she tried to take the dominant position. I couldn't allow that and managed a punch on the side of her face that was a lot harder than the earlier one.

I thought that would be the end of the fight. My hit had knocked her off me, and I started to stand, but then that little bitch grabbed my hair and jerked me back down. I twisted out of her hold—though I'm pretty sure she took some hair away with her—and this time managed to fully pin her, throwing all my weight and strength into it as I pressed down. I knew it had to be painful but didn't really care. She'd started it. Besides, this skirmish had gone beyond defense. Pulling someone's hair was just playing dirty.

Angeline made a few more attempts to break away, but when it became clear she couldn't, those around us began whistling and cheering. A few moments later, that dark and furious look vanished from Angeline's face, replaced by resignation. I eyed her warily, not about to let down my guard.

"Fine," she said. "I guess it's okay. Go ahead."

"Huh? What's okay?" I demanded.

"It's okay if you marry my brother."

THIRTEEN

"IT'S NOT FUNNY!"

"You're right," agreed Sydney. "It's not funny. It's *hilarious*."

We were back at Raymond's house, in the privacy of our room. It had taken forever for us to get away from the fireside festivities, particularly after learning a terrible fact about a Keeper custom. Well, I thought it was terrible, at least. It turned out that if someone wanted to marry someone else around here, the prospective bride and groom each had to battle it out with the other's nearest relative of the same sex. Angeline had spotted Joshua's interest from the moment I'd arrived, and when she'd seen the bracelet, she'd assumed some sort of arrangement had been made. It therefore fell on her, as his sister, to make sure I was worthy. She still didn't like or entirely trust me, but proving myself a capable fighter had shot me up in her esteem, allowing her to consent to our "engagement." It had then taken a lot of fast-talking to convince everyone—including Joshua—that there was no engagement. Had there been, I'd learned, Dimitri would have had to stand in as my "relative" and fight Joshua.

"Stop that," I chastised. Dimitri leaned against one of the room's walls, arms crossed, watching as I rubbed where Angeline had hit my cheekbone. It was hardly the worst injury I'd ever had, but I'd definitely have a bruise tomorrow. There was a small smile on his face.

"I told you not to encourage him," came Dimitri's calm response.

"Whatever. You didn't see this coming. You just didn't want me to—" I bit off my words. I wouldn't say what was on my mind: that Dimitri was jealous. Or possessive. Or whatever. I just knew he'd been irritated to see me friendly with Joshua . . . and very amused at my outrage over Angeline's attack. I abruptly turned to Sydney, who was just as entertained as Dimitri. In fact, I was pretty sure I'd never seen her smile so much. "Did *you* know about this custom?"

"No," she admitted, "but I'm not surprised. I told you they're savage. A lot of ordinary problems are settled by fights like that."

"It's stupid," I said, not caring that I was whining. I touched the top of my head, wishing I had a mirror to see if Angeline had taken a noticeable chunk of hair. "Although . . . she wasn't bad. Unpolished, but not bad. Are they all that tough? The humans and Moroi too?"

"That's my understanding."

I pondered that. I was annoyed and embarrassed by what had happened, but I had to admit the Keepers were suddenly way more interesting. How ironic that such a backward group had the insight to teach everyone to fight, no matter their race. Meanwhile, my own "enlightened" culture still refused to teach defense.

"And that's why Strigoi don't bother them," I murmured,

recalling breakfast. I didn't even realize what I'd said until Dimitri's smile dropped. He glanced toward the window, face grim.

"I should check in with Boris again and see what he's found." He turned back toward Sydney. "It won't take long. We don't all need to go. Should I just take your car since I only have to go a little ways?"

She shrugged and reached for her keys. We'd learned earlier that Sydney's phone could pick up a signal about ten minutes from the village. He was right. There really was no reason for us all to go for a quick phone call. After my fight, Sydney and I were reasonably safe. No one would mess with me now. Still . . . I didn't like the thought of Dimitri reliving his Strigoi days alone.

"You should still go," I told her, thinking fast. "I need to check in on Lissa." Not entirely a lie. What my friends had heard from Joe was still weighing on me. "I can usually still keep track of what's going on around me at the same time, but it might be better if you're away—especially in case Alchemists do show up."

My logic was faulty, though her colleagues were still a concern. "I doubt they'd come while it's dark," she said, "but I don't really want to hang out if you're just going to stare into space." She didn't admit it, and I didn't need to say anything, but I suspected she didn't want someone else driving her car anyway.

Dimitri thought her coming was unnecessary and said as much, but apparently, he didn't feel like he could boss her around as much as me. So, they both set out, leaving me alone in the room. I watched them wistfully. Despite how annoying his earlier mockery had been, I was worried about him. I'd seen the effect of the last call and wished I could be there now to comfort him. I had a feeling he wouldn't have allowed that, so I accepted Sydney's accompaniment as a small victory.

With them gone, I decided I really would check in with Lissa. I'd said it more as an excuse, but truthfully, it beat the alternative—going back out and socializing. I didn't want any more people congratulating me, and apparently, Joshua had read my "maybe" and acceptance of the bracelet as a real commitment. I still thought he was devastatingly cute but couldn't handle seeing his adoration.

Sitting cross-legged on Angeline's bed, I opened myself to the bond and what Lissa was experiencing. She was walking through the halls of a building I didn't recognize at first. A moment later, I got my bearings. It was a building at Court that housed a large spa and salon—as well as the hideout of Rhonda the gypsy. It seemed weird that Lissa would be going to get her fortune told, but once I got a glimpse of her companions, I knew she was up to something else.

The usual suspects were with her: Adrian and Christian. My heart leapt at seeing Adrian again—especially after the Joshua Incident. My last spirit dream had been too brief.

Christian was holding Lissa's hand as they walked, his grip warm and reassuring. He looked confident and determined—though with that typically snarky half-smile of his. Lissa was the one who felt nervous and was clearly bracing herself for something. I could feel her dreading her next task, even though she believed it was necessary.

"Is this it?" she asked, coming to a halt in front of a door.

"I think so," said Christian. "That receptionist said it was the red one."

Lissa hesitated only a moment and then knocked. Nothing. Either the room was empty or she was being ignored. She held up her hand again, and the door opened. Ambrose stood there, stunning as always, even in jeans and a casual blue T-shirt. The clothing hugged his body in a way that showed off every muscle. He could have walked straight off the cover of *GQ*.

"Hey," he said, clearly surprised.

"Hey," said Lissa back. "We were wondering if we could talk to you?"

Ambrose ever so slightly inclined his head toward the room. "I'm kind of busy right now."

Beyond him, Lissa could see a massage table with a Moroi woman lying face down. The lower half of her body had a towel over it, but her back was bare, shining in the dim lighting with oil. Scented candles burned in the room, and a calming kind of New Age music played softly.

"Wow," said Adrian. "You don't waste any time, do you? She's only been in her grave a few hours, and you've already got someone new." Tatiana had finally been laid to rest earlier in the day, just before sunset. The burial had had much less fanfare than the original attempt.

Ambrose gave Adrian a sharp look. "She's my client. It's my job. You forget that some of us have to work for a living."

"Please?" asked Lissa, hastily stepping in front of Adrian. "It won't take long."

Ambrose looked my friends over a moment and then sighed. He glanced behind him. "Lorraine? I have to step outside. I'll be right back, okay?"

"Okay," called the woman. She shifted, facing him. She was older than I'd expected, mid-forties or so. I guess if you were paying for a massage, there was no reason not to have a masseuse half your age. "Hurry back."

He gave her a dazzling smile as he shut the door, a smile that dropped once he was alone with my friends. "Okay, what's going on? I don't like the looks on your faces."

Ambrose might have radically deviated from a dhampir man's normal life, but he'd had the same training as any guardian. He was observant. He was always on the lookout for potential threats.

"We, uh, wanted to talk to you about . . ." Lissa hesitated. Talking about investigations and interrogations was one thing. Carrying them out was another. "About Tatiana's murder."

Ambrose's eyebrows rose. "Ah. I see. Not sure what there is to say, except that I don't think Rose did it. I don't think you believe that either, despite what's going around. Everyone's talking about how shocked and upset you are. You're getting a lot of sympathy over having been tricked by such a dangerous and sinister 'friend.'"

Lissa felt her cheeks flush. By publicly condemning me and renouncing our friendship, Lissa was keeping herself out of trouble. It had been Abe and Tasha's advice, and Lissa knew it was sound. Yet, even though it was an act, she still felt guilty. Christian stepped to her defense.

"Back off. That's not what this is about."

"What *is* it about then?" asked Ambrose.

Lissa jumped in, worried Christian and Adrian might upset Ambrose and make it difficult to get answers. "Abe Mazur told us that in the courtroom, you said or, uh, did something to Rose."

Ambrose looked shocked, and I had to give him points for being convincing. "Did something? What does that mean? Does Mazur think I, like, hit on her in front of all those people?"

"I don't know," admitted Lissa. "He just saw something, that's all."

"I wished her good luck," said Ambrose, still looking offended. "Is that okay?"

"Yeah, yeah." Lissa had made a point to talk to Ambrose before Abe could, fearing Abe's methods would involve threats and a lot of physical force. Now, she was wondering if she was doing so great a job. "Look, we're just trying to find out who really killed the queen. You were close to her. If there's anything—*anything*—at all you've got that can help us, we'd appreciate it. We need it."

Ambrose glanced curiously between them. Then, he suddenly understood. "You think I did it! That's what this is about." None of them said anything. "I can't believe this! I already got this from the guardians . . . but from you? I thought you knew me better."

"We don't know you at all," said Adrian flatly. "All we

know is you had lots of access to my aunt." He pointed at the door. "And obviously, it didn't take you long to move on."

"Did you miss the part where I said that's my job? I'm giving her a massage, that's it. Not everything is sordid and dirty." Ambrose shook his head in frustration and ran a hand through his brown hair. "My relationship with Tatiana wasn't dirty either. I cared about her. I would never do anything to hurt her."

"Don't statistics say most murders happen between close people?" asked Christian.

Lissa glared at him and Adrian. "Stop it. Both of you." She looked back at Ambrose. "No one's accusing you of anything. But you were around her a lot. And Rose told me you were upset about the age law."

"When I first heard about it, yeah," Ambrose said. "And even then, I told Rose there was some mistake—that there must be something we didn't know. Tatiana would have never put those dhampirs in danger without a good reason."

"Like making herself look good in front of all those terrified royals?" asked Christian.

"Watch it," warned Adrian. Lissa couldn't decide which was more annoying: her two guys teaming up to spar against Ambrose or them throwing barbs at each other.

"No!" Ambrose's voice rang throughout the narrow hall. "She didn't want to do that. But if she didn't, worse things were going to happen. There are people who wanted—still want—to round up all the dhampirs who don't fight and force them into it. Tatiana passed the age law as a way to stall that."

Silence fell. I'd already learned this from Tatiana's note, but it was shocking news to my friends. Ambrose kept going, seeing he was gaining ground.

"She was actually open to lots of other options. She wanted to explore spirit. She approved of Moroi learning to fight."

That got a reaction from Adrian. He still wore that sardonic expression, but I could also see faint lines of pain and sorrow on his face. The burial earlier must have been hard on him, and hearing others reveal information you hadn't known about a loved one had to hurt.

"Well, I obviously wasn't sleeping with her like you were," said Adrian, "but I knew her pretty well, too. She never said a word about anything like that."

"Not publicly," agreed Ambrose. "Not even privately. Only a few people knew. She was having a small group of Moroi trained in secret—men and women, different ages. She wanted to see how well Moroi could learn. If it was possible for them to defend themselves. But she knew people'd be upset about it, so she made the group and their trainer keep quiet."

Adrian gave no response to this, and I could see his thoughts had turned inward. Ambrose's revelation wasn't bad news, exactly, but Adrian was still hurt at the thought that his aunt had kept so much from him. Lissa, meanwhile, was eating the news up, seizing and analyzing every piece of info.

"Who were they? The Moroi being trained?"

"I don't know," said Ambrose. "Tatiana was quiet about it. I never found out their names, just their instructor."

"Who was . . . ?" prompted Christian.

"Grant."

Christian and Lissa exchanged startled looks. "My Grant?" she asked. "The one Tatiana assigned to me?"

Ambrose nodded. "That's why she gave him to you. She trusted him."

Lissa said nothing, but I heard her thoughts loud and clear. She'd been pleased and surprised when Grant and Serena—the guardians who had replaced Dimitri and me—had offered to teach Lissa and Christian basic defense moves. Lissa had thought she'd simply stumbled onto a progressive-thinking guardian, not realizing she had one of the pioneers in teaching combat to Moroi.

Some piece of this was important, she and I were both certain, though neither of us could make the connection. Lissa puzzled it over, not protesting when Adrian and Christian threw in some questions of their own. Ambrose was still clearly offended by the inquisition, but he answered everything with forced patience. He had alibis, and his affection and regard for Tatiana never wavered. Lissa believed him, though Christian and Adrian still seemed skeptical.

"Everyone's been all over me about her death," said Ambrose, "but nobody questioned Blake very long."

"Blake?" asked Lissa.

"Blake Lazar. Someone else she was . . ."

"Involved with?" suggested Christian, rolling his eyes.

"Him?" exclaimed Adrian in disgust. "No way. She wouldn't stoop that low."

Lissa racked her brain through the Lazar family but couldn't peg the name. There were just too many of them. "Who is he?"

"An idiot," said Adrian. "Makes me look like an upstanding member of society."

That actually brought a smile to Ambrose's face. "I agree. But he's a pretty idiot, and Tatiana liked that." I heard affection in his voice as he spoke her name.

"She was sleeping with him too?" Lissa asked. Adrian winced at the mention of his great-aunt's sex life, but a whole new world of possibilities had opened up. More lovers meant more suspects. "How did you feel about that?"

Ambrose's amusement faded. He gave her a sharp look. "Not jealous enough to kill her, if that's what you're getting at. We had an understanding. She and I were close—yes, 'involved'—but we both saw other people too."

"Wait," said Christian. I had the feeling he was really enjoying this now. Tatiana's murder was no joke, but a soap opera was definitely unfolding before them. "*You* were sleeping with other people too? This is getting hard to follow."

Not for Lissa. In fact, it was becoming clearer and clearer that Tatiana's murder could have been a crime of passion, rather than anything political. Like Abe had said, someone with access to her bedroom was a likely suspect. And some woman jealous over sharing a lover with Tatiana? That was perhaps the most convincing motive thus far—if only we knew the women.

"Who?" Lissa asked. "Who else were you seeing?"

"No one who'd kill her," said Ambrose sternly. "I'm not giving you names. I'm entitled to some privacy—so are they."

"Not if one of them was jealous and killed my aunt," growled Adrian. Joshua had looked down on Adrian for not "protecting" me, but in that moment, defending his aunt's honor, he looked as fierce as any guardian or Keeper warrior. It was kind of sexy.

"None of them killed her, I'm certain," said Ambrose. "And as much as I despise him, I don't think Blake did either. He's not smart enough to pull it off and frame Rose." Ambrose gestured to the door. His teeth were clenched, and lines of frustration marred his handsome face. "Look, I don't know what else I can say to convince you. I need to get back in there. I'm sorry if I seem difficult, but this has been kind of hard on me, okay? Believe me, I'd love it if you could find out who did that to her." Pain flashed through his eyes. He swallowed and looked down for a moment, as though he didn't want them to know just how much he'd cared about Tatiana. When he looked up again, his expression was fierce and determined again. "I *want* you to and will help if I can. But I'm telling you, look for someone with political motives. Not romantic ones."

Lissa still had a million more questions. Ambrose might be convinced the murder was free of jealousy and sex, but she wasn't. She would have really liked the names of his other women but didn't want to push too hard. For a moment, she considered compelling him as she had Joe. But no. She wouldn't cross that line again, especially with someone she considered a friend. At least not yet. "Okay," she said reluctantly. "Thank you. Thank you for helping us."

Ambrose seemed surprised at her politeness, and his face

softened. "I'll see if I can dig up anything to help you. They're keeping her rooms and possessions locked down, but I might still be able to get in there. I'll let you know."

Lissa smiled, genuinely grateful. "Thank you. That'd be great."

A touch on my arm brought me back to the drab little room in West Virginia. Sydney and Dimitri were looking down at me. "Rose?" asked Dimitri. I had a feeling this wasn't the first time he'd tried to get my attention.

"Hey," I said. I blinked a couple of times, settling myself back into this reality. "You're back. You called the Strigoi?"

He didn't visibly react to the word, but I knew he hated hearing it. "Yes. I got a hold of Boris's contact."

Sydney wrapped her arms around herself. "Crazy conversation. Some of it was in English. It was even scarier than before."

I shivered involuntarily, glad that I'd missed it. "But did you find out anything?"

"Boris gave me the name of a Strigoi who knows Sonya and probably knows where she is," Dimitri said. "It's actually someone I've met. But phone calls only go so far with Strigoi. There's no way to contact him—except to go in person. Boris only had his address."

"Where is it?" I asked.

"Lexington, Kentucky."

"Oh for God's sake," I moaned. "Why not the Bahamas? Or the Corn Palace?"

Dimitri tried to hide a smile. It might have been at my

expense, but if I'd lightened his mood, I was grateful. "If we leave right now, we can reach him before morning."

I glanced around. "Tough choice. Leave all this for electricity and plumbing?"

Now Sydney grinned. "And no more marriage proposals."

"And we'll probably have to fight Strigoi," added Dimitri.

I jumped to my feet. "How soon can we go?"

FOURTEEN

THE KEEPERS HAD MIXED REACTIONS to us leaving. They were usually glad to see outsiders go, especially since we had Sydney with us. But after the fight, they held me up as some kind of superhero and were enchanted by the idea of me marrying into their "family." Seeing me in action meant some of the women were beginning to eye Dimitri now too. I wasn't in the mood to watch them flirt with him—especially since, according to their courtship rules, I would apparently have to be the one to battle it out with any prospective fiancée.

Naturally, we didn't tell the Keepers our exact plans, but we did mention we'd likely be encountering Strigoi—which caused quite a reaction. Most of that reaction was excitement and awe, which continued to boost our reputations as fierce warriors. Angeline's response, however, was totally unexpected.

"Take me with you," she said, grabbing a hold of my arm, just as I started down the forest path toward the car.

"Sorry," I said, still a little weirded out after her earlier hostility. "We have to do this alone."

"I can help! You beat me . . . but you saw what I can do. I'm good. I could take a Strigoi."

For all her fierceness, I knew Angeline didn't have a clue

about what she'd be facing if she ever met an actual Strigoi. The few Keepers who bore *molnija* marks spoke little about the encounters, faces grave. They understood. Angeline didn't. She also didn't realize that any novice at St. Vladimir's in the secondary school could probably take her out. She had raw potential, true, but it needed a lot of work.

"You might be able to," I said, not wanting to hurt her feelings. "But it's just not possible for you to come with us." I would have lied and given her a vague "Maybe sometime," but since that had led Joshua to thinking we were semi-engaged, I decided I'd better not.

I expected more boasts about her battle prowess. We'd learned she was regarded as one of the best young fighters in the compound, and with her pretty looks, she had plenty of admirers too. A lot of it had gone to her head, and she liked to talk about how she could beat anyone or anything up. Again, I was reminded of Jill. Jill also had a lot to learn about the true meaning of battle but was still eager to jump in. She was quieter and more cautious than Angeline, though, so Angeline's next direction caught me off guard.

"Please. It's not just the Strigoi! I want to see the world. I *need* to see something else outside of this place!" Her voice was pitched low, out of the range of the others. "I've only been to Rubysville twice, and they say that's nothing compared to other cities."

"It's not," I agreed. I didn't even consider it a city.

"Please," she begged again, this time her voice trembling. "Take me with you."

Suddenly, I felt sad for her. Her brother had also shown a little longing for the outside world, but nothing like this. He'd joked that electricity would be nice, but I knew he was happy enough without the perks of the modern world. But for Angeline, the situation was much more desperate. I too knew what it was like to feel trapped in one's life and was legitimately sorry for what I had to say.

"I can't, Angeline. We have to go on our own. I'm sorry. I really am."

Her blue eyes shimmered, and she raced off into the woods before I could see her cry. I felt horrible after that and couldn't stop thinking about her as we made our farewells. I was so distracted, I even let Joshua hug me goodbye.

Getting back on the road was a relief. I was glad to be away from the Keepers and was ready to spring into action and start helping Lissa. Lexington was our first step. We had a six-hour drive ahead of us, and Sydney, per usual, seemed adamant that no one else was going to drive her car. Dimitri and I made futile protests, finally giving up when we realized that if we were going to be facing Strigoi soon, it was probably best we rest and conserve our strength. The address for Donovan—the Strigoi who allegedly knew Sonya—was only where he could be found at night. That meant we had to make it to Lexington before sunrise, so we wouldn't lose him when he went to his daytime lair. It also meant we'd be meeting Strigoi in the dark. Certain that little would happen on the drive—especially once we were out of West Virginia—Dimitri and I agreed we could doze a little, seeing as neither of us had had a full night's sleep.

Even though the lulling of the car was soothing, I drifted in and out of restless sleep. After a few hours of this, I simply settled into the trancelike state that brought me to Lissa. It was a good thing too: I'd stumbled into one of the biggest events facing the Moroi. The nomination process to elect the new king or queen was about to begin. It was the first of many steps, and everyone was excited, given how rare monarch elections truly were. This was an event none of my friends had expected to see anytime soon in our lives, and considering recent events . . . well, we all had especial interest. The future of the Moroi was at stake here.

Lissa was sitting on the edge of a chair in one of the royal ballrooms, a huge sweeping space with vaulted ceilings and gold detailing everywhere. I'd been in this dazzling room before, with its murals and elaborate molding. Chandeliers glittered above. It had held the graduate luncheon, where newly made guardians put on their best faces and hoped to attract a good assignment. Now, the room was arranged like the Council chamber, with a long table on one side of the room that was set with twelve chairs. Opposite that table were rows and rows of other chairs—where the audience sat when the Council was in session. Except, now there were about four times as many chairs as usual, which probably explained the need for this room. Every single chair was filled. In fact, people were even standing, crowding in as best they could. Agitated-looking guardians moved among the herd, keeping them out of doorways and making sure the bystanders were arranged in a way that allowed for optimal security.

Christian sat on one side of Lissa, and Adrian sat beside Christian. To my pleasant surprise, Eddie and Mia sat nearby too. Mia was a Moroi friend of ours who had gone to St. Vladimir's and was nearly as hardcore as Tasha about Moroi needing to defend themselves. My beloved father was nowhere in sight. None of them spoke. Conversation would have been difficult among the buzzing and humming of so many people, and besides, my friends were too awestruck by what was about to happen. There was so much to see and experience, and none of them had realized just how big the crowd would be. Abe had said things would move fast once Tatiana was buried, and they certainly had.

"Do you know who I am?"

A loud voice caught Lissa's attention, just barely carrying above the din. Lissa glanced down the row, a few seats away from Adrian. Two Moroi, a man and a woman, sat side by side and were looking up at a very angry woman. Her hands were on her hips, and the pink velvet dress she wore seemed outlandish next to the couple's jeans and T-shirts. It also wasn't going to hold up so well once she stepped outside of air conditioning.

A glare twisted her face. "I am Marcella Badica." When that didn't get a reaction from the couple, she added, "Prince Badica is my brother, and our late queen was my third cousin twice removed. There are no seats left, and someone like me *cannot* stand against the wall with the rest of that mob."

The couple exchanged glances. "I guess you should have gotten here earlier, Lady Badica," said the man.

Marcella gaped in outrage. "Didn't you just hear who I am? Don't you know who your betters are? I *insist* you give up your seats."

The couple still seemed unfazed. "This session is open to everyone, and there weren't assigned seats, last time I checked," said the woman. "We're entitled to ours as much as you are."

Marcella turned to the guardian beside her in outrage. He shrugged. His job was to protect her from threats. He wasn't going to oust others from their chairs, particularly when they weren't breaking any rules. Marcella gave a haughty "humph!" before turning sharply and stalking away, no doubt to harass some other poor soul.

"This," said Adrian, "is going to be delightful."

Lissa smiled and turned back to studying the rest of the room. As she did, I became aware of something startling. I couldn't tell exactly who was who, but the crowd wasn't composed entirely of royals—as most Council sessions were. There were tons of "commoners," just like the couple sitting near my friends. Most Moroi didn't bother with Court. They were out in the world, living their lives and trying to survive while the royals pranced around at Court and made laws. But not today. A new leader was going to be chosen, and that was of interest to all Moroi.

The milling and chaos continued for a while until one of the guardians finally declared the room to be at capacity. Those outside were outraged, but their cries were quickly silenced when the guardians closed the doors, sealing off the ballroom.

Shortly thereafter, the eleven Council members took their seats, and—to my shock—Adrian's father, Nathan Ivashkov, took the twelfth chair. The Court's herald yelled and called everyone to attention. He was someone who'd been chosen because of his remarkable voice, though I always wondered why they didn't just use a microphone in these situations. More old-world traditions, I supposed. That, and excellent acoustics.

Nathan spoke once the room settled down. "In the absence of our beloved queen . . ." He paused looking down mournfully to offer a moment of respect before continuing.

In anyone else, I might have suspected his feelings were faked, particularly after seeing him grovel so much in front of Tatiana. But, no. Nathan had loved his prickly aunt as much as Adrian had.

"And in the wake of this terrible tragedy, I will be moderating the upcoming trials and elections."

"What'd I tell you?" muttered Adrian. He had no fuzzy affection for his father. "De-lightful."

Nathan droned on a bit about the importance of what was to come and some other points about Moroi tradition. It was obvious, though, that like me, everyone in the room really wanted to get down to the main event: the nominations. He seemed to realize that too and sped up the formalities. Finally, he got to the good stuff.

"Each family, if they choose, may have one nominee for the crown who will take the tests all monarchs have endured since the beginning of time." I thought that "beginning of time" part was a bold and probably unverified exaggeration, but whatever. "The only exclusion is the Ivashkovs, since back-to-back monarchs from the same family aren't allowed. For candidacy, three nominations are required from Moroi of royal blood and proper age." He then added some stuff about what happened in the event more than one person was nominated from the same family, but even I knew the chances of that happening were non-existent. Each royal house wanted to get the best advantage here, and that would involve a unified standing behind one candidate.

Satisfied everyone understood, Nathan nodded and gestured grandly to the audience. "Let the nominations begin."

For a moment, nothing happened. It kind of reminded me of when I'd been back in school, when a teacher would say something like, "Who'd like to present their paper first?" Everyone kind of waited for someone else to get things going, and at last, it happened.

A man I didn't recognize stood up. "I nominate Princess Ariana Szelsky."

Ariana, as princess, sat on the Council and was an expected choice. She gave a gracious nod to the man. A second man, presumably from their family, also stood and gave the second nomination. The third and final nomination came from another Szelsky—a very unexpected one. He was Ariana's brother, a world traveler who was almost never at Court, and also the man my mother guarded. Janine Hathaway was most likely in this room, I realized. I wished Lissa would look around and find her, but Lissa was too focused on the proceedings. After everything I'd been through, I suddenly had a desperate longing to see my mother.

With three nominations, Nathan declared, "Princess Ariana Szelsky is entered as a candidate." He scrawled something on a piece of paper in front of him, his motions full of flourish. "Continue."

After that, the nominations came in rapid succession. Many were princes and princesses, but others were respected—and still high-ranking—members of the families. The Ozera candidate, Ronald, was not the family's Council member, nor was he anyone I knew. "He's not one of Aunt Tasha's 'ideal' candidates," Christian murmured to Lissa. "But she admits he's not a moron."

I didn't know much about most of the other candidates either. A couple, like Ariana Szelsky, I had a good impression of. There were also a couple I'd always found appalling. The tenth candidate was Rufus Tarus, Daniella's cousin. She'd married into the Ivashkovs from the Tarus family and seemed delighted to see her cousin declared a nominee.

"I don't like him," said Adrian, making a face. "He's always telling me to do something useful with my life."

Nathan wrote down Rufus's name and then rolled up the paper like a scroll. Despite the appearance of antique customs, I suspected a secretary in the audience was typing up everything being said here on a laptop.

"Well," declared Nathan, "that concludes—"

"I nominate Princess Vasilisa Dragomir."

Lissa's head jerked to the left, and through her eyes, I recognized a familiar figure. Tasha Ozera. She'd stood and spoken the words loudly and confidently, glancing around with those ice-blue eyes as if daring anyone to disagree.

The room froze. No whispers, no shifting in chairs. Just utter and complete silence. Judging from the faces, the Ozera family's nominee was the second-most astonished person in the room to hear Tasha speak. The first, of course, was Lissa herself.

It took a moment for Nathan to get his mouth working. "That's not—"

Beside Lissa, Christian suddenly stood up. "I second the nomination."

And before Christian had even sat down, Adrian was on his feet. "I confirm the nomination."

All eyes in the room were on Lissa and her friends, and then, as one, the crowd turned toward Nathan Ivashkov. Again, he seemed to have trouble finding his voice.

"That," he managed at last, "is not a legal nomination. Due to its current Council standing, the Dragomir line is regrettably not eligible to present a candidate."

Tasha, never afraid of talking in a crowd or taking on impossible odds, leapt back up. I could tell she was eager to. She was good at making speeches and challenging the system. "Monarch nominees don't need a Council position or quorum to run for the throne."

"That makes no sense," said Nathan. There were mutters of agreement.

"Check the law books, Nate—I mean, Lord Ivashkov."

Yes, there he was at last. My tactful father had joined the

conversation. Abe had been leaning against a wall near the doorway, dressed splendidly in a black suit with a shirt and tie that were exactly the same shade of emerald green. My mother stood beside him, the slightest hint of a smile on her face. For a moment, I was captivated as I studied them side by side. My mother: the perfect picture of guardian excellence and decorum. My father: always capable of achieving his goals, no matter how twisted the means. Uneasily, I began to understand how I'd inherited my bizarre personality.

"Nominees have no requirements concerning how many people are in their family," continued Abe jovially. "They only need three royal nominations to be confirmed."

Nathan gestured angrily toward where his own wayward son and Christian sat. "They aren't from her family!"

"They don't need to be," countered Abe. "They just need to be from *a* royal family. They are. Her candidacy is within the law—so long as the princess accepts."

All heads swiveled toward Lissa now, as though they were suddenly just noticing her. Lissa hadn't twitched since the startling events began. She was in too much shock. Her thoughts seemed to move both fast and slow. Part of her couldn't even start to process what was happening around her. The rest of her mind was spinning with questions.

What was going on? Was this a joke? Or maybe a spirit-induced hallucination? Had she finally gone crazy? Was she dreaming? Was it a trick? If so, why would her own friends have been the ones to do it? Why would they do this to her? And for the love of God, would everyone stop staring at her?

She could handle attention. She'd been born and raised for it, and like Tasha, Lissa could address a crowd and make bold statements—when she supported them and was prepared. Neither of those things applied to this situation. This was pretty much the last thing in the world she had expected or wanted. And so, she couldn't bring herself to react or even consider a response. She stayed where she was, silent and shell-shocked.

Then, something snapped her from her trance. Christian's hand. He'd taken Lissa's, wrapping his fingers with hers. He gave her a gentle squeeze, and the warmth and energy he sent brought her back to life. Slowly, she looked around the room, meeting the eyes of those all watching her. She saw Tasha's determined gaze, my father's cunning look, and even my mother's expectation. That last one proved most startling of all. How could Janine Hathaway—who always did what was right and could barely crack a joke—be going along with this? How could any of Lissa's friends be going along with this? Didn't they love and care about her?

Rose, she thought. *I wish you were here to tell me what to do.*

Me too. Damned one-way bond.

She trusted me more than anyone else in the world, but she realized then that she trusted all of these friends too—well, except maybe Abe, but that was understandable. And if they were doing this, then surely—*surely*—there was a reason, right?

Right?

It made no sense to her, yet Lissa felt her legs move as she rose to her feet. And despite the fear and confusion still running through her, she found her voice inexplicably clear and confident as it rang out through the room.

"I accept the nomination."

FIFTEEN

I DIDN'T LIKE TO SEE Victor Dashkov proven right. But, oh, was he ever.

With Lissa's proclamation, the room that had been holding its breath suddenly exploded. I wondered if there had ever been a peaceful Council session in Moroi history or if I just kept coincidentally tuning into controversial ones. What followed today reminded me a lot of the day the dhampir age decree had passed. Shouting, arguments, people out of their chairs . . . Guardians who normally lined the walls and watched were out among the people, looks of concern on their faces as they prepared for any disputes that might go beyond words.

As quickly as Lissa had been at the center of everything, the room seemed to forget her. She sat back down, and Christian found her hand again. She squeezed it tightly, so much so I wondered if she was cutting off his circulation. She stared straight ahead, still reeling. Her mind wasn't focused on all the chaos, but everything her eyes and ears perceived came through to me. Really, the only attention my friends received was when Daniella came over and scolded Adrian for nominating outside his family. He shrugged it off in his usual way, and she huffed off, realizing—like many of us—that there was really no point in trying to reason with Adrian.

You'd think that in a room where everyone was scrambling to push their own family's advantage, every single person would therefore be arguing that Lissa's nomination was invalid. That wasn't the case, however—particularly because not everyone in the room *was* royal. Just as I'd noted earlier, Moroi from all over had come to witness the events that would determine their future. And a number of them were watching this Dragomir girl with interest, this princess from a dying line who could allegedly work miracles. They weren't ravenously chanting her name, but many were in the thick of the arguments, saying she had every right to step up for her family. Part of me also suspected that some of her "common" supporters simply liked the idea of thwarting the royal agenda. The young couple that had been harassed by Lady Badica weren't the only ones there who'd been pushed around by their "betters."

Most surprisingly, there were some royals speaking up for Lissa too. They might be loyal to their own families, but not all of them were heartless, selfish connivers. Many had a sense of right and wrong—and if Lissa had the law on her side, then she was in the right. Plus, lots of royals simply liked and respected her. Ariana was one person who advocated for Lissa's nomination, despite the competition it created. Ariana knew the law well and undoubtedly realized the loophole that allowed Lissa to run would fail when election time came. Still, Ariana stood her ground, which endeared her to me even more. When the real voting did come, I hoped Ariana would win the crown. She was intelligent and fair—exactly what the Moroi needed.

Of course, Ariana wasn't the only one who knew the law. Others picked up on the loophole and argued the nomination of a candidate that no one could vote for was pointless. Normally, I would have agreed. On and on the debate raged while my friends sat quietly in the hurricane's eye. At long last, the matter was settled the way most decisions should be: through voting. With Lissa still denied her Council seat, that left eleven members to determine her future. Six of them approved her candidacy, making it official. She could run. I suspected some of those who voted for her didn't truly want her running, but their respect for the law prevailed.

Many Moroi didn't care what the Council said. They made it clear they considered this matter far from over, proving what Victor had said: this was going to rage on for a while, getting worse if she actually passed the tests and made it to the voting stages. For now, the crowd dispersed, seeming relieved—not only because they wanted to escape the yelling but also because they wanted to spread this sensational news.

Lissa continued saying little as she and our friends left. Walking past the gawkers, she remained a model of regality and calmness, like she'd already been declared queen. But when she finally escaped it all and was back in her room with the others, all those locked-up, frozen feelings exploded.

"What the *hell* were you guys thinking?" she yelled. "What have you done to me?"

Along with Adrian, Christian, and Eddie, the rest of the conspirators had shown up: Tasha, Abe, and my mom. All of them were so completely stunned by this reaction from sweet

Lissa that none of them could reply now. Lissa took advantage of their silence.

"You set me up! You've put me in the middle of a political nightmare! Do you think I want this? Do you really think I want to be queen?"

Abe recovered first, naturally. "You won't be queen," he said, voice uncharacteristically soothing. "The people arguing about the other part of the law are right: no one can actually vote for you. You need family for that."

"Then what's the point?" she exclaimed. She was furious. She had every right to be. But that outrage, that anger . . . it was fueled by something worse than this situation alone. Spirit was coming to claim its price and making her even more upset than she would have been.

"The point," said Tasha, "is everything crazy you just saw in the Council room. For every argument, for every time someone drags out the law books again, we have more time to save Rose and find out who killed Tatiana."

"Whoever did it must have an interest in the throne," explained Christian. He rested a hand on Lissa's shoulder, and she jerked away. "Either for themselves or someone they know. The longer we delay their plans, the more time we have to find out who it is."

Lissa raked her hands through her long hair in frustration. I tried to pull that coil of fury from her, taking it into myself. I succeeded a little, enough that she dropped her hands to her side. But she was still pissed off.

"How am I supposed to look for the murderer when

I'm tied up doing all those stupid tests?" she demanded.

"You won't be looking," said Abe. "We will."

Her eyes widened. "That was never part of the plan! I'm not going to jump through royal hoops when Rose needs me. I want to help her!"

It was almost comical. Almost. Neither Lissa nor I could handle "sitting around" when we thought the other needed our help. We wanted to be out there, actively doing what we could to fix the situation.

"You are helping her," said Christian. His hand twitched, but he didn't try to touch her again. "It's in a different way than you expected, but in the end, it's going to help her."

The same argument everyone kept using on me. It also made her just as angry as it had made me, and I desperately tugged at the wave of instability spirit kept sending through her.

Lissa peered around the room, looking accusingly at each face. "Who in the world thought of this idea?"

More uncomfortable silence followed.

"Rose did," said Adrian at last.

Lissa spun around and glared at him. "She did not! She wouldn't do this to me!"

"She did," he said. "I talked to her in a dream. It was her idea, and . . . it was a good one." I didn't really like how that seemed to come as a surprise to him. "Besides, you kind of put her in a bad situation too. She kept going on about how much the town she's in sucks."

"Okay," snapped Lissa, ignoring the part about my plight.

"Supposing that's true, that Rose passes this 'brilliant' idea on to you, then why didn't anyone bother *to tell me*? Didn't you think a little warning might help?" Again, it was just like me complaining about how my jailbreak had been kept a secret from me.

"Not really," said Adrian. "We figured you'd react exactly like this and have time to plan a refusal. We kind of gambled that if you were caught on the spot, you'd accept."

"That was kind of risky," she said.

"But it worked," came Tasha's blunt response. "We knew you'd come through for us." She winked. "And for what it's worth, I think you'd make a great queen."

Lissa gave her a sharp look, and I made one more attempt to drag away some of the darkness. I concentrated on those churning emotions, imagining them in me instead of her. I didn't pull it all but managed enough to take the fight out of her. Rage suddenly flared in me, blinding me momentarily, but I was able to push it off to a corner of my mind. She suddenly felt exhausted. I kind of did too.

"The first test is tomorrow," she said quietly. "If I fail it, I'm out. The plan falls apart."

Christian made another attempt to put his arm around her, and this time, she let him. "You won't."

Lissa didn't say anything else, and I could see the relief on everyone's faces. No one believed for a second she liked this, but they seemed to think she wasn't going to withdraw her nomination, which was as much as they could hope for.

My mother and Eddie had said nothing this entire time. As

was common for guardians, they'd kept to the background, remaining shadows while Moroi business was conducted. With the initial storm passing over, my mother stepped forward. She nodded toward Eddie. "One of us is going to try to stay near you at all times."

"Why?" asked Lissa, startled.

"Because we know there's someone out there who isn't afraid to kill to get what they want," said Tasha. She nodded toward Eddie and my mom. "These two and Mikhail are really the only guardians we can trust."

"Are you sure?" Abe gave Tasha a sly look. "I'm surprised you didn't get your special guardian 'friend' on board."

"What special friend?" demanded Christian, instantly picking up on the insinuation.

Tasha, to my astonishment, flushed. "Just a guy I know."

"Who follows you with puppy-dog eyes," continued Abe. "What's his name? Evan?"

"Ethan," she corrected.

My mother, looking exasperated by such ridiculous talk, promptly put an end to it—which was just as well since Christian looked like he had a few things to say. "Leave her alone," she warned Abe. "We don't have time for it. Ethan's a good guy, but the fewer people who know about this, the better. Since Mikhail has a permanent post, Eddie and I will do security."

I agreed with all of what she'd just said, but it struck me that to get my mother on board, someone—probably Abe—had filled her in on all the illicit activity that had occurred recently.

He was either really convincing or she loved me a lot. Grudgingly, I suspected both were true. When Moroi were at Court, their guardians didn't need to accompany them everywhere, meaning my mom would most likely be free of her assignment while Lord Szelsky stayed here. Eddie didn't have an assignment yet, which also gave him flexibility.

Lissa started to say something else when a sharp jolt in my own reality snapped me away from her.

"Sorry," said Sydney. Her slamming on the brakes was what had brought me back. "That jerk cut me off."

It wasn't Sydney's fault, but I felt irritated at the interruption and wanted to yell at her. With a deep breath, I reminded myself that I was simply feeling spirit's side effects and that I couldn't allow it to make me act irrationally. It would fade, like always, yet some part of me knew I couldn't keep taking that darkness from Lissa forever. I wouldn't always be able to control it.

Now that I was back to myself, I looked out the windows, taking in our new surroundings. We weren't in the mountains anymore. We'd reached an urban area, and while the traffic was hardly heavy (seeing as it was still the middle of the human night), there were definitely more cars on the road than we'd seen in a while.

"Where are we?" I asked.

"Outskirts of Lexington," Sydney said. She pulled over to a nearby gas station, both to refill and so we could plug Donovan's address into her GPS. His place was about five miles away.

"Not a great part of town, from what I hear," Dimitri said. "Donovan runs a tattoo parlor that's only open at night. A couple of other Strigoi work with him. They get partiers, drunk kids . . . the kind of people that can easily disappear. The kind Strigoi love."

"Seems like the police would eventually notice that every time someone went for a tattoo, they disappeared," I pointed out.

Dimitri gave a harsh laugh. "Well, the 'funny' thing is that they don't kill everyone who comes in. They actually give tattoos to some of them and let them go. They smuggle drugs through the place too."

I regarded him curiously, as Sydney slipped back into the car. "You sure know a lot."

"I made it my business to know a lot, and Strigoi have to keep a roof over their heads too. I actually met Donovan once and got most of this straight from the source. I just didn't know where exactly he worked out of until now."

"Okay, so, we've got the info on him. What do we do with it?"

"Lure him out. Send in a 'customer' with a message from me needing to meet him. I'm not the kind of person he can ignore—well, that he used to not—never mind. Once he's out, we get him to a place *we* choose."

I nodded. "I can do that."

"No," said Dimitri. "You can't."

"Why not?" I asked, wondering if he thought it was too dangerous for me.

"Because they'll know you're a dhampir the instant they see you. They'll probably smell it first. No Strigoi would have a dhampir working for him—only humans."

There was an uncomfortable silence in the car.

"No!" said Sydney. "I am *not* doing that!"

Dimitri shook his head. "I don't like it either, but we don't have a lot of options. If he thinks you work for me, he won't hurt you."

"Yeah? And what happens if he doesn't believe me?" she demanded.

"I don't think he can take the chance. He'll probably go with you to check things out, with the idea that if you're lying, they'll just kill you then."

This didn't seem to make her feel any better. She groaned.

"You can't send her in," I said. "They'll know she's an Alchemist. One of those wouldn't work for Strigoi either."

Surprisingly, Dimitri hadn't considered that. We grew quiet again, and it was Sydney who unexpectedly came up with a solution.

"When I was inside the gas station," she said slowly, "they had, like, one rack of makeup. We could probably cover most of my tattoo up with powder."

And we did. The only compact the station sold wasn't a great match for her skin tone, but we caked enough of it on to obscure the golden lily on her cheek. Brushing her hair forward helped a little. Satisfied we'd done all we could, we headed off to Donovan's.

It was indeed in a rundown part of town. A few blocks away

from the tattoo parlor, we spotted what looked like a nightclub, but otherwise, the neighborhood appeared deserted. I wasn't fooled, though. This was no place you'd want to walk around alone at night. It screamed "mugging." Or worse.

We checked out the area until Dimitri found a spot he felt good about. It was a back alley two buildings away from the parlor. A gnarled wired fence stood on one side while a low brick building flanked the other. Dimitri instructed Sydney on how to lead the Strigoi to us. She took it all in, nodding along, but I could see the fear in her eyes.

"You want to look awed," he told her. "Humans who serve Strigoi worship them—they're eager to please. Since they're around Strigoi so much, they aren't as startled or terrified. Still a little afraid, of course, but not as much as you look now."

She swallowed. "I can't really help it."

I felt bad for her. She strongly believed all vampires were evil, and we were sending her into a nest of the worst kind, putting her at great risk. I knew also that she'd only ever seen one live Strigoi, and despite Dimitri's coaching, seeing more could completely shell shock her. If she froze in front of Donovan, everything could fall apart. On impulse, I gave her a hug. To my surprise, she didn't resist.

"You can do this," I said. "You're strong—and they're too afraid of Dimitri. Okay?"

After a few deep breaths, Sydney nodded. We gave her a few more encouraging words, and then she turned the corner of the building, heading toward the street, and disappeared from our sight. I glanced at Dimitri.

"We may have just sent her to her death."

His face was grim. "I know—but we can't do anything now. You'd better get into position."

With his help, I managed to make it onto the roof of the low building. There was nothing intimate in the way he hoisted me up, but I couldn't help but have the same electric feeling all contact with him caused or note how easily we worked together. Once I was securely positioned, Dimitri headed for the opposite side of the building Sydney had gone around. He lurked just around the corner, and then there was nothing to do but wait.

It was agonizing—and not just because we were on the verge of a fight. I kept thinking about Sydney, what we'd asked her to do. My job was to protect the innocent from evil—not thrust them into the middle of it. What if our plan failed? Several minutes passed, and I finally heard footsteps and muttered voices at the same time a familiar wave of nausea moved through me. We'd pulled the Strigoi out.

Three of them walked around the building's corner, Sydney in the lead. They came to a halt, and I spotted Donovan. He was the tallest—a former Moroi—with dark hair and a beard that reminded me of Abe's. Dimitri had given me his description so I wouldn't (hopefully) kill him. Donovan's henchmen hovered behind him, all of them alert and on guard. I tensed, my stake gripped tightly in my right hand.

"Belikov?" demanded Donovan, voice harsh. "Where are you?"

"I'm here," came Dimitri's response—in that cold, terrible

Strigoi voice. He appeared from around the building's opposite corner, keeping to the shadows.

Donovan relaxed slightly, recognizing Dimitri—but even in darkness, Dimitri's true appearance materialized. Donovan went rigid—suddenly seeing a threat, even if it was one that confused him and defied what he knew. At the exact same moment, one of his guys jerked his head around. "Dhampirs!" he exclaimed. It wasn't Dimitri's features that tipped him off. It was our scent, and I breathed a silent prayer of thanks that it had taken them this long to notice.

Then, I leapt off the roof. It wasn't an easy distance to jump—but not one that would kill me. Plus, my fall was broken by a Strigoi.

I landed on one of Donovan's guys, knocking him to the ground. I aimed my stake at his heart, but his reflexes were quick. With my lighter weight, I was easy to shove off. I'd expected it and managed to keep my footing. Out of the corner of my eye, I saw Sydney dropping low and hurrying off out of here, per our instructions. We wanted her away from the crossfire and had told her to go to the car, readying herself to take off if things went bad.

Of course, with Strigoi, things were always bad. Donovan and his other guy had both gone for Dimitri, assessing him as the greater threat. My opponent, judging from his fanged smile, didn't seem to regard me as a threat at all. He lunged toward me, and I dodged away, but not before snaking out a kick that took him in the knee. My hit didn't seem to hurt him, but it did ruin his balance. I made another strike at staking and was thrown off again, hitting the ground hard. My bare legs scraped against the rough cement, tearing skin. Because my jeans had grown too dirty and torn, I'd been forced to wear a pair of shorts from the backpack Sydney had brought me. I ignored the pain, shooting right back up with speed the Strigoi didn't expect. My stake found his heart. The hit wasn't as hard as I would have liked, but it was enough to throw him off, then allowing me to drive the stake in further and finish him. Not even waiting to see him fall, I jerked my stake out and turned toward the others.

I hadn't hesitated once in the battle I'd just fought, but now, I paused at what I saw. Dimitri's face. It was . . . terrifying. Ferocious. He'd had a similar look when he'd defended me at my arrest—that badass warrior god expression that said he could take on hell itself. The way he looked now . . . well, it took that fierceness to a whole new level. This was personal, I realized. Fighting these Strigoi wasn't just about finding Sonya and helping Lissa. This was about redemption, an attempt to destroy his past by destroying the evil directly in his path.

I moved to join him, just as he staked the second henchman. There was power in that strike, much more power than Dimitri needed as he shoved the Strigoi against the brick wall and pierced his heart. It was impossible, but I could imagine that stake going straight through the body and into the wall. Dimitri put more attention and effort into that kill than he should have. He should have responded like I had and immediately turned to the next threat, once the Strigoi was dead. Instead, Dimitri was so fixated on his victim that he didn't notice Donovan taking advantage of the situation. Fortunately for Dimitri, I had his back.

I slammed my body into Donovan's, shoving him away from Dimitri. As I did, I saw Dimitri pull out his stake and then slam the body against the wall again. Meanwhile, I'd successfully drawn Donovan's attention and was now having a difficult time eluding him without killing him.

"Dimitri!" I yelled. "Come help me. I need you!"

I couldn't see what Dimitri was doing, but a few seconds later, he was by my side. With what almost sounded like a roar, he leapt at Donovan, stake out, and knocked the Strigoi to the ground. I breathed a sigh of relief and moved in to help with the restraint. Then, I saw Dimitri line up his stake with Donovan's heart.

"No!" I dropped to the ground, trying to both hold Donovan and push away Dimitri's arm. "We need him! Don't kill him!"

From the look on Dimitri's face, it was unclear if he even heard me. There was death in his eyes. He wanted to kill Donovan. The desire had suddenly taken precedence.

Still trying to hold Donovan with one arm, I smacked Dimitri in the face with my other hand—going for the side I hadn't punched the other night. I don't think he felt the pain in his adrenaline rage, but the hit got his attention. "Don't kill him!" I repeated.

The command made it through to Dimitri. Our struggle, unfortunately, gave Donovan maneuvering room. He started to break free of us, but then, as one, Dimitri and I threw ourselves into holding Donovan. I was reminded of the time I'd questioned Strigoi in Russia. It had taken a whole group of dhampirs to restrain one Strigoi, but Dimitri seemed to have unnatural strength.

"When we were interrogating, we used to—"

My words were interrupted when Dimitri decided to utilize his own method of interrogation. He gripped Donovan by the shoulders and shook him hard, causing the Strigoi to keep hitting his head against the cement.

"Where is Sonya Karp?" roared Dimitri.

"I don't—" began Donovan. But Dimitri had no patience for Strigoi evasion.

"Where is she? I know you know her!"

"I—"

"Where is she?"

I saw something on Donovan's face that I'd never seen in a Strigoi before: fear. I'd thought it was an emotion they simply didn't possess. Or, if they did, it was only in the battles they fought with one another. They wouldn't waste time with fear around lowly dhampirs.

But oh, Donovan was scared of Dimitri. And to be honest, I was too.

Those red-ringed eyes were wide—wide, desperate, and terrified. When Donovan blurted out his next words, something told me they were true. His fear wasn't giving him a chance to lie. He was too shocked and unprepared by all of this.

"Paris," he gasped out. "She's in Paris!"

"Christ," I exclaimed. "We *cannot* road trip to Paris."

Donovan shook his head (in as much as he could with Dimitri shaking him in return). "It's a small town—an hour away. There's this tiny lake. Hardly anyone on it. Blue house."

Vague directions. We needed more. "Do you have an addr—"

Dimitri apparently didn't share my need for more information. Before I could finish speaking, his stake was out—and in Donovan's heart. The Strigoi made a horrible, blood-curdling scream that faded as death took him. I winced. How long until someone heard all this and called the police?

Dimitri pulled his stake out—and then stabbed Donovan again. And again. I stared in disbelief and horror, frozen for a few moments. Then, I grabbed Dimitri's arm and began shaking him, though I felt like I would have had more effect shaking the building behind me.

"He's dead, Dimitri! He's dead! Stop this. Please."

Dimitri's face still wore that terrible, terrible expression—rage, now marked with a bit of desperation. Desperation that told him if he could only obliterate Donovan, then maybe he could obliterate everything else bad in his life.

I didn't know what to do. We had to get out of here. We had to get Sydney to disintegrate the bodies. Time was ticking, and I just kept repeating myself.

"He's dead! Let it go. *Please*. He's dead."

Then, somewhere, somehow, I broke through to Dimitri. His motions slowed and finally stopped. The hand holding the stake dropping weakly to his side as he stared at what was left of Donovan—which wasn't pretty. The rage on Dimitri's face completely gave way to desperation . . . and then that gave way to despair.

I tugged gently on his arm. "It's over. You've done enough."

"It's never enough, Roza," he whispered. The grief in his voice killed me. "It'll never be enough."

"It is for now," I said. I pulled him to me. Unresisting, he let go of his stake and buried his face against my shoulder. I dropped my stake as well and embraced him, drawing him closer. He wrapped his arms around me in return, seeking the contact of another living being, the contact I'd long known he needed.

"You're the only one." He clung more tightly to me. "The only one who understands. The only one who saw how I was. I could never explain it to anyone . . . you're the only one. The only one I can tell this to . . ."

I closed my eyes for a moment, overpowered by what he was saying. He might have sworn allegiance to Lissa, but that didn't mean he'd fully revealed his heart to her. For so long, he and I had been in perfect sync, always understanding each other. That was still the case, no matter if we were together, no matter if I was with Adrian. Dimitri had always kept his heart and feelings guarded until meeting me. I thought he'd locked them back up, but apparently, he still trusted me enough to reveal what was killing him inside.

I opened my eyes and met his dark, earnest gaze. "It's okay," I said. "It's okay now. I'm here. I'll always be here for you."

"I dream about them, you know. All the innocents I killed." His eyes drifted back to Donovan's body. "I keep thinking . . . maybe if I destroy enough Strigoi, the nightmares will go away. That I'll be certain I'm not one of them."

I touched his chin, turning his face back toward mine and away from Donovan. "No. You have to destroy Strigoi because they're evil. Because that's what we do. If you want the nightmares to go away, you have to *live*. That's the only way. We could have died just now. We didn't. Maybe we'll die tomorrow. I don't know. What matters is that we're alive now."

I was rambling at this point. I had never seen Dimitri so low, not since his restoration. He'd claimed being Strigoi had killed so many of his emotions. It hadn't. They were there, I realized. Everything he had been was still inside, only coming out in bursts—like this moment of rage and despair. Or when he'd defended me from the arresting guardians. The old Dimitri wasn't gone. He was just locked away, and I didn't know how to let him out. This wasn't what I did. He was always the one with words of wisdom and insight. Not me. Still, he was listening now. I had his attention. What could I say? What could get through to him?

"Remember what you said earlier?" I asked. "Back in Rubysville? Living is in the details. You've got to appreciate the details. That's the only way to defeat what the Strigoi did to you. The only way to bring back who you really are. You said it yourself: you escaped with me to feel the world again. Its beauty."

Dimitri started to turn toward Donovan again, but I

wouldn't let him. "There's nothing beautiful here. Only death."

"That's only true if you let *them* make it true," I said desperately, still feeling the press of time. "Find one thing. One thing that's beautiful. Anything. Anything that shows you're not one of them."

His eyes were back on me, studying my face silently. Panic raced through me. It wasn't working. I couldn't do this. We were going to have to get out of here, regardless of whatever state he was in. I knew he'd leave, too. If I'd learned anything, it was that Dimitri's warrior instincts were still working. If I said danger was coming, he would respond instantly, no matter the self-torment he felt. I didn't want that, though. I didn't want him to leave in despair. I wanted him to leave here one step closer to being the man I knew he could be. I wanted him to have one less nightmare.

It was beyond my abilities, though. I was no therapist. I was about to tell him we had to get out there, about to make his soldier reflexes kick in, when he suddenly spoke. His voice was barely a whisper. "Your hair."

"What?" For a second, I wondered if it was on fire or something. I touched a stray lock. No, nothing wrong except that it was a mess. I'd bound it up for battle to prevent the Strigoi from using it as a handhold, like Angeline had. Much of it had come undone in the struggle, though.

"Your hair," repeated Dimitri. His eyes were wide, almost awestruck. "Your hair is beautiful."

I didn't think so, not in its current state. Of course, considering we were in a dark alley filled with bodies, the choices were kind of limited. "You see? You're not one of them. Strigoi don't see beauty. Only death. You found something beautiful. One thing that's beautiful."

Hesitantly, nervously, he ran his fingers along the strands I'd touched earlier. "But is it enough?"

"It is for now." I pressed a kiss to his forehead and helped him stand. "It is for now."

SIXTEEN

CONSIDERING SYDNEY DESTROYED dead bodies on a regular basis, it was kind of surprising that she was so shocked by our post-fight appearances. Maybe dead Strigoi were just objects to her. Dimitri and I were real live people, and we were a mess.

"I hope you guys don't stain the car," she said, once the bodies were disposed of and we were on our way. I think it was her best attempt at a joke, in an effort to cover up her discomfort over our torn and bloody clothes.

"Are we going to Paris?" I asked, turning to look back at Dimitri.

"Paris?" asked Sydney, startled.

"Not yet," said Dimitri, leaning his head back against the seat. He was back to looking like a controlled guardian. All signs of his earlier breakdown were gone, and I had no intention of giving away what had happened before we'd fetched Sydney. So small . . . yet so monumental. And very private. For now, he mostly looked tired. "We should wait until daytime. We had to go for Donovan now, but if Sonya's got a house, she's probably there all the time. Safer for us in daylight."

"How do you know he wasn't lying?" asked Sydney. She was driving with no real destination, merely getting us out of the neighborhood as fast as possible and before people reported screams and the sounds of fighting.

I thought back to the terror on Donovan's face and shivered. "I don't think he was lying."

Sydney didn't ask any more questions, except about which direction she should drive. Dimitri suggested we find another hotel so that we could clean up and get some rest before tomorrow's task. Fortunately, Lexington had a much broader selection of hotels than our last town. We didn't go for luxury, but the large, modern-looking place we chose was part of a chain, clean and stylish. Sydney checked us in and then led us inside through a side door, so as not to startle any guests who might be up in the middle of the night.

We got one room with two double beds. No one commented on it, but I think we all shared a need to stay together after our earlier Strigoi encounter. Dimitri was much more of a mess than me, thanks to his mutilation of Donovan, so I sent him to shower first.

"You did great," I told Sydney as we waited. I sat on the floor (which was much cleaner than the last room's) so that I wouldn't wreck the beds. "That was really brave of you."

She crooked me a smile. "Typical. You get beat up and nearly killed, but I'm the one you're praising?"

"Hey, I do this all the time. Going in there alone like you did . . . well, it was pretty hardcore. And I'm not *that* beat up."

I was brushing off my injuries, just as Dimitri would. Sydney, eyeing me, knew it too. My legs were scraped more than

I'd realized, the skin torn and bleeding from where I'd fallen on the cement. One of my ankles was complaining over the roof-jump, and I had a number of cuts and bruises scattered over the rest of me. I had no clue where most had come from.

Sydney shook her head. "How you guys don't catch gangrene more often is beyond me." We both knew why, though. It was part of the natural resistance I'd been born with as a dhampir, getting the best of both races' traits. Moroi were actually pretty healthy too, though they sometimes caught diseases unique to their race. Victor was an example. He had a chronic disease and had once forced Lissa to heal him. Her magic had restored him to full health at the time, but the illness was slowly creeping back.

I showered after Dimitri finished, and then Sydney forced her first aid kit on both of us. When we were bandaged and disinfected to her satisfaction, she got out her laptop and pulled up a map of Paris, Kentucky. The three of us huddled around the screen.

"Lots of creeks and rivers," she mused, scrolling around. "Not much in the way of lakes."

I pointed. "Do you think that's it?" It was a tiny body of water, marked APPLEWOOD POND.

"Maybe. Ah, there's another pond. That could be a suspect too or—oh! Right here?" She tapped the screen on another body of water, a bit bigger than the ponds: MARTIN LAKE.

Dimitri sat back and ran a hand over his eyes as he yawned. "That looks like the most likely option. If not, I don't think it'll take long to drive around the other ones."

"That's your plan?" asked Sydney. "Just drive around and look for a blue house?"

I exchanged glances with Dimitri and shrugged. Sydney might be showing her bravery on this trip, but I knew her idea of "a plan" was a little different from ours. Hers were structured, well-thought out, and had a clear purpose. Also, details.

"It's more solid than most of our plans," I said at last.

The sun was going to be up in another hour or so. I was restless to go after Sonya, but Dimitri insisted sleep until midday. He took one bed, and Sydney and I shared the other. I didn't really think I needed the rest he claimed, but my body disagreed. I fell asleep almost instantly.

And like always lately, I eventually was pulled into a spirit dream. I hoped it was Adrian, coming to finish our last conversation. Instead, the conservatory materialized around me, complete with harp and cushioned furniture. I sighed and faced the Brothers Dashkov.

"Great," I said. "Another conference call. I have *really* got to start blocking your number."

Victor gave me a small bow. "Always a pleasure, Rose." Robert merely stared off into space again. Nice to know some things never changed.

"What do you want?" I demanded.

"You know what we want. We're here to help you help Vasilisa." I didn't believe that for an instant. Victor had some scheme in mind, but my hope was to capture him before he could do any further damage. He studied me expectantly. "Have you found the other Dragomir yet?"

I stared incredulously. "It's only been a day!" I almost had to redo my math on that one. It felt more like ten years. Nope. Only a day since I'd last spoken to Victor.

"And?" Victor asked.

"And, how good do you think we are?"

He considered. "Pretty good."

"Well, thanks for the vote of confidence, but it's not as easy as it seems. And actually . . . considering what a cover-up this has all been, it really doesn't seem easy at all."

"But you have found something?" Victor pressed.

I didn't answer.

An eager gleam lit his eyes, and he took a step forward. I promptly took one back. "You *have* found something."

"Maybe." Again, I had the same indecision as before. Did Victor, with all his scheming and manipulating, know something that could help us? Last time, he'd given me nothing, but now we had more information. What had he said? If we found a thread, he could unravel it?

"Rose." Victor was speaking to me like I was a child, as he often did to Robert. It made me scowl. "I told you before: It doesn't matter if you trust me or my intentions. For now, we're both interested in the same short-term goal. Don't let future worries ruin your chance here."

It was funny, but that was similar to the principle I'd operated on for most of my life. Live in the now. Jump right in and worry about the consequences later. Now, I hesitated and tried to think things over before making a decision. At last, I chose to take the risk, again hoping Victor might be able to help.

"We think the mother . . . the mother of Lissa's brother or sister . . . is related to Sonya Karp." Victor's eyebrows rose. "You know who that is?"

"Of course. She turned Strigoi—allegedly because she went insane. But we both know it was a little more complicated than that."

I nodded reluctantly. "She was a spirit user. No one knew."

Robert's head whipped around so fast that I nearly jumped. "Who's a spirit user?"

"*Former* spirit user," said Victor, instantly switching to soothing mode. "She became a Strigoi to get away from it."

The sharp focus Robert had directed toward the two of us melted into soft dreaminess once more. "Yes . . . always a lure to that . . . kill to live, live to kill. Immortality and freedom from these chains, but oh, what a loss . . ."

They were crazy ramblings, but they had an eerie similarity to some of the things Adrian said sometimes. I didn't like that at all. Trying to pretend Robert wasn't in the room, I turned back to Victor. "Do you know anything about her? Who she's related to?"

He shook his head. "She has a large family."

I threw up my hands in exasperation. "Could you be any more useless? You keep acting like you know so much, but you're just telling us what we've already found out! You aren't helping!"

"Help comes in many forms, Rose. Have you found Sonya?"

"Yes." I reconsidered. "Well, not quite. We know where she is. We're going to see her tomorrow and question her."

The look on Victor's face spoke legions about how ridiculous he thought that was. "And I'm sure she'll be eager to help."

I shrugged. "Dimitri's pretty persuasive."

"So I've heard," said Victor. "But Sonya Karp isn't an impressionable teenager." I sized up a punch but worried Robert might have his force field up again. Victor appeared oblivious to my anger. "Tell me where you are. We'll come to you."

Once more, a dilemma. I didn't think there was much the brothers could do. But this might present an opportunity to recapture him. Besides, if we had him in person, maybe he'd stop interrupting my dreams.

"We're in Kentucky," I said at last. "Paris, Kentucky." I gave him what other info we had about the blue house.

"We'll be there tomorrow," Victor said.

"Then where are you now—"

And just like last time, Robert ended the dream abruptly, leaving me hanging. What had I gotten myself into with them? Before I could consider it, I was immediately taken to another spirit dream. Good Lord. It really was déjà vu. Everyone wanted to talk to me in my sleep. Fortunately, like last time, my second visit was from Adrian.

This one was in the ballroom where the Council had met. There were no chairs or people, and my steps echoed on the hard wood floor. The room that seemed so grand and powerful when in use now had a lonely, ominous feel.

Adrian stood near one of the tall, arched windows, giving me one of his roguish smiles when I hugged him. Compared to how dirty and bloody everything was in the real world, he seemed pristine and perfect.

"You did it." I gave him a quick kiss on the lips. "You got them to nominate Lissa." After our last dream visit, when I'd realized there might be some merit to Victor's suggestion, I'd had to work hard to convince Adrian that the nomination idea was a good one—particularly since I hadn't been sure myself.

"Yeah, getting that group on board was easy." He seemed to like my admiration, but his face grew grimmer as he pondered my words. "She's not happy about it, though. Boy, she let us have it afterward."

"I saw it. You're right that she doesn't like it—but it was more than that. It was spirit-darkness. I took some of it away, but yeah . . . it was bad." I remembered how taking her anger had caused it to flare up briefly in me. Spirit didn't hit me as hard as it did her—but that was only temporary. Eventually, if I pulled enough over the years, it would take over. I caught hold of Adrian's hand and gave him as pleading a look as I could manage. "You've got to look after her. I'll do what I can, but you know as well as I do how stress and worry can agitate spirit. I'm afraid it'll come back like it used to. I wish I could be there to take care of her. Please—help her."

He tucked a loose piece of hair behind my ear, concern in his deep green eyes. At first, I thought his worry was just for Lissa. "I will," he said. "I'll do what I can. But Rose . . . will it happen to me? Is that what I'll become? Like her and the others?"

Adrian had never shown the extreme side effects Lissa had,

largely because he didn't use as much spirit and because he did so much self-medicating with alcohol. I didn't know how long that would last, though. From what I'd seen, there were only a few things to delay the insanity: self-discipline, antidepressants, and bonding to someone shadow-kissed. Adrian didn't seem interested in any of those options.

It was weird, but in this moment of vulnerability, I was reminded of what had just happened with Dimitri. Both of these men, so strong and confident in their ways, yet each needing me for support. *You're the strong one, Rose,* a voice whispered inside my head.

Adrian gazed off. "Sometimes . . . sometimes I can believe the insanity is all imagined, you know? I've never felt it like the others . . . like Lissa or old Vlad. But once in a while . . ." he paused. "I don't know. I feel so close, Rose. So close to the edge. Like if I allow myself one small misstep, I'll plunge away and never come back. It's like I'll lose myself."

I'd heard him say stuff like this before, when he'd go off on some weird tangent that only half made sense. It was the closest he ever came to showing that spirit might be messing with his mind too. I'd never realized he was aware of these moments or what they could mean.

He looked back down at me. "When I drink . . . I don't worry about it. I don't worry about going crazy. But then I think . . . maybe I already I am. Maybe I am, but no one can tell the difference when I'm drunk."

"You're not crazy," I said fiercely, pulling him to me. I loved his warmth and the way he felt against my skin.

"You'll be okay. You're strong."

He pressed his cheek to my forehead. "I don't know," he said. "I think you're my strength."

It was a sweet and romantic statement, but something about it bothered me. "That's not quite right," I said, wondering how I could put my feelings into words. I knew you could help someone else in a relationship. You could strengthen them and support them. But you couldn't actually do *everything* for them. You couldn't solve all their problems. "You have to find it within your—"

The hotel room's alarm clock blared and broke me from the dream, leaving me frustrated both because I missed Adrian and hadn't been able to say all I wanted to. Well, there was nothing I could do for him now. I could only hope he'd manage on his own.

Sydney and I were both sluggish and squinty-eyed. It made sense that she'd be exhausted, since her whole sleeping schedule—when she actually got sleep—had been thrown off. Me? My fatigue was mental. So many people, I thought. So many people needed me . . . but it was so hard to help all of them.

Naturally, Dimitri was up and ready to go. He'd woken before us. Last night's breakdown might as well have never happened. It turned out he'd been dying for coffee and had patiently waited for us, not wanting to leave us sleeping and undefended. I shooed him off, and twenty minutes later, he returned with coffee and a box of donuts. He also had purchased an industrial-strength chain at a hardware store across the street "for when we find Sonya," which made me uneasy.

By then Sydney and I were ready to go, and I decided to hold off on my questions. I wasn't crazy about wearing shorts again, not with my legs in this condition, but I was too eager to get to Sonya to insist we stop at a mall.

I did, however, decide it was time to get my companions up to speed.

"So," I began casually, "Victor Dashkov might be joining us soon."

It was to Sydney's credit that she didn't drive off the road. "*What*? That guy who escaped?"

I could see in Dimitri's eyes that he was just as shocked, but he kept cool and under control, like always. "Why," he began slowly, "is Victor Dashkov joining us?"

"Well, it's kind of a funny story . . ."

And with that intro, I gave them as brief yet thorough a recap as I could, starting with the background on Robert Doru and ending with the brothers' recent dream visits. I glossed over Victor's "mysterious" escape a few weeks ago, but something told me that Dimitri, in that uncanny way we had of guessing each other's thoughts, was probably putting the pieces together. Both Lissa and I had told Dimitri we'd gone through a lot to learn how to restore him, but we'd never explained the full story—especially the part about breaking out Victor so that he could help us find his brother.

"Look, whether he can help or not, this is our chance to catch him," I added hastily. "That's a good thing, right?"

"It's an issue we'll deal with . . . later." I recognized the tone in Dimitri's voice. He'd used it a lot at St. Vladimir's. It usually meant there was a private talk in my future, where I'd be grilled for more details.

Kentucky turned out to be pretty beautiful as we drove out to Paris. The land was rolling and green as we got out of the city, and it was easy to imagine wanting to live in a little house out here. I wondered idly if that had been Sonya's motivation and then caught myself. I'd just told Dimitri that Strigoi saw no beauty. Was I wrong? Would gorgeous scenery matter to her?

I found my answer when our GPS led us to Martin Lake. There were only a few houses scattered around it, and among those, only one was blue. Stopping a fair distance away from the house, Sydney parked the car off to the side of the road as much as she could. It was narrow, the shoulders covered in trees and high grass. We all got out of the car and walked a little ways, still keeping our distance.

"Well. It's a blue house," declared Sydney pragmatically. "But is it hers? I don't see a mailbox or anything."

I looked closer at the yard. Rose bushes, full of pink and red blossoms, grew in front of the porch. Baskets thick with white flowers I didn't know the names of hung from the roof, and blue morning glories climbed up a trellis. Around the house, I could just barely make out a wood fence. A vine with orange, trumpet-shaped flowers crawled over it.

Then, an image flickered into my mind, gone as quickly as it had come. Ms. Karp watering pots of flowers in her classroom, flowers that seemed to grow impossibly fast and tall. As a teenager more interested in dodging homework, I hadn't thought much about them. It was only later, after watching Lissa make plants grow and bloom during spirit experiments, that I understood what had been happening in Ms. Karp's classroom. And now, even deprived of spirit and possessed by evil, Sonya Karp was still tending her flowers.

"Yeah," I said. "This is her house." Dimitri approached the front porch, studying every detail. I started to follow but held back. "What are you doing?" I kept my voice low. "She might see you."

He returned to my side. "Those are black-out curtains. They aren't letting in any light, so she isn't going to see anything. It also means she likely spends her time on the house's main floor, rather than a basement."

I could easily follow his line of thinking. "That's good news for us." When I'd been captured by Strigoi last year, my friends and I had been held in a basement. Not only was it convenient for Strigoi wanting to avoid the sun, it also meant fewer escape and entry options. It was easy for Strigoi to trap prey in a basement. The more doors and windows we had, the better.

"I'll scout the other side," he said, starting for the backyard.

I hurried up to him and caught him by the arm. "Let me. I'll sense any Strigoi—not that she's going outside, but, well, just in case."

He hesitated, and I grew irate, thinking he didn't believe me capable. Then, he said, "Okay. Be careful." I realized he was just worried about me.

I moved as smoothly and quietly as I could around the house, soon discovering the wooden fence was going to create difficulty in seeing the backyard. I feared climbing over might alert Sonya to my presence and pondered what to do. My solution came in the form of a large rock lying near the fence's edge. I dragged the stone over and stood on top. It wasn't enough to let me look completely over, but I was able to easily put my hands on top of the fence and hoist myself up for a peek with minimal noise.

It was like looking into the Garden of Eden. The flowers in the front had merely been the warm-up act. More roses, magnolia and apple trees, irises, and a billion other flowers I didn't recognize. Sonya's backyard was a paradise of lush color. I scoped out what I needed to and hurried back to Dimitri. Sydney still stood by the car.

"A patio door and two windows," I reported. "All curtained. There's also a wooden deck chair, a shovel, and a wheelbarrow."

"Any pitchforks?"

"Unfortunately, no, but there's a big-ass rock sitting outside the fence. It'd be hard to get it into the yard, though. We're better off using it to help us climb over. No gate in the fence. She's made a fortress."

He nodded in understanding, and without any conversation, I knew what to do. We got the chain from the car and entrusted it to Sydney. We told her to wait for us outside—with the strict instructions to leave if we weren't back in thirty minutes. I hated to say that kind of thing—and Sydney's face indicated she didn't like hearing it—but it was inevitable. If we hadn't subdued Sonya in that amount of time, we weren't going to subdue her at all—or leave alive. If we did manage to overtake her, we'd give some signal for Sydney to come in with the chain.

Sydney's amber-brown eyes were filled with anxiety as she watched us head back around the house. I nearly teased her for caring about evil creatures of the night but stopped myself just in time. She might loathe every other dhampir and Moroi in the world, but somewhere along the way, she'd come to like Dimitri and me. That wasn't something to mock.

Dimitri stood on the rock and surveyed the yard. He murmured a few last-minute instructions to me before taking my hands and boosting me up over the fence. His height went a long way to make the maneuver as easy and quiet—though not silent—as possible. He followed me shortly thereafter, landing beside me with a small thud.

After that, we sprang forward with no delay. If Sonya had heard us, then there was no point in wasting time. We needed every advantage we could get. Dimitri grabbed the shovel and swung it hard into the glass—once, twice. The first strike was about the height of my head, the second lower. The glass fractured more with each impact. Right on the heels of the second hit, I pushed forward and shoved the wheelbarrow into the door. Lifting it and throwing it against the glass would have been a lot cooler, but it was too unwieldy to raise very high. When the wheelbarrow struck the already weakened glass, the cracked areas broke and crumbled altogether, creating a hole big enough for both of us to get through. We both had to duck—especially Dimitri.

A simultaneous attack through both sides of the house would have been ideal, but it wasn't like Sonya could run out the front door. Nausea had started to creep over me as soon as we were near the patio, and the sensation hit full force as we entered a living room. I ignored my stomach in the way I'd perfected and braced myself for what was to come. We'd broken in pretty quickly but not quickly enough to truly get the jump on Strigoi reflexes.

Sonya Karp was right there, ready for us, doing all she could to avoid the sunlight spilling into the living room. When I'd first seen Dimitri as a Strigoi, I'd been so shocked that I'd frozen up. It had allowed him to capture me, so I'd mentally braced myself this time, knowing I'd feel the same shock when I saw my former teacher as a Strigoi. And it *was* shocking. Just like with him, so many of Sonya's features were the same as before: the auburn hair and high cheek bones . . . but her beauty was twisted by all the other terrible conditions: chalky skin, red eyes, and the expression of cruelty that all Strigoi seemed to wear.

If she recognized us, she gave no sign and lunged toward Dimitri with a snarl. It was a common Strigoi tactic to take out the bigger threat first, and it annoyed me that they always believed that was Dimitri. He'd shoved his stake in his belt in order to carry the shovel inside with him. The shovel wouldn't kill a Strigoi, but with enough strength and momentum, it would definitely keep Sonya at arm's length. He struck her with it in the shoulder after her first attempt, and while she didn't fall over, she definitely waited before trying another attack. They circled each other, like wolves readying for a battle, as she sized up her odds. One charge, and her greater strength would push him down, shovel or not.

All of this took place in a matter of seconds, and Sonya's calculations had left me out of the equation. I made my own charge, slamming into her other side, but she saw me coming out of the corner of her eye and responded instantly, throwing me down while never taking her eyes off Dimitri. I wished I had the shovel and could hit her in the back from a safe distance. All I carried was my stake, and I had to be careful with it since it could kill her. I did a quick scan of her eerily normal living room and couldn't see any other potential weapons.

She feinted, and Dimitri went for it. He just barely corrected himself as she leapt forward to take advantage of the situation. She thrust him against the wall, pinning him there and knocking the shovel from his grasp. He struggled against her, trying to break free as her hands found his throat. If I tried to pull her off, my strength combined with Dimitri's would probably free him. I wanted this over as quickly as possible, however, and decided to make a power play.

I ran toward her, stake in hand, and plunged it through her right shoulder blade, hoping I was nowhere near her heart. The charmed silver, so agonizing to Strigoi skin, made her scream. Frantic, she shoved me away with force that was astonishing even for a Strigoi. I fell backward, stumbling, and whacked my head against a coffee table. My vision dimmed slightly, but instinct and adrenaline drove me back to my feet.

My attack gave Dimitri the split second he needed. He

knocked Sonya to the ground and grabbed my stake, pushing it against her throat. She screamed and flailed, and I moved forward to help him, knowing how hard it was to pin a Strigoi.

"Get Sydney . . ." he grunted. "The chain . . ."

I moved as quickly as I could, stars and shadows dancing in front of me. I unlocked the front door and kicked it open as a signal, then ran back to Dimitri. Sonya was making good progress in fighting him off. I dropped to my knees, working with Dimitri to keep her restrained. He had that battle lust in his eyes again, a look that said he wanted to destroy her right here and now. But there was something else, too. Something that made me think he had more control, that my words in the alley had actually had an impact. Still, I uttered a warning.

"We need her . . . remember we need her."

He gave me a slight nod, just as Sydney showed up lugging the chain. She stared at the scene wide-eyed, pausing only a moment before hurrying over to us. *We'll make a warrior of her yet*, I thought.

Dimitri and I moved to our next task. We'd already spotted the best place to bind Sonya: a heavy, reclining armchair in the corner. Lifting her—which was dangerous since she was still thrashing wildly—we thrust her into the chair. Then, keeping the stake at her neck, Dimitri attempted to hold her down while I grabbed hold of the chain.

There was no time to think of a precise system. I just started wrapping it, first around her legs and then as best as I could around her torso, trying to lock her arms against her. Dimitri had bought *a lot* of chain, thankfully, and I hurriedly wrapped it around the chair in a crazy manner, doing everything I could to keep her down.

When I finally ran out of chain, Sonya was pretty well locked into place. Was it something she could break out of? Absolutely. But with a silver stake against her? Not so easy. With both in place . . . well, we had her trapped for now. It was the best we could do.

Dimitri and I exchanged brief, weary looks. I felt dizzy but fought through it, knowing our task was far from over.

"Time for questioning," I said grimly.

SEVENTEEN

THE INTERROGATION DIDN'T go so well.

Oh, sure, we made plenty of threats and used the stakes as torture devices, but not much came of it. Dimitri was still scary when dealing with Sonya, but after his breakdown with Donovan, he was careful not to fall into that berserk rage again. This was healthier for him in the long run but not so good for scaring up answers out of Sonya. It didn't help matters that we didn't exactly have a concrete question to ask her. We mostly had a series to throw at her. Did she know about another Dragomir? Was she related to the mother? Where were the mother and child? Things also went bad when Sonya realized we needed her too much to kill her, no matter how much silver stake torture we did.

We'd been at it for over an hour and were getting exhausted. At least, I was. I leaned against a wall near Sonya, and though I had my stake out and ready, I was relying on the wall a bit more than I liked to admit to keep me upright. None of us had spoken in a while. Even Sonya had given up on her snarling threats. She simply waited and stayed watchful, undoubtedly planning for escape, probably figuring we'd tire before she did. That silence was scarier than all the threats in the world. I was used to Strigoi using words to intimidate me. I'd never expected the power simply being quiet and staring menacingly could have.

"What happened to your head, Rose?" asked Dimitri, suddenly catching a glimpse of it.

I'd been tuning out a little and realized he was talking to me. "Huh?" I brushed aside hair that had been obscuring part of my forehead. My fingers came away sticky with blood, triggering vague memories of crashing into the table. I shrugged, ignoring the dizziness I'd been feeling. "I'm fine."

Dimitri gave Sydney the quickest of glances. "Go lay her down and clean it up. Don't let her sleep until we can figure out if it's a concussion."

"No, I can't," I argued. "I can't leave you alone with her . . ."

"I'm fine," he said. "Rest up so that you can help me later. You're no good to me if you're just going to fall over."

I still protested, but when Sydney gently took my arm, my stumbling gave me away. She led me to the house's one bedroom, much to my dismay. There was something creepy about knowing I was in a Strigoi's bed—even if it was covered with a blue-and-white floral quilt.

"Man," I said, lying back against the pillow once Sydney had cleaned my forehead. Despite my earlier denial, it felt great to rest. "I can't get used to the weirdness of a Strigoi living in a place so . . . normal. How are you holding up?"

"Better than you guys," said Sydney. She wrapped her arms around herself and eyed the room uncomfortably. "Being around Strigoi is starting to make you guys seem not so bad."

"Well, at least some good's come out of this," I remarked.

Despite her joke, I knew she had to be terrified. I started to close my eyes and was jolted awake when Sydney poked my arm.

"No sleep," she chastised. "Stay up and talk to me."

"It's not a concussion," I muttered. "But I suppose we can go over plans to get Sonya to talk."

Sydney sat at the foot of the bed and grimaced. "No offense? But I don't think she's going to crack."

"She will once she's gone a few days without blood."

Sydney blanched. "A few days?"

"Well, whatever it takes to—" A spike of emotion flitted through the bond, and I froze. Sydney jumped up, her eyes darting around as though a group of Strigoi might have burst into the room.

"What's wrong?" she exclaimed.

"I have to go to Lissa."

"You're not supposed to sleep—"

"It's not sleeping," I said bluntly. And with that, I jumped away from Sonya's bedroom and into Lissa's perspective.

She was riding in a van with five other people whom I immediately recognized as other royal nominees. It was an eight-person van and also included a guardian driver with another in the passenger seat who was looking back at Lissa and her companions.

"Each of you will be dropped off in a separate location on the outskirts of a forest and given a map and compass. The ultimate goal is for you to reach the destination on the map and wait out the daylight until we come for you."

Lissa and the other nominees exchanged glances and then, almost as one, peered out the van's windows. It was almost noon, and the sunlight was pouring down. "Waiting out the daylight" was not going to be pleasant but didn't sound impossible. Idly, she scratched at a small bandage on her arm and quickly stopped herself. I read from her thoughts what it was: a tiny, barely noticeable dot tattooed into her skin. It was actually similar to Sydney's: blood and earth, mixed with compulsion. Compulsion might be taboo among Moroi, but this was a special situation. The spell in the tattoo prevented the candidates from revealing the monarch tests to others not involved with the process. This was the first test.

"What kind of terrain are you sending us to?" demanded Marcus Lazar. "We're not all in the same physical shape. It's not fair when some of us have an advantage." His eyes were on Lissa as he spoke.

"There *is* a lot of walking," said the guardian, face serious. "But it's nothing that any candidate—of any age—shouldn't be able to handle. And, to be honest, part of the requirements for a king or queen is a certain amount of stamina. Age brings wisdom, but a monarch needs to be healthy. Not an athlete by any means," added the guardian quickly, seeing Marcus start to open his mouth. "But it's no good for the Moroi to have a sickly monarch elected who dies within a year. Harsh, but true. And you also need to be able to endure uncomfortable situations. If you can't handle a day in the sun, you can't handle a Council meeting." I think he intended that as a joke, but it was hard to tell since he didn't smile. "It's not a race, though. Take your time getting to the end if you need it. Marked along the map are spots where certain items are hidden—items that'll make this more bearable, if you can decipher the clues."

"Can we use our magic?" asked Ariana Szelsky. She wasn't young either, but she looked tough and ready to accept a challenge of endurance.

"Yes, you can," said the guardian solemnly.

"Are we in danger out there?" asked another candidate, Ronald Ozera. "Aside from the sun?"

"That," said the guardian mysteriously, "is something you'll need to learn for yourselves. But, if at any time you want out . . ." He produced a bag of cell phones and distributed them. Maps and compasses followed. "Call the programmed number, and we'll come for you."

Nobody had to ask about the hidden message behind that. Calling the number would get you out of the long day of endurance. It would also mean you'd failed the test and were out of the running for the throne. Lissa glanced at her phone, half-surprised there was even a signal. They'd left Court about an hour ago and were well into the countryside. A line of trees made Lissa think they were nearing their destination.

So. A test of physical endurance. It wasn't quite what she'd expected. The trials a monarch went through had long been shrouded in mystery, gaining an almost mystical reputation. This one was pretty practical, and Lissa could understand the reasoning, even if Marcus didn't. It truly wasn't an athletic competition, and the guardian had a point in saying that the future monarch should possess a certain level of fitness. Glancing at the back of her map, which listed the clues, Lissa realized this would also test their reasoning skills. All very basic stuff—but essential to ruling a nation.

The van dropped them off one by one at different starting points. With each departing candidate, Lissa's anxiety grew. *There's nothing to worry about*, she thought. *I've just got to sit through a sunny day*. She was the next to last person dropped off, with only Ariana remaining behind. Ariana patted Lissa's arm as the van door opened.

"Good luck, dear."

Lissa gave her a quick smile. These tests might all be a ruse on Lissa's part, but Ariana was the real deal, and Lissa prayed the older woman could get through this successfully.

Left alone as the van drove away, unease spread through Lissa. The simple endurance test suddenly seemed much more daunting and difficult. She was on her own, something that didn't happen very often. I'd been there for most of her life, and even when I'd left, she'd had friends around her. But now? It was just her, the map, and the cell phone. And the cell phone was her enemy.

She walked to the edge of the forest and studied her map. A drawing of a large oak tree marked the beginning, with directions to go northwest. Scanning the trees, Lissa saw three maples, a fir, and—an oak. Heading toward it, she couldn't help a smile. If anyone else had botanical landmarks and didn't know their plants and trees, they could lose candidacy right there.

The compass was a classic one. No digital GPS convenience

here. Lissa had never used a compass like this, and the protective part of me wished I could jump in and help. I should have known better, though. Lissa was smart and easily figured it out. Heading northwest, she stepped into the woods. While there was no clear path, the forest's floor wasn't *too* covered with overgrowth or obstacles.

The nice part about being in the forest was that the trees blocked out some of the sun. It still wasn't an ideal Moroi condition, but it beat being dropped in a desert. Birds sang, and the scenery was lush and green. Keeping an eye out for the next landmark, Lissa tried to relax and pretend she was simply on a pleasant hike.

Yet . . . it was difficult to do that with so much on her mind. Abe and our other friends were now in charge of working and asking questions about the murder. All of them were asleep right now—it was the middle of the Moroi night—but Lissa didn't know when she'd return and couldn't help resenting this test for taking up her time. No, *wasting* her time. She'd finally accepted the logic behind her friends' nomination—but she still didn't like it. She wanted to actively help them.

Her churning thoughts almost led her right past her next landmark: a tree that had fallen ages ago. Moss covered it, and much of the wood was rotten. A star on the map marked it as a place with a clue. She flipped over the map and read:

I grow and I shrink. I run and I crawl.
Follow my voice, though I have none at all.
I never do leave here, but I travel around—

I float through the sky and I creep through the ground.
I keep my cache in a vault although I have no wealth,
Seek out my decay to safeguard your health.

Um.

My mind went blank right about then, but Lissa's spun. She read it over and over again, examining the individual words and how each line played off the other. *I never do leave here.* That was the starting point, she decided. Something permanent. She looked around, considered the trees, then dismissed them. They could always be cut and removed. Careful not to stray too far from the fallen tree, she circled the area searching for more. Everything was theoretically transient. What stayed?

Follow my voice. She came to a halt and closed her eyes, absorbing the sounds around her. Mostly birds. The occasional rustle of leaves. And—

She opened her eyes and walked briskly to her right. The sound she'd heard grew louder, bubbling and trickling. There. A small creek ran through the woods, hardly noticeable. Indeed, it seemed too tiny for the streambed carved out around it.

"But I bet you grow when it rains," she murmured, uncaring that she was speaking to a stream. She looked back down at the clue, and I felt her clever mind rapidly piece it all together. The stream was permanent—but traveled. It changed size. It had a voice. It ran in deep parts, crawled when there were obstacles. And when it evaporated, it floated in the air. She frowned, still puzzling the riddle aloud. "But you don't decay."

Lissa studied the area once more, uneasily thinking decay could apply to any plant life. Her gaze moved past a large maple tree and then jerked back. At its base grew a clump of brown and white mushrooms, several wilting and turning black. She hurried over and knelt down, and that was when she saw it: a small hole dug into the earth nearby. Leaning closer, she saw a flash of color: a purple drawstring bag.

Triumphantly, Lissa pulled it out and stood up. The bag was made of canvas and had long strings that would allow it to hang over her shoulder as she walked. She opened the bag and peered inside. There, tucked inside the fluffy and fuzzy lining, was the best thing of all: a bottle of water. Until now, Lissa hadn't realized how hot and dehydrated she'd grown—or how wearying the sun was. The candidates had been told to wear sturdy shoes and practical clothing but hadn't been allowed any other supplies. Finding this bottle was priceless.

Sitting on the log, she took a break, careful to conserve her water. While the map indicated a few more clues and "rewards," she knew she couldn't necessarily count on any more helpful bags. So, after several minutes' rest, she put away the water and slung the little tote over her shoulder. The map directed her due west, so that was the way she went.

The heat beat on her as she continued her walk, forcing her to take a few more (conservative) water breaks. She kept reminding herself it wasn't a race and that she should take it easy. After a few more clues, she discovered the map wasn't quite to scale, so it wasn't always obvious how long each leg of the hike was. Nonetheless, she was delighted to successfully solve each clue, though the rewards became more and more baffling.

One of them was a bunch of sticks sitting on a rock, something she would have sworn was a mistake, but someone civilized had clearly tied the bundle together. She added that into her bag, along with a neatly folded green plastic tarp. By now, sweat was pouring off her, and rolling up the sleeves of her button-down cotton shirt did little to help. She took more frequent breaks. Sunburn became a serious concern, so it was a huge relief when her next clue led to a bottle of sunscreen.

After a couple hours of battling the intense summer heat, Lissa became so hot and tired that she no longer had the mental energy to be annoyed about missing out on whatever was happening at Court. All that mattered was getting to the end of this test. The map showed two more clues, which she took as a promising sign. She would reach the end soon and then could simply wait for someone to get her. A flash of realization hit her. The tarp. The tarp was a sun block, she decided. She could use it at the end.

This cheered her up, as did the next prize: more water and a floppy, wide-brimmed hat that helped keep the sunlight from her face. Unfortunately, after that, what appeared to be a short leg of the trip turned out to be twice as long as she expected. By the time she finally reached the next clue, she was more interested in taking a water break than digging out whatever else the guardians had left her.

My heart went out to her. I wished so, so badly that I could help. That was my job, to protect her. She shouldn't be alone.

Or should she? Was that also part of the test? In a world where royals were almost always surrounded by guardians, this solitude had to be a total shock. Moroi were hardy and had excellent senses, but they weren't built for extreme heat and challenging terrain. I could have probably jogged the course easily. Admittedly, I wasn't sure I would have had Lissa's deductive skills in figuring out the clues.

Lissa's last reward was flint and steel, not that she had any idea what they were. I recognized them instantly as the tools of a fire-making kit but couldn't for the world figure out why she'd need to build a fire on a day like this. With a shrug, she added the items to her bag and kept going.

And that's when things started to get cold. Really cold.

She didn't entirely process it at first, mainly because the sun was still shining so brilliantly. Her brain said what she felt was impossible, but her goose bumps and chattering teeth said otherwise. She rolled her sleeves back down and quickened her pace, wishing that the sudden cold had at least come with cloud cover. Walking faster and exerting herself more helped heat her body.

Until it began to rain.

It started off as a mist, then changed to drizzle, and finally turned into a steady curtain of water. Her hair and clothing became soaked, making the cold temperature that much worse. Yet . . . the sun still shone, its light an annoyance to her sensitive skin but offering no warmth in compensation.

Magic, she realized. *This weather is magical*. It was part of the test. Somehow, Moroi air and water magic users had united to defy the hot, sunny weather. That was why she had a tarp—to block the sun *and* the rain. She considered getting it out now and wearing it like a cloak but quickly decided to wait until she reached the endpoint. She had no idea how far away that really was, though. Twenty feet? Twenty miles? The chill of the rain crept over her, seeping under her skin. It was miserable.

The cell phone in the bag was her ticket out. It was barely late afternoon. She had a long time to wait before this test ended. All she had to do was make one call . . . one call, and she'd be out of this mess and back to working on what she should be at Court. *No*. A kernel of determination flared up within her. This challenge was no longer about the Moroi throne or Tatiana's murder. It was a test she would take on for herself. She'd led a soft and sheltered life, letting others protect her. She would endure this on her own—and she would pass.

This determination took her to the map's end, a clearing ringed in trees. Two of the trees were small and close enough together that Lissa thought she might be able to drape the tarp into some sort of reasonable shelter. With cold, fumbling fingers, she managed to get it out of the bag and unfold it to its full size—which was fortunately much larger than she'd suspected. Her mood began to lift as she worked with the tarp and figured out how to create a small canopy. She crawled inside once it was complete, glad to be out of the falling rain.

But that didn't change the fact that she was wet. Or that the ground was also wet—and muddy. The tarp also didn't protect her against the cold. She felt a flash of bitterness, recalling the guardians saying magic was allowed in this test.

She hadn't thought magic would be useful at the time, but now, she could certainly see the perks of being a water user to control the rain and keep it off her. Or, better yet: being a fire user. She wished Christian was with her. She would have welcomed the warmth of both his magic and his embrace. For this kind of situation, spirit seriously sucked—unless, perhaps, she got hypothermia and needed to try to heal herself (which never worked as well as it did on other people). No, she decided. There could be no question: water and fire users had the advantage in this test.

That's when it hit her.

Fire!

Lissa straightened up from where she'd been huddled. She hadn't recognized the iron and flint for what they were, but now, vague recollections of fire-making were coming back to her. She'd never been taught those skills directly but was pretty sure striking the stones together would make a spark—if she only had dry wood. Everything out there was soaked. . . .

Except for the bundle of sticks in her bag. Laughing out loud, she untied the sticks and set them in a place shielded from the rain. After arranging them in what seemed like a campfire-friendly pattern, she tried to figure out what to do with the steel and flint. In movies, she thought she'd seen people just hit them to make sparks fly. So, that's what she did.

Nothing happened.

She tried three more times, and her earlier excitement gave way to spirit-darkened frustration. I pulled some of that from her, needing her to stay focused. On the fourth try, a spark flew off and faded away—but it was what she needed to understand the principle. Before long she could easily make sparks, but they did nothing when they landed on the wood. Up and down: her mood was a rollercoaster of hope and disappointment. *Don't give up,* I wanted to say as I drew off more negativity. *Don't give up.* I also wanted to give her a lesson on kindling, but that was pushing my limits.

Watching her, I was beginning to realize how much I underestimated Lissa's intelligence. I knew she was brilliant, but I always imagined her being helpless in these situations. She wasn't. She could reason things out. That tiny spark couldn't penetrate the wood of the sticks. She needed a bigger flame. She needed something the sparks could ignite. But what? Surely nothing in this waterlogged forest.

Her eyes fell on the map poking out of her bag. She hesitated only a moment before ripping and shredding the paper into a pile on top of the twigs. Supposedly, she'd reached the end of the hike and didn't need the map. Supposedly. But it was too late now, and Lissa pushed forward with her plan. First, she pulled out some of the bag's fluffy lining, adding the bits of fuzz to the paper. Then she took up the flint and steel again.

A spark jumped out and immediately caught a piece of the paper. It flared orange before fading out, leaving a wisp of smoke. She tried again, leaning forward to gently blow on the paper when the spark landed. A tiny flame appeared, caught a neighboring shred, and then faded. Steeling herself up, Lissa tried a final time.

"Come on, come on," she muttered, as though she might compel a fire into existence.

This time, the spark caught and held, turning into a small flame, then a larger flame that soon consumed her kindling. I prayed it would take to the wood, or else she was out of luck. Brighter and larger the flame grew, eating the last of the paper and fuzz . . . and then spreading along the sticks. Lissa blew softly to keep it going, and before long, the campfire was in full blaze.

The fire couldn't change the piercing cold, but as far as she was concerned, she had the warmth of the entire sun in her hands. She smiled, and a sense of pride that she hadn't felt in a while spread within her. Finally able to relax, she glanced out at the rainy forest and caught the faintest flashes of color in the distance. Channeling spirit, she used her magic to intensify her ability to see auras. Sure enough—hidden far, far out among the trees, she could see two auras filled with strong, steady colors. Their owners stood still, staying quiet and covered. Lissa's smile grew. Guardians. Or maybe the air and water users controlling the weather. None of the candidates were alone out here. Ronald Ozera had had no need to worry—but then, he wouldn't know that. Only she did. Maybe spirit wasn't so useless out here after all.

The rain began to lighten, and the fire's warmth continued to soothe her. She couldn't read the time from the sky, but somehow, she knew she would have no problem waiting out the day and—

"Rose?" A voice summoned me out of Lissa's wilderness

survival. "Rose, wake up or . . . whatever."

I blinked, focusing on Sydney's face, which was a few inches from mine. "What?" I demanded. "Why are you bothering me?"

She flinched and jerked away, momentarily speechless. Pulling away Lissa's darkness while joined with her hadn't affected me at the time, but now, conscious in my own body, I felt anger and irritation flood me. *It's not you, it's not Sydney,* I told myself. *It's spirit. Calm down.* I took a deep breath, refusing to let spirit master me. I was stronger than it was. I hoped.

As I fought to push those feelings down, I looked around and remembered I was in Sonya Karp's bedroom. All my problems came rushing back. There was a bound Strigoi in the other room, one we were barely keeping constrained and who didn't seem like she would give us answers anytime soon.

I looked back at Sydney, who still seemed afraid of me. "I'm sorry . . . I didn't mean to snap at you. I was just startled." She hesitated a few moments and then nodded, accepting my apology. As the fear faded from her face, I could see that something else was bothering her. "What's wrong?" I asked. As long as we were alive and Sonya was still trapped, things couldn't be *that* bad, right?

Sydney stepped back and crossed her arms. "Victor Dashkov and his brother are here."

EIGHTEEN

I SPRANG UP FROM THE bed, relieved that I didn't fall over. My head still hurt, but I no longer felt dizzy, which hopefully meant I really had evaded a concussion. Glancing at an alarm clock as I left Sonya's bedroom, I saw that I'd been in Lissa's head for a few hours. Her test had been far more extensive than I'd realized.

In the living room, I found an almost comical sight. Victor and Robert stood there, in the flesh, taking in the surrounding details. Even Robert seemed to be with us mentally this time. Only, whereas Victor was studying everything in his calculating way, Robert's attention was fixed on Sonya. His eyes bugged out in astonishment. Dimitri, meanwhile, hadn't altered his position near Sonya or put away the stake at her throat. It was clear from his stance and watchful gaze, however, that he regarded the brothers as a new threat and was trying—impossibly—to stay on guard against everything. He seemed relieved to see me and have some backup.

Sonya had gone perfectly still within her chains, which I didn't like at all. It made me think she was planning something. Her red eyes narrowed.

The whole situation was tense and dangerous, but a tiny part of me felt smug satisfaction as I studied Victor more closely. The dream meetings had been deceptive. Just as I could shift my appearance in dreams, Victor had made himself look stronger and healthier in those visits than he actually was in real life. Age, disease, and life on the run were taking their toll. Dark shadows lined his eyes, and his graying hair seemed thinner than it had a month ago. He looked haggard and tired, but I knew he was still dangerous.

"So," I said, hands on hips. "You managed to find us."

"There's one lake in this town," said Victor. "One blue house. Maybe you had trouble with those directions, but for the rest of us, it wasn't that difficult."

"Well, if you're so smart, what's your plan now?" I asked. I was trying to stall as I frantically thought about what *my* plan was. I'd wanted to capture Victor and Robert but didn't know how. Since we had to split our attention between them and Sonya, Dimitri and I couldn't team up. I wished we had leftover chain. Aside from physically subduing the brothers, we would also specifically need to restrain their hands to reduce their ability to use magic.

"Since *you're* so smart," countered Victor, "I assumed you'd have already obtained the needed information."

I gestured toward Sonya. "She's not exactly forthcoming."

Victor's eyes fell on her. "Sonya Karp. You've changed since I last saw you."

"I'm going to kill you all," Sonya snarled. "And consume you one by one. Normally, I'd start with the human and work up to the Moroi, but . . ." She glanced at Dimitri and me, her face full of rage. "I think I'll save you two for last and drag out your suffering." She paused and almost comically added, "You've annoyed me the most."

"Do all Strigoi go through some boot camp and learn all the same threats? It's a wonder you don't cackle too." I turned back to Victor. "See? Not that easy. We've tried everything. Beating it out, torturing it out. Sydney went through the names of all her relatives. No reaction."

Victor studied Sydney in detail for the first time. "So. Your pet Alchemist."

Sydney didn't move. I knew she had to be scared of facing someone who was both a vampire *and* a dangerous criminal. I had to give her points for meeting his stare unflinchingly.

"Young," Victor mused. "But of course she would be. I imagine it's the only way you could manipulate her into this little escapade."

"I'm here by choice," replied Sydney. Her expression stayed calm and confident. "No one manipulated me." Abe's blackmail wasn't really relevant at the moment.

"Look, if you wanted to keep torturing me with your not-funny comments, you could have just kept invading my dreams," I snapped. "If you don't have anything useful to offer, then get out of here and let us wait until hunger weakens Sonya." And by *get out of here*, I meant: *foolishly think you're going to leave so that I can knock your heads together and drag you back to the guardians.*

"We can help," said Victor. He touched his brother lightly on the arm. Robert flinched, jerking his eyes from Sonya to Victor. "Your methods were destined to fail. If you want answers, there's only one way to—"

Sonya made her move. Dimitri was still right next to her, but he'd also been keeping an eye on the rest of us. And of course, I'd been completely focused on the Victor drama as well. It was probably the best opening Sonya could have hoped for.

With crazy Strigoi strength, she bucked up from the chair. The chain was wrapped around her over and over, but her quick movement and strength were enough to snap the chain in two places. The rest still encircled her, but I knew perfectly well even one opening was enough for her to eventually bust out. Distracted or not, Dimitri was on her in a flash, and a second later, so was I. She was flailing in the chair, using every bit of her strength and speed to shake off the chains. If she got loose, I knew she'd put up another fierce fight. Dimitri and I met eyes briefly, and I knew we were thinking the same things. First, how were we going to re-restrain her? The chain could probably be rebound, but we'd need to unwind it and start over, which would be next to impossible. We also both knew he and I might not be able to take her down a second time, and now we had innocents around. They couldn't fight, but Sonya might be able to use them to her advantage somehow.

All we could do was try to keep her down. Holding her against a flat surface like the floor would have been much easier than the unwieldy recliner. It shook as she fought against us, and we struggled to get a good position on the chair. Dimitri had his stake—I'd set mine down earlier—and he raked it against her skin, giving us some advantage in the struggle. She screamed in rage, and I clung to the hope we might tire her out. Probably not. We'd break first. My aching head was proof enough that I wasn't in peak condition.

I saw a flash of movement in my periphery, setting off new alarms. Robert Doru was heading toward us—and he had a silver stake in his hand. The sight was so bizarre and unexpected that I was slow to alert Dimitri. When my sluggish mind suddenly kicked back to life, it was too late.

"No!" I shrieked, seeing Robert raise the stake. "Don't kill her!"

Dimitri turned and saw Robert then, but there was nothing he could do. Dimitri and I had created the perfect opportunity. We were holding Sonya still, and with her chest vulnerable, Robert had a clean shot. Frantically, I wondered what to do. If I stopped him, I'd release Sonya. If I didn't stop him, he might kill our only chance at finding out who—

Too late. The stake plunged down with a force that astonished me. Lissa had had a very difficult time staking Dimitri, and I'd assumed the same would be true for someone like Robert, who was older and seemed so fragile. But, no. He still had to use two hands, but the stake went firmly into Sonya's chest, piercing her heart.

Sonya let out an intense scream. A brilliant, blinding white light suddenly filled the room, just as an unseen force blasted me away. I hit a wall, my brain barely registering the pain. The small house shook, and with one hand, I tried to grab something and brace myself. I squeezed my eyes shut but could still see starbursts. Time slowed. My heartbeat slowed.

Then—it all stopped. Everything. The light. The tremors. I

breathed normally. All was quiet and still, as though I'd imagined what had just happened.

I blinked, trying to bring my eyes back into focus and assess the situation. I did my best to scramble clumsily to my feet and saw Dimitri was doing the same. He looked like he'd also been knocked over but had caught the wall for support, rather than smashing into it. Robert was lying flat out on the floor, and Victor rushed over to help him. Sydney just stood frozen.

And Sonya?

"Unbelievable," I whispered.

Sonya was still in the armchair, and from the way she was sitting back, it was obvious that she'd been blasted by the same force that had hit the rest of us. The chains were still around her, but she'd stopped struggling. On her lap was the silver stake Robert had held only moments ago. Sonya managed to wiggle a hand out of the chain, just enough for her fingers to brush against the stake's surface. Her eyes widened with wonder—eyes that were a rich, azure blue.

Robert had brought Sonya Karp back to life. She was no longer Strigoi.

When Lissa had saved Dimitri, I'd felt the magic's power through the bond, giving me the full and overwhelming experience of it all. Witnessing it now, without the firsthand knowledge provided from Lissa, was still just as incredible. Victor was preoccupied with Robert, but the rest of us couldn't stop staring at Sonya in amazement. I kept looking for anything—*anything*—that might give the slightest hint of her previous existence.

There was none. Her skin bore the typical Moroi paleness, but it was still filled with the warmth of life, with the faintest tinge of color—not like the Strigoi, who were completely devoid of pigment. Her eyes were bloodshot, but that was from her rapidly forming tears. There was no red ring around her irises. And the look in those eyes . . . there was no cruelty or malice. They were not the eyes of someone who had just threatened to kill us all. Her eyes were all shock and fear and confusion. I couldn't tear my gaze from her.

A miracle. Another miracle. Even after seeing Lissa restore Dimitri, some secret part of me had believed I would never witness anything like it again. That was how miracles worked. Once in a lifetime. There'd been a lot of talk about using spirit to save Strigoi everywhere, talk that had faded when other drama—such as the murder of a queen—took precedence at Court. The shortage of spirit users had also made the idea unpopular, and besides, everyone knew the difficulties involved with a Moroi staking a Strigoi. If trained guardians died fighting Strigoi, how could a Moroi stake one? Well, here was the answer: a subdued Strigoi. A Moroi could manage staking one with two hands, especially with guardian backup. The possibilities made me reel. Robert's magic was strong, but he was old and frail. Yet, if he had still done this, could any spirit user? He'd almost made it look easy. Could Adrian do it? Could Lissa do it again?

A miracle. Sonya Karp was a living, breathing miracle.

And suddenly, she began screaming.

It started off as kind of a low wail and rapidly grew in

volume. The noise snapped me to attention, but I didn't exactly know how to respond. Dimitri did. His stake fell from his hand, and he rushed to Sonya's side, where he began trying to free her from the chains. She floundered at his touch, but her efforts no longer packed the supernatural strength of an undead monster seeking revenge. These were the motions of someone desperately, terribly afraid.

I'd wrapped those chains pretty securely, but Dimitri had them off in seconds. Once Sonya was free, he sat in the chair and pulled her to him, letting her bury her face against his chest and sob. I swallowed. Dimitri had also wept when he had been changed back. An odd image of newborn babies flashed through my mind. Was crying the natural reaction for anyone being born—or, in this case, reborn—into the world?

A sudden movement grabbed my attention. Sydney's eyes were wide, and she was actually moving toward Dimitri—to stop him. "What are you doing?" she cried. "Don't release her!"

Dimitri ignored Sydney, and I caught hold of her, pulling her back. "It's okay, it's okay," I said. Sydney was the most stable factor in this whole operation. I couldn't have her freaking out. "She's not Strigoi. Look. Look at her. She's Moroi."

Sydney slowly shook her head. "She can't be. I just saw her."

"It's what happened to Dimitri. Exactly the same. You don't think he's a Strigoi, do you? You trust him." I released my hold on her, and she stayed put, her face wary.

Looking down at the brothers, I realized theirs might be a

more serious situation than I had realized. Robert, while not a Strigoi, looked pale enough to be one. His eyes were vacant, drool escaping his partially open mouth. I reassessed my earlier observation about Robert making Strigoi restoration look easy. He'd staked her like a pro, but obviously, there were a few side effects. Victor was trying to support his brother and murmured soothing and encouraging words. And on Victor's face . . . well, there was a look of compassion and fear that I'd never seen before. My brain didn't entirely know how to reconcile it with my well-defined and villainous image of him. He seemed like a real person.

Victor glanced up at me, his lips twisting into a bitter smile. "What, no witty quips now? You should be happy. We've given you what you wanted. You need answers from Sonya Karp?" He nodded toward her. "Go get them. They've certainly come at a high price."

"No!" exclaimed Dimitri. He still held Sonya against him, but his gentle expression turned hard at Victor's words. "Are you crazy? Didn't you see what just happened?"

Victor arched an eyebrow. "Yes. I noticed."

"She's in no condition to answer anything! She's in shock. Leave her alone."

"Don't act like *she's* the one who's suffering here," snapped Victor. Turning back to Robert, Victor helped his brother stand and go toward the couch. Robert barely managed it, his legs trembling and then giving way as he sat down. Victor put an arm around Robert. "You'll be all right. Everything's all right."

"Will he be?" I asked uncertainly. Robert didn't look like he was in all that good of shape. My earlier thoughts about spirit users saving Strigoi continued growing unrealistic. "He . . . he did it before and recovered, right? And Lissa's fine."

"Robert was much younger—as is Vasilisa," replied Victor, patting Robert's shoulder. "And this is hardly a simple spell. Doing it even once is monumental. Twice? Well, you and I both know how spirit works, and this feat takes a toll on both body and mind. Robert has made a great sacrifice for you."

He had, I supposed. "Thank you, Robert," I said. The words came hesitantly to my lips. Robert didn't seem to hear.

Dimitri stood up, lifting Sonya easily in his arms. She was still crying, but her sobs were quieter now.

"She needs to rest," he said gruffly. "Believe me, you have no idea what's going on inside her right now."

"Oh, I believe you," I said.

"You're idiots," snapped Victor. "Both of you."

It was a wonder Dimitri's glare didn't pin Victor to the floor. "No interrogation yet."

I nodded my agreement, not knowing what else to do. When Lissa had changed Dimitri, she'd taken on a fierce, similarly protective attitude. He might not have been the one to change Sonya, but he was the only one here who had any idea what she was going through. I knew he'd had a hard adjustment and that the initial effects of the restoration had been disorienting. That wasn't even taking into account the subsequent depression.

He swept past all of us, taking Sonya to her bedroom. Sydney watched them go and then glanced over to the sofa, where

Victor still had his arm wrapped around his brother. The Alchemist met my eyes wonderingly.

"I heard . . . but I didn't believe."

"Sometimes," I told her, "I still don't. It goes against every rule of the universe."

To my surprise, she touched the small gold cross around her neck. "Some rules are bigger than the universe."

Victor rose from the couch, apparently satisfied Robert was resting. I tensed up. Miracles aside, he was still a criminal, one I intended to capture. He took a step toward me, pitching his voice low.

"Sorry to interrupt Metaphysics 101, but you need to listen to me," he said. "Be careful, Rose. Very careful. A lot rests on you now. Don't let your pet wolf keep you from finding out what Sonya knows."

"But he's right," I exclaimed. "It's been five minutes! What she went through . . . what they both went through . . . well, it's kind of a big deal. Literally life-changing. He had to recover too and adjust to being saved. Once she does, she'll help us."

"Are you sure?" he asked, narrowing his eyes. "Will *she* think she's been saved? You forget: Belikov was turned against his will. She wasn't."

"W-what are you saying? That she's going to try to become Strigoi again?"

He shrugged. "I'm saying get your answers soon. And don't leave her alone."

With that, Victor turned and headed toward the kitchen. He soon returned with a glass of water. Robert drank it greedily and then fell into a heavy sleep. I sighed and leaned against a wall near Sydney, totally worn out. I still hurt from the earlier fight.

"What now?" asked Sydney.

I shook my head. "I don't know. We wait, I guess."

Dimitri returned a little while later and spared a small glance for Robert. "She's sleeping too," he told me. "The transformation . . . it's difficult." I could see a haunted look in his eyes and wondered what memory was tormenting him now. The memory of being changed? The memory of being Strigoi?

"I don't think we should leave Sonya alone," I said. Out of the corner of my eye, I saw Victor smirk. "Someone should stay with her in case she wakes up. She won't know what's going on."

Dimitri didn't answer for a few seconds as he scrutinized me. He knew me well enough to sense there might be something else on my mind. Fortunately, he couldn't find a fault in my logic.

"You're right. Do you mind sitting with her?" he asked Sydney.

I groped for something to say. No, no. Not Sydney. If Sonya did turn on us, we needed someone else on guard—someone who could fight back. Sydney, probably guessing my problem, saved me from lying to Dimitri—or from telling him the truth about my concerns.

"She doesn't know me. It might make things worse when she wakes up. Besides . . ." Sydney put on that disgusted expression that Alchemists excelled at. "I don't really feel that comfortable with someone who was a monster five minutes ago."

"She's not Strigoi," he exclaimed. "She's absolutely, completely Moroi again!" Even I felt a little cowed by the harshness of his voice, but I wasn't entirely surprised at his vehement reaction. He'd had a hard time convincing others he'd changed. His face softened a little. "I know it's hard to believe, but she really has changed."

"I'll stay with her then," I said.

"No, no." Dimitri shook his head. "Sydney's right about one thing: Sonya might be confused. It's better if someone's there who understands what's happened."

I started to argue that I was the only one Sonya really knew but then decided I'd rather stay with the brothers. They seemed harmless now, but I didn't trust them. Dimitri apparently didn't either. He took a few steps forward and leaned down, speaking only an inch from my ear.

"Keep an eye on them," he murmured. "Robert's down right now but might recover sooner than we think."

"I know."

He started to turn, then glanced back at me. His commander face had softened into something thoughtful and awestruck. "Rose?"

"Yeah?"

"That . . . was that what it was like when Lissa changed me?"

"More or less."

"I didn't realize . . . it was . . ." He struggled for words. It was uncharacteristic. "The way that light filled the room, the way she changed. Seeing that life emerge from death . . . it was . . ."

"Beautiful?"

He nodded. "Life like that . . . you don't—no, you *can't* waste it."

"No," I agreed. "You can't."

I saw something shift in him then. It was small, just like in the alley, but I knew then another piece of the Strigoi-trauma had peeled away.

He said no more, and I watched as he walked back down the hall. With nothing else to do, Sydney sat down cross-legged on the floor, holding a book in her lap. It was closed, her thoughts clearly elsewhere. Meanwhile, Victor sat back in the armchair and reclined it. He didn't look as bad as Robert, but lines of fatigue showed on both brothers. Good. The longer they were out of commission, the better. I brought in a chair from the kitchen so I could sit and survey the room. Everything was peaceful.

I felt like a babysitter, which I suppose I kind of was. It had been a long day, and night soon turned the windows black. This made worried me. For all I knew, Sonya had some Strigoi pals who might stop by. The fact that Donovan knew her certainly indicated she wasn't a total outcast among them. It made me extra-vigilant, but at the same time, I was exhausted. The brothers were already asleep. Sydney, perhaps in an attempt to keep her human schedule, eventually found a spare blanket and pillow and curled up in a makeshift bed on the floor.

And me? I was halfway between human and vampiric

schedules. I had a feeling Dimitri was the same. Really, we were on a do-what's-necessary schedule, in which extensive sleep was not an option.

A hum of excitement and astonishment suddenly sang through the bond. I sensed no danger or threat, but curiosity made me decide to check in with Lissa anyway. Even if I was in her mind, I knew my body would stay watchful, and I wanted to know how the rest of Lissa's test had gone.

Beautifully, of course. She rode back to Court, exhausted but proud of herself. She wasn't the only one. The rest of her companions all wore similar expressions . . . all except for Ava Drozdov. She had been the only one to break and use the cell phone to call for help. Lissa was surprised that Ava had cracked. After his earlier bitching, Marcus Lazar had seemed the most likely to bail. But no, the old man had managed it somehow, meaning he'd continue on in the monarch trials. Ava refused to make eye contact with anyone, instead staring bleakly out the window as they traveled back to Court. She would still hold a Council spot, but her shot at being queen was gone.

Lissa felt bad for her but couldn't spare too much concern. It was the way of the trials, the way they determined the best candidates. Besides, Lissa had her own issues. Staying out in the daytime had run contrary to the normal vampiric schedule. Now, she simply wanted to get back to Court, find her room, and sleep for a few hours. She wanted some peace.

Instead, she found a mob waiting for her.

Nineteen

The vans parked in a semi-remote part of Court, so seeing the area packed with eager Moroi was quite a shock to Lissa. Guardians moved through the people like ghosts, just as they had at the nomination session, keeping as much order as possible. The crowd kept getting in the way as the vans attempted to reach the garages, and faces looked in the windows, trying to get a glimpse of the royal candidates.

Lissa stared at the masses in shock, almost afraid to get out. Ariana gave her a comforting smile. "This is normal. They all want to know who made it and who didn't. *They* especially want to know." She inclined her head toward the front of the van. Peering through the windshield, Lissa spied the other six candidates. Because the forest course could only accommodate so many people, the group had been split in half. The rest of the candidates would take the same test tomorrow and were no doubt curious who among their competitors had passed today.

Lissa was used to order and decorum around royals, so she was astonished to see such eagerness and frenzy among them now. And of course, the "common" Moroi who'd been arriving at Court were mixed into the crowd too. Everyone was pushing, peering over the heads of others to find out what had happened. People were shouting some of the candidates' names, and I was half-surprised they hadn't come up with songs and banners.

Lissa and her companions exited the van and were met with a wave of cheers that rippled through the crowd. It became obvious pretty quickly who had passed and who hadn't. This sent the crowd abuzz even more. Lissa stood rooted to the spot, staring around and feeling lost. It was one thing to rationally discuss the pros of her running for queen with her friends. It was an entirely different matter to suddenly be thrust into what the elections truly meant.

Her focus had been limited to a few things: my safety, finding the murderer, and surviving the tests. Now, as she took in the crowd, she realized the election was bigger than her, bigger than anything she could have imagined. For these people, it wasn't a joke. It wasn't a scam to twist the law and stall for time. Their lives were figuratively on the line. Moroi and dhampirs lived inside various countries and obeyed those laws, but they also obeyed *this* government, the one that operated out of the Court. It reached around the world and affected every dhampir and Moroi who chose to stay in our society. We had some voting, yes, but the king or queen shaped our futures.

The guardians in charge of the crowds finally gave the okay for family members to push through the masses and collect their nominees. Lissa had no one. Both Janine and Eddie—despite earlier claims—were occasionally given temporary tasks that prevented them from being with Lissa 24/7, and she certainly had no family to come for her. Adrift, she felt dizzy in the chaos, still stunned by her moment of clarity. Conflicting emotions warred within her. Deceiving everyone made her feel unworthy, like she should resign her candidacy right now. At the same time, she suddenly wanted to be worthy of the elections. She wanted to hold her head high and walk into the tests proudly, even if she was taking them for ulterior motives.

A strong hand at last caught hold of her arm. Christian. "Come on. Let's get out of here." He pulled her away, shouldering through the onlookers. "Hey," he called to a couple guardians on the crowd's periphery. "A little help here for the princess?"

It was the first time I had ever seen him act like a royal, throwing around the authority of his bloodline. To me, he was snarky, cynical Christian. In Moroi society, at eighteen, he could now technically be addressed as Lord Ozera. I'd forgotten that. The two guardians hadn't. They rushed to Lissa's side, helping Christian part the crowd. The faces around her were a blur, the noise a dull roar. Yet, every once in a while, something would come through to her. The chanting of her name. Declarations about the return of the dragon, which was the symbol of the Dragomir family. *This is real*, she kept thinking. *This is real.*

The guardians efficiently led her out of it all and back across the Court's grounds to her building. They released her once they considered her safe, and she graciously thanked them for their help. When she and Christian were in her room, she sank onto the bed, stunned.

"Oh my God," she said. "That was insane."

Christian smiled. "Which part? Your welcome home party?

Or the test itself? You look like you just . . . well, I'm not really sure *what* you just did."

Lissa took a quick survey of herself. They'd given her dry towels on the ride home, but her clothing was still damp and was wrinkling as it dried. Her shoes and jeans had mud all over them, and she didn't even want to think about what her hair looked like.

"Yeah, we—"

The words stuck on her tongue—and not because she suddenly decided not to tell him.

"I can't say," she murmured. "It really worked. The spell won't let me."

"What spell?" he asked.

Lissa rolled up her sleeve and lifted the bandage to show him the tiny tattooed dot on her arm. "It's a compulsion spell so I won't talk about the test. Like the Alchemists have."

"Wow," he said, truly impressed. "I never actually thought those worked."

"I guess so. It's really weird. I want to talk about it, but I just . . . can't."

"It's okay," he said, brushing some of her damp hair aside. "You passed. That's what matters. Just focus on that."

"The only thing I want to focus on right now is a shower—which is kind of ironic, considering how soaked I am." She didn't move, though, and instead stared off at the far wall.

"Hey," said Christian gently. "What's wrong? Did the crowd scare you?"

She turned back to him. "No, that's the thing. I mean, they

were intimidating, yeah. But I just realized . . . I don't know. I realized I'm part of a major process, one that's gone on since—"

"The beginning of time?" teased Christian, quoting Nathan's nonsensical statement.

"Nearly," she answered, with a small smile that soon faded. "This goes beyond tradition, Christian. The elections are a core part of our society. Ingrained. We can talk about changing age laws or fighting or whatever, but this is ancient. And far-reaching. Those people out there? They're not all Americans. They've come from other countries. I forget sometimes that even though the Court is here, it rules Moroi everywhere. What happens here affects the whole world."

"Where are you going with this?" he asked. She was lost in her own thoughts and couldn't see Christian as objectively as I could. He knew Lissa. He understood her and loved her. The two of them had a synchronicity similar to what Dimitri and I shared. Sometimes, however, Lissa's thoughts spun in directions he couldn't guess. He'd never admit it, but I knew part of why he loved her was that—unlike me, who everyone knew was impetuous—Lissa always seemed the picture of calmness and rationality. Then, she'd do something totally unexpected. Those moments delighted him—but sometimes scared him because he never knew just how much a role spirit was playing in her actions. Now was one of those times. He knew the elections were stressing her, and like me, he knew that could bring out the worst.

"I'm going to take these tests seriously," she said. "It's—it's shameful not to. An insult to our society. My ultimate goal is to find out who framed Rose, but in the meantime? I'm going to go through the trials like someone who intends to be queen."

Christian hesitated before speaking, a rarity for him. "Do you *want* to be queen?"

That snapped Lissa from her dreamy philosophizing about tradition and honor. "No! Of course not. I'm eighteen. I can't even drink yet."

"That's never stopped you from doing it," he pointed out, becoming more like his usual self.

"I'm serious! I want to go to college. I want Rose back. I *don't* want to rule the Moroi nation."

A sly look lit Christian's blue eyes. "You know, Aunt Tasha makes jokes about how you'd actually be a better queen than the others, except sometimes . . . I don't think she's joking."

Lissa groaned and stretched back on the bed. "I love her, but we've got to keep her in check. If anyone could actually get that law changed, it would be her and her activist friends."

"Well, don't worry. The thing about her 'activist friends' is that they have so much to protest, they don't usually get behind one thing at the same time." Christian stretched out beside her and pulled her close. "But for what it's worth, I think you'd be a great queen too, Princess Dragomir."

"You're going to get dirty," she warned.

"Already am. Oh, you mean from your clothes?" He wrapped his arms around her, heedless of her damp and muddy state. "I spent most of my childhood hiding in a dusty attic and own exactly one dress shirt. You really think I care about this T-shirt?"

She laughed and then kissed him, letting her mind free itself of worry for a moment and just savor the feel of his lips. Considering they were on a bed, I wondered if it was time for me to go. After several seconds, she pulled back and sighed contentedly.

"You know, sometimes I think I love you."

"Sometimes?" he asked in mock outrage.

She ruffled his hair. "All the time. But I've got to keep you on your toes."

"Consider me kept."

He brought his lips toward hers again but stopped when a knock sounded at the door. Lissa pulled back from the near-kiss, but neither of them broke from the embrace.

"Don't answer," said Christian.

Lissa frowned, peering toward the living room. She slipped out of his arms, stood up, and walked toward the door. When she was several feet from it, she nodded knowingly. "It's Adrian."

"More reason not to answer," said Christian.

Lissa ignored him and opened the door, and sure enough, my devil-may-care boyfriend stood there. From behind Lissa, I heard Christian say, "Worst. Timing. Ever."

Adrian studied Lissa and then looked at Christian sprawling on the bed on the far side of the suite. "Huh," Adrian said, letting himself in. "So that's how you're going to fix the family problem. Little Dragomirs. Good idea."

Christian sat up and strolled toward them. "Yeah, that's exactly it. You're interrupting official Council business."

Adrian was dressed casually for him, jeans and a black T-shirt, though he made it look like designer clothing. Actually, it probably was. God, I missed him. I missed them all.

"What's going on?" asked Lissa. While Christian seemed to consider Adrian's arrival a personal offense, Lissa knew that Adrian wouldn't be here without a good reason—especially this early in the Moroi day. Although he had on his normal lazy smile, there was an excited and eager glitter in his aura. He had news.

"I've got him," said Adrian. "Got him trapped."

"Who?" asked Lissa, startled.

"That idiot Blake Lazar."

"What do you mean trapped?" asked Christian, as perplexed as Lissa. "Did you set out a bear trap on the tennis courts or something?"

"I wish. He's over at the Burning Arrow. I just bought another round, so he should still be there if we hurry. He thinks I went out for a cigarette."

Judging from the scent wreathing Adrian, Lissa had a feeling he actually had been out for a cigarette. And likely shared in the round. "You've been at a bar this early?"

Adrian shrugged. "It's not early for humans."

"But you're not—"

"Come *on*, cousin." Adrian's aura didn't have the muted colors of someone who was completely drunk, but yes, he'd definitely had a few drinks. "If pretty boy Ambrose was right about Aunt Tatiana, then this guy can tell us the names of other jealous women."

"Why didn't you ask him yourself?" asked Christian.

"Because me asking about my aunt's sex life would be sick and wrong," said Adrian. "Whereas Blake will be more than happy to talk to our charming princess here."

Lissa really wanted her bed, but finding out anything to help me sparked a new rush of energy within her. "Okay, let me at least get some different clothes and brush my hair."

While she was changing in the bathroom, she heard Adrian say to Christian, "You know, your shirt's kind of grungy-looking. Seems like you could put in a little more effort since you're dating a princess."

Fifteen minutes or so later, the threesome were on their way across Court to a tucked away bar inside an administrative building. I'd been there before and had originally thought it was a weird place to house a bar. But, after a recent stint of filing, I'd decided that if I were doing office work for living, I'd probably want a quick source of alcohol on hand, too.

The bar was dimly lit, both for mood and Moroi comfort. Adrian's joking aside, it really was early for Moroi, and only a couple patrons were there. Adrian made a small gesture to the bartender, which I presumed was some kind of ordering signal because the woman immediately turned and began pouring a drink.

"Hey, Ivashkov! Where'd you go?"

A voice called over to Lissa and the others, and after a few moments, she spotted a lone guy sitting at a corner table. As Adrian led them closer, Lissa saw that the guy was young—about Adrian's age, with curly black hair and brilliant teal eyes, kind of like Abe's recent tie. It was as though someone had taken the stunning color of both Adrian and Christian's eyes and mixed them together. He had a leanly muscled body—about as buff as any Moroi could manage—and, even with a boyfriend, Lissa could admire how hot he was.

"To get better-looking company," replied Adrian, pulling out a chair.

The Moroi then noticed Adrian's companions and jumped up. He caught hold of Lissa's hand, leaned over, and kissed it. "Princess Dragomir. It's an honor to meet you at last. Seeing you from a distance was beautiful. Up close? Divine."

"This," said Adrian grandly, "is Blake Lazar."

"It's nice to meet you," she said.

Blake smiled radiantly. "May I call you Vasilisa?"

"You can call me Lissa."

"You can also," added Christian, "let go of her hand now."

Blake looked over at Christian, taking a few more moments to release Lissa's hand—seeming very proud about those extra seconds. "I've seen you too. Ozera. Crispin, right?"

"Christian," corrected Lissa.

"Right." Blake pulled out a chair, still playing the over-the-top gentleman. "Please. Join us." He made no such offer to Christian, who went out of his way to sit close to Lissa. "What would you like to drink? It's on me."

"Nothing," said Lissa.

The bartender appeared just then, bringing Adrian's drink and another for Blake. "Never too early. Ask Ivashkov. You drink as soon as you roll out of bed, right?"

"There's a bottle of scotch right on my nightstand," said Adrian, still keeping his tone light. Lissa opened her eyes to his aura. It bore the bright gold all spirit users had, still muddled slightly from alcohol. It also had the faintest tinge of red—not true anger, but definite annoyance. Lissa recalled that neither Adrian nor Ambrose had had a good opinion of this Blake guy.

"So what brings you and Christopher here?" asked Blake. He finished a glass of something amber colored and set it down beside the new drink.

"*Christian*," said Christian.

"We were talking about my aunt earlier," said Adrian. Again, he managed to sound very conversational, but no matter how much he might want to clear my name, delving into the details of Tatiana's murder obviously bothered him.

Blake's smile diminished a little. "How depressing. For both of you." That was directed to Adrian and Lissa. Christian might as well have not existed. "Sorry about Hathaway too," he added to Lissa alone. "I've heard how upset you've been. Who'd have seen that coming?"

Lissa realized he was referring to how she'd been pretending to be angry and hurt by me. "Well," she said bitterly. "I guess you just don't know people. There were a million clues beforehand. I just didn't pay attention."

"You must be upset too," said Christian. "We heard you and the queen were kind of close."

Blake's grin returned. "Yeah . . . we knew each other pretty well. I'm going to miss her. She might have seemed cold to some people, but believe me, she knew how to have a good time." Blake glanced at Adrian. "You must have known that."

"Not in the way you did." Adrian paused to take a sip of his own drink. I think he needed it to restrain any snippy remarks, and honestly, I didn't begrudge him it. I actually admired his self-control. If I'd been in his place, I would have long since punched Blake. "Or Ambrose."

Blake's pretty smile transformed into a full-fledged scowl. "Him? That blood whore? He didn't deserve to be in her presence. I can't even believe they let him stay at Court."

"He actually thinks *you* killed the queen." Lissa then added hastily, "Which is ridiculous when all the evidence proves Rose did it." Those hadn't been Ambrose's exact words, but she wanted to see if she could elicit a reaction. She did.

"He thinks *what*?" Yes. Definitely no smile now. Without it, Blake suddenly didn't seem as good-looking as earlier. "That lying bastard! I have an alibi, and he knows it. He's just pissed off because she liked me better."

"Then why'd she keep him around?" asked Christian, face almost angelic. "Weren't you enough?"

Blake fixed him with a glare while finishing the new drink in nearly one gulp. Almost by magic, the bartender appeared with another. Blake nodded his thanks before continuing. "Oh, I was more than enough. More than enough for a dozen women, but *I* didn't fool around on the side like he did."

Adrian's expression was growing increasingly pained at each mention of Tatiana's sex life. Still, he played his role. "I suppose you're talking about Ambrose's other girlfriends?"

"Yup. But 'girl' is kind of extreme. They were all older, and honestly, I think they paid him. Not that your mom needed to pay anyone," added Blake. "I mean, she's actually pretty hot. But you know, she couldn't really be with him in any real way."

It seemed to take all of them a moment to follow what Blake was alluding to. Adrian caught on first. "*What* did you just say?"

"Oh." Blake looked legitimately surprised, but it was hard to say if it was an act. "I thought you knew. Your mom and Ambrose . . . well, who could blame her? With your dad? Though just between you and me, I think she could have done better." Blake's tone implied exactly whom he thought Daniella could have done better with.

In Lissa's vision, Adrian's aura flared red. "You son of a bitch!" Adrian was not the fighting type, but there was a first time for everything—and Blake had just crossed a serious line. "My mom was *not* cheating on my dad. And even if she was . . . she sure as hell wouldn't have to pay for it."

Blake didn't seem fazed, but maybe things would have been different if Adrian actually had hit him. Lissa rested her hand on Adrian's arm and squeezed it gently. "Easy," she murmured. I felt the smallest tingle of calming compulsion move from her into him. Adrian recognized it immediately and pulled his arm back, giving her a look that said he didn't appreciate her "help."

"I thought you didn't like your dad," said Blake, utterly clueless that his news *might* be upsetting. "And besides, don't get all pissy at me. *I* wasn't sleeping with her. I'm just telling you what I heard. Like I said, if you want to start accusing random people, go after someone like Ambrose."

Lissa jumped in to keep Adrian from saying anything. "How many women? Do you know who else he was involved with?"

"Three others." Blake ticked off names on his hand. "Marta Drozdov and Mirabel Conta. Wait. That's two. I was thinking with Daniella; that's three. But then, that's four with the queen. Yeah, four."

Lissa didn't concern herself with Blake's faulty math skills, though it did support Adrian's previous "idiot" claims. Marta Drozdov was a semi-notorious royal who had taken to traveling the world in her old age. By Lissa's estimation, Marta was hardly in the U.S. most of the year, let alone Court. She didn't seem invested enough to murder Tatiana. As for Mirabel Conta . . . she was notorious in a different way. She was known for sleeping with half the guys at Court, married or otherwise. Lissa didn't know her well, but Mirabel had never seemed overly interested in any one guy.

"Sleeping with other women wouldn't really give him a motive for killing the queen," pointed out Lissa.

"No," agreed Blake. "Like I said, it's obvious that Hathaway girl did it." He paused. "Damned shame too. She's pretty hot. God, that body. Anyway, if Ambrose had killed her, he'd have done it because he was jealous of me, because Tatiana liked me better. Not because of all those other women he was doing."

"Why wouldn't Ambrose just kill you?" asked Christian. "Makes more sense."

Blake didn't have a chance to respond because Adrian was still back on the earlier topic, his eyes flashing with anger. "My mother wasn't sleeping with anybody. She doesn't even sleep with my father."

Blake continued in his oblivious way. "Hey, I saw them. They were all over each other. Did I mention how hot your—"

"Stop it," warned Lissa. "It's not helping."

Adrian clenched his glass. "None of this is helping!" Clearly, things weren't going the way he'd hoped when he'd first summoned Lissa and Christian from her room. "And I'm not going to sit and listen to this bullshit." Adrian downed the drink and shot up from his chair, turning abruptly for the exit. He tossed some cash on the bar before walking out the door.

"Poor guy," said Blake. He was back to his calm, arrogant self. "He's been through a lot between his aunt, mom, and murdering girlfriend. That's why really, at the end of the day, you just can't trust women." He winked at Lissa. "Present company excluded, of course."

Lissa felt as disgusted as Adrian, and a quick glance at Christian's stormy face showed he felt the same. It was time to go before someone really did punch Blake. "Well, it's been great talking to you, but we need to go."

Blake gave her puppy-dog eyes. "But you just got here! I was hoping we could get to know each other." It went without saying what he meant by that. "Oh. And Kreskin too."

Christian didn't even bother with a correction this time. He simply took hold of Lissa's hand. "We have to go."

"Yeah," agreed Lissa.

Blake shrugged and waved for another drink. "Well, any time you want to really experience the world, come find me."

Christian and Lissa headed for the door, with Christian muttering, "I really hope that last part was meant for you, not me."

"That's no world I want to experience," said Lissa with a grimace. They stepped outside, and she glanced around, in case Adrian had lingered. Nope. He was gone, and she didn't blame him. "I can see now why Ambrose and Adrian don't like him. He's such a . . ."

"Asshole?" supplied Christian. They turned toward her building.

"I suppose so."

"Enough to commit murder?"

"Honestly? No." Lissa sighed. "I kind of agree with Ambrose . . . I don't think Blake's smart enough for murder. Or that the motive's really there. I can't tell if people are lying or not from their auras, but his didn't reveal anything overly dishonest. You joked, but if anyone was going to commit a jealous murder, why wouldn't the guys want to kill each other? A lot easier."

"They did both have easy access to Tatiana," Christian reminded her.

"I know. But if there *is* love and sex involved here . . . it seems like it'd be someone jealous of the queen. A woman."

A long, meaningful pause hung between them, neither of them wanting to say what they were both likely thinking. Finally, Christian broke the silence.

"Say, like, Daniella Ivashkov?"

Lissa shook her head. "I can't believe that. She doesn't seem like the type."

"Murderers never seem like the type. That's why they get away with it."

"Have you been studying up on your criminology or something?"

"No." They reached her building's front door, and he opened it for Lissa. "Just laying out some facts. We know Adrian's mom never liked Tatiana for personality reasons. Now we find out that they were sharing the same guy."

"She has an alibi," said Lissa stonily.

"Everyone has an alibi," he reminded her. "And as we've learned, those can be paid for. In fact, Daniella's already paid for one."

"I still can't believe it. Not without more proof. Ambrose swore this was more political than personal."

"Ambrose isn't off the list either."

They came to Lissa's room. "This is harder than I thought it would be." They went inside, and Christian wrapped his arms around her.

"I know. But we'll do it together. We'll figure it out. But . . . we might want to keep some of this to ourselves. Maybe I'm overreacting here, but I think it'd be best if we don't ever,

ever tell Adrian his mom has an excellent motive for having killed his aunt."

"Oh, you think?" She rested her head against his chest and yawned.

"Naptime," said Christian, leading her toward the bed.

"I still need a shower."

"Sleep first. Shower later." He pulled back the covers. "I'll sleep with you."

"Sleep or *sleep*?" she asked dryly, sliding gratefully into bed.

"Real sleep. You need it." He crawled in beside her, spooning against her and resting his face on her shoulder. "Of course, afterward, if you want to conduct any official Council business . . ."

"I swear, if you say 'Little Dragomirs,' you can sleep in the hall."

I'm sure there was a patented Christian retort coming, but another knock cut him off. He looked up in exasperation. "Don't answer it. For real this time."

But Lissa couldn't help herself. She broke from his embrace and climbed out of bed. "It's not Adrian . . ."

"Then it's probably not important," said Christian.

"We don't know that." She got up and opened the door, revealing—my mother.

Janine Hathaway swept into the room as casually as Adrian had, her eyes sharp as she studied every detail around her for a threat. "Sorry I was away," she told Lissa. "Eddie and I wanted to set up an alternating system, but we both got pulled for duty earlier." She glanced over at the rumpled bed, with Christian in it, but being who she was, she came to a pragmatic conclusion, not a romantic one. "Just in time. I figured you'd want to sleep after the test. Don't worry—I'll keep watch and make sure nothing happens."

Christian and Lissa exchanged rueful looks.

"Thanks," said Lissa.

TWENTY

"YOU SHOULD SLEEP."

Sydney's soft voice nearly made me leap out of my skin, proving that even while in Lissa's mind, I could still stay alert. I tuned back to Sonya's dark living room. Aside from Sydney, everything was quiet and at peace.

"You look like the walking dead," she continued. "And I don't say that lightly."

"I've got to stay on watch," I said.

"I'll watch. You sleep."

"You're not trained like me," I pointed out. "You might miss something."

"Even I wouldn't miss Strigoi beating down the door," she replied. "Look, I know you guys are tough. You don't have to convince me. But I have a feeling things are going to get harder, and I don't want you passing out at some crucial moment. If you sleep now, you can relieve Dimitri later."

Only the mention of Dimitri made me give in. We *would* need to relieve each other eventually. So, reluctantly, I crawled into Sydney's bed on the floor, giving her all sorts of instructions that I think she rolled her eyes at. I fell asleep almost instantly and then woke up just as quickly when I heard the sound of a door closing.

I immediately sat upright, expecting to see Strigoi busting down the door. Instead, I found sunlight creeping in through the windows and Sydney watching me with amusement. In the living room, Robert was sitting up on the couch, rubbing his eyes. Victor was gone. I turned to Sydney in alarm.

"He's in the bathroom," she said, anticipating my question.

That was the sound I'd heard. I exhaled in relief and stood up, surprised at how even a few hours of sleep had energized me. If I only had food, I'd be ready for anything. Sonya didn't have any, of course, but I settled for a glass of water in the kitchen. As I stood there drinking, I noticed that the Dashkov brothers had made themselves at home: coats hanging on hooks, car keys on the counter. I quietly grabbed hold of the keys and called for Sydney.

She came in, and I slipped her the keys, trying not to let them rattle.

"Do you still know about cars?" I murmured.

In one exquisite look, she told me that was a ridiculous and insulting question.

"Okay. Can you go do a grocery run? We're going to need food. And maybe on your way out, you can, um, make sure their car has engine trouble or something? Anything that keeps it here. But not something obvious, like slashed tires."

She put the keys in her pocket. "Easy. Got any food requests?"

I thought about it. "Something with sugar. And coffee for Dimitri."

"Coffee's a given," she said.

Victor stepped into the kitchen, his typically unconcerned expression making me think he hadn't heard me instructing Sydney to sabotage his car. "Sydney's getting groceries," I said, hoping to distract him before he might notice the missing keys. "Need anything?"

"A feeder would be nice, but barring that, Robert has an especial liking for Cheerios. The apple cinnamon kind." He smiled at Sydney. "I never thought I'd see the day an Alchemist would be an errand girl. It's charming."

Sydney opened her mouth, no doubt to make some biting comment, and I quickly shook my head. "Just go," I said.

She went, and Victor soon returned to Robert's side. Convinced the brothers wouldn't be going anywhere in full daylight without a car, I decided it was time to check on Dimitri. To my surprise, Sonya was awake. She sat cross-legged on the bed with him, and the two spoke in hushed tones. Her hair was disheveled from both sleep and fighting, but otherwise, she showed no cuts or bruises from the battle. Dimitri had been the same after his transformation, escaping terrible burns. The power of a Strigoi restoration healed all injuries. Between my skinned legs and pseudo-concussion, I kind of wished someone had transformed me from a Strigoi.

Sonya turned from Dimitri as I entered. A sequence of emotions passed across her face. Fear. Astonishment. Recognition.

"Rose?" There was hesitancy in the word, like she wondered if I was a hallucination.

I forced a smile. "It's good to see you again." I chose not to add, "Now that you're not trying to suck the life out of me."

She averted her eyes down to her hands, studying her fingers like they were magical and wonderful. Of course, after being a monster, maybe having her "old hands" back really was wondrous. The day after his change, Dimitri hadn't seemed quite so fragile, but he'd certainly been in shock. That was also when he'd grown depressed. Was she? Or did she want to turn again, as Victor had suggested?

I didn't know what to say. It was all so strange and awkward. "Sydney went for groceries," I told Dimitri lamely. "She also stayed up so that I could sleep last night."

"I know," he said with a small smile. "I got up once to check on you."

I felt myself flushing, somehow embarrassed that I'd been caught in weakness. "You can rest too," I told him. "Get some breakfast, and then I'll keep an eye on everything. I have it on good authority that Victor's going to have car trouble. Also that Robert really likes Cheerios, so if you want some, you're out of luck. He doesn't seem like the sharing type."

Dimitri's smile grew. Sonya suddenly lifted her head.

"There's another spirit user here," she said, voice frantic. "I can feel it. I remember him." She looked between Dimitri and me. "It's not safe. We're not safe. You shouldn't have us around."

"Everything's fine," said Dimitri, voice so, so gentle. That tone was rare for him, but I'd heard it before. He'd used it on me in some of my most desperate moments. "Don't worry."

Sonya shook her head. "No. You don't understand. We . . . we're capable of terrible things. To ourselves, to others.

It's why I changed, to stop the madness. And it did, except . . . it was worse. In its way. The things I did . . ."

There it was, the same remorse Dimitri had felt. Half-afraid he'd start telling her there was no redemption for her either, I said, "It wasn't you. You were controlled by something else."

She buried her face in her hands. "But I chose it. *Me*. I made it happen."

"That was spirit," I said. "It's hard to fight. Like you said, it can make you do terrible things. You weren't thinking clearly. Lissa battles with the same thing all the time."

"Vasilisa?" Sonya lifted her eyes and stared off into space. I think she was digging through memories. In fact, despite her ramblings now, I didn't believe she was quite as unstable as she'd been just before becoming Strigoi. We'd heard healings could lessen spirit's madness, and I think Robert's transformation had lightened some of the darkness within her for now. "Yes, of course. Vasilisa has it too." She turned to me in a panic. "Did you help her? Did you get her out of there?"

"I did," I said, trying to emulate Dimitri's gentleness. Lissa and I fled St. Vladimir's for a while, partly because of warnings from Sonya. "We left and then came back and, uh, were able to stop what was hunting her." I didn't think it was a good idea for Sonya to know that the thing—or rather, person—hunting Lissa was now sitting out in the living room. I took a step forward. "And you can help Lissa too. We need to know if—"

"No," said Dimitri. No gentleness now in the warning look he gave me. "Not yet."

"But—"

"Not yet."

I shot him a glare in return but said no more. I was all for giving Sonya her recuperation time, but we didn't have forever. The clock was ticking, and we had to find out what Sonya knew. I felt like Dimitri would have been able to give us this information immediately after he'd been changed back. Of course, he hadn't been unstable beforehand, so he'd kind of had an edge. Still. We couldn't play house in Kentucky forever.

"Can I see my flowers?" asked Sonya. "Can I go outside and see my flowers?"

Dimitri and I exchanged glances. "Of course," he said.

We all moved toward the door, and that's when I had to ask. "Why did you grow flowers when you were . . . like you were?"

She paused. "I've always grown flowers."

"I know. I remember. They were gorgeous. The ones here are gorgeous too. Is that why . . . I mean, did you just want a pretty garden, even as a Strigoi?"

The question was unexpected and seemed to throw her off. I was about to give up on an answer when she finally said, "No. I never thought about *pretty*. They were . . . I don't know. Something to do. I'd always grown flowers. I had to see if I still could. It was like . . . a test of my skills, I guess."

I met Dimitri's eyes again. So. Beauty hadn't been part of her world. It was just like I'd told him. Strigoi were notoriously arrogant, and it seemed the flowers had simply been a show of prowess. Growing them had also been a familiar habit for her, and I recalled how Dimitri had read Western novels while Strigoi. Being Strigoi might cost someone their sense of goodness and morality, but old behaviors and hobbies remained.

We took her out to the living room, interrupting a conversation between Victor and Robert. Sonya and Robert both froze, sizing each other up. Victor gave us one of his knowing smiles.

"Up and around. Have we found out what we need yet?"

Dimitri shot him a look similar to what I'd received when asking about interrogation. "Not yet."

Sonya dragged her gaze from Robert and moved quickly toward the patio door, pausing when she saw our shoddy patch job. "You broke my door," she said.

"Collateral damage," I said. In my periphery, I think Dimitri rolled his eyes.

Needing no guidance from us, Sonya opened the door and stepped outside. With a gasp, she came to a halt and stared upward. The sky was a perfect, cloudless blue, and the sun had crossed the horizon now, illuminating everything in gold. I went outside too, feeling the warmth of that light on my skin. Some of the night's coldness lingered, but we were in store for a hot day.

Everyone else came out too, but Sonya was oblivious. She lifted her hands upward, as though maybe she could grab hold of the sun and wrap it in her arms. "It's so beautiful." She finally looked away and met my eyes. "Isn't it? Have you ever seen anything so beautiful?"

"Beautiful," I reiterated. For some reason, I felt both happy and sad.

She walked around her yard, examining every plant and

flower. She touched the petals and inhaled their fragrance. "So different . . ." she kept saying to herself. "So different in the sun . . ." Several especially caught her attention. "These don't open at night! Do you see it? Do you see the colors? Can you smell that?"

The questions didn't seem to be for anyone in particular. We watched, all of us kind of hypnotized. At last, she settled into the patio chair, happily gazing around, lost in sensory overload—in that beauty that had been denied to her as a Strigoi. When it became obvious she wasn't leaving for a while, I turned to Dimitri and repeated Sydney's advice about him taking a turn at sleeping while we waited for Sonya to recover. To my surprise, he actually agreed.

"That's smart. Once Sonya's able to talk, we'll need to move." He smiled. "Sydney's turning into a battle mastermind."

"Hey, she's not in charge here," I teased. "She's just a soldier."

"Right." He lightly brushed his fingers against my cheek. "Sorry, Captain."

"General," I corrected, catching my breath at that brief touch.

He gave Sonya a kind goodbye before disappearing into the house. She nodded, but I don't know if she really heard. Victor and Robert brought out two wooden kitchen chairs and set them in the shade. I chose a spot on the ground. Nobody spoke. It wasn't the weirdest thing I'd ever experienced, but it was certainly strange.

Sydney returned later with the groceries, and I briefly abandoned the group to check in with her. Victor's keys were lying back on the counter, which I took as a good sign. Sydney unloaded an assortment of food and handed me a box of a dozen donuts.

"Hope that's enough for you," she remarked.

I made a face at her presumption but took the donuts anyway. "Come on outside when you're done," I told her. "It's like the barbecue of the damned. Except . . . there's no grill."

She looked puzzled, but when she joined us later, she seemed to get what I'd been saying. Robert brought out a bowl of Cheerios, but neither Sydney nor Victor ate. I gave Sonya a donut, the first thing that took her attention from her yard. She held it in her hands, turning it over and over.

"I don't know if I can. I don't know if I can eat it."

"Of course you can." I recalled how Dimitri had regarded food uncertainly too. "It's chocolate-glazed. Good stuff."

She took a tentative, rabbit-sized bite. She chewed it a billion times and finally swallowed. She closed her eyes briefly and sighed. "Such sweetness." Slowly, she continued taking more tiny bites. It took forever for her to get halfway through the donut, and at that point, she finally stopped. I'd polished off three donuts by then, and my impatience to accomplish something was growing. Part of it was still the irritability from spirit, and part of it was just my continual restlessness to help Lissa.

"Sonya," I said pleasantly, fully aware of how pissed off Dimitri was going to be at me defying his instructions. "We wanted to talk to you about something."

"Mm-hmm," she said, gazing at bees hovering around some honeysuckle.

"Is there a relative of yours . . . someone who, uh, had a baby a while ago . . . ?"

"Sure," she said. One of the bees flew from the honeysuckle to a rose, and she never looked away. "Lots."

"Articulate, Rosemarie," remarked Victor. "Very articulate."

I bit my lip, knowing an outburst would upset Sonya. And probably Robert too.

"This would be a secret baby," I told her. "And you were the beneficiary on a bank account that took care of the baby . . . an account paid for by Eric Dragomir."

Sonya's head whipped toward me, and there was no dreamy absentmindedness in her blue eyes now. A few seconds passed before she spoke. Her voice was cold and hard—not a Strigoi voice, but definitely a *back off* voice. "No. I don't know anything about that."

"She's lying," said Robert.

"I didn't need any powers to figure that out," scoffed Sydney.

I ignored both of them. "Sonya, we know you know, and it's really important we find this baby . . . er, child. Person." We'd made guesses on the age but weren't 100 percent sure. "You said you were worried about Lissa earlier. This will help her. She *needs* to know. She needs to know she has another family member."

Sonya turned her attention back to the bees, but I knew she was no longer watching them. "I don't know anything." There was a trembling in her voice, and something told me that maybe I shouldn't push this after all. I couldn't tell if she was afraid or on the verge of rage.

"Then why were you on the account?" This came from Victor.

"I don't know anything," she repeated. Her voice could have made icicles form on the ornamental trees. "Nothing."

"Stop lying," snapped Victor. "You know something, and you're going to tell us."

"Hey!" I exclaimed. "Be quiet. You don't have interrogation rights here."

"You didn't seem to be doing a very good job."

"Just shut up, okay?" I looked back at Sonya, replacing my glare with a smile. "Please," I begged. "Lissa's in trouble. This will help her. I thought you said before that you wanted to help her?"

"I promised . . ." said Sonya. Her voice was so low, I could barely hear it.

"Promised what?" I asked. *Patience, patience.* I had to remain calm. I couldn't risk a breakdown.

She squeezed her eyes shut and raked her hands through her hair violently, almost like a child about to have a tantrum. "Promised not to tell. Promised not to tell anyone . . ."

I had the urge to run over and shake her. *Patience, patience,* I repeated to myself. *Don't upset her.* "We wouldn't ask you to break your promise if it wasn't important. Maybe . . . maybe you can get in touch with this person . . ." Who had she promised? Eric's mistress? "And see if it's okay to tell us?"

"Oh for God's sake," said Victor irritably. "This is ridiculous and getting us nowhere." He glanced at his brother. "Robert?"

Robert hadn't done much so far today, but at Victor's command, Robert leaned forward. "Sonya?"

Still obviously distraught, she turned to look at him . . . and her face went still.

"Tell us what we need to know," said Robert. His voice wasn't kind so much as smooth and lulling, with a faintly sinister touch. "Tell us who and where this child is. Tell us who the mother is."

This time, I did jump to my feet. Robert was using compulsion on her to get the answers. Sonya's eyes stayed locked on him, but her body began to shake. Her lips parted, though no sound came out. A tangle of thoughts swirled in my mind. Compulsion would get us what we needed to know, but something told me, it wasn't right—

Sonya stopped me from any more pondering. She shot up almost as quickly as I had. She was still staring at Robert, but no longer in that transfixed, hypnotized way. She'd broken the compulsion, and now . . . now she was pissed. The features that had been scared and fragile earlier were filled with fury. I had no magical senses, but after being with Lissa, I knew raging spirit when I saw it. Sonya was a bomb, about to explode.

"How dare you . . ." she hissed. "How *dare* you try to compel me?"

Plants and vines near Robert suddenly sprang to life, growing to impossible heights. They reached out, tangled themselves around his chair's legs, and pulled. The chair toppled over, Robert along with it. Victor moved to help his brother, but Robert was already taking matters into his own hands. Recovering remarkably fast, he narrowed his eyes at Sonya, and she went flying backward, slamming against the wooden fence. Air users could do that trick sometimes, but this wasn't air blowing her back. This was spirit's telekinetic abilities. He apparently possessed them outside of dreams too. Lovely.

I'd seen spirit users battle it out before, when Avery Lazar and Lissa had gone one on one. That hadn't been pretty, particularly since more than this exterior psychic phenomena had occurred. Avery had actually dug into Lissa's mind—and mine. I didn't know Robert or Sonya's full skill set, but this couldn't end well.

"Dimitri!" I yelled, springing toward Sonya. I didn't exactly know what I was going to do, but tackling her seemed like a sound plan. From what I'd observed, a lot of spirit involved eye contact with the target.

And sure enough, when I managed to wrestle her to the ground, she struggled half-heartedly but mostly fought to keep her gaze on Robert. He screamed in sudden alarm, looking down at his own body in terror. Sonya was planting visions into his head. His expression hardened. He had to know it was an illusion, and a few moments later, he looked up, having broken her spell like she'd broken his earlier compulsion.

Dimitri came tearing out the door at that point, just as Robert used his mind to fling one of the chairs toward Sonya. Of course, I was on top of her, so the chair hit *me* in the back. Dimitri picked up pretty quickly what was going on and ran toward Robert, attempting the same tactic as me. Victor, possibly thinking his brother was in physical danger, tried to pry Dimitri away, which was futile. More vines began to reach toward Robert, and I realized constraining Sonya wasn't all that useful.

"Get him inside!" I yelled to Dimitri. "Get him away from her!"

Dimitri had already guessed that and began dragging Robert toward the door. Even with Victor interfering, Dimitri's strength was enough to get Robert out of there and back into the house. As soon as her target was gone, all the energy seemed to fade out of Sonya. She made no more efforts to fight me and collapsed to the ground. I was relieved, having feared she'd turn on me once Robert was gone. Tentatively, still on guard, I helped Sonya sit up. She leaned against me, weak as a rag doll, and cried into my shoulder. Another breakdown.

After that, it was a matter of damage control. In order to keep the spirit users apart, Dimitri had taken Robert to the bedroom and left Victor with him. Robert seemed as worn out as Sonya, and Dimitri deemed the brothers safe enough to leave alone. Sonya collapsed on the couch, and after both Dimitri and I had tried to calm her down, we stepped away while Sydney held the Moroi woman's hand.

I briefly recapped what had happened. Dimitri's face grew more and more incredulous as I did.

"I told you it wasn't time!" he exclaimed. "What were you thinking? She's too weak!"

"You call that weak? And hey, I was doing fine! It wasn't until Victor and Robert got involved that things went to hell."

Dimitri took a step toward me, anger radiating off him. "They should never have gotten involved. This is you, acting irrational again, jumping in foolishly with no thought of the consequences."

Outrage shot through me in return. "Hey, I was trying to make progress here. If being rational is sitting around and doing therapy, then I'm happy to jump over the edge. I'm not afraid to get in the game."

"You have no idea what you're saying," he growled. We were standing closer now, hardly any space left between us as we engaged in our battle of wills. "This may have set us back."

"This set us *forward*. We found out she knows about Eric Dragomir. The problem is she promised not to tell anyone about this baby."

"Yes, I promised," piped up Sonya. Dimitri and I turned as one, realizing our argument was fully visible and audible to Sonya and Sydney. "I promised." Her voice was very small and weak, pleading with us.

Sydney squeezed her hand. "We know. It's okay. It's okay to keep promises. I understand."

Sonya looked at her gratefully. "Thank you. Thank you."

"But," said Sydney carefully, "I heard that you care about Lissa Dragomir."

"I can't," interrupted Sonya, turning fearful again.

"I know, I know. But what if there was a way to help her without breaking your promise?"

Sonya stared at Sydney. Dimitri glanced at me questioningly. I shrugged and then stared at Sydney too. If someone had asked who could stage the best intervention with a crazy woman who'd formerly been an undead monster, Sydney Sage would have been my last guess.

Sonya frowned, all attention on Sydney. "W-what do you mean?"

"Well . . . what did you promise exactly? Not to tell anyone that Eric Dragomir had a mistress and baby?"

Sonya nodded.

"And not to tell who they were?"

Sonya nodded again.

Sydney gave Sonya the warmest, friendliest smile I'd ever seen on the Alchemist. "Did you promise not to tell anyone where they are?" Sonya nodded, and Sydney's smile faltered a little. Then, her eyes lit up. "Did you promise not to *lead* anyone to where they are?"

Sonya hesitated, no doubt turning every word over in her mind. Slowly, she shook her head. "No."

"So . . . you could lead us to them. But not tell us where they actually are. You wouldn't be breaking the promise that way."

It was the most convoluted, ridiculous piece of logic I'd heard in a while. It was something I would have come up with.

"Maybe . . ." said Sonya, still uncertain.

"You wouldn't break the promise," Sydney repeated. "And it would really, really help Lissa."

I stepped forward. "It would help Mikhail too."

Sonya's mouth dropped open at the mention of her former lover. "Mikhail? You know him?"

"He's my friend. He's Lissa's friend too." I almost said that if we found the missing Dragomir, we could then take Sonya to Mikhail. Recalling Dimitri's feelings of unworthiness, I decided to avoid that tactic just now. I didn't know how Sonya would react to a reunion with her beloved. "And he wants to help Lissa. But he can't. None of us can. We don't have enough information."

"Mikhail . . ." Sonya looked down at her hands again, small tears running down her cheeks.

"You won't break your promise." Sydney was so compelling she could have been a spirit user. "Just lead us. It's what Mikhail and Lissa would want. It's the right thing to do."

I don't know which argument convinced Sonya the most. It could have been the part about Mikhail. Or it could have been the idea of doing "the right thing." Maybe, like Dimitri, Sonya wanted redemption for her Strigoi crimes and saw this as a chance. Looking up, she swallowed and met my eyes.

"I'll lead you there," she whispered.

"We're going on another road trip," Sydney declared. "Get ready."

Dimitri and I were still standing right next to each other, the anger between us beginning to diffuse. Sydney looked proud and continued trying her best to soothe Sonya.

Dimitri looked down at me with a small smile that shifted slightly when he seemed to become aware of just how close we were. I couldn't say for sure, though. His face gave little away. As for me, I was very aware of our proximity and felt intoxicated by his body and scent. Damn. Why did fighting with him always increase my attraction to him? His smile returned as he tilted his head toward Sydney. "You were wrong. She really is the new general in town."

I smiled back, hoping he wasn't aware of my body's reaction to us standing so close. "Maybe. But, it's okay. You can still be colonel."

He arched an eyebrow. "Oh? Did you demote yourself? Colonel's right below general. What's that make you?"

I reached into my pocket and triumphantly flashed the CR-V keys I'd swiped when we'd come back inside. "The driver," I said.

TWENTY-ONE

I DIDN'T GET TO DRIVE.

"General" Sydney didn't either, much to her outrage, though Dimitri did some fast-talking to explain why.

It all started when Victor discovered his car was having "engine trouble." He wasn't very happy about that. He made no accusations, but I think everyone there—even Sonya and Robert—could guess the malfunction wasn't coincidental. This meant we all had to pile in the CR-V, which hadn't been designed to seat so many people—which was why Dimitri had come up with a creative seating plan. Of course, one of those "seats" turned out to be the cargo space in the back. It was good-sized, but when Sydney learned it was *her* seat, she accused Dimitri of adding insult to the injury of taking her keys.

I wouldn't tell her so, but putting her back there was a sound choice. Dimitri's seating chart was configured to minimize threats inside the car. Dimitri drove, with Robert going shotgun, and me between Victor and Sonya in the backseat. This put a guardian in each row, separated the brothers, and kept the spirit users apart too. When I argued that he and I could switch spots and still maintain the same security, Dimitri pointed out that having me at the wheel wouldn't be safe if I had to suddenly flip to Lissa's mind. It was a fair point. As for Sydney . . . well, she was neither a threat nor a fighting force, so she got offloaded to the back. And speaking of dead weight . . .

"We have *got* to get rid of Victor and Robert now," I murmured to Dimitri, as we loaded the CR-V with groceries and our meager luggage (further reducing Sydney's space, much to her outrage). "They've done what we needed. Keeping them is dangerous. It's time to turn them over to the guardians." The brothers wanted to continue on with us in order to find Lissa's sibling. We were letting them—but not out of generosity. We simply couldn't let them out of our sights yet.

"Agreed," Dimitri said, frowning slightly. "But there's no good way to do it. Not yet. We can't leave them tied up beside the road; I wouldn't put it past them to escape and hitchhike. We also can't turn them in ourselves, for obvious reasons."

I set a bag inside the car and leaned against the bumper. "Sydney could turn them in."

Dimitri nodded. "That's probably our best bet—but I don't want to part with her until we get to . . . well, wherever we're going. We might need her help."

I sighed. "And so, we drag them along."

"Afraid so," he said. He gave me wary look. "You know, when they are in custody, there's a very good chance they'll have quite a story to tell the authorities about us."

"Yeah." I'd been thinking about that too. "I guess that's a problem for later. Gotta deal with the immediate problems first."

To my surprise, Dimitri smiled at me. I would have expected

some prudent, wise remark. "Well, that's always been our strategy, hasn't it?" he asked.

I smiled in return, but it was short-lived, once we hit the road. Mercifully, Victor wasn't his usual annoying chatty self—which I suspected was because he was growing weak from lack of blood. Sonya and Robert had to be feeling the same way. This was going to be a problem if we didn't get a feeder soon, but I didn't know how we were going to pull that off. I had the impression Sydney hadn't realized any of this yet, which was just as well. Being a human among a group of hungry vampires would certainly make me nervous. She was actually probably safer sequestered in the back from everyone else.

Sonya's directions were vague and very need-to-know. She only gave us short-term information and often wouldn't warn about a turn until we were right on top of it. We had no idea where we were going or how long it would take. She scanned a map and then told Dimitri to go north on I-75. When we asked how long our trip would take, her response was: "Not long. A few hours. Maybe more."

And with that mysterious explanation, she settled back in her seat and said no more. There was a haunted, pensive expression on her face, and I tried to imagine how she felt. Only a day ago she'd been Strigoi. Was she still processing what had happened? Was she seeing the faces of her victims as Dimitri had? Was she tormenting herself with guilt? Did she want to become Strigoi again?

I left her alone. Now wasn't the time for therapy. I settled back, preparing myself to be patient. A tingle of consciousness suddenly sparked in the bond, shifting my attention inward. Lissa was awake. I blinked and looked at the dashboard clock. Afternoon for humans. The Moroi at Court should have been long asleep by now. But no, something had awakened her.

Two guardians stood at her door, faces impassive. "You have to come with us," one of them said. "It's time for the next test."

Astonishment filled Lissa. She'd known the next test was "coming soon" but hadn't heard any further details since returning from the endurance test. That trip had taken place during the Moroi night too, but she'd at least had fair warning. Eddie stood nearby in her room, having replaced my mother as Lissa's protection a few hours ago. Christian sat up in Lissa's bed, yawning. They hadn't gotten hot and heavy, but Lissa liked having him around. Snuggling with her boyfriend while Eddie was in the room didn't seem as weird to her as it did when my mom was there. I didn't blame her.

"Can I change?" Lissa asked.

"Be quick," said the guardian.

She grabbed the first outfit she could and hurried to the bathroom, feeling confused and nervous. When she came out, Christian had pulled on his jeans already and was reaching for his T-shirt. Eddie meanwhile was sizing up the guardians, and I could guess his thoughts because I would have shared the same ones. This wakeup call seemed official, but he didn't know these guardians and didn't totally trust them.

"Can I escort her?" he asked.

"Only as far as the testing area," said the second guardian.

"What about me?" asked Christian.

"Only as far as the testing area."

The guardians' answers surprised me, but then, I realized it was probably common for monarch candidates to go to their tests with entourages—even unexpected tests in the middle of the night. Or maybe not so unexpected. The Court's grounds were virtually deserted, but when her group reached their destination—a small, out of the way section of an old brick building—she had to pass several groups of Moroi lining the halls. Apparently, word had gotten out.

Those gathered stepped aside respectfully. Some—probably advocates of other families—gave her scowls. But lots of other people smiled at her and called out about "the dragon's return." A few even brushed their hands against her arms, as though taking luck or power from her. The crowd was much smaller than the one who'd greeted her after the first test. This eased her anxiety but didn't shake her earlier resolve to take the tests seriously. The faces of the onlookers shone with awe and curiosity, wondering if she might be the next to rule them.

A doorway at the end of the hall marked the conclusion of her journey. Neither Christian nor Eddie needed to be told that this was as far as they could go. Lissa glanced at the two of them over her shoulder before following one of the guardians inside, taking comfort from her loved ones' supportive faces.

After the epic adventure of the first test, Lissa expected something equally intimidating. What she found instead was an old Moroi woman sitting comfortably in a chair in a mostly empty room. Her hands were folded in her lap, holding something wrapped in cloth. The woman hummed, seeming very content. And when I say old, I mean she was *old*. Moroi could live until their early 100s, and this woman had clearly crossed that mark. Her pale skin was a maze of wrinkles, and her gray hair was wispy and thin. She smiled when she saw Lissa and nodded toward an empty chair. A small table sat beside it with a glass pitcher of water. The guardians left the women alone.

Lissa glanced around her surroundings. There were no other furnishings, though there was a plain door opposite the one she had come through. She sat down and then turned toward the old woman. "Hello," said Lissa, trying to keep her voice strong. "I'm Vasilisa Dragomir."

The woman's small smile grew, showing her yellowed teeth. One of her fangs was missing. "Always such manners in your family," she croaked. "Most people come in here and demand we get down to business. But I remember your grandfather. He was polite during his test as well."

"You knew my grandfather?" exclaimed Lissa. He had died when she was very, very young. Then, she picked up another meaning in the woman's words. "He ran for king?"

The woman nodded. "Passed all his tests. I think he would have won the election, if he hadn't withdrawn at the last moment. After that, it was a coin's toss between Tatiana Ivashkov and Jacob Tarus. Very close, that one. The Taruses still hold a grudge."

Lissa had never heard any of this. "Why'd my grandfather withdraw?"

"Because your brother had just been born. Frederick

decided he needed to devote his energy to his fledgling family, instead of a nation."

Lissa could understand this. How many Dragomirs were there back then? Her grandfather, her father, and Andre—and her mother, but only by marriage. Eric Dragomir hadn't had any brothers or sisters. Lissa knew little about her grandfather, but in his place, she decided that she too would have rather spent time with her son and grandson, instead of listening to the endless speeches Tatiana had had to deal with.

Lissa's mind had wandered, and the old woman was watching her carefully. "Is . . . this the test?" asked Lissa, once the silence had gone on too long. "Is it, like, an interview?"

The old woman shook her head. "No. It's this." She unwrapped the object in her lap. It was a cup—a chalice or a goblet. I'm not sure which. But it was beautiful, made of silver that seemed to glow with its own light. Blood-red rubies were scattered along the sides, glittering with each turn of the cup. The woman regarded it fondly.

"Over a thousand years old, and it still gleams." She took the pitcher and filled the chalice with water while Lissa and I processed the words. A thousand years? I was no metal expert, but even I knew silver should have tarnished in that time. The woman held out the cup to Lissa. "Drink from it. And when you want to stop, say 'stop.'"

Lissa reached for the cup, more confused than ever by the odd instructions. What was she supposed to stop? Drinking? As soon as her fingers touched the metal, she understood. Well, kind of. A tingle ran through her, one she knew well.

"This is charmed," she said.

The old woman nodded. "Infused with all four elements and a spell long since forgotten."

Charmed with spirit too, thought Lissa. That too must have been forgotten, and it put her on edge. Elemental charms had different effects. Earth charms—like the tattoo she'd been given—were often tied with minor compulsion spells. The combination of all four in a stake or ward provided a unified blast of life that blocked the undead. But spirit . . . well, she was quickly learning that spirit charms covered a wide range of unpredictable effects. The water no doubt activated the spell, but Lissa had a feeling that spirit was going to be the key player. Even though it was the power that burned in her blood, it still scared her. The spell woven into this cup was complex, far beyond her skills, and she feared what it would do. The old woman stared unblinkingly.

Lissa hesitated only a moment more. She drank.

The world faded away, then rematerialized into something completely different. She and I both recognized what this was: a spirit dream.

She no longer stood in the plain room. She was outdoors, wind whipping her long hair in front of her face. She brushed it aside as best she could. Other people stood around her, all of them in black, and she soon recognized the Court's church and graveyard. Lissa herself wore black, along with a long wool coat to protect against the chill. They were gathered around a grave, and a priest stood near it, his robes of office offering the only color on that gray day.

Lissa took a few steps over, trying to see whose name was on the tombstone. What she discovered shocked me more than her: ROSEMARIE HATHAWAY.

My name was carved into the granite in regal, elaborate font. Below my name was the star of battle, signifying that I'd killed more Strigoi than could be counted. Go me. Beneath that were three lines of text in Russian, Romanian, and English. I didn't need the English translation to know what each line said because it was standard for a guardian's grave: "Eternal Service."

The priest spoke customary funeral words, giving me the blessings of a religion I wasn't sure I believed in. That was the least weird thing here, however, seeing as I was watching my own funeral. When he finished, Alberta took his place. Lauding the deceased's achievements was also normal at a guardian's funeral—and Alberta had plenty to say about mine. Had I been there, I would have been moved to tears. She concluded by describing my last battle, how I'd died defending Lissa.

That actually didn't weird me out so much. I mean, don't get me wrong. Everything going on here was completely insane. But, reasonably speaking, if I was actually watching my own funeral, it made sense that I would have died protecting her.

Lissa didn't share my feelings. The news was a slap in the face to her. She suddenly became aware of a horrible empty feeling in her chest, like part of her was gone. The bond only worked one way, yet Robert had sworn losing his bondmate had left him in agony. Lissa understood it now, that terrible, lonely ache. She was missing something she'd never even known she'd had. Tears brimmed in her eyes.

This is a dream, she told herself. *That's all.* But she'd never had a spirit dream like this. Her experiences had always been with Adrian, and the dreams had felt like telephone calls.

When the mourners dispersed from the graveyard, Lissa felt a hand touch her shoulder. Christian. She threw herself gratefully into his arms, trying hard to hold back sobs. He felt real and solid. Safe. "How did this happen?" she asked. "How could it have happened?"

Christian released her, his crystal-blue eyes more serious and sorrowful than I'd ever seen. "You know how. Those Strigoi were trying to kill you. She sacrificed herself to save you."

Lissa had no memory of this, but it didn't matter. "I can't . . . I can't believe this is happening." That agonizing emptiness grew within her.

"I have more bad news," said Christian.

She stared in astonishment. "How could this get any worse?"

"I'm leaving."

"Leaving . . . what? Court?"

"Yes. Leaving everything." The sadness on his face grew. "Leaving you."

Her jaw nearly dropped. "What . . . what's wrong? What did I do?"

"Nothing." He squeezed her hand and let it go. "I love you. I'll always love you. But you are who you are. You're the last Dragomir. There'll always be something taking you away . . . I'd just get in your way. You need to rebuild your family.

I'm not the one you need."

"Of course you are! You are the *only* one! The only one I want to build my future with."

"You say that now, but just wait. There are better choices. You heard Adrian's joke. 'Little Dragomirs'? When you're ready for kids in a few years, you're going to need a bunch. The Dragomirs need to be solid again. And me? I'm not responsible enough to handle that."

"You'd be a great father," she argued.

"Yeah," he scoffed, "and I'd be a big asset to you too—the princess married to the guy from the Strigoi family."

"I don't care about any of that, and you know it!" She clutched at his shirt, forcing him to look at her. "I love you. I want you to be part of my life. None of this makes sense. Are you scared? Is that it? Are you scared of the weight of my family name?"

He averted his eyes. "Let's just say it's not an easy name to carry."

She shook him. "I don't believe you! You're not afraid of anything! You never back down."

"I'm backing down now." He gently removed himself from her. "I really do love you. That's why I'm doing this. It's for the best."

"But you can't . . ." Lissa gestured toward my grave, but he was already walking away. "You can't! She's gone. If you're gone too, there'll be no one . . ."

But Christian *was* gone, disappearing into fog that hadn't been there minutes ago. Lissa was left with only my tombstone for company. And for the first time in her life, she was really and truly alone. She had felt alone when her family died, but I'd been her anchor, always at her back, protecting her. When Christian had come along, he too had kept the loneliness away, filling her heart with love.

But now . . . now we were both gone. Her family was gone. That hole inside threatened to consume her, and it was more than just the loss of the bond. Being alone is a terrible, terrible thing. There's no one to run to, no one to confide in, no one who cares what happens to you. She'd been alone in the woods, but that was nothing like this. Nothing like it at all.

Staring around, she wished she could go sink into my grave and end her torment. No . . . wait. She really could end it. *Say "stop,"* the old woman had said. That was all it took to stop this pain. This was a spirit dream, right? True, it was more realistic and all-consuming than any she'd ever faced, but in the end, all dreamers woke up. One word, and this would become a fading nightmare.

Staring around at the empty Court, she almost said the word. But . . . did she want to end things? She'd vowed to fight through these trials. Would she give up over a dream? A dream about being alone? It seemed like such a minor thing, but that cold truth hit her again: *I've never been alone.* She didn't know if she could carry on by herself, but then, she realized that if this wasn't a dream—and dear God, did it feel real—there was no magic "stop" in real life. If she couldn't deal with loneliness in a dream, she never would be able to while waking. And as much as it scared her, she decided she would not back down from this. Something urged her toward the fog, and she walked toward it—alone.

The fog should have led her into the church's garden. Instead, the world rematerialized and she found herself in a Council session. It was an open one, with a Moroi audience watching. Unlike usual, Lissa didn't sit with the audience. She was at the Council's table, with its thirteen chairs. She sat in the Dragomir seat. The middle chair, the monarch's chair, was occupied by Ariana Szelsky. *Definitely a dream,* some wry part of her thought. She had a Council spot and Ariana was queen. Too good to be true.

Like always, the Council was in a heated debate, and the topic was familiar: the age decree. Some Council members argued that it was immoral. Others argued that the Strigoi threat was too great. Desperate times called for desperate actions, those people said.

Ariana peered down the table at Lissa. "What does the Dragomir family think?" Ariana was neither as kind as she'd been in the van nor as hostile as Tatiana had been. Ariana was neutral, a queen running a Council and gathering the information she needed. Every set of eyes in the room turned toward Lissa.

For some reason, every coherent idea had fled out of her head. Her tongue felt thick in her mouth. What did she think? What was her opinion of the age decree? She desperately tried to dredge up an answer.

"I . . . I think it's bad."

Lee Szelsky, who must have taken the family spot when

Ariana became queen, snorted in disgust. "Can you elaborate, princess?"

Lissa swallowed. "Lowering the guardian age isn't the way to protect us. We need . . . we need to learn to protect ourselves too."

Her words were met with more contempt and shock. "And pray tell," said Howard Zeklos, "how do you plan to do that? What's your proposal? Mandatory training for all ages? Start a program in the schools?"

Again Lissa groped for words. What *was* the plan? She and Tasha had discussed it lots of times, strategizing this very issue of how to implement training. Tasha had practically pounded those details into her head in the hopes Lissa could make her voice heard. Here she was now, representing her family on the Council, with the chance to change things and improve Moroi life. All she had to do was explain herself. So many were counting on her, so many waiting to hear the words she felt so passionately about. But what were they? Why couldn't Lissa remember? She must have taken too long to answer because Howard threw his hands up in disgust.

"I knew it. We were idiots to let a little girl on this Council. She has nothing useful to offer. The Dragomirs are gone. They've died with her, and we need to accept that."

They've died with her. The pressure of being the last of her line had weighed on Lissa since the moment a doctor had told her that her parents and brother had died. The last of a line that had empowered the Moroi and produced some of the greatest kings and queens. She'd vowed to herself over and over that she wouldn't disappoint that lineage, that she would see her family's pride restored. And now it was all falling apart.

Even Ariana, whom Lissa had considered a supporter, looked disappointed. The audience began to jeer, echoing the call of removing this tongue-tied child from the Council. They yelled for her to leave. Then, worse still: "The dragon is dead! The dragon is dead!"

Lissa almost tried again to make her speech, but then something made her look behind her. There, the twelve family seals hung on the wall. A man had appeared out of nowhere and was taking down the Dragomir's crest, with its dragon and Romanian inscription. Lissa's heart sank as the shouts in the room became louder and her humiliation grew. She rose, wanting to run out of there and hide from the disgrace. Instead, her feet took her to the wall with its seals. With more strength than she thought herself capable of possessing, she jerked the dragon seal away from the man.

"No!" she yelled. She turned her gaze to the audience and held up the seal, challenging any of them to come take it from her or deny her her rightful place on the Council. "This. Is. Mine. Do you hear me? *This is mine!*"

She would never know if they heard because they disappeared, just like the graveyard. Silence fell. She now sat in one of the medical examining rooms back at St. Vladimir's. The familiar details were oddly comforting: the sink with its orange hand soap, the neatly labeled cupboards and drawers, and even the informative health posters on the walls. STUDENTS: PRACTICE SAFE SEX!

Equally welcome was the school's resident physician: Dr. Olendzki. The doctor wasn't alone. Standing around Lissa—who sat on top of an examination bed—were a therapist named Deirdre and . . . me. Seeing myself there was pretty wacky, but after the funeral, I was just starting to roll with all of this.

A surprising mix of feelings raced through Lissa, feelings out of her control. Happiness to see us. Despair at life. Confusion. Suspicion. She couldn't seem to get a hold of one emotion or thought. It was a very different feeling from the Council, when she just hadn't been able to explain herself. Her mind had been orderly—she'd just lost track of her point. Here, there was nothing to keep track of. She was a mental mess.

"Do you understand?" asked Dr. Olendzki. Lissa suspected the doctor had already asked this question. "It's beyond what we can control. Medication no longer works."

"Believe me, we don't want you hurting yourself. But now that others are at risk . . . well, you understand why we have to take action." This was Deirdre. I'd always thought of her as smug, particularly since her therapeutic method involved answering questions with questions. There was no sly humor now. Deirdre was deadly earnest.

None of their words made sense to Lissa, but the *hurting yourself* part triggered something in her. She looked down at her arms. They were bare . . . and marred with cuts. The cuts she used to make when the pressure of spirit grew too great. They'd been her only outlet, a horrible type of release. Studying them now, Lissa saw the cuts were bigger and deeper than before. The kinds of cuts that danced with suicide. She looked back up.

"Who . . . who did I hurt?"

"You don't remember?" asked Dr. Olendzki.

Lissa shook her head, looking desperately from face to face, seeking answers. Her gaze fell on me, and my face was as dark and somber as Deirdre's. "It's okay, Liss," I said. "It's all going to be okay."

I wasn't surprised at that. Naturally, it was what I would say. I would always reassure Lissa. I would always take care of her.

"It's not important," said Deirdre, voice soft and soothing. "What's important is no one else ever gets hurt. You don't want to hurt anyone, do you?"

Of course Lissa didn't, but her troubled mind shifted elsewhere. "Don't talk to me like a child!" The loudness of her voice filled the room.

"I didn't mean to," said Deirdre, the paragon of patience. "We just want to help you. We want you to be safe."

Paranoia rose to the forefront of Lissa's emotions. Nowhere was safe. She was certain about that . . . but nothing else. Except maybe something about a dream. A dream, a dream . . .

"They'll be able to take care of you in Tarasov," explained Dr. Olendzki. "They'll make sure you're comfortable."

"Tarasov?" Lissa and I spoke in unison. This other Rose clenched her fists and glared. Again, a typical reaction for me.

"She is *not* going to that place," growled Rose.

"Do you think we want to do this?" asked Deirdre. It was the first time I'd really seen her cool façade crumble. "We don't. But the spirit . . . what it's doing . . . we have no choice . . ."

Images of our trip to Tarasov flashed through Lissa's mind. The cold, cold corridors. The moans. The tiny cells. She remembered seeing the psychiatric ward, the section other spirit users were locked up in. Locked up indefinitely.

"No!" she cried, jumping up from the table. "Don't send me to Tarasov!" She looked around for escape. The women stood between her and the door. Lissa couldn't run. What magic could she use? Surely there was something. Her mind touched spirit, as she rifled for a spell.

Other-Rose grabbed a hold of her hand, likely because she'd felt the stirrings of spirit and wanted to stop Lissa. "There's another way," my alter ego told Deirdre and Dr. Olendzki. "I can pull it from her. I can pull it all from her, like Anna did for St. Vladimir. I can take away the darkness and instability. Lissa will be sane again."

Everyone stared at me. Well, the other me.

"But then it'll be in you, right?" asked Dr. Olendzki. "It won't disappear."

"I don't care," I told them stubbornly. "I'll go to Tarasov. Don't send her. I can do it as long as she needs me to."

Lissa watched me, scarcely believing what she heard. Her chaotic thoughts turned joyous. *Yes! Escape.* She wouldn't go crazy. She wouldn't go to Tarasov. Then, somewhere in the jumble of her memories . . .

"Anna committed suicide," murmured Lissa. Her grasp on reality was still tenuous, but that sobering thought was enough to momentarily calm her racing mind. "She went crazy from helping St. Vladimir."

My other self refused to look at Lissa. "It's just a story. I'll take the darkness. Send me."

Lissa didn't know what to do or think. She didn't want to go to Tarasov. That prison gave her nightmares. And here I was, offering her escape, offering to save her like I always did. Lissa wanted that. She wanted to be saved. She didn't want to go insane like all the other spirit users. If she accepted my offer, she would be free.

Yet . . . on the edge or not, she cared about me too much. I had made too many sacrifices for her. How could she let me do this? What kind of friend would she be, to condemn me to that life? Tarasov scared Lissa. A life in a cage scared Lissa. But me facing that scared her even more.

There was no good outcome here. She wished it would all just go away. Maybe if she just closed her eyes . . . wait. She remembered again. The dream. She was in a spirit dream. All she had to do was wake up.

Say "stop."

It was easier this time. Saying that word was the simple way out, the perfect solution. No Tarasov for either of us, right? Then, she felt a lightening of the pressure on her mind, a stilling of those chaotic feelings. Her eyes widened as she realized I had already started pulling away the darkness. *"Stop"* was forgotten.

"No!" Spirit burned through her, and she threw up a wall in the bond, blocking me from her.

"What are you doing?" my other self asked.

"Saving you," said Lissa. "Saving myself." She turned to

Dr. Olendzki and Deirdre. "I understand what you have to do. It's okay. Take me to Tarasov. Take me where I won't hurt anyone else." Tarasov. A place where real nightmares walked the halls. She braced herself as the office faded away, ready for the next part of the dream: a cold stone cell, with chains on the walls and people wailing down the halls. . . .

But when the world put itself back together, there was no Tarasov. There was an empty room with an old woman and a silver chalice. Lissa looked around. Her heart was racing, and her sense of time was off. The things she'd seen had lasted an eternity. Yet, simultaneously, it felt like only a couple seconds had passed since she and the old woman had conversed.

"What . . . what was that?" asked Lissa. Her mouth was dry, and the water sounded good now . . . but the chalice was empty.

"Your fear," said the old woman, eyes twinkling. "All your fears, laid out neatly in a row."

Lissa placed the chalice on the table with shaking hands. "It was awful. It was spirit, but it . . . it wasn't anything I've seen before. It invaded my mind, rifling through it. It was so real. There were times I believed it was real."

"But you didn't stop it."

Lissa frowned, thinking of how close she had come. "No."

The old woman smiled and said nothing.

"Am I . . . am I done?" asked Lissa, confused. "Can I go?"

The old woman nodded. Lissa stood and glanced between the two doors, the one she'd entered through and the plain one in the back. Still in shock, Lissa automatically turned toward the door she'd come through. She didn't really want to see those people lined up in the hall again but swore she'd put on a good princess face. Besides, there'd only been a fraction here compared to the group who'd greeted her after the last test. Her steps were halted when the old woman spoke again and pointed toward the back of the room.

"No. That's for those who fail. You go out this door."

Lissa turned and approached the plain door. It looked like it led outdoors, which was probably just as well. Peace and quiet. She felt like she should say something to her companion but didn't know what. So, she simply turned the knob and stepped outside . . .

Into a crowd cheering for the dragon.

TWENTY-TWO

"YOU'RE AWFULLY HAPPY."

I blinked and found Sonya staring at me. The CR-V and smooth stretch of I-75 hummed around us, the outside revealing little except Midwestern plains and trees. Sonya didn't seem quite as creepy crazy as she had back at school or even at her house. Mostly, she still just seemed scattered and confused, which was to be expected. I hesitated before answering but finally decided there was no reason to hold back.

"Lissa passed her second monarch test."

"Of course she did," said Victor. He was staring out the window away from me. The tone of his voice suggested I'd just wasted his time by saying something that was a given.

"Is she okay?" asked Dimitri. "Injured?"

Once, that would have sparked jealousy in me. Now, it was just a sign of our shared concern for Lissa.

"She's fine," I said, wondering if that was entirely true. She wasn't physically injured, but after what she'd seen . . . well, that had to leave scars of a different type. The back door had been quite a surprise too. When she'd seen a small crowd by the first door, she'd thought it meant only a few people were up that late to see the candidates. Nope. Turned out everyone was just waiting out back to see the victors. True to her promise, Lissa hadn't let it faze her. She walked out with her head held high, smiling at her onlookers and fans as though she already owned the crown.

I was growing sleepy but Lissa's triumph kept me smiling for a long time. There's something tiring about an endless, unknown stretch of highway. Victor had closed his eyes and was leaning against the glass. I couldn't see Sydney when I twisted around to check on her, meaning she also had decided on a nap or was just lying down. I yawned, wondering if I dared risk sleeping. Dimitri had urged me to when we left Sonya's house, knowing that I could use more than the couple hours Sydney had given me.

I tipped my head against the seat and closed my eyes, falling instantly asleep. The blackness of that sleep gave way to the feel of a spirit dream, and my heart leapt with both panic and joy. After living through Lissa's test, spirit dreams suddenly had a sinister feel. At the same time, this might be a chance to see Adrian. And . . . it was.

Only we appeared somewhere entirely unexpected: Sonya's garden. I stared in wonder at the clear blue sky and the brilliant flowers, nearly overlooking Adrian in the process. He wore a dark green cashmere sweater that made him blend in. To me, he was more gorgeous than any of the garden's other wonders.

"Adrian!"

I ran to him, and he lifted me easily, spinning me around. When he placed me back on my feet, he studied the garden and nodded in approval. "I should let you pick the place more often. You have good taste. Of course, since you're dating me, we already knew that."

"What do you mean, 'pick the place?'" I asked, lacing my hands behind his neck.

He shrugged. "When I reached out and sensed you were sleeping, I summoned the dream but didn't feel like thinking up a place. So I left it to your subconscious." Irritably, he plucked at the cashmere. "I'm not dressed for the occasion, though." The sweater shimmered, soon replaced by a light gray T-shirt with an abstract design on the front. "Better?"

"Much."

He grinned and kissed the top of my forehead. "I've missed you, little dhampir. You can spy on Lissa and us all the time, but the best I get are these dreams, and honestly, I can't figure out what schedule you're on."

I realized that with my "spying," I knew more about what had just happened at Court than he did. "Lissa took her second test," I told him.

Yup. His expression verified it. He hadn't known about the test, probably because he'd been sleeping. "When?"

"Just now. It was a tough one, but she passed."

"Much to her delight, no doubt. Still . . . that keeps buying us time to clear you and get you home. Not sure I'd want to come home if I were you, though." He looked around the garden again. "West Virginia's a lot better than I thought."

I laughed. "It's not West Virginia—which isn't that bad, by the way. It's Sonya Karp's—"

I froze, unable to believe what I'd nearly said. I'd been

so happy to see him, so at ease . . . I'd let myself screw up. Adrian's face grew very, very serious.

"Did you say Sonya Karp?"

Several options played out in my head. Lying was the easiest. I could claim this was some place I'd been a long time ago, like maybe she'd taken us on a field trip to her house. That was pretty flimsy, though. Plus, I was guessing the look on my face screamed guilt. I'd been caught. A pretty lie wouldn't fool Adrian.

"Yes," I said finally.

"Rose. Sonya Karp's a Strigoi."

"Not anymore."

Adrian sighed. "I knew you staying out of trouble was too good to be true. What happened?"

"Um, Robert Doru restored her."

"Robert." Adrian's lip curled in disdain. The two spirit users hadn't gotten along well. "And just because I feel like we're marching into full-fledged Crazy Territory—which means something, coming from me—I'm going to take a guess that Victor Dashkov is also with you."

I nodded, wishing desperately then that someone would wake me up and get me away from Adrian's interrogation. Damn it. How could I have slipped up like this?

Adrian released me and walked around in small circles. "Okay, so. You, Belikov, the Alchemist, Sonya Karp, Victor Dashkov, and Robert Doru are all hanging out in West Virginia together."

"No," I said.

"No?"

"We're, uh, not in West Virginia."

"Rose!" Adrian halted his pacing and strode back over to me. "Where the hell are you then? Your old man, Lissa—everyone thinks you're safe and sound."

"I am," I said haughtily. "Just not in West Virginia."

"Then where?"

"I can't . . . I can't tell you." I hated saying those words to him and seeing the look they elicited. "Part of it's for safety. Part of it's because . . . well, um, I don't actually know."

He caught hold of my hands. "You can't do this. You can't run off on some crazy whim this time. Don't you get it? They'll kill you if they find you."

"It's not a crazy whim! We're doing something important. Something that's going to help all of us."

"Something you can't tell me," he guessed.

"It's better if you're not involved," I said, squeezing his hands tightly. "Better if you don't know the details."

"And in the meantime, I can rest easy knowing you've got an elite team at your back."

"Adrian, please! Please just trust me. Trust that I've got a good reason," I begged.

He let go of my hands. "I believe you *think* you've got a good reason. I just can't imagine one that justifies you risking your life."

"It's what I do," I said, surprised at how serious I sounded. "Some things are worth it."

Pieces of static flickered across my vision, like TV reception going bad. The world started to fade. "What's going on?" I asked.

He scowled. "Someone or something's waking me up. Probably my mom checking in for the hundredth time."

I reached for him, but he was fading away. "Adrian! Please don't tell anyone! *Anyone*."

I don't know if he heard my pleas or not because the dream completely disappeared. I woke up in the car. My immediate reaction was to swear, but I didn't want to give away the idiotic thing I'd done. Glancing over, I nearly jumped out of my seat when I saw Sonya watching me intently.

"You were having a spirit dream," she said.

"How'd you know?"

"Your aura."

I made a face. "Auras used to be cool, but now they're just starting to get annoying."

She laughed softly, the first time I'd heard her do so since being restored. "They're very informative if you know how to read them. Were you with Vasilisa?"

"No. My boyfriend. He's a spirit user too."

Her eyes widened in surprise. "That's who you were with?"

"Yeah. Why? What's wrong?"

She frowned, looking puzzled. A few moments later, she glanced up toward the front seat, where Dimitri and Robert sat, and then studied me in a scrutinizing way that sent chills down my spine.

"Nothing," she said. "Nothing's wrong."

I had to scoff at that. "Come on, it sure seemed like—"

"There!" Sonya abruptly turned from me, leaned forward, and pointed. "Take that exit."

We were nearly past "that exit," and Dimitri had to do some fancy maneuvering—kind of like in our escape back in Pennsylvania—to make it. The car jerked and lurched, and I heard Sydney yelp behind me.

"A little warning next time would be helpful," Dimitri noted.

Sonya wasn't listening. Her gaze was totally fixated on the road we'd pulled off onto. We came to a red light, where I caught sight of a cheery sign: WELCOME TO ANN ARBOR, MICHIGAN. The spark of life I'd seen in her moments ago was gone. Sonya had returned to her tense, almost robotic self. Despite Sydney's clever negotiating, Sonya still seemed uncomfortable about this trip. She still felt guilty and traitorous.

"Are we here?" I asked eagerly. "And how long were we on the road?" I'd hardly noticed the drive. I'd stayed awake for the first part of it, but the rest had been a blur of Lissa and Adrian.

"Six hours," said Dimitri.

"Go left at that second light," said Sonya. "Now right at the corner."

Tension built in the car. Everyone was awake now, and my heart raced as we pushed deeper and deeper into suburbia. Which house? Were we close? Was one of these it? It was a fast drive but seemed to stretch forever. We all let out a collective breath when Sonya suddenly pointed.

"There."

Dimitri pulled into the driveway of a cute brick house with a perfectly trimmed lawn. "Do you know if your relatives still live here?" I asked Sonya.

She said nothing, and I realized we were back to promise territory. Lockdown mode.

So much for progress. "I guess there's only one way to find out," I said, unbuckling my seatbelt. "Same plan?"

Earlier, Dimitri and I had discussed who would go and who would stay behind if Sonya got us to the right place. Leaving the brothers behind was a no-brainer. The question had been who would guard them, and we'd decided Dimitri would while Sydney and I went with Sonya to meet her relatives—who were undoubtedly in for a shocking visit.

"Same plan," agreed Dimitri. "You go to the house. You look less threatening."

"Hey!"

He smiled. "I said 'look.'"

But his reasoning made sense. Even at ease, there was something powerful and intimidating about Dimitri. Three women going up to the door would freak these people out less—especially if it turned out Sonya's relatives had moved. Hell, for all I knew, she'd purposely led us to the wrong house.

"Be careful," Dimitri said, as we got out of the car.

"You too," I replied. That got me another smile, one a little warmer and deeper.

The feelings that stirred in me flitted away as Sonya, Sydney, and I walked up the sidewalk. My chest tightened. This was it. Or was it? Were we about to reach the conclusion of our journey? Had we really found the last Dragomir, against all odds? Or had I been played from the beginning?

I wasn't the only one who was nervous. I could feel Sydney and Sonya crackling with tension too. We reached the front step. I took a deep breath and rang the doorbell.

Several seconds later, a man answered—and he was Moroi. A promising sign.

He looked at each of our faces, no doubt wondering what a Moroi, a dhampir, and a human were doing at his door. It sounded like the start of a bad joke.

"Can I help you?" he asked.

I was suddenly at a loss. Our plan had covered the big stuff: find Eric's mistress and love child. What we'd say once we actually got there wasn't so clear. I waited for one of my companions to speak up now, but there was no need. The Moroi man's head suddenly whipped to my side as he did a double take.

"Sonya?" he gasped. "Is that you?"

Then, I heard a young female voice behind him call, "Hey, who's here?"

Someone squeezed in beside him, someone tall and slim—someone I knew. My breath caught as I stared at waves of unruly light brown hair and light green eyes—eyes that should have tipped me off a long time ago. I couldn't speak.

"Rose," exclaimed Jill Mastrano. "What are you doing here?"

TWENTY-THREE

THE FEW SECONDS OF SILENCE that followed seemed to stretch out to eternity. Everyone was confused, each for totally different reasons. Jill's initial surprise had been laced with excitement, but as she stared around from face to face, her smile faded and faded until she looked as bewildered as the rest of us.

"What's going on?" asked a new voice. Moments later, Emily Mastrano appeared beside her daughter. Emily glanced at me and Sydney with curiosity and then gasped when she saw the third member of our group. "Sonya!" Emily jerked Jill back, her face filled with panic. Emily wasn't guardian-fast, but I admired her responsiveness.

"Emily . . . ?" Sonya's voice was very small, on the verge of cracking. "It . . . it's me . . . *really* me . . ."

Emily tried to tug the man inside as well but stopped when she got a good look at Sonya. Like anyone else, Emily had to acknowledge the obvious. Sonya had no Strigoi features. Plus, she was out in broad daylight. Emily faltered and opened her mouth to speak, but her lips couldn't quite manage it. She finally turned to me.

"Rose . . . what's going on?"

I was surprised that she would regard me as an authority,

both because we'd only met once and because I honestly wasn't sure what was going on either. It took me a few attempts to find my voice. "I think . . . I think we should come inside . . ."

Emily's gaze fell back on Sonya. Jill tried to push forward to see what all the drama was about, but Emily continued blocking the door, still not totally convinced it was safe. I couldn't blame her. At last, she gave a slow nod and stepped away to give us access.

Sydney's eyes flicked toward the car, where Victor, Robert, and Dimitri were waiting. "What about them?" she asked me.

I hesitated. I wanted Dimitri to be with me to drop the bombshell, but Emily might only be able to handle one thing at a time here. Moroi didn't have to run in royal circles to know who Victor Dashkov was or what he looked like. Our trip to Las Vegas had been proof of that. I shook my head at Sydney. "They can wait."

We settled into the family's living room and learned the guy who'd answered the door was Emily's husband, John Mastrano. Emily went through the motions of offering us beverages, like this was a perfectly ordinary visit, but the look on her face confirmed she was still in shock. She handed us glasses of water like a robot, her face so pale she might have been Strigoi.

John rested his hand on Emily's once she sat down. He kept giving us wary looks, but for her, he was all affection and concern. "What's going on?"

Emily's eyes were still dazed. "I . . . don't know. My cousin is here . . . but I don't understand how . . ." She looked back and forth at me, Sydney, and Sonya. "How is this possible?" Her voice shook.

"It was Lissa, wasn't it?" exclaimed Jill, who undoubtedly knew this relative's sordid history. She was understandably shocked—and a little nervous—but excitement was beginning to stir. "I heard what happened with Dimitri. It's true, isn't it? Lissa can heal Strigoi. She saved him. She saved . . ." Jill turned toward Sonya, enthusiasm wavering a little. I wondered what kind of stories she'd heard about Sonya. "She saved you."

"Lissa didn't do it," I said. "Another, uh, spirit user did."

Jill's face lit up. "Adrian?" I'd forgotten about her crush on him.

"No . . . someone else. It's not important," I added hastily. "Sonya's . . . well, she's Moroi again. Confused, though. Not quite herself."

Sonya had been drinking in the sight of her cousin but now turned to me with a wry, knowing smile. "I can speak for myself, Rose."

"Sorry," I said.

Emily turned to Sydney and frowned. They'd been introduced, but no more. "Why are you here?" Emily didn't have to say what she really meant. She wanted to know why a *human* was here. "Are you a feeder?"

"No!" exclaimed Sydney, jumping up from her spot beside me on the loveseat. I had never seen her filled with such outrage and disgust. "Say that again, and I'll walk right out of here! I'm an Alchemist."

She was met with blank stares, and I pulled Sydney back down. "Easy, girl. I don't think they don't know what Alchemists are." Secretly, I was glad. When I'd first discovered the Alchemists, I'd felt like I was the last person in the world to find out. It was nice to know others were out of the loop too. Keeping things simple for now, I explained to Emily, "Sydney's been helping us."

Tears brimmed in Emily's blue eyes as she turned back to her cousin. Emily Mastrano was one of the most stunning women I'd ever met. Even tears were beautiful on her. "It's really you, isn't it? They brought you back to me. Oh God." Emily rose and walked over to hold her cousin in a deep embrace. "I've missed you so much. I can't believe this."

I almost felt like crying, too, but sternly reminded myself that we had come with a mission. I knew how startling this all was. We had just turned the Mastrano family's world upside down . . . and I was about to complicate things even more. I hated to do it. I wished they could have the time they needed to adjust, to celebrate the miracle of having Sonya back. But the clock at Court—and on my life—was ticking.

"We brought her . . ." I said at last. "But there's another reason we're here."

I don't know what tone my voice conveyed, but Emily stiffened and stepped back from Sonya, sitting down beside her husband. Somehow, in that moment, I think she knew why we were here. I could see in her eyes that she was afraid—as if she'd been dreading this type of visit for years, as if she'd imagined it a hundred times.

I pushed forward. "We know . . . we know about Eric Dragomir."

"No," said Emily, her voice an odd mixture of harshness and desperateness. Her obstinate manner was remarkably similar to Sonya's initial refusal to aid us. "No. We are not doing this."

The instant I'd seen Jill, the instant I'd recognized those eyes, I'd known we had the right place. Emily's words—more importantly, her lack of a denial—confirmed it.

"We have to," I said. "This is serious."

Emily turned to Sonya. "You promised! You promised you wouldn't tell!"

"I didn't," said Sonya, but her face wore its earlier doubt.

"She didn't," I said firmly, hoping to reassure them both. "It's hard to explain . . . but she kept her promise."

"No," repeated Emily. "This isn't happening. We cannot talk about this."

"What . . . what's going on?" demanded John. Anger kindled in his eyes. He didn't like seeing strangers upset his wife.

I directed my words to Emily. "We *have* to talk about this. Please. We need your help. We need *her* help." I gestured to Jill.

"What do you mean?" asked Jill. That earlier eager spark was gone, cooled by her mother's reaction.

"It's about your—" I came to a stop. I'd rushed into this, ready to find Lissa's sibling—her sister, we now knew—with little thought of the implications. I should have known this would be a secret from everyone—including the child in question. I hadn't considered what a shock this would be to her. And this wasn't just some random stranger. This was *Jill*. Jill. My friend. The girl who was like a little sister to all of us, the one we looked out for. What was I about to do to her? Looking at John, I realized things were worse still. Did Jill think he was her father? This family was about to be shaken to its core—and I was responsible.

"Don't!" cried Emily, jumping up again. "Get out! All of you! I don't want you here!"

"Mrs. Mastrano . . ." I began. "You can't pretend this isn't real. You have to face it."

"No!" she pointed to the door. "Get out! Get out, or I'll . . . I'll call the police! Or the guardians! You . . ." Realization flashed over her now that the initial shock of seeing Sonya had faded. Victor wasn't the only criminal Moroi would be on guard for. "You're a fugitive! A murderer!"

"She is not!" said Jill, leaning forward. "I told you, Mom. I told you before it was a mistake—"

"Get out," repeated Emily.

"Sending us away won't change the truth," I said, forcing myself to stay calm.

"Will someone please tell me what the *hell* is going on?" John's face was flushed red, angry and defensive. "If I don't have an answer within thirty seconds, I'm calling the guardians *and* the police."

I looked over at Jill and couldn't speak. I didn't know how to say what I needed to, at least not tactfully. Sydney, however, didn't have that problem.

"He's not your father," she said bluntly, pointing at John.

There was a slight pause in the room. Jill almost looked disappointed, like she'd hoped for more exciting news.

"I know that. He's my stepdad. Or, well, my dad as far as I'm concerned."

Emily sank back on the couch, burying her face in her hands. She seemed to be crying, but I was pretty sure she could jump up at any moment and call the authorities. We had to get through this fast, no matter how painful.

"Right. He's not your biological father," I said, looking steadily at Jill. *The eyes. How had I never noticed the eyes?* "Eric Dragomir is."

Emily made a low keening sound. "No," she begged. "Please don't do this."

John's anger morphed back to the confusion that seemed to be so in fashion in this room. "*What?*"

"That . . . no." Jill slowly shook her head. "That's impossible. My father was just . . . just some guy who ran out on us."

In some ways, that wasn't far from the truth, I supposed. "It was Eric Dragomir," I said. "You're part of their family. Lissa's sister. You're . . ." I startled myself, realizing I had to look at Jill in a whole new way. "You're royalty."

Jill was always full of energy and optimism, operating in the world with a naive hope and charm. But now her face was grim and sober, making her look older than her fifteen years. "No. This is a joke. My dad was a lowlife. I'm not . . . no. Rose, stop."

"Emily." I flinched at the sound of Sonya's voice, surprised to hear her speak. I was more surprised at her expression. Authoritative. Serious. Determined. Sonya was younger than Emily by—what? Ten years, if I had to guess. But Sonya had fixed her cousin with a stare that made Emily look like a naughty child. "Emily, it's time to give this up. You have to tell her. For God's sake, you have to tell John. You can't keep this buried anymore."

Emily looked up and met Sonya's eyes. "I can't tell. You know what will happen . . . I can't do that to her."

"None of us know what will happen," said Sonya. "But things will get worse if you don't take control now."

After a long moment, Emily finally looked away, staring at the floor. The sad, sad look on her face broke my heart. And not just mine.

"Mom?" asked Jill, voice trembling. "What's happening? This is all a big mix-up, right?"

Emily sighed and looked up at her daughter. "No. You are Eric Dragomir's daughter. Rose is right." John made a small, strangled sound but didn't interrupt his wife. She squeezed his hand again. "What I told you both over the years . . . it was true. Mostly. We did just have a brief . . . relationship. Not a cheap one, exactly. But brief." She paused and glanced over at John this time, her expression softening. "I told you . . ."

He nodded. "And I told *you* the past didn't matter to me. Never affected how I felt about you, about Jill. But I never imagined . . ."

"Me neither," she agreed. "I didn't even know who he was when we first met. It was back when I lived in Las Vegas and had my first job, dancing in a show at the Witching Hour."

I felt my eyes go wide. No one seemed to notice. *The Witching Hour*. My friends and I had been to that casino while hunting for Robert, and a man there had made a joke about Lissa's father being interested in showgirls. I knew Emily worked in a Detroit ballet company now; it was why they lived in Michigan. Never would I have guessed that she'd started as a feather-and-sequin-clad dancer in a Las Vegas show. But why not? She would have had to start somewhere, and her tall, graceful frame would lend itself well to any type of dancing.

"He was so sweet . . . and so sad," Emily continued. "His father had just died, and he'd come to sort of drown his sorrows. I understood how a death would devastate him, but now . . . well, I *really* understand. It was another loss to his family. The numbers were dropping." She frowned thoughtfully and then shrugged. "He was a good man, and I think he truly loved his wife. But he was in a dark, low place. I don't think he was using me. He cared about me, though I doubt what happened between us would have in other circumstances. Anyway, I was fine with the way things ended and was content to move on with my life . . . until Jill came along. I contacted Eric because I thought he should know—though I made it clear I didn't expect anything from him. And at that point, knowing who he was, I didn't *want* anything. If I'd let him, I think he would have acknowledged you, had a role in your life." Emily's eyes were on Jill now. "But I've seen what that world is like. Court life is politics and lies and backstabbing. In the end, the only thing I'd accept from him was money. I still didn't want that. I didn't want to feel like I was blackmailing him—but I *did* want to make sure your future was secure."

I spoke without thinking. "You don't really live like you're using that money." I regretted the words as soon as they were out. Their home was perfectly nice, hardly the depths of poverty. But it also didn't match the funds I'd seen moved around in those bank accounts.

"I'm not," said Emily. "It's on hand for emergencies, of course, but mostly I set it all aside for Jill, for her future. To do whatever she wants."

"What do you mean?" asked Jill, aghast. "What kind of money are you talking about?"

"You're an heiress," I said. "*And* royalty."

"I'm not any of those things," she said. She was frantic now, looking around at all of us. She reminded me of a deer, ready to bolt. "There's a mistake. You've all made some mistake."

Emily stood up and walked over to Jill's chair, kneeling on the floor before it. Emily clasped her daughter's hand. "It *is* all true. And I'm sorry you have to find out like this. But it doesn't change anything. Our lives aren't going to change. We'll go on just like we have before."

A range of emotions raced over Jill's features—especially fear and confusion—but she leaned down and buried her face against her mother's shoulder in acceptance. "Okay."

It was a touching moment, and again, I almost felt like crying. I'd had my own share of family drama and parental issues. Like before, I wanted the Mastranos to have this moment—but they couldn't.

"You can't," I told them. "You can't go on like before. Jill . . . Jill has to go to Court."

Emily jerked away from Jill and stared at me. Only a second ago, Emily had been full of grief and distress. Now, I saw intense anger and ferocity. Her blue eyes were stormy, fixing me with a sharp glare. "*No*. She is not going there. She is never going there."

Jill had already visited Court before, but both Emily and I knew that I wasn't referring to some casual sightseeing trip. Jill had to go with her true identity. Well—maybe *true* wasn't the right word. Illicit royalty wasn't part of her nature, at least not yet. She was who she'd always been, but her name had changed. That change had to be acknowledged, and the Moroi Court would be shaken.

"She has to," I urged. "The Court's getting corrupted, and the Dragomir family has to play its part to help fix things. Lissa has no power alone, not without a family quorum. All the other royals . . . they're trampling her. They're going to push laws that won't help any of us."

Emily still knelt by the chair, as though shielding Jill from my words. "And that's exactly why Jill can't go. It's why I wouldn't let Eric acknowledge her. I don't want Jill involved. That place is poison. Tatiana's murder is proof." Emily paused and gave me a sharp look, reminding me that I was the chief suspect. Apparently we weren't past that yet. "All those royals . . . they're vicious. I don't want Jill turning into one of them. I *won't* let her turn into one of them."

"Not all royals are like that," I argued. "Lissa's not. She's trying to change the system."

Emily gave me a bitter smile. "And how do you think the others feel about her reform? I'm sure there are royals who are happy to see her silenced—royals who wouldn't like to see her family reemerge. I told you: Eric was a good man. Sometimes I don't think it's a coincidence their family has died out."

I gaped. "That's ridiculous." But I suddenly wasn't so sure.

"Is it?" Emily's eyes were on me, as though guessing my doubts. "What do you think they'd do if another Dragomir came forward? The people who oppose Vasilisa? What do you think they'd do if only one person stood between them and her family's power?"

Her implications were shocking . . . yet, I knew they weren't impossible. Glancing over at Jill, I felt an empty, sinking feeling in my stomach. What would I be subjecting her to? Sweet, innocent Jill. Jill wanted adventure out of life and could still barely talk to guys without blushing. Her desire to learn to fight was half–youthful impulse and half-instinct to defend her people. Stepping into the royal world could technically help her people too—though not in a way she'd ever expected. And it would mean getting involved with the dark and sinister nature that sometimes filled the Court.

Emily seemed to read my silence as agreement. A mix of triumph and relief crossed her face, all of which vanished when Jill suddenly spoke up.

"I'll do it."

We all turned to stare. Thus far, I'd been regarding her with pity, thinking of her as a victim. Now, I was startled at how brave and resolved she looked. Her expression was still underscored with a little fear and shock, but there was a steel in her I'd never seen before.

"What?" exclaimed Emily.

"I'll do it," said Jill, voice steadier. "I'll help Lissa and . . . and the Dragomirs. I'll go with Rose back to Court."

I decided mentioning the myriad difficulties of me getting anywhere near Court wasn't important just then. Honestly, I had reached a point where I was playing all of this by ear, though it was a relief to see Emily's fury shifted away from me.

"You will not! I'm not letting you near there."

"You can't make this choice for me!" cried Jill. "I'm not a child."

"And you're certainly not an adult," retorted Emily.

The two began arguing back and forth, and soon John jumped in to support his wife. In the midst of the family bickering, Sydney leaned toward me and murmured, "I bet you never thought the hardest part of finding your 'savior' would be getting her mom to let her stay out past curfew."

The unfortunate part about her joke was that it was kind of true. We needed Jill, and I certainly hadn't envisioned this complication. What if Emily refused? Clearly, keeping Jill's heritage a secret was something she'd been pretty adamant about for a while—say, like, fifteen years. I had a feeling Jill wouldn't be beyond running away to Court if it came down to that. And I wouldn't be beyond helping her.

Once more, Sonya jumped into the conversation unexpectedly. "Emily, didn't you hear me? This is all going to happen eventually, with or without your consent. If you don't let Jill go now, she'll go next week. Or next year. Or in five years. The point is, it *will* happen."

Emily sank back against the chair, face crumpling. "No. I don't want this."

Sonya's pretty face turned bitter. "Life, unfortunately, doesn't seem to care what we want. Act now while you can actually stop it from being a disaster."

"Please, Mom," begged Jill. Her jade Dragomir eyes regarded Emily with affection. I knew Jill might indeed disobey and run off—but she didn't want to, not if she didn't have to.

Emily stared into the distance, long-lashed eyes vacant and defeated. And although she was standing in the way of my plans, I knew she did it out of legitimate love and concern—traits that had probably drawn Eric to her.

"Okay," said Emily at last. She sighed. "Jill can go—but I'm going too. You aren't facing that place without me."

"Or me," said John. He still seemed bewildered but was determined to support his wife and stepdaughter. Jill regarded them both with gratitude, reminding me again that I'd just turned a functional family dysfunctional. Emily and John coming with us hadn't been part of my plans, but I couldn't blame them and didn't see what harm they'd cause. We'd need Emily anyway to tell everyone about Eric.

"Thank you," I said. "Thank you so much."

John eyed me. "We still haven't dealt with the fact that there's a fugitive in our home."

"Rose didn't do it!" That fierceness was still in Jill. "It was a setup."

"It was." I hesitated to speak my next words. "Probably

by the people opposing Lissa."

Emily paled, but I felt the need for honesty, even if it reaffirmed her fears. She took a steadying breath. "I believe you. Believe that you didn't do it. I don't know why . . . but I do." She almost smiled. "No, I do know why. It's because of what I said before, about those vipers at Court. They're the ones who do this kind of thing. Not you."

"Are you sure?" asked John uneasily. "This mess with Jill is bad enough without us housing a criminal."

"I'm certain," said Emily. "Sonya and Jill trust Rose, and so I do. You're all welcome to stay here tonight since we can hardly head out to Court right now."

I opened my mouth to say we most certainly could leave right now, but Sydney elbowed me sharply. "Thank you, Mrs. Mastrano," she said, summoning up that Alchemist diplomacy. "That would be great."

I repressed a scowl. Time was still pressing on me, but I knew the Mastranos were entitled to make some preparations. It was probably better to travel in the daytime too. A rough check of my mental map made me think we could do the whole drive back to Court in one day. I nodded in agreement with Sydney, resigning myself to a sleepover at the Mastrano house.

"Thanks. We appreciate it." Suddenly, something occurred to me, summoning back John's words. *This mess with Jill is bad enough without us housing a criminal.* I gave Emily as convincing and reassuring a smile as I could muster. "We, um, also have some friends with us waiting out in the car . . ."

TWENTY-FOUR

CONSIDERING THEIR EARLIER antagonism, I was a bit surprised to see Sonya and Robert combine their powers to create an illusion for the Dashkov brothers. It obscured their appearances, and with the addition of some fake names, the Mastrano family just assumed the guys were part of our increasingly bizarre entourage. Considering the distress and upheaval already going on in the house, a couple more people seemed the least of the Mastranos' worries.

In playing good Moroi hosts, it wasn't enough to just cook up dinner. Emily also managed to get a feeder to come by—a sort of "blood delivery service." Normally, Moroi who lived outside sheltered areas and intermingled among humans had access to secret feeders living nearby. Usually, these feeders had a keeper of sorts, a Moroi who made money off the service. It was common for Moroi to simply show up at the home of the feeder's "owner," but in this case, Emily had made arrangements for the feeder to be brought to her house.

She was doing it as a courtesy, the kind she'd do for any Moroi guests—even ones who were delivering news she'd dreaded receiving for most of her life. Little did she know just how desperately welcome blood was to the Moroi we'd brought along. I didn't mind the brothers suffering a little weakness, but Sonya definitely needed blood if she was going to continue her recovery.

Indeed, when the feeder and her keeper showed, Sonya was the first to drink. Dimitri and I had to stay out of sight upstairs. Sonya and Robert could only manage so much spirit-illusion, and hiding Robert and Victor's identities from the feeder's Moroi was imperative. Obscuring both me and Dimitri would have been too much, and considering our most-wanted status, it was essential we not take any risks.

Leaving the brothers unsupervised made Dimitri and me nervous, but the two of them seemed too desperate for blood to attempt anything. Dimitri and I wanted to clean up anyways, since we hadn't had time for showers this morning. We flipped a coin, and I got to go first. Only, when I finished and was rummaging through my clothes, I discovered I'd gone through my clean "casual wear" supply and was down to the dress Sydney had included in the backpack. I grimaced but figured it wouldn't hurt to put the dress on for one night. We wouldn't be doing much more than waiting around for tomorrow's departure, and maybe Emily would let me do laundry before we left. After decent hair styling with a blow dryer, I finally felt civilized again.

Sydney and I had been given a guestroom to share, and the brothers occupied another. Sonya was going to stay in Jill's room, and Dimitri had been offered the couch. I didn't doubt for a second he'd be stalking the halls as the household slept and that I'd be trading shifts with him. For now, he was still showering, and I crept out into the hall and peered down over a railing to check out the first floor. The Mastranos, Sonya, and the brothers were all gathered with the feeder and her keeper. Nothing seemed amiss. Relieved, I returned to my room and used the downtime to check on Lissa.

After the initial excitement of passing her test, I'd felt her calm down and had assumed she was getting much-needed sleep. But, no. She hadn't gone to bed. She'd taken Eddie and Christian over to Adrian's, and I realized she was the one who'd woken him up from the dream I'd shared with him in the car. A skimming of her recent memories gave me a replay of what had happened since the time he left me and staggered to his door.

"What's going on?" he asked, looking from face to face. "I was having a good dream."

"I need you," said Lissa.

"I hear that from women a lot," said Adrian. Christian made a gagging sound, but the faintest glimmer of a smile crossed Eddie's lips, despite his otherwise tough guardian-stance.

"I'm serious," she told him. "I just got a message from Ambrose. He's got something important to tell us, and . . . I don't know. I'm still not certain of his role in everything. I want another set of eyes on him. I want your opinion."

"That," Adrian said, "is *not* something I hear a lot."

"Just hurry up and get dressed, okay?" ordered Christian.

Honestly, it was a wonder anyone slept anymore, considering how often we were all pulled out of sleep. Adrian nonetheless did dress quickly, and despite his flippant comments, I knew he was interested in anything related to clearing my name. What I was uncertain of was whether he'd tell anyone about the mess I'd gotten myself into, now that I'd slipped and revealed some of my true activities.

My friends hurried over to the building they'd visited before, the one where Ambrose lived and worked. The Court had woken up, and people were out and about, many undoubtedly wanting to find out about the second monarch test. In fact, a few people catching sight of Lissa called out happy greetings.

"I had another trial tonight," Lissa told Adrian. Someone had just congratulated her. "An unexpected one."

Adrian hesitated, and I waited for him to say he'd already heard that from me. I also waited for him to deliver the shocking news about my current company and whereabouts. "How'd it go?" he asked instead.

"I passed," she replied. "That's all that matters."

She couldn't bring herself to tell him about the cheering people, those who didn't just simply support her because of the law but because they actually believed in her. Tasha, Mia, and some surprise friends from school had been among the onlookers, grinning at her. Even Daniella, there to wait for Rufus's turn, had grudgingly congratulated Lissa, seeming surprised Lissa had made it through. The whole experience had been surreal, and Lissa had simply wanted to get out of there.

Eddie had gotten pulled away to assist other guardians, despite his protests that he was Lissa's escort. So, Christian and Tasha had ended up having to take Lissa home alone. Well, almost alone. A guardian named Ethan Moore joined them, the one Abe had teased Tasha about. Abe exaggerated some things, but he'd been right this time. Ethan looked as tough as any guardian, but his kickass attitude occasionally faltered whenever he looked at Tasha. He adored her. She clearly liked him too and flirted along the way—much to Christian's discomfort. I thought it was cute. Some guys probably wouldn't go near Tasha because of her scars. It was nice to see someone who appreciated her for her character, no matter how disgusted Christian was by the thought of *anyone* dating his aunt. And I actually kind of liked seeing Christian so obviously tormented. It was good for him.

Ethan and Tasha left once Lissa was securely back in her room. Within minutes, Eddie showed back up, grumbling about how they'd delayed him with some "crap task" when they knew he had better things to do. He'd apparently made such a fuss that they'd finally released him, so he could hurry back to Lissa's side. He made it just ten minutes before Ambrose's note arrived, which was lucky timing. Eddie would have freaked out if he'd come to her room and found her gone. He would have thought Strigoi had kidnapped his charge in his absence.

That was the series of events leading up to what was happening now: Lissa and the three guys going off to Ambrose's secret meeting.

"You're early," he said, letting them in before Lissa could even knock a second time. They stood inside Ambrose's own room now, not a fancy parlor for clients. It resembled a dorm room—a very nice one. Much nicer than anything I'd endured.

Lissa's attention was all on Ambrose, so she didn't notice, out of the corner of her eye, Eddie quickly scanning the room. I was glad he was on his game and guessed he didn't trust Ambrose—or anyone not in our immediate circle.

"What's going on?" asked Lissa, as soon as Ambrose shut the door. "Why the urgent visit?"

"Because I have to show you something," he said. On his bed was a pile of papers, and he took the top one. "Remember when I said they were locking off Tatiana's belongings? Well now they're inventorying and removing them." Adrian shifted uncomfortably—again, only something I noticed. "She had a safe where she kept important documents—secret ones, obviously. And . . ."

"And?" prompted Lissa.

"And, I didn't want anyone to find them," Ambrose continued. "I didn't know what most of them were, but if she wanted them secret . . . I just felt they should stay that way. I knew the combination, and so . . . I stole them." Guilt shone on his face, but it wasn't murderous guilt. It was guilt for the theft.

Lissa eyed the stack eagerly. "And?"

"None of them have anything to do with what you're looking for . . . except maybe this one." He handed her the piece of paper. Adrian and Christian crowded around her.

Darling Tatiana,

I'm a bit surprised to see how these latest developments have unfolded. I thought we had an understanding that the safety of our people required more than just bringing in a younger crop of guardians. We have let too many of them go to waste, particularly the women. If you took actions to force them back—and you know what I'm talking about—the guardian ranks would swell. This current law is completely inadequate, particularly after seeing how your "training" experiment failed.

I'm equally shocked to hear that you are considering releasing Dimitri Belikov from his guards. I don't understand exactly what happened, but you cannot trust mere appearances. You may be unleashing a monster—or at the very least, a spy—in our midst, and he needs to be under much stricter guard than he currently is. In fact, your continued support of the study of spirit is troubling altogether and no doubt led to this unnatural situation. I believe there is a reason this element was lost to us for so long: our ancestors realized its danger and stamped it out. Avery Lazar stands as proof of that, and your prodigy, Vasilisa Dragomir, is certain to follow. In encouraging Vasilisa, you encourage the degradation of the Dragomir line, a line that should be allowed to fade into history with honor and not the disgrace of insanity. Your support of her may also put your own great-nephew at risk, something neither of us would like to see happen.

I'm sorry to burden you with so much condemnation. I hold you in the highest regard and have nothing but respect for the way you have so skillfully governed our people these long years. I'm certain you will soon come to the appropriate decisions—though I worry others may not share my confidence in you. Said people might attempt to take matters into their own hands, and I fear for what may follow.

The letter was typed, with no signature. For a moment, Lissa couldn't process it as a whole. She was completely consumed by the part about the Dragomir line fading into disgrace. It hit too close to the vision she'd seen in the test.

It was Christian who pulled her back. "Well. It would seem Tatiana had enemies. But I guess that's kind of obvious at this point in the game."

"Who's this from?" demanded Adrian. His face was dark, furious at this thinly veiled threat to his aunt.

"I don't know," said Ambrose. "This is exactly the way I found it. Maybe she didn't even know who the sender was."

Lissa nodded her agreement. "There's certainly an anonymous feel to it . . . and yet, at the same time, I feel like it's someone Tatiana must have known well."

Adrian gave Ambrose a suspicious look. "How do we know you didn't just type this yourself to throw us off?"

"Adrian," chastised Lissa. She didn't say it but was hoping to urge Adrian to feel out Ambrose's aura for anything she might not be able to detect.

"This is crazy," said Christian, tapping the piece of paper. "The part about rounding up dhampirs and forcing them to be guardians. What do you think that means—the "actions" that Tatiana knows about?"

I knew because I'd been tipped off about a lot of this earlier. Compulsion, Tatiana's note had said.

"I'm not sure," said Lissa. She reread the letter to herself. "What about the 'experiments' part? Do you think that's the training sessions Grant did with Moroi?"

"That was what I thought," said Ambrose. "But I'm not sure."

"Can we see the rest?" asked Adrian, gesturing to the stack of papers. I couldn't tell if his suspicion was legitimate distrust of Ambrose or just the result of how upset his aunt's murder made him.

Ambrose handed over the papers, but after going through the pages, Lissa agreed: there was nothing of use in them. The documents mostly consisted of legalese and personal correspondence. It occurred to Lissa—as it had to me—that Ambrose might not be showing everything he'd found. There was no way to prove that for now. Stifling a yawn, she thanked him and left with the others.

She was hoping for sleep, but her mind couldn't help but analyze the letter's possibilities. If it was legitimate.

"That letter's evidence that someone had a lot more reason to be pissed off at Tatiana than Rose did," observed Christian as they wound their way back upstairs toward the building's exit. "Aunt Tasha once said that anger based on calculated reason is more dangerous than anger based on blind hate."

"Your aunt's a regular philosopher," said Adrian wearily. "But everything we've got is still circumstantial."

Ambrose had let Lissa keep the letter, and she'd folded it and put it in her jeans pocket. "I'm curious what Tasha will have to say about this. And Abe too." She sighed. "I wish Grant was still alive. He was a good man—and might have some insight into this."

They reached a side exit on the main floor, and Eddie pushed the door open for them. Christian glanced over at Lissa as they stepped outside. "How close were Grant and Serena—"

Eddie moved a fraction of a second before Lissa saw the problem, but of course, Eddie would have already been watching for problems. A man—a Moroi, actually—had been waiting among trees in the courtyard that separated Ambrose's building from the neighboring one. It wasn't exactly a secluded spot, but it was far enough off of the main paths that it often stayed deserted.

The man moved forward and looked startled when he saw Eddie racing toward him. I was able to analyze the fight in a way Lissa couldn't. Judging by the man's angle and movement, he'd been heading for Lissa—with a knife in his hand. Lissa froze in fear, an expected reaction for someone not trained to react in this situation. But when Christian jerked her back, she came to life and quickly retreated with him and Adrian.

The attacker and Eddie were deadlocked for a moment, each trying to take the other down. I heard Lissa yell for help, but my attention was all on the fighters. The guy was strong for a Moroi and his maneuvers suggested he'd been trained to fight. I doubted, however, that he'd been trained since elementary school, nor did he have the muscle a dhampir did.

Sure enough, Eddie broke through and forced the guy to the ground. Eddie reached out to pin the man's right hand and get the knife out of the equation. Moroi or not, the man was actually quite skilled with the blade, particularly when I (and probably Eddie too) noticed scarring and what looked like a bent finger on his left hand. The guy had probably gone to great extents to hone his knife-hand's reflexes. Even restrained, he was still able to snake up with the blade, aiming unhesitatingly for Eddie's neck. Eddie was too fast to let that happen and blocked the blow with his arm, which took the blade's cut.

Eddie's block gave the Moroi a bit more room to move, and he bucked up, throwing Eddie off. Without missing a beat—really, this guy was impressive—the Moroi swung for Eddie again. There could be no doubt about the man's intentions. He wasn't holding back. He was there to kill. That blade was out for blood. Guardians knew how to subdue and take prisoners, but we'd also been trained that when things were moving too fast, when it was an us-or-them situation—well, we made sure it was them. Eddie was faster than his opponent and was being driven by instincts pounded into us for years: stop what was trying to kill you. Eddie had no gun or knife, not at Court. When the man came at him a second time, knife again pointed straight at Eddie's neck, Eddie used the only weapon left that he could be sure would save his life.

Eddie staked the Moroi.

Dimitri had once jokingly commented that you didn't have to be Strigoi to be hurt by a stake through your heart. And, let's face it, a stake through the heart didn't actually hurt. It killed. Tatiana was proof. The man's knife actually made contact with Eddie's neck—and then fell before piercing skin. The man's eyes went wide in shock and pain and then saw nothing at all. He was dead. Eddie leaned back on his heels, staring at his victim with the adrenaline-charged battle lust that followed any situation. Shouting suddenly caught his attention, and he leapt to his feet, ready for the next threat.

What he found was a group of guardians, ones who had responded to Lissa's earlier cries for help. They took one look at the scene and immediately acted on and the conclusions their training drove them to. There was a dead Moroi and someone holding a bloody weapon. The guardians went for Eddie, throwing him against the wall and prying his stake away. Lissa shouted to them that they had it all wrong, that Eddie had saved her life and—

"Rose!"

Dimitri's frantic voice shocked me back to the Mastrano house. I was sitting on the bed, and he knelt before me, face full of fear as he gripped my shoulders. "Rose, what's wrong? Are you okay?"

"No!"

I pushed him aside and moved toward the door. "I have to—I have to go back to Court. Now. Lissa's in danger. She needs me."

"Rose. *Roza*. Slow down." He'd caught hold of my arm, and there was no escaping from that grip. He turned me so I faced him. His hair was still damp from the shower, and the clean scent of soap and wet skin surrounded us. "Tell me what happened."

I quickly repeated what I'd seen. "Someone tried to kill her, Dimitri! And I wasn't there!"

"But Eddie was," said Dimitri quietly. "She's okay. She's alive." He released me, and I leaned wearily against the wall. My heart was racing, and even though my friends were safe, I couldn't shake my panic.

"And now he's in trouble. Those guardians were pissed—"

"Only because they don't know the whole story. They see a dead body and a weapon, that's it. Once they get facts and testimonies, everything will be okay. Eddie saved a Moroi. It's his job."

"But he killed another Moroi to do it," I pointed out. "We're not supposed to do that." It sounded like an obvious—and even stupid—statement, but I knew Dimitri understood what I meant. The guardians' purpose was to protect Moroi. *They come first*. Killing one was unimaginable. But then, so was them trying to kill each other.

"This wasn't a normal situation," Dimitri affirmed.

I tipped my head back. "I know, I know. I just can't stand leaving her undefended. I want so badly to go back and keep her safe. Right now." Tomorrow seemed years away. "What if it happens again?"

"Other people are there to protect her." Dimitri walked over to me, and I was surprised to see a smile on his lips, in light of the grim events. "Believe me, I want to protect her too, but we'd risk our lives for nothing if we take off right now. Wait a little longer and at least risk your life for something important."

A little of the panic faded. "And Jill is important, isn't she?"

"Very."

I straightened up. Part of my brain kept trying to calm me about Lissa's attack while the other fully processed what we'd accomplished here. "We did it," I said, feeling a smile slowly spread to my own lips. "Against all reason . . . somehow, we found Lissa's lost sister. Do you realize what this means? Lissa can have everything she's entitled to now. They can't deny her anything. Hell, she *could* be queen if she wanted. And Jill . . ."

I hesitated. "Well, she's part of an ancient royal family. That's got to be a good thing, right?"

"I think it depends on Jill," said Dimitri. "And what the after-effects of all this are."

Guilt over potentially ruining Jill's life returned, and I stared down at my feet. "Hey, it's okay," he said, tilting my chin back up. His brown eyes were warm and affectionate. "You did the right thing. No one else would have tried something this impossible. Only Rose Hathaway. You took a gamble to find Jill. You risked your life by breaking Abe's rules—and it paid off. It was worth it."

"I hope Adrian thinks so," I mused. "He thinks me leaving our 'safe house' was the stupidest thing ever."

Dimitri's hand dropped. "You told him about all this?"

"Not about Jill. But I accidentally told him we weren't in West Virginia anymore. He's kept it secret, though," I added hastily. "No one else knows."

"I can believe that," said Dimitri, though he'd lost some of his earlier warmth. It was such a fleeting thing. "He . . . he seems pretty loyal to you."

"He is. I trust him completely."

"And he makes you happy?" Dimitri's tone wasn't harsh, but there was an intensity to it that put the exchange on par with a police interrogation.

I thought about my time with Adrian: the bantering, the parties, the games, and of course, the kissing. "Yeah. He does. I have fun with him. I mean he's infuriating sometimes—okay, a lot of the time—but don't be fooled by all the vices. He's not a bad person."

"I know he isn't," said Dimitri. "He's a good man. It's not easy for everyone to see, but I can. He's still getting himself together, but he's on his way. I saw it in the escape. And after . . ." The words caught on Dimitri's tongue. "After Siberia, he was there for you? He helped you?"

I nodded, puzzled by all these questions. Turns out they were only the warm-up for the big one.

"Do you love him?"

There were only a few people in the world who could ask me such insanely personal questions without getting punched. Dimitri was one of them. With us, there were no walls, but our complicated relationship made this topic surreal. How could I describe loving someone else to a man I'd once loved? *A man you still love*, a voice whispered inside my head. Maybe. Probably. Again, I reminded myself that it was natural to carry lingering feelings for Dimitri. They would fade. They *had* to fade, just like his had. He was the past. Adrian was my future.

"Yeah," I said, taking longer than I probably should have. "I . . . I do love him."

"Good. I'm glad." The thing was, Dimitri's face didn't look all that glad as he stared blankly out the window. My confusion grew. Why was he upset? His actions and words no longer seemed to match lately.

I approached him. "What's wrong?

"Nothing. I just want to make sure that you're okay. That you're happy." He turned back to me, putting on a forced smile. He'd spoken the truth—but not the whole truth. "Things have been changing, that's all. It's making me reconsider so much. Ever since Donovan . . . and then Sonya . . . it's strange. I thought it all changed the night Lissa saved me. But it didn't. There's been so much more, more to the healing than I realized." He started to slip into pensive mode but caught himself. "Every day I figure out something new. Some new emotion I'd forgotten to feel. Some revelation I totally missed. Some beauty I didn't see."

"Hey, my hair in the alley does *not* go on that list, okay?" I teased. "You were in shock."

The forced smile grew natural. "No, Roza. It *was* beautiful. It's beautiful now."

"The dress is just throwing you off," I said, attempting a joke. In reality, I felt dizzy under his gaze.

Those dark, dark eyes looked at me—*really* looked at me, I think, for the first time since he'd entered the room. A mixed expression came over him that made no sense to me. I could pick out the emotions it contained but not what caused them. Awe. Wonder. Sadness. Regret.

"What?" I asked uneasily. "Why are you looking at me like that?"

He shook his head, the smile rueful now. "Because sometimes, a person can get so caught up in the details that they miss the whole. It's not just the dress or the hair. It's *you*. You're beautiful. So beautiful, it hurts me."

I felt a strange fluttering sensation in my chest. Butterflies, cardiac arrest . . . it was hard to say what exactly. Yet, in that moment, I was no longer standing in the Mastrano guestroom.

He'd said those words before, or something very close. *So beautiful, it hurts me.* It was back in the cabin at St. Vladimir's, the one and only time we'd had sex. He'd looked at me in a very similar way, too, only there'd been less sadness. Nonetheless, as I heard those words again, a door I'd kept locked in my heart suddenly burst open, and with it came all the feelings and experiences and sense of oneness we'd always shared. Looking at him, just for the space of a heartbeat, I had a surreal sensation wash over me, liked I'd known him forever. Like we were bound . . . but not in the way Lissa and I were, by a bond forced on us.

"Hey, guys, have you—oh." Sydney came to a halt in the half-open doorway and promptly took two steps back. "Sorry. I—that is—"

Dimitri and I immediately pulled back from each other. I felt warm and shaky and only then noticed how close we had been. I didn't even remember moving, but only a breath had separated us. What had happened? It was like a trance. A dream.

I swallowed and tried to slow my pulse. "No problem. What's going on?"

Sydney glanced between us, still looking uncomfortable. Her dating life might be non-existent, but even she knew what she'd walked in on. I was glad one of us did. "I . . . that is . . . I just wanted to come hang out. I can't handle *that* going on downstairs."

I attempted a smile, still utterly confused by my feelings. *Why did Dimitri look at me like that? Why did he say that? He can't still want me. He said he didn't. He told me to leave him alone.*

"Sure. We were just . . . talking," I said. She obviously didn't believe me. I tried harder to convince her . . . and myself. "We were talking about Jill. Do you have any ideas on how to get her to Court—seeing as we're all outlaws?"

Sydney might not be an expert in personal relationships, but puzzles were familiar territory. She relaxed, her attention focusing inward as she tried to figure our problem out.

"Well, you could always have her mother—"

A loud crashing from downstairs abruptly cut her off. As one, Dimitri and I sprang for the door, ready to combat whatever mess Victor and Robert had caused. We both came screeching to a halt at the top of the stairs when we heard lots of shouts for everyone to get down.

"Guardians," Dimitri said. "There are guardians raiding the house."

TWENTY-FIVE

WE COULD ALREADY HEAR footsteps thundering through the house and knew we were seconds from the army downstairs heading up to the second floor. The three of us backed away, and to my surprise, it was Sydney who reacted first.

"Get out. I'll distract them."

Her distracting them would probably just mean momentarily blocking their way until they pushed her aside, but those extra seconds could make a huge difference. Still, I couldn't stand the thought of abandoning her. Dimitri had no such reservations, particularly when we heard feet on the stairs.

"Come on!" he shouted, grabbing hold of my arm.

We raced down the hall to the farthest bedroom, Victor and Robert's. Just before we entered, I yelled back to Sydney, "Get Jill to Court!" I don't know if she heard because by the sounds of it, the guardians had reached her. Dimitri immediately opened the room's one large window and looked at me knowingly. As always, we needed no vocal communication.

He jumped out first, no doubt wanting to take the full brunt of whatever danger waited below. I immediately followed. I dropped onto the first floor's roof, slid down it, and then made the longer drop to the ground. Dimitri caught my arm, steadying my landing—but not before one of my ankles twisted slightly in on itself. It was the same one that had taken the brunt of the fall outside Donovan's, and I winced as pain shot through me, pain I then promptly ignored.

Dark figures moved toward us, emerging from evening shadows and hidden spots around the backyard. Of course. Guardians wouldn't just come busting down a door. They'd also have the place staked out. With our natural rhythm, Dimitri and I fought back-to-back against our attackers. Like usual, it was hard to incapacitate our foes without killing them. Hard, but necessary if we could manage it. I didn't want to kill my own people, people who were just doing their job to apprehend fugitives. The long dress didn't do me any favors either. My legs kept getting caught in the fabric.

"The others will be out any minute," Dimitri grunted, slamming a guardian to the ground. "We need to move—there. That gate."

I couldn't respond but followed his lead as we made our way to a door in the fence while still defending ourselves. We'd just taken out the backyard squad when more spilled from the house. We slipped through the gate, emerging onto a quiet side road flanking the Mastrano house, and ran. It soon became clear, however, that I couldn't keep up with Dimitri. My mind could ignore the pain, but my body couldn't make my injured ankle work properly.

Without missing a beat, Dimitri slid his arm around me, helping me run and take the weight off the ankle. We turned off the road, cutting through yards that would make it more difficult—but not impossible—for them to track us.

"We can't outrun them," I said. "I'm slowing us down. You need to—"

"Do *not* say leave you," he interrupted. "We're doing this together."

Snick, snick. A flowerpot near us suddenly exploded into a pile of dirt and clay.

"They're shooting at us," I said incredulously. "They're actually shooting at us!" With so much hand-to-hand training, I always felt like guns were cheating. But when it came to hunting down a queen-killing murderer and her accomplice? Honor wasn't the issue. Results were.

Another bullet zinged by, dangerously close. "With a silencer," said Dimitri. "Even so, they'll be cautious. They don't want the neighborhood thinking it's under attack. We need cover. Fast." We might've been literally dodging bullets, but my ankle wouldn't last much longer.

He made another sharp turn, completely immersing us in suburban backyards. I couldn't look behind us, but I heard shouting voices that let me know we weren't free yet.

"There," said Dimitri.

Ahead of us was a dark house with a large glass patio reminiscent of Sonya's. The glass door was open, though a screen blocked the way inside. Dimitri tugged on its latch. Locked. But a screen was hardly a deterrent for us. Poor, trusting family. He took out his stake and slashed a long, vertical line that we hastily slipped through. Immediately, he jerked me to the side, out of view. He put a finger to his lips, holding me close to his body, shattering me in his warmth.

Seconds later, we saw guardians coming through and searching the yards. Some kept moving on in case we'd run farther. Others lingered, investigating places that made good hiding spots as the evening grew darker and darker. I glanced at the screen. The cut had been clean, not an obvious hole, but it was still something our pursuers might notice.

Sensing this as well, Dimitri carefully moved off into the living room, doing his best to avoid windows and keep out of sight. We cut through to the kitchen and found a door leading to the garage. In the garage was a red Ford Mustang.

"Two car family," he murmured. "I was hoping for that."

"Or they're out for a walk and about to come home when they notice a SWAT team in their neighborhood," I whispered.

"The guardians won't let themselves be seen." We began searching for obvious key locations. At last, I found a set hanging on the side of a cupboard and scooped them up.

"Got 'em," I said. Since I had the keys, I think Dimitri actually would have let me jump into the driver's seat. Thanks to my right ankle, however, I had to toss him the keys. The universe had a sick sense of humor.

"Will they spot us in this?" I asked, as Dimitri opened the garage door and backed out. "It's, uh, a bit flashier than our usual stolen car profile." It was also awesome. Sydney, car geek that she was, would have loved it. I bit my lip, still guilty that we'd left her behind. I tried to push the thought out of my head for now.

"It is," agreed Dimitri. "But other cars will be driving down the street. Some guardians will still be searching the yards, and some will be guarding the Mastranos. They don't have infinite numbers. They can't watch everything at once, though they'll certainly try."

I held my breath anyway as we drove out of the subdivision. Twice, I thought I spotted stealthy figures by the side of the road, but Dimitri was right: they couldn't check every car in a busy suburban neighborhood. The darkness also obscured our faces.

Dimitri remembered the way we'd driven in because a few turns later, we were merging onto the freeway. I knew he had no destination in mind, except for *away*. With no obvious indications that we'd been followed, I shifted my body and stretched out my throbbing leg. My chest had that light, nebulous feeling you got when too much adrenaline was pumping through you.

"They turned us in, didn't they?" I asked. "Victor and Robert called us in and then took off. I should have kept watch."

"I don't know," Dimitri said. "It's possible. I saw them just before I talked to you, and everything seemed fine. They wanted to go with us to find Jill, but they knew it was only a matter of time before we turned them over to the authorities. I'm not surprised they came up with an escape plan. They could have used the feeding as a distraction to call the guardians and get rid of us."

"Crap." I sighed and pushed my hair back, wishing I had a ponytail holder. "We should've gotten rid of *them* when we had the chance. What'll happen now?"

Dimitri was silent for a few seconds. "The Mastranos will be questioned . . . extensively. Well, all of them will, really. They'll lock Sonya up for investigation, like me, and Sydney will be shipped back to the Alchemists."

"And what will they do to her?"

"I don't know. But I'm guessing her helping vampire fugitives won't go over well with her superiors."

"Crap," I repeated. Everything had fallen apart. "And what are *we* going to do?"

"Put some distance between us and those guardians. Hide somewhere. Wrap up your ankle."

I gave him a sidelong look. "Wow. You've got everything planned out."

"Not really," he said, a small frown on his face. "That's the easy stuff. What happens *after* that is going to be the hard part."

My heart sank. He was right. Provided the Mastranos weren't indicted by Moroi authorities for helping criminals, Emily now had no one forcing her to acknowledge Jill's heritage. If Sydney was being hauled back to her own people—well. She couldn't help either. I was going to have to tell someone else, I realized. The next time I made contact with Adrian, I'd have to divulge the truth so that my friends could do something about Jill. We couldn't sit on this secret any longer.

Dimitri took the next exit, and I tuned back into the world. "Hotel?" I asked.

"Not quite," he said. We were in a busy, commercial area, not far from Ann Arbor, I thought. One of the Detroit suburbs.

Restaurants and stores lined the road, and he turned us toward a twenty-four-hour superstore that promised to carry "everything." He parked and opened his door. "Stay here."

"But—"

Dimitri looked meaningfully at me, and I glanced down. I'd come away from our fight more scuffed up than I realized, and the dress had torn. My ragged appearance would attract attention, as would my limping. I nodded, and he left.

I spent the time turning over our problems, cursing myself for not having found a way to turn in the brothers once Robert had restored Sonya. I'd been bracing myself for betrayal in the form of some magical attack. I hadn't expected something as simple as a call to the guardians.

Dimitri, ever the efficient shopper, returned soon with two large bags and something slung over his shoulder. He tossed it all in the backseat, and I peered back curiously. "What's that?" It was long and cylindrical, covered in canvas.

"A tent."

"Why are we—" I groaned. "No hotel, huh?"

"We'll be harder to find at a campground. The car will especially be harder to find. We can't get rid of it quite yet, not with your foot."

"Those poor people," I said. "I hope their car insurance covers theft."

Back on the freeway, we soon left the urban sprawl, and it wasn't long before we saw advertisements for campgrounds and RV parks. Dimitri pulled over at a place called Peaceful Pines. He negotiated with the man working in the office and produced a number of crisp bills. That was another reason we couldn't get a hotel, I realized. Most required credit cards, and Sydney had had all those (in fake names, of course). We were living off cash now.

The clerk gave us directions along a gravel road that led to a spot on the opposite end of the campground. The place was busy with vacationing families, but no one paid much attention to us. Dimitri made sure to park as close to a cluster of trees as possible, in order to obscure the car and its plates. Despite my protests, he wouldn't let me help with the tent. He claimed he could do it faster without me and that I should stay off my feet. I started to argue until he began assembling the tent. My jaw dropped a little as I watched how quickly he put it together. He didn't even need the directions. It had to be some kind of record.

The tent was small and sturdy, giving us both room to sit and lie, though he had to hunch just a little when we were sitting. Once inside, I got to see the rest of his purchases. A lot of it was first aid. There was also a flashlight he propped up, a kind of makeshift lamp.

"Let me see the ankle," he ordered.

I stretched out my leg, and he pushed my dress's skirt up to my knee, fingers light against my skin. I shivered as a sense of déjà vu swept me. It seemed to be happening to me a lot lately. I thought back to all the times he had helped me with other injuries. We could have been right back in St. Vladimir's gym. He gently tested the ankle's mobility and did a little poking and prodding. His fingers never ceased to amaze me. They could break a man's neck, bandage a wound, and slide sensually across bare skin.

"I don't think it's broken," he said at last. He lifted his hands, and I noticed how warm I'd been while he touched me. "Just sprained."

"That kind of thing happens when you keep jumping off roofs," I said. Jokes were my old standby to hide discomfort. "You know, we never practiced that in our training."

He smiled and took out bandaging material, wrapping the ankle until it was supported and stabilized. After that, he produced—

"A bag of frozen peas?"

Dimitri shrugged and rested the bag on my ankle. The coolness instantly made me feel better. "Easier than buying a full bag of ice."

"You're pretty resourceful, Belikov. What else do you have stashed away?"

The rest of the bags' contents turned out to be blankets and some food. I gave him a big grin when I saw he'd gotten me sour cream potato chips and a bar of chocolate. I loved that he remembered such little details about me. My smile faded when another problem quickly popped up.

"You didn't buy any clothes, did you?"

"Clothes?" he asked, like it was a foreign word.

I gestured to my torn dress. "I can't wear this for long. What am I going to do? Make a toga out of a blanket? You're such a guy, never thinking of this stuff."

"I was thinking of injury and survival. Fresh clothing's

a luxury, not a necessity."

"Not even your duster?" I asked slyly.

Dimitri froze for a moment and then swore. He'd had no need to wear his coat indoors at the Mastranos'—honestly, he didn't need to outside either—and had left it there in the ensuing fight.

"Don't worry, comrade," I teased. "Plenty more where that came from."

He spread blankets over the tent's floor and laid back on them. There was a look of woe on his face that was almost comical. Raids, bullets, criminals . . . no problem. A missing duster? Crisis. "We'll get you another one," I said. "You know, once we find Jill, clear my name, and save the world."

"Just those things, huh?" he asked, making both of us laugh. But when I stretched myself out beside him, both our faces sobered.

"What are we going to do?" I asked. Tonight's most popular question.

"Sleep," he said, clicking off the flashlight. "Tomorrow we'll get a hold of Abe or Tasha or . . . someone. We'll let them handle it and get Jill where she needs to be."

I was surprised how small my voice sounded when I spoke. "I feel like we failed. I was so happy back there. I thought we'd done the impossible, but it was for nothing. All this work for nothing."

"Nothing?" he asked in astonishment. "What we did . . . this is huge. You found Lissa's sister. Another Dragomir. I don't think you still really understand the weight of that. We had almost nothing to go on, yet you pushed forward and made it happen."

"And I lost Victor Dashkov. Again."

"Well, the thing about him is that he doesn't stay hidden for long. He's one of those people who always has to be in control. He'll have to make a move eventually and when he does—we'll get him."

The smile returned to my lips, though I knew he couldn't see it. "And I thought *I* was the optimistic one here."

"It's contagious," he replied. Then, to my surprise, his hand found mine in the dark. He laced our fingers together. "You did good, Roza. Very good. Now sleep."

We touched in no other way, but his hand held all the warmth in the world. This was hardly a perfect moment, like in the library, but our familiar connection and the understanding between us burned brighter than ever, and it felt good. Right. Natural. I didn't want to sleep. I just wanted to stay there and savor being with him. It wasn't cheating, I decided, thinking of Adrian. It was just enjoying this closeness.

Still, sleep was essential. We worked out a schedule where each of us took shifts. He would stay awake now while I rested, and I had a feeling if I didn't sleep, he wouldn't either when the shift change came. I closed my eyes, and it wasn't my heart I had to slow down this time. It was my mind, the hamster wheel that went nowhere trying to figure out what to do next. *Just get Jill to Court. Just get Jill to Court.* That was all that mattered. We'd contact someone who could reach Jill. Dimitri and I would lie low, everything would soon fix itself. . . .

"Thank God."

I spun around, not even realizing I'd fallen into a spirit dream. I was back in Sonya's garden with all its sunshine and color, and she sat back in a chair, looking expectant.

"I was afraid you'd be up all night, watching your back," she continued.

"I would if I had my choice," I replied, strolling over to her. She wasn't quite whom I'd expected to see in my dreams, but at least I'd made contact with the outside world. I wore the black-and-white dress here, but unlike reality, it was clean and intact. "Dimitri thinks we're in a secure location—though he's awake, of course."

"Of course." There was a glimmer of amusement in her eyes, but it was brief.

"Where are you?" I asked. "Did the guardians put you in holding?"

"They didn't get me," she said smugly. "You were their priority, and a little compulsion made sure they didn't see me. I took off . . . I hated to leave Emily, though."

I empathized but was too excited at Sonya's escape. Good news, finally. "But you can get Jill to Court. You're free."

Sonya looked at me as those I'd just spoken French. "I can't get to Jill."

I frowned. "Is she under that much security?"

"Rose," said Sonya. "Jill isn't with the guardians at all. Victor and Robert took her."

Twenty-Six

"SHE'S WHAT?" I EXCLAIMED. The dream birds singing in the garden fell silent. "With *them*? Is that why they called the guardians?"

Sonya's calmness continued, but she frowned slightly. "Victor and Robert didn't call the guardians. Why would they?"

"Because . . . because they wanted to get rid of Dimitri and me . . ."

"Perhaps," said Sonya. "But not while they were still in the house. Victor's as wanted as you are. It was only Robert's magic that got them out."

"Then who . . ." The answer hit me. I groaned. "John and Emily. I should have known it wouldn't be that easy. They were too quick to accept fugitives into their house."

"I actually think it was just John. Emily really did seem to believe you were innocent . . . even if she didn't like why you were there. I also suspect she'd worry calling guardians would just draw more attention to Jill's identity. It wouldn't surprise me if John didn't even warn her about calling them. He probably thought he was doing everyone a favor."

"And instead, he lost his stepdaughter," I said. "But why would Victor and Robert take her? And how the hell did two old men subdue a teenage girl anyway?"

Sonya shrugged. "They're probably stronger than they seem. Compulsion also likely played a role. And as for why? Hard to say. But Victor wants power and control. Keeping the missing Dragomir with him is a good way to possess that."

I slumped against a tree. "We'll never get her to Court."

"We just have to find her," said Sonya. "Which I should be able to do once she's asleep."

"More dream-walking," I said. My hope began to rekindle. "You should go to her now. Find out—"

"I've tried. She's not asleep. And I'm willing to bet they're keeping her awake for that very reason so they can put some distance between us. I'll keep trying, though."

It wasn't ideal but was the best we could hope for right now. "And Sydney and the Mastranos?"

"Facing a lot of questions." Sonya's face fell. I knew she still felt bad about abandoning her cousin, just as I felt bad about Sydney.

I gently touched Sonya's arm. "It's okay. They'll be okay. What you did will help Jill."

She nodded. "How are we going to stay in touch? I can't always wait for you to be asleep."

Silence. Excellent point.

"Maybe we could get a cell phone today . . . God knows we've needed one. And well . . . why don't you just come to us? Where are you anyway?"

I wondered if I was making a mistake in inviting her to join us. Dimitri and I had gone to great pains to keep our location secret, and that run-in with the guardians had already been a bit closer than I would have liked. Aside from the obvious problems—imprisonment, execution, et cetera—being captured would take us out of the picture for helping Lissa. Yet, I was pretty sure Sonya was one of our allies, and at this point, she might be our only link to Jill.

I'd made a similar gamble in revealing where we were to Victor. And while he had technically helped us, that help had obviously backfired. Nonetheless, I told Sonya the name of our campground and the best directions I could. She said she'd come—I didn't know how she'd manage it but suspected she was resourceful—and would keep trying to reach Jill.

"Sonya . . ." I hesitated to speak, knowing I should just let her end the dream. We had important problems, more serious than what I was about to ask. Plus, this was personal territory. "What did you mean in the car . . . when I said I'd shared a dream with my boyfriend? You looked surprised."

Sonya studied me for a long moment, those blue eyes looking deeper into me than I would have liked. Sometimes she seemed safer in crazy mode. "Auras tell a lot, Rose, and I'm very good at reading them. Much better than your friends probably are. A spirit dream wraps your own aura in gold, which is how I knew. Your personal aura is unique to you, though it fluctuates with your feelings and soul. When people are in love, it shows. Their auras shine. When you were dreaming, yours was bright. The colors were bright . . . but not what I expected from a boyfriend. Of course, not every relationship is the same. People are at different stages. I would have brushed it off, except . . ."

"Except what?"

"Except, when you're with Dimitri, your aura's like the sun. So is his." She smiled when I simply stared in stunned silence. "You're surprised by this?"

"I . . . that is, we're over. We used to be together, but after his change, he didn't want me anymore. I moved on." Where moving on apparently meant holding hands and having close, heated moments. "That's why I'm with Adrian. I'm happy with Adrian." That last sentence sounded almost defensive. Who was I trying to convince? Her or myself?

"Behaviors and feelings rarely line up," she said, sounding very Dimitri Zen-like. "Don't take this the wrong way, but you've got some issues to work out."

Great. Therapy from a crazy woman. "Okay, let's suppose there's something to this. I only really gave up on Dimitri a couple weeks ago. It's *possible* I'm probably still holding onto some feelings." Possible? I thought about how acutely aware of his physical presence I always was in the car, the carefree harmony in the library, how good it felt to work with him in that way of ours, both so determined and almost never second-guessing the other. And only hours ago, in the guestroom . . .

Sonya had the audacity to laugh. "Possible? After only two weeks? Rose, you're wise in so many ways . . . and so young in others."

I hated being judged by my age but had no time for temper tantrums. "Okay, whatever. I've still got feelings. But not him. You didn't see him after he was changed. It was horrible. He was depressed. He said he wanted to avoid me at all costs, that he couldn't love anyone again. It wasn't until this escape madness that he even started acting like his old self."

"He and I talked about that," she said, face serious again. "About the depression. I understand it. After being Strigoi . . . doing what we did . . . you don't feel worthy of life. There's just guilt and darkness and the crushing memories of that evil." She shuddered.

"You . . . you've acted differently from him. I mean, you look so sad sometimes, but at others . . . it's like nothing happened. You're already back to your old self. Mostly. Why the difference in you two?"

"Oh, I've still got the guilt, believe me. After Robert changed me . . ." There was venom when she spoke his name. "Well, I didn't want to leave my house, my bed. I hated myself for what I'd done. I wished I'd been staked to death. Then Dimitri talked to me. . . . He said that guilt was inevitable. The fact that I can feel it proves I'm not Strigoi. But he told me I can't let that stop me from embracing life again. We've been given second chances, he and I. We can't throw them away. He also said it took him a while to realize it and that he didn't want me to make the same mistakes. He told me to embrace life and its beauty and the people I love before it was too late—even though it'd be difficult. Shaking that Strigoi past . . . it's like a weight, always pressing on me. He swore he wasn't going to let it control him anymore—which, believe me, sounds noble but is very hard to do—and that he wouldn't let his life be pointless. He'd already lost some things forever but refused to let go of the rest."

"He said all that? I . . . I'm not even sure what half of it means." *He told me to embrace life and its beauty and the people I love before it was too late.*

"Sometimes I don't either. Like I said, it's much easier said than done. Still, I think he has helped me recover more quickly than I would have on my own. I'm grateful. And as for you and your auras . . ." That small smile returned. "Well, you've got to figure it out. I don't believe in soul mates, not exactly. I think it's ridiculous to think there's only one person out there for us. What if your 'soul mate' lives in Zimbabwe? What if he dies young? I also think 'two souls becoming one' is ridiculous. You need to hold onto yourself. But I do believe in souls being in sync, souls that mirror each other. I see that synchronicity in auras. I can see love too. And I see all of that in his aura and in yours. Only you can choose what to do with that information—if you even believe it."

"No pressure," I muttered.

She looked like she was about to end the dream but then stopped and gave me a piercing look. "One thing to be careful of, Rose. Your auras match, but they aren't identical. Dimitri's is spiked with bits of darkness, leftover from his trauma. That darkness fades a little each day. You carry darkness too—but it's not fading."

I shivered. "Lissa. It's the darkness I'm taking from her, isn't it?"

"Yes. I don't know much about bonds, but what you're doing—even if it's helping her—is very dangerous. Spirit tears us apart, no question, but in some ways . . . I think we spirit users are built for it a little better. Not that it's always obvious," she added wryly. "But you? No. And if you take too much, I don't know what'll happen. I'm afraid of it building and building. I'm afraid it's just going to take one spark—one catalyst—to make it explode inside you."

"What happens then?" I whispered.

She shook her head slowly. "I don't know."

With that, the dream faded.

I fell back into dreamless sleep, though my body—as if knowing it was time to take my shift—woke on its own a few hours later. Night's blackness surrounded me once more, and nearby, I could hear Dimitri's even, steady breathing and sense his warmth. Everything I'd just discussed with Sonya came pouring back to me. Too much, too much. I didn't know where to begin processing it. And no, I didn't know if I could believe it, not with what I'd seen in real life. *Behaviors and feelings rarely line up.* With a deep breath, I forced myself to be a guardian, not an emotionally distraught girl.

"Your time for sleep, comrade."

His voice came to me like light in the darkness, soft and low. "You can get more rest if you need it."

"No, I'm fine," I told him. "And remember, you're not—"

"I know, I know," he chuckled. "I'm not the general." Oh lord. We finished each other's jokes. *I do believe in souls that are in sync.* Sternly reminding myself that Sonya's visit hadn't actually been about my love life, I recounted the rest of the dream to Dimitri, describing John's betrayal and Jill's abduction. "Did I . . . did I do the right thing telling

Sonya where we are?"

Several moments passed before he replied. "Yes. You're right that we need her help—and she can find Jill. The problem is, Victor and Robert have to know that too." He sighed. "And you're right that I'd better rest up for what's to come."

So, in that efficient way of his, he said no more. Soon, his breathing shifted as he fell back into sleep. It was amazing how he could do that with so little effort. Of course, that was something we'd been taught as guardians: sleep when you can because you don't know when you'll be able to again. It was a trick I'd never picked up. Staring into the darkness, I kept my senses sharp, listening for any sounds that might indicate danger.

I might not have a talent for falling asleep instantly, but I *could* keep my waking body alert while still checking in with Lissa. Jill and our escape had occupied me today, but events at Court still weighed heavily on me. Someone had tried to *kill* Lissa, and a group of guardians had just dragged off Eddie.

When I looked through her eyes, it was no surprise that I found most of my friends together. They were in a stark, intimidating room similar to the one she'd been questioned in about my escape—except it was larger. And with good reason. It was packed with all sorts of people. Adrian and Christian stood by Lissa, and I needed no aura reading to know the two guys were as uneasy as she was. Hans stood behind a table, hands pressed on it as he leaned forward and glared at everyone. Opposite Lissa, against the far wall, Eddie sat stone-faced in a chair with a guardian on either side of him. Both of his guards were tense, braced to leap into action. They thought Eddie was a threat, I realized, which was ridiculous. Yet, Hans seemed to share their opinion.

He jabbed his finger at a photograph lying on the table. Taking a step forward, Lissa saw that the picture was of the guy who'd attacked her—a picture taken after his death. His eyes were closed, his skin gone pale—but it provided a detailed look at his facial features, bland as they were.

"You killed a Moroi!" exclaimed Hans. I'd apparently tuned in to the middle of the conversation. "How is that not a problem? You're trained to protect them!"

"I did," said Eddie. He was so calm, so serious that the part of me that could still muster a sense of humor thought he was like Dimitri Junior. "I protected her. What difference does it make if the threat's Moroi or Strigoi?"

"We have no proof of any of the details of this attack," growled Hans.

"You have three witnesses!" snapped Christian. "Are you saying our reports are worthless?"

"I'm saying you're his friends, which makes your reports questionable. I would have liked to have had a guardian around to verify this."

Now Lissa's temper flared. "You did! Eddie was there."

"And there was no way you could have protected her *without* killing him?" asked Hans.

Eddie didn't answer, and I knew he was seriously considering the question, wondering if he might truly have made a mistake. At last, he shook his head. "If I hadn't killed him, he would have killed me."

Hans sighed, his eyes weary. It was easy for me to be angry at him right now, and I had to remind myself he was just doing his job. He held up the picture. "And none of you—*none* of you—have ever seen this man?"

Lissa studied the face once more, repressing a shiver. No, she hadn't recognized him during the attack and didn't recognize him now. There was really nothing remarkable about him—no notable feature you could point out. Our other friends shook their heads, but Lissa felt herself frowning.

"Yes?" asked Hans, immediately jumping on that subtle shift.

"I don't know him . . ." she said slowly. The conversation with Joe the janitor popped into her mind.

"What'd the guy look like?" she'd asked Joe.

"Plain. Ordinary. Except the hand."

Lissa stared at the picture a moment longer, which just barely showed a scarred hand with a couple of bent fingers. I had also noticed it in the fight. She lifted her eyes to Hans. "I don't know him," she repeated. "But I think I know someone who does. There's a janitor . . . well, a former janitor. The one who testified about Rose. I think he's seen this guy before. They have an interesting business relationship. Mikhail was going to make sure he didn't leave Court."

Adrian did not look happy at all about having Joe brought up, seeing as it implicated his mother for bribery. "They'll have a hard time making him talk."

Hans narrowed his eyes. "Oh, if he knows something, we'll

make him talk." He gave a sharp nod toward the door, and one of the guardians by Eddie moved toward it. "Find this guy. And send in our 'guests.'" The guardian nodded and left the room.

"What guests?" asked Lissa.

"Well," said Hans, "it's funny you mention Hathaway. Because we just had a sighting of her."

Lissa stiffened, panic flashing through her. *They found Rose. But how?* Abe had assured her I was safe in that town in West Virginia.

"She and Belikov were spotted outside of Detroit, where they kidnapped a girl."

"They'd never—" Lissa stopped. "Did you say Detroit?" It was with great restraint that she didn't shoot questioning looks at Christian and Adrian.

Hans nodded, and although he gave the appearance of just passing on information, I knew he was watching for some sort of telling reaction from my friends. "They had a few other people with them. Some of them got away, but we caught one."

"Who did they kidnap?" asked Christian. His astonishment wasn't faked either. He too had thought we were safely stashed.

"Mastrano," said Hans. "Something Mastrano."

"*Jill* Mastrano?" exclaimed Lissa.

"Jailbait?" asked Adrian.

Hans clearly wasn't up to date on this nickname but didn't have a chance to question it because just then, the door opened. Three guardians entered, and with them was—Sydney.

TWENTY-SEVEN

I WOULD HAVE GAPED IF I were there, both from the shock of seeing Sydney and at the sight of a human on Court grounds. Humans, actually, because there were two others with her, a man and a woman. The man was young, only a little older than Sydney, with deep brown hair and eyes. The woman was older and wore the tough, seasoned look I associated with Alberta. This woman was dark-skinned, but I could still see the golden tattoo she and the other humans had. All Alchemists.

And it was obvious these Alchemists were not happy. That older woman was putting on a good show, but her darting eyes made it clear she wanted to be somewhere—anywhere—else. Sydney and the guy didn't hide their fear at all. Sydney might have gotten used to me and Dimitri, but she and her associates had just walked into a den of evil, as far as they were probably concerned.

The Alchemists weren't alone in their discomfort. As soon as they'd entered, the guardians no longer regarded Eddie as the room's threat. Their eyes were all on the humans, scrutinizing them as though they were Strigoi. My friends seemed more curious than afraid. Lissa and I had lived among humans, but Christian and Adrian had had very little exposure, other than feeders. Seeing the Alchemists on "our turf" added an extra element of intrigue.

I was certainly astonished to see Sydney there so quickly. Or was it quickly? Hours had passed since we'd escaped Jill's house. Not enough time to drive to Court but certainly enough to fly. Sydney hadn't changed clothes since I'd last seen her, and there were shadows under her eyes. I had a feeling she'd been grilled to no end since her capture. The mystery was, why bring the Alchemists here to the meeting about Eddie killing the unknown Moroi? There were two completely different issues at stake.

Lissa was thinking the same thing. "Who are these guys?" she asked, although she had a pretty good idea who Sydney was. She'd heard enough description from me. Sydney gave Lissa a once-over, and I suspected she had guessed Lissa's identity as well.

"Alchemists," said Hans gruffly. "You know what that means?"

Lissa and my friends nodded. "What do they have to do with Eddie and that guy who attacked me?" she asked.

"Maybe something. Maybe nothing." Hans shrugged. "But I know there's something strange going on, something you're all involved in, and I need to figure out what. She"—Hans pointed at Sydney—"was with Hathaway in Detroit, and I still have trouble believing *none* of you know anything about it."

Adrian crossed his arms and leaned against the wall, the perfect picture of indifference. "Keep believing that, but I don't know *any* of these people. Don't Alchemists hate us? Why are they here?" Adrian, ironically, was the only one of my friends who knew I hadn't been in West Virginia, but you'd never tell from his demeanor.

"Because we have an escaped murderess to deal with and needed to question her accomplice in person," was Hans's crisp response.

A denial of my guilt was on Lissa's lips, but the older Alchemist jumped in first. "You have no proof that Miss Sage was an 'accomplice' to your criminal. And I still think it's ridiculous that you wouldn't let us do our *own* questioning and leave it at that."

"In any other situation, we would, Miss Stanton," replied Hans. Ice was forming between the two of them. "But this one, as you can imagine, is a bit more serious than most. Our queen was murdered."

Tension ramped up even more between the guardians and the Alchemists. Their working relationship was not a happy one, I realized. It also occurred to me that even if Sydney's superiors thought she'd committed some crime, they would never admit as much to my people—which meant Hans's paranoia wasn't entirely unfounded. When none of the Alchemists responded, Hans seemed to read this as approval to begin interrogating Sydney.

"Do you know these three?" He gestured to my friends, and Sydney shook her head. "Ever communicated with them?"

"No."

He paused, as though hoping she'd change her answer. She didn't. "Then how did you get involved with Hathaway?"

She studied him intently, fear in her brown eyes. I wasn't sure if it was because of him exactly. Really, she had a lot of things to be nervous about right now, like being here at all and the eventual punishment the Alchemists would dole out. Then, of course, there was Abe. Technically, he was the reason she had gotten ensnared in this mess. All she had to do was tell on him, say he'd blackmailed her. It'd get her off the hook—but incur his wrath. Sydney swallowed and forced a defiant look.

"I met Rose in Siberia."

"Yes, yes," said Hans. "But how did you end up helping her escape here?"

"I had nothing to do with her escaping this place!" said Sydney. It was a half-truth, I supposed. "She contacted me a few days ago and asked for help to get to a house near Detroit. She claimed she was innocent and that this would help prove it."

"The Alchemists knew by then she was a fugitive," pointed out Hans. "Everyone had orders to look out for her. You could have turned her in."

"When I first met Rose, she didn't seem like the murdering type—I mean, aside from killing Strigoi. Which isn't murder at all, really." Sydney threw in a little Alchemist disdain. It was a nice touch. "So, when she said she was innocent and could prove it, I decided to help her. I gave her a ride."

"We already asked her about this," Stanton said irritably. "And we already told you that we did. What she did was foolish—a naive lapse in judgment. It's something for us to deal with, not you. You worry about your murdering fiend." Her words were light, like they were going to take Sydney home and chastise a naughty child. I doubted it would be that simple.

"Who were the people with her?" asked Hans, ignoring Stanton.

Sydney's contempt grew. "One was that guy . . . Dimitri Belikov. The one you think was 'cured.' I don't know who the others were. Two guys and a woman. They never introduced us." It was a well-done lie, her faked disgust about Dimitri masking her knowledge of the rest of our associates.

Lissa leaned forward eagerly, speaking just before Hans could. "What was in Detroit? How was Rose going to clear herself? Especially with Jill?"

Hans didn't look happy about the interruption, but I knew he had to be curious about Jill and Detroit as well. He said nothing, perhaps hoping someone might slip and reveal a key piece of knowledge. Sydney, however, continued playing distant and cold.

"I have no idea. That Jill girl didn't seem to know either. Rose just said we had to get to her, so I helped her."

"Blindly?" asked Hans. "You really expect me to believe that you just trusted her like that?"

"She's my—" Sydney bit her lip on what I suspected was "friend." She turned her professional mode back on. "There was something believable about her, and I figured it'd be a waste of resources if the Alchemists had been helping you hunt the wrong murderer. If I decided she was guilty, I could always turn her in. And I thought . . . I thought if I was the one who solved this, I'd get the credit and a promotion." That was a good, good lie. An ambitious girl trying to improve her career on the sly? Very good. Well, not to everyone.

Hans shook his head. "I don't believe any of you."

The guy Alchemist took a step forward that made every guardian tense to jump him. "If she says that's the way it happened, then that's the way it happened." He had the same fierceness and mistrust that Stanton had, but there seemed to be more. A sort of protectiveness toward Sydney that was as personal as professional. Lissa picked up on it too.

"Easy, Ian," said Stanton, still keeping her eyes on Hans. Her composure reminded me more and more of Alberta. She couldn't be at ease with a roomful of guardians but wasn't showing it. "It doesn't matter if you believe her or not. The point remains: Miss Sage answered your questions. We're finished."

"Do Jill's parents know anything?" asked Lissa. She was still in shock at all of these developments—not to mention worried about me being out of my safe mountain town—but this mysterious shot at clearing my name was powerful. She couldn't let it go.

Sydney turned to Lissa, and I could practically read the Alchemist's thoughts. She knew how close Lissa and I were and would have liked to give Lissa some sort of comfort. There was no way, though, that Sydney could do that with these people in the room. She also had to be aware of the fact that I myself hadn't told Lissa anything about Jill.

"No," said Sydney. "We just went there, and Rose said Jill had to come with her. The Mastranos don't know why. And then—and then Rose did take her. Or Jill went with her. I'm not sure what happened. It all turned to chaos."

Neither the Alchemists nor guardians disputed me taking Jill, which made me think it was a story they'd gotten—and accepted—from both Jill's parents and Sydney. It had just enough truth to be plausible—and explain Jill's disappearance. It didn't mention the Dragomir secret, however, which Emily was probably more than happy to keep quiet for now.

"There," said Stanton. "This is exactly what we told you before. We need to leave now." She turned toward the door, but guardians blocked the way.

"Impossible," said Hans. "This is a serious matter, and Miss Sage is the only link we have to a murder—a royal murder. And a kidnapping."

Stanton scoffed, and I remembered Sydney once saying the Alchemists thought the Moroi royalty system was silly. "She doesn't seem to be of much more use to you. But don't worry—we'll be holding her. Contact us if you have more questions."

"Unacceptable," said Hans. "She stays here."

Ian, the other Alchemist, joined the argument, moving protectively in front of Sydney. "We're not leaving one of our own here!" Again, I had that funny feeling about him. A crush, that was it. He had a crush on her and was treating this as more than just business. Stanton gave him a look that said she would handle this matter. He fell silent.

"You can all stay here, then," said Hans. "Makes no difference to me. We'll get you rooms."

"*That* is unacceptable." From there, she and Hans got into

a raging argument. I didn't think it would come to blows, but the other guardians had closed in slightly as a precaution.

Ian's eyes darted between Stanton and Sydney, but he didn't get into the fray. Once, his gaze passed over the table Hans leaned against, and Ian suddenly did a double take at the photograph. It was only a brief pause, a slight widening of the eyes . . . but Lissa caught it.

She took a step toward Ian and Sydney. One of the guardians glanced at the movement, deemed Lissa safe, and returned to watching Stanton. "You know him," Lissa murmured, keeping her voice below the shouts. In fact, it was a little too low because she got blank looks from Sydney and Ian. Their ears couldn't hear what a Moroi or dhampir could have.

Lissa glanced uneasily around, not wanting to attract attention. She raised her volume slightly. "You know him. The guy in the picture."

Ian stared at Lissa, a bit of wonder and wariness on his face. He undoubtedly bore that same standoffish attitude toward vampires, but her words had caught him off guard. And, even if she was an evil creature of the night, she was a very pretty one.

"Ian," said Sydney softly. "What is it?" There was a note of urging in her voice, one that inadvertently played upon his crush, I think. He opened his mouth to speak, but then, the "conversation" among the others wrapped up. Sydney again became the center of attention, and Ian turned away from Lissa.

The compromise Stanton and Hans had reached was exactly

that—a compromise. Neither was happy with it. There was a small town less than forty-five minutes away from Court, and the Alchemists would stay there—with several guardians on hand. It sounded like a house arrest to me, and Stanton's expression seemed to agree. I think she only consented because it was a human town. Before he'd let everyone go, Hans questioned my friends a final time, his eyes studying every face carefully.

"And none of you—*none* of you—know this Alchemist girl or have been in contact with her? Or know about her involvement with Hathaway?"

Again, Lissa and the others denied it, and again, Hans had no choice but to grudgingly accept the responses. Everyone moved toward the door, but Hans wouldn't let Eddie leave. "Not you, Castile. You're staying here until other matters are settled."

Lissa gasped. "What? But he—"

"Don't worry about it," said Eddie with a small smile. "Everything'll be okay. Just look after yourself."

Lissa hesitated, despite Christian tugging her arm to go. Although all accounts said Eddie had defended Lissa's life, he'd still killed a Moroi. That wouldn't be taken lightly. The guardians had to be 100 percent convinced he'd had no other choice before they'd release him. Seeing the strong, calm look on his face, Lissa knew he was prepared to handle whatever came.

"Thank you," she said, walking past him. "Thank you for saving me."

His answer was a slight nod, and Lissa stepped into the hallway—to find herself in more chaos.

"Where are they? I insist on—ah."

My friends and the Alchemists had been heading toward the exit while a group of guardians escorted them. Meanwhile, someone had entered the hall and was now being stopped and challenged by the guardians. It was Abe.

He took in every piece of the bizarre scenario in less than a heartbeat, his eyes passing over Sydney and the Alchemists as though he'd never seen them before. Through Lissa's eyes, I saw Sydney blanch, but nobody else noticed. Abe smiled at Lissa and sidled up to walk out with her.

"There you are. They want you for the last monarch test."

"And they sent you?" asked Christian skeptically.

"Well, I volunteered," replied Abe. "I'd heard there was some, er, excitement. Murder, fanatical religious humans, interrogations. All things I'm interested in, you know."

Lissa rolled her eyes but said nothing until the whole group emerged from the building. The Alchemists and their unwelcome escort went one way while Lissa and our friends went the other. Lissa longed to glance at Sydney and Ian—I did too—but knew it was best to keep moving forward and follow Abe's lead, particularly since some of those guardians were watching more than just the Alchemists.

As soon as Lissa's group was far enough away from the authorities, Abe's amiable smile vanished, and he turned on my friends. "What the hell happened? I've heard all sorts of crazy stories. Someone said you were dead."

"Nearly," said Lissa. She told him about the attack, expressing her fear over Eddie.

"He'll be fine," said Abe dismissively. "They have nothing to hold him on. The worst he'll get is a mark on his record."

Lissa was relieved by Abe's easy assurance, but I still felt guilty. Thanks to me, Eddie's record was already marred. His sterling reputation was declining on a daily basis.

"That was Sydney Sage," said Lissa. "I thought they were all in West Virginia. Why isn't she with Rose?"

"That," said Abe darkly, "is an excellent question."

"Because they were apparently kidnapping Jill Mastrano in Detroit," said Christian. "Which is weird. But not the craziest thing I can think of Rose doing." I appreciated the support.

Abe got a recap of this new development too, at least as much as my friends knew of it—which was only a fraction of the whole story. Abe picked up immediately that he'd been played, and it was obvious from his angry expression that he didn't like being kept in the dark. *Welcome to the club, old man,* I thought with small satisfaction. I hadn't forgotten how no one had filled me in on the escape plan. My smugness was short-lived because I was worried about what would happen to Sydney, now that Abe was on to her.

"That girl was lying to me," he growled. "Every day, all these reports about how quiet and boring it was in West Virginia. I wonder if they even made it to that town. I *have* to go talk to her."

"Good luck," said Adrian, pulling a cigarette out and lighting it. Apparently, in my absence, the dating contract he'd jokingly made up that said he would "cut back" on his vices didn't apply. "I don't think her cronies or the guardians are going to let you near her."

"Oh, I'll get to her," said Abe. "She's got a lot of answers. If she hid them from those other idiots, then good for her. But she's going to tell *me*."

A sudden thought sparked into Lissa's mind. "You have to talk to Ian. That guy with the Alchemists. He knows the man in the picture—er, I mean, the guy Eddie killed."

"You're certain?" asked Abe.

"Yes," said Adrian, surprising them all. "Ian definitely had a reaction. He's also got a crush on that Sydney girl."

"I saw that too," said Lissa.

"She seems kind of uptight." Adrian frowned. "But maybe their kind go for that."

"That crush might actually be useful," mused Abe. "You women don't know the power you wield. Have you seen that guardian your aunt's dating? Ethan Moore?"

"Yes," groaned Christian. "Don't remind me."

"Tasha *is* pretty hot, though," noted Adrian.

"That is not cool," said Christian.

"Don't get so huffy," said Abe. "Ethan's a palace guard. He was there the night of the murder—which could be very useful to us if she can keep him interested."

Christian shook his head. "Those guards already testified. It won't matter. Ethan's told what he knows."

"I'm not so sure," said Abe. "There are always things that

occur off the official record, and I'm positive the guards were all debriefed with strict orders on what to reveal and not to reveal. Your aunt might be charming enough to find out something for us." Abe sighed, still looking very unhappy at the sudden upsetting of his orderly plans. "If only Sydney had been charming enough to talk her way out of that interrogation so that *I* could go interrogate her. Now I've got to break through those Alchemists and the guardians to get to her and figure out where Rose is. Oh, and you do actually have to go to your test, princess."

"I thought that was just a line you used to find me," Lissa said.

"No, they want you." He gave her directions to the test. It was in the building she'd had the second test in. "All of you go together and then get a guardian to walk you back. Don't leave your room until Janine or Tad come by." Tad was one of Abe's henchmen. "No more surprise attacks."

Lissa wanted to argue that she most certainly wasn't going to put herself under house arrest but decided it was best to just let Abe go for now. He hurried off, still radiating agitation, and she and the guys turned toward the testing site.

"Boy, is he pissed," said Adrian.

"Do you blame him?" asked Christian. "He just lost membership in the evil mastermind club. His brilliant plan fell apart, and now his daughter's missing when he thought she was somewhere safe."

Adrian stayed pointedly silent.

"I hope she's okay," sighed Lissa, a knot forming in her

stomach. "And what in the world does Jill have to do with any of this?"

Nobody had an answer for that one. When they reached the testing site, Lissa found a situation almost identical to before. Lots of spectators lining the hall. Guardians blocking the door. More people than ever were cheering her name as she approached, some who were "common" Moroi and others who were royals whose candidates were out of the running. A number of nominees hadn't passed the fear test, so those families had switched their loyalties.

Again, Lissa was ushered into the room alone. Her heart began to pound when she saw the same old woman. Were more terrible images to come? Lissa couldn't see the chalice, but that was no guarantee of safety. There was no extra chair, so Lissa simply stood in front of the old woman.

"Hello," Lissa said respectfully. "It's nice to see you again."

The woman grinned, showing those missing teeth. "I doubt that, but you say it very convincingly. You have politics in your blood."

"Thank . . . you . . ." said Lissa, unsure if she'd been complimented or not. "What would you like me to do for this test?"

"Just listen. That's all. It's an easy one."

A twinkle in the woman's eye made Lissa think this would not be easy.

"All you have to do is answer a question for me. Answer correctly, and you're through to the vote. And won't that be entertaining." The old woman seemed to say those last words more to herself than Lissa.

"Okay," said Lissa uneasily. "I'm ready."

The woman sized Lissa up and seemed to like what she saw. "Here it is then: What must a queen possess in order to truly rule her people?"

Lissa's mind went blank for a moment, and then a jumble of words popped into her head. *Integrity? Wisdom? Sanity?*

"No, no, don't answer," said the old woman, watching Lissa carefully. "Not yet. You have until tomorrow, at this same time, to think about it. Come back with the right answer, and you'll have passed the trials. And . . ." She winked. "It goes without saying you won't talk to anyone about this."

Lissa nodded, rubbing the small tattooed spot on her arm. She'd get no help with the answer from anyone else. Lissa left the room, turning the question over and over in her mind. There were too many answers to a question like that, she thought. Any of them could—

Movement in my reality instantly snapped me out of her head. I half expected Sonya to come bursting into our tent, but no, that wasn't what had caught my attention. It was a much smaller motion . . . and something infinitely more powerful.

Dimitri was in my arms.

TWENTY-EIGHT

I STOPPED BREATHING. WE'D each had our own blankets, but even in the middle of summer, the temperature had dropped during the night. Dimitri, in his sleep, had rolled over against me, merging our blankets into one pile and resting his head on my chest. His body lay against mine, warm and familiar, and he even snuggled a little closer.

He was more exhausted than I'd realized if he was doing this in his sleep. After all, this was the guy who slept with one eye open. But his guard was down now, his body unconsciously seeking . . . what? Simple warmth? *Me*? Damn it. Why had I asked Sonya my question? Why couldn't I keep going with my easy role as Adrian's girlfriend and Dimitri's friend? Because honestly, I wasn't doing a very good job at either one right now.

Tentatively, fearfully, I shifted slightly so that I could put one arm around Dimitri and draw him closer. I knew it was a risk, one that might wake him and break this spell. But it didn't. If anything, he seemed to relax more. Feeling him like that . . . holding him . . . it churned up a swarm of emotions within me. The ache I had felt since his loss burned within me. At the same time, holding him like this also seemed to fill that ache, as though a piece of me that had been missing was now restored. I hadn't even realized that piece was missing. I'd blocked it all out until Sonya's words had shaken my fragile new acceptance of life.

I don't know how long I stayed like that with Dimitri. It was long enough that the rising sun began to illuminate the tent's translucent fabric. That was all the light my eyes needed to now see Dimitri, to see the finely carved lines of his face and softness of his hair as he lay against me. I wanted so badly to touch that hair, to see if it felt like it used to. That was a silly sentiment, of course. His hair wouldn't have changed. Still . . . the urge was there, and I finally gave in, gently running my fingers over some stray locks. They were smooth and silky, and that barest touch sent chills through me. It also woke him up.

His eyes opened, instantly alert. I expected him to jump away from me, but instead, he only assessed the situation—and didn't move. I left my hand where it was on the side of his face, still stroking his hair. Our gazes locked, so much passing between us. In those moments, I wasn't in a tent with him, on the run from those who regarded us as villains. There was no murderer to catch, no Strigoi trauma to overcome. There was just him and me and the feelings that had burned between us for so long.

When he did move, it wasn't to get away. Instead, he lifted his head so that he looked down at me. Only a few inches separated us, and his eyes betrayed him. He wanted to kiss me—and I wanted him to. He leaned over me, one hand resting against my cheek. I readied myself for his lips—I needed them—and then he froze. He pulled back and sat up, exhaling in frustration as he looked away from me. I sat up as well, my breathing rapid and shallow.

"Wh-what's wrong?" I asked.

He glanced back at me. "Pick. There are lots of choices."

I ran a finger along my lips. So close. So, so close. "I know . . . I know things have changed. I know you were wrong. I know you can feel love again."

His mask was back up as he formulated his answer. "This isn't about love."

The last minute replayed in my head, that perfect connection, the way he'd looked at me and made my heart feel. Hell, Sonya claimed we even had some mystical connection. "If it's not about love, then what is it about?" I exclaimed.

"It's about doing the right thing," he said quietly.

The right thing? Right and wrong had been perennial topics at St. Vladimir's. I wasn't eighteen. He was my teacher. We were slated to be Lissa's guardians and had to give her our full attention. All of those were arguments for why staying apart had been necessary back then. But those had long since fallen by the wayside.

I would have questioned him more—if someone hadn't scratched at our door.

Both of us sprang up and apart, reaching for the stakes we'd slept near. Grabbing my stake was instinct because I knew there was no Strigoi out there. But lately, Strigoi had been the least of our worries.

"Rose? Dimitri?"

The voice was barely audible—but familiar. Relaxing slightly, I unzipped the tent's entrance and revealed Sonya kneeling in front of it. Like us, she wore the same clothes from earlier, and her auburn hair was messy. Otherwise, she seemed to have escaped her pursuers unscathed. I scooted aside so that she could enter.

"Cozy," she said, glancing around. "You've got the farthest spot out on the campground. Took me forever to find the car you described."

"How'd you get here?" I asked.

She winked. "You're not the only ones who can steal cars. Or, in my case, get people to 'willingly' lend them."

"Were you followed?" asked Dimitri. He was all seriousness again, with no sign of what had passed moments ago.

"Not that I could tell," she said, shifting into a cross-legged position. "A couple guardians followed me back in the neighborhood, but I lost them a while ago. Most of them seemed more interested in you two."

"Imagine that," I muttered. "Too bad Victor was long gone—he might have taken priority."

"He didn't kill a queen," she said ruefully. We'd had to eventually tell her why Victor was wanted and that he'd been the one Sonya had sensed was stalking Lissa back at St. Vladimir's. "But the good news is I know where they're at now."

"Where?" asked Dimitri and I in unison.

A small, knowing smile came to her lips at that. "West Michigan," she said. "They took off in the opposite direction from Court."

"Damn," I muttered. Dimitri and I had gone southeast from Ann Arbor, clipping the Detroit suburbs and just crossing into Ohio. We'd picked the wrong direction. "But you saw Jill? Is she okay?"

Sonya nodded. "Fine. Scared, but fine. She described enough landmarks that I think we can locate their motel. I found her in a dream a couple hours ago; they had to rest. Victor wasn't feeling well. They might still be there."

"Then we need to leave now," said Dimitri, instantly in action. "Once they're moving, Jill will be awake and out of contact."

We packed up our campsite with amazing speed. My ankle felt better but was still sore. Noticing my limp, Sonya called a halt just before we got in her car.

"Hang on."

She knelt before me, examining the swelling ankle that was easily exposed by my torn dress. Taking a deep breath, she rested her hands on me, and a surge of electricity shot through my leg, followed by waves of heat and cold. When it was over and she stood up, the pain and swelling were gone, as were the scrapes on my legs. Probably the cuts on my head too. Spirit users had healed me so often that you'd think I'd be used to it, but it was still a little startling.

"Thank you," I said. "But you shouldn't have done that . . . shouldn't have used the magic . . ."

"You need to be in peak condition," she said. Her gaze drifted from me, staring off at the trees. "And the magic . . . well, it's hard to stay away from."

Indeed it was, and I felt guilty that she was using it on me—and moving closer to insanity. Robert's restoration had healed her mind a little, and she needed to take advantage of that. This was no time for a lecture, though, and Dimitri's expression told me he too thought it best I get back in shape.

We took off toward where Sonya told us Jill was, and this time, her directions were as specific as she could make them. No more vagueness or binding promises. We stopped once to "acquire" a new car and get a map. The info Sonya had gleaned from Jill led us to a town called Sturgis. While it was in the western half of Michigan, it was also south—meaning the distance wasn't quite as long as we'd expected. Nonetheless, Dimitri drove at least fifteen miles per hour over the speed limit the whole time.

"There," said Sonya, as we rolled into downtown Sturgis—which wasn't much of a downtown. We were near a modest-looking motel on a side street. "That's what she described. The Sunshine Motel."

Dimitri pulled into the lot behind the building, and we all sat there, staring at the motel, which didn't look as cheerful as its name. Like me, I presumed my companions were trying to figure out how to approach this. Jill's dream info had gotten us here, but Sonya had nothing else to help us find their room—if they were even still here. They certainly wouldn't have checked in under real names. I was going to suggest we just walk past the doors and hope Sonya would sense Robert when she suddenly pointed.

"That's their car," she said. "They're here."

Sure enough. There was the CR-V we'd taken to Jill's house. Talk about karma. I'd swiped Victor's keys, and he'd repaid the favor by taking ours. None of us had thought much about his escape vehicle in the ensuing chaos.

"Sloppy," murmured Dimitri, eyes narrowed thoughtfully. "They should have switched cars."

"That's Sydney's," I pointed out. "It's not technically stolen, so it's not on any police lists. Besides, something tells me Victor and Robert aren't hot-wiring pros like *some* people are." We'd left a string of stolen cars across the Midwest.

Dimitri nodded, like I'd actually just complimented him. "Whatever the reason, it helps us."

"How do we find them?" asked Sonya.

I was about to suggest the aura plan but dismissed it. Robert would sense Sonya at the same moment, giving him brief warning. Plus, when we found the brothers, there'd likely be a fight. Doing it in the motel would attract attention. This parking lot was in back, away from the main road.

"We wait," I said. "It's amazing enough that they even stopped this long. If they have any sense, they'll leave soon."

"Agreed," said Dimitri, catching my eyes. *Souls in sync*. The memory of that near-kiss returned, and I looked away, fearing what my face would betray. "The lot's easy to defend too. Not much room for escape." It was true. The motel flanked one side, a concrete wall the other. There weren't many other buildings nearby either.

He moved our car to the farthest spot he could in the lot,

providing us with a full view of it and the motel's exit—but keeping us semi-concealed. We considered sitting in the car, but Dimitri and I decided we should wait outside, giving us more mobility. We left Sonya inside. This wasn't her fight.

Standing behind the car with Dimitri, in the shadow of a leafy maple, I became acutely aware of his proximity and fierce warrior stance. He might be missing his duster, but I had to admit I liked the view of him I got without the coat.

"I don't suppose," I said softly, "that we're going to talk about this morning?"

Dimitri's eyes were fixed so hard on the CR-V that he might have been trying to make Jill and the brothers materialize inside it. I wasn't fooled. He was just avoiding looking at me. "There's nothing to talk about."

"I knew you'd say that. Actually, it was a toss-up between that and 'I don't know what you're talking about.'"

Dimitri sighed.

"But," I continued, "there *is* something to talk about. Like when you almost kissed me. And what did you mean about 'the right thing'?"

Silence.

"You wanted to kiss me!" It was hard to keep my voice low. "I saw it."

"Just because we want something doesn't mean it's right."

"What I said . . . it's true, isn't it? You *can* love, can't you? I realize now that right after the transformation, you really didn't think you could. And you probably couldn't. But things have changed. You're getting yourself back."

Dimitri gave me a sidelong look. "Yes. Things have changed . . . and some haven't."

"Okay, Mr. Enigma. That doesn't help explain the 'right thing' comment."

Frustration filled his features. "Rose, I've done a lot of bad things, most of which I can never fix or find redemption for. My only choice now, if I want to reclaim my life, is to go forward, stopping evil and doing what's right. And what is *not* right is taking a woman from another man, a man I like and respect. I'll steal cars. I'll break into houses. But there are lines I *will* not cross, no matter what I—"

The motel's back door opening jolted us to attention. It was no wonder my love life was so messed up when the most profound and intimate moments were always being interrupted by dire situations. It was just as well because I had never, ever seen that line coming: *What is* not *right is taking a woman from another man, a man I like and respect.*

New drama took precedence. Victor stepped outside, with Robert and Jill walking side by side behind him. I'd half expected to see her tied up and was surprised that she accompanied them so calmly. Too calmly, I soon realized. It wasn't natural. There was an almost robotic feel to her movements: she was being compelled into docility.

"Compulsion," said Dimitri quietly, recognizing it as well. "Go for Victor. I'll get Robert."

I nodded. "Jill will run as soon as the compulsion's broken. I hope." I didn't put it past her to join our fight, which could cause more harm than good. We'd find out soon enough.

Mercifully, no one else was around. It was still fairly early in the morning. Dimitri and I sprang out from our hiding spots, crossing the distance of the parking lot in a matter of moments. Two healthy dhampirs could outrace two old Moroi any day. And as crafty as they might be, the brothers hadn't expected us.

In my periphery, I just barely saw Dimitri kicking into warrior god mode, fierce and unstoppable. Then, I focused entirely on Victor, throwing my full weight at him and knocking him to the ground. He hit hard against the asphalt, and I pinned him down, slamming my fist into his face and making his nose bleed.

"Well done," he gasped out.

"I've been wanting to do that for a very long time," I growled.

Victor smiled through the pain and the blood. "Of course you have. I used to think Belikov was the savage one, but it's really you, isn't it? You're the animal with no control, no higher reasoning except to fight and kill."

I clenched his shirt and leaned him over him. "Me? I'm not the one who tortured Lissa for my own benefit. I'm not the one who turned my daughter Strigoi. And I'm sure as hell not the one who used compulsion to kidnap a fifteen-year-old girl!"

To my disgust, he kept that maddening smile on his face. "She's valuable, Rose. So, so valuable. You have no idea how much so."

"She's not an object for you to manipulate!" I cried. "She's a—ahh!"

The ground suddenly rolled up beneath me, a mini-earthquake centered around us. The asphalt bucked up, giving Victor the leverage to push me off. It wasn't a strong push, and I could have easily recovered my balance if not for the ground rippling and surrounding me, rolling like ocean waves to knock me over. Victor was using his earth magic to control the area where I stood. Faint cries of surprise told me others were feeling a little of it, but the magic was clearly focused on me.

Not without cost, though. Victor was an old man—an old man I'd just shoved onto asphalt and punched. Pain and fatigue were all over him, and his labored breathing told me wielding magic this powerful—something I'd never seen an earth user do—was pushing every ounce of strength he had left.

One good punch. That was all I needed. One good punch would knock him down and take him out of this fight. Only, *I* was the one being taken down. Literally. Try as I might, my personal earthquake got the best of me, knocking me to my knees. I was still in that stupid dress too, meaning my newly healed legs got scraped again. And once I was down, the asphalt rose around me. I realized Victor was going to ensnare me by creating a stone prison. I couldn't let that happen.

"All that brawn for nothing," gasped out Victor, sweat pouring off his face. "It does you no good in the end. Real power is in the mind. In cunning. In controlling Jillian, I control Vasilisa. With Vasilisa, I control the Dragomirs, and from there—the Moroi. That's power. *That's* strength."

Most of his smug tirade went over me. But part of it stuck: *In controlling Jillian, I control Vasilisa.* Lissa. I couldn't let him hurt her. I couldn't let him use her. In fact, I couldn't let him use Jill either. Lissa had given me a *chotki,* which was kind of a cross between a bracelet and a rosary. It was a Dragomir heirloom, bestowed upon those who protected the family. That was my duty: to protect all the Dragomirs. The old guardian mantra rang in my mind: *They come first.*

With skill I didn't know I possessed, I sized up the shaking ground and attempted to stand again. I made it, practically dancing in that parking lot. And as I stared at Victor, I felt what Sonya had warned about: the catalyst. The spark that would ignite the darkness I'd gathered and gathered from Lissa. In looking at him, I saw all the evils of my life in one man. Was that entirely accurate? No, not exactly. But he had hurt my best friend—nearly killed her. He'd toyed with Dimitri and me, complicating what was already a mess of a relationship. He was now trying to control others. When would it end? When would his evil stop? Red and black tinged my vision. I heard a voice call my name—Sonya's, I think. But in that moment, there was nothing else in the world but Victor and my hate for him.

I sprang at him, fueled by rage and adrenaline, leaping out of the epicenter of shaking ground that threatened to seize me. Once more, I threw myself at him, but we didn't hit the ground. We'd shifted position slightly, and instead, we hit the concrete wall—with just as much force as I might have thrown a Strigoi. His head bent back at the impact. I heard an odd cracking sound, and Victor slumped to the ground. I immediate dropped down, grabbing his arms and shaking him.

"Get up!" I screamed. "Get up and fight me!" But no matter how much I shook him or yelled, Victor would not stand. He wouldn't move on his own.

Hands grabbed me, trying futilely to pull me away. "Rose—Rose! Stop. *Stop this.*"

I ignored the voice, ignored the hands. I was all anger and power, wanting—no, *needing*—Victor to face me once and for all. Suddenly, a strange sensation crept along me, like fingertips across my skin. *Let him go.* I didn't want to, but for half a second, it seemed like a reasonable idea. I loosened my hold slightly, just enough for those hands to jerk me away. Like that, I snapped out of the haze and realized what had happened. The person who'd pulled me was Sonya, and she'd used a tiny bit of compulsion to get me away and let go of Victor. She was strong enough in her power that she didn't even need eye contact. She held onto me, even though she had to know it was wasted effort.

"I have to stop him," I said, wriggling from her grasp. "He has to pay." I reached for him again.

Sonya gave up on physical restraint, appealing to words instead. "Rose, he has! He's *dead*. Can't you see that? Dead. Victor's dead!"

No, I didn't see that—not at first. All I saw was my blind obsession, my need to get to Victor. But then, her words broke through to me. As I gripped Victor, I felt the limpness in his body. I saw the eyes that looked blankly at . . . nothing. That crazy, churning emotion in me faded, transforming into shock. My grip slackened as I stared at him and truly understood what she had said.

Understood what I had done.

Then, I heard a terrible sound. A low wailing broke through the frozen horror in my mind. I glanced back in alarm and saw Dimitri standing with Robert. Robert's arms were pinned behind his back as Dimitri effortlessly held him, but the Moroi was doing everything in his power—and failing—to break free. Jill stood nearby, looking uneasily at all of us, confused and afraid.

"Victor! Victor!"

Robert's pleas were muffled by sobs and as useless as my own efforts to get Victor up. I dragged my gaze back down to the body before me, barely believing what I had just done. I'd thought the guardians had been crazy in their reaction to Eddie killing a Moroi, but now, I was starting to understand. A monster like a Strigoi was one thing. But the life of a person, even a person who—

"Get him out of here!"

Sonya was so near me that the unexpected exclamation made me wince. She'd been kneeling too but now jumped to her feet, turning toward Dimitri.

"Get him out of here! As far as you can!"

Dimitri looked surprised, but the powerful command in her voice drove him to instant action. He began dragging Robert away. After a few moments, Dimitri simply opted to toss the man over his shoulder and cart him off. I would have expected cries of protest, but Robert had fallen silent. His eyes were on Victor's body—their gaze so sharp, so focused that they seemed like they could burn a hole through someone. Sonya, not having my fanciful impression, thrust herself between the brothers and dropped to the ground again, covering Victor's body with her own.

"Get him out of here!" she called again. "He's trying to bring Victor back! He'll be shadow-kissed!"

I was still confused and upset, still appalled at what I'd done, but the danger of what she said hit me hard. Robert couldn't be allowed to bring back Victor back. The brothers were dangerous enough without being bonded. Victor couldn't be allowed to summon ghosts the way I could. Victor had to stay dead.

"Doesn't he have to touch the body?" I asked.

"To finish the bond, yes. But he was wielding tons of spirit just now, calling Victor's soul back and keeping it around," she explained.

When Dimitri and Robert were gone, Sonya told me to help her move the body. We'd made too much noise, and it was a wonder no one had come out yet. Jill joined us, and I moved without really being aware of what I was doing. Sonya found the keys to the CR-V on Victor and flattened the backseats to increase the rear cargo space. We crawled into it, the three of us having to hunch down to stay out of sight. We soon heard voices, people coming to see what had happened. I don't know long they were in the parking lot, only that they mercifully didn't search cars. Honestly? I had few coherent thoughts at all. That rage was gone, but my mind was a mess.

I couldn't seem to get a hold of anything concrete. I felt sick and just followed Sonya's orders, staying low as I tried not to look at Victor's body.

Even after the voices were gone, she kept us in the car. At last, she exhaled a deep breath and focused on me. "Rose?" I didn't answer right away. "Rose?"

"Yeah?" I asked, voice cracking.

Her voice was soothing and cajoling. I felt that crawling on my skin again and a need to please her. "I need you to look at the dead. Open your eyes to them."

The dead? No. My mind felt out of control, and I had enough sense to know bringing ghosts here would be a bad idea. "I can't."

"You can," she said. "I'll help you. Please."

I couldn't refuse her compulsion. Expanding my senses, I let down the walls I kept around me. They were the walls that blocked me from the world of the dead and the ghosts that followed me around. Within moments, translucent faces appeared before me, some like normal people and others terrible and ghastly. Their mouths opened, wanting to speak but unable to.

"What do you see?" asked Sonya.

"Spirits," I whispered.

"Do you see Victor?"

I peered into the swarm of faces, seeking anyone familiar. "No."

"Push them back," she said. "Put your walls back up."

I tried to do as she said, but it was hard. I didn't have the will. I felt outside encouragement and realized Sonya was still compelling me. She couldn't make the ghosts disappear, but feelings of support and determination strengthened me. I shut out the restless dead.

"He's gone then," Sonya said. "He's either completely consumed by the world of the dead or is wandering as a restless spirit. Regardless, any lingering threads to life are gone. He can't come back to life." She turned to Jill. "Go get Dimitri."

"I don't know where he is," said Jill, startled.

Sonya smiled, but it didn't reach her eyes. "Close, I'm sure. And watching. Go walk around the motel, the block, whatever. He'll find you."

Jill left, needing no compulsion. When she was gone, I buried my face in my hands. "Oh God. Oh God. All this time, I denied it, but it's true: I *am* a murderer."

"Don't think about that yet," said Sonya. Her take-charge attitude was almost comforting. Almost. It was easier to take orders than fend for yourself. "Deal with your guilt later. For now, we have to get rid of the body."

I uncovered my eyes and forced myself to look at Victor. Nausea welled up within me, and those crazy feelings spun even more out of control. I gave a harsh laugh. "Yes. The body. I wish Sydney was here. But we don't have any magic potions. The sun won't destroy him. Weird, isn't it? Strigoi are harder to kill . . . harder to kill, easier to clean up." I laughed again because there was something familiar about my rambling . . . it was like Adrian in one of his weird moments. Or Lissa when spirit had pushed her to the edge. "This is it, isn't it?" I asked

Sonya. "The flood . . . the flood you warned me about. Lissa escaped spirit, but it finally defeated me . . . just like Anna . . . just like the dream . . . oh God. This is the dream, isn't it? But I won't wake up . . ."

Sonya was staring at me, her blue eyes wide with . . . fear? Mockery? Alarm? She reached out and took my hand. "Stay with me, Rose. We'll push it back."

A knock at the window startled us both, and Sonya let Jill and Dimitri in.

"Where's Robert?" asked Sonya.

Dimitri glanced down at Victor and then promptly looked away. "Unconscious, hidden in some bushes around the corner."

"Charming," said Sonya. "Do you think that's smart? Leaving him?"

He shrugged. "I figured I shouldn't be seen carrying an unconscious guy in my arms. In fact . . . yes, I think we should just leave him there. He'll wake up. He's not a fugitive. And without Victor, he's . . . well, not harmless. But less harmful. We can't keep dragging him with us anyway."

I laughed again, that laugh that seemed unhinged and hysterical even to me. "He's unconscious. Of course. Of course. You can do that. You can do the right thing. Not me." I looked down at Victor. "'An animal,' he said. He was right. No higher reasoning . . ." I wrapped my arms around myself, my fingernails digging into my skin so hard they drew blood. *Physical pain to make the mental pain go away.* Wasn't that what Lissa had always said?

Dimitri stared at me and then turned to Sonya. "What's wrong?" he demanded. I'd seen him risk his life over and over, but never, until now, had he truly looked afraid.

"Spirit," said Sonya. "She's pulled and pulled for so long . . . and managed to hold it back. It's been waiting, though. Always waiting . . ." She frowned slightly, maybe realizing she was starting to sound like me. She turned to Jill. "Is that silver?"

Jill looked down at the heart-shaped locket around her neck. "I think so."

"Can I have it?"

Jill undid the clasp and passed it over. Sonya held it between her palms and closed her eyes a moment, pursing her lips. A few seconds later, her eyes opened, and she handed me the locket. "Put it on."

Just touching it gave me a strange tingling in my skin. "The heart . . ." I looked at Dimitri as I fastened the clasp. "Do you remember that? 'Where's the heart?' you asked. And here it is. Here it . . ."

I stopped. The world suddenly became crisper. My jumbled thoughts slowly began to move back together, forming some semblance of rationality. I stared at my companions—the living ones—truly seeing them now. I touched the locket.

"This is a healing charm."

Sonya nodded. "I didn't know if it'd work on the mind. I don't think it's a permanent fix . . . but between it and your own will, you'll be okay for a while."

I tried not to focus on those last words. *For a while.* Instead,

I tried to make sense of the world around me. Of the body in front of me.

"What have I done?" I whispered.

Jill put her arm around me, but it was Dimitri who spoke. "What you had to."

TWENTY-NINE

THE EVENTS THAT FOLLOWED were a blur. Sonya might have kept spirit's touch at bay, but it didn't matter. I was still in shock, still unable to think. They put me in the front seat, as far from Victor as possible. Dimitri drove us somewhere—I didn't pay much attention—where he and Sonya disposed of the body. They didn't say what they did, only that it was "taken care of." I didn't ask for details.

After that, we were back and headed toward Court. Sonya and Dimitri tossed around options on what to do when we got there. Seeing as no one had yet cleared my name, the current plan was that Sonya would have to escort Jill into Court. Jill asked if she could call her parents to let them know she was okay, but Dimitri felt that was a security risk. Sonya said she'd try to reach Emily in a dream, which made Jill feel a little better.

I coped during the drive by checking in on Lissa. Focusing on her took me away from the horrible guilt and emptiness I felt, the horror at what I'd done to Victor. When I was with Lissa, I wasn't me, and just then, that was my greatest desire. I didn't want to be me.

But things weren't perfect for her either. Like always, a number of issues were weighing her down. She felt close—so, so close—to unraveling who had killed Tatiana. The answer seemed within her grasp, if only she could reach just a little farther. The guardians had dragged Joe the janitor in, and after a fair amount of coercion—they had methods that didn't require magical compulsion—he'd admitted to having seen the twisted-handed Moroi in my building on the night of the murder. No amount of pushing would get Joe to admit he had been paid off—by either the man or Daniella. The most he'd admit was that he might have been "a little off" in his times that night. It was by no means hard evidence to save me.

Lissa had Ambrose's letter too, which had subtly threatened Tatiana. The writer had opposed the age law for being soft, disapproved of Tatiana's endorsement of spirit, and resented the secret training sessions. The letter might have been perfectly polite, but whoever penned it had had a serious grudge against the queen. That supported the political motive theories.

Of course, there were still lots of personal motives for the murder too. The sordid mess with Ambrose, Blake, and the women involved pegged any of them as the murderer. Daniella Ivashkov being on that list was a constant point of stress for Lissa, and she dared not breathe a word to Adrian. The saving grace there was that Daniella's bribery had been to get Adrian out of trouble—not solidify my guilt. The unknown Moroi had funded that bribe. Surely, if she had killed Tatiana, Daniella would have paid for both of Joe's lies.

And of course, there was the last test pressing against Lissa's mind. The riddle. The riddle that seemed to have so many answers—and yet, none at all. *What must a queen possess in order to truly rule her people?* In some ways, it was more difficult than the other tests. Those had had a hands-on component, so to speak. This? This was her own intellect. No fire to build. No fear to look in the eye.

She hated that she took the riddle so seriously too. She didn't need its stress, not with everything else going on. Life would have been simpler if she'd kept treating the trials simply as a scam to buy us time. The Court was continually swelling with those who had come to see the election, and more and more of them—much to her disbelief—were throwing their support behind her. She could hardly walk anywhere without people calling out about "the Dragon" or "Alexandra reborn." Word of her attack had gotten out too, which seemed to have fueled her supporters even more.

But, of course, Lissa still had plenty of opposition. The biggest case against her was the same old legal one: that she wouldn't be eligible for votes when the time came. Another mark against her was her age. She was too young, her opponents said. Who would want a child on the throne? But Lissa's admirers wouldn't hear any of it. They kept citing young Alexandra's rule and the miracles Lissa had wrought with her healing. Age was irrelevant. The Moroi needed young blood, they cried. They also demanded the voting laws be changed.

Unsurprisingly, her opponents also kept bringing up the fact that she was tied to a queen-killing murderer. I'd have thought that would have been the biggest issue in her candidacy, but she'd been so convincing about how I'd shocked and betrayed her that many felt her being queen would actually right the wrong I'd committed. She'd used bits of compulsion whenever the topic came up, which also went a long way in making others think she was now completely dissociated from me.

"I'm so tired of this," Lissa told Christian, back in her room. She'd sought escape there and was lying on her bed in his arms. My mom was there, on guard. "This queen thing was a horrible idea."

Christian stroked her hair. "It's not. Abe said the election will be delayed because of the uproar. And no matter how much you complain, I know you're proud you made it this far."

It was true. The chalice test had cut the nominees in half. Only five remained. Ariana Szelsky was one of them, as was Daniella's cousin, Rufus Tarus. Lissa was the third, with Marcus Lazar and Marie Conta rounding out the group. Ronald Ozera hadn't made it through.

My mother spoke up. "I've never seen anything like this—it's incredible how much support you're getting. The Council and other royals are under no obligations to change the law. But the mob's loud . . . and gaining the love of 'commoners' could benefit certain royals. Standing by your claim to run would certainly reflect well on a couple families that are out of favor. What's holding them back is the thought that you might actually win. So they'll just keep arguing and arguing."

Lissa stiffened. "Winning . . . that's not really possible, is it? Ariana's got it sealed . . . right?" Winning had never been a part of this crazy plan, and now, with so few candidates, the pressure was even greater to get Ariana on the throne. As far as Lissa was concerned, the other candidates showed no promise of improving Moroi life. Ariana *had* to win.

"I'd say so," said Janine. There was pride in her voice, seeing how close she was to the Szelsky family. "Ariana's brilliant and competent, and most people know it. She'd treat dhampirs fairly—more so than some of the other candidates. She's already spoken about reversing the age law."

The thought of worse laws oppressing the dhampirs made Lissa's stomach sink. "God, I hope she wins. We can't have anything else go wrong."

A knock at the door snapped my mom into full guardian mode until Lissa said, "It's Adrian."

"Well," muttered Christian, "at least his timing's better than usual."

Sure enough, my boyfriend entered, wreathed in his now usual scent of smoke and liquor. True, his vices were the least of my concerns, but it kept bugging me that he needed *me* to be there in person to enforce his good behavior. It reminded me of when he said I was his strength.

"Get up, guys," he said. He looked very pleased with himself. "We've got a visit to pay."

Lissa sat up, puzzled. "What are you talking about?"

"I am *not* hanging out with Blake Lazar again," warned Christian.

"You and me both," said Adrian. "I've got someone better. And more attractive. Remember how you were wondering how close Serena was to Grant? Well, looks like you can ask her yourself. I found her. And yes, you're welcome."

A frown crossed my mother's face. "Last I heard, Serena had been sent away to teach at a school. One on the east coast, I think." After the Strigoi attack that had killed Grant and several others, the guardians had decided to pull Serena from active bodyguard duty for a while. She'd been the only guardian to survive.

"She is, but since it's summer, they brought her back to help with election crowd control. She's working the front gates."

Lissa and Christian exchanged looks. "We have to talk to her," said Lissa excitedly. "She might have known who Grant was secretly teaching."

"That doesn't mean one of them killed Tatiana," warned my mother.

Lissa nodded. "No, but there's a connection, if Ambrose's letter is right. She's there now? At the gates?"

"Yup," said Adrian. "And we probably don't even need to buy her a drink."

"Then let's go." Lissa stood and reached for her shoes.

"Are you sure?" asked Christian. "You know what's waiting out there."

Lissa hesitated. It was late at "night" for Moroi, but that didn't mean everyone was in bed—especially at the gates, which was always jam-packed with people lately. Clearing my name was too important, Lissa decided. "Yeah. Let's do it."

With my mother leading the way, my friends made their way to the Court's entrance. (The "door" that Abe had made had been patched up.) The Court was surrounded in high, multicolored stone walls that helped further the human image that this was actually an elite school. Wrought iron gates at the entrance stood open, but a group of guardians blocked the road leading into Court grounds. Normally, only two guardians would have manned the booth at the gate. The extra numbers were both for greater interrogation of cars and for crowd control. Spectators lined the road's sides, watching the arriving cars as though they were at a red carpet premiere. Janine knew a roundabout way that avoided some people—but not all.

"Don't cringe," Christian told Lissa as they passed a particularly vocal group, which had noticed her. "You're a queenly nominee. Act like it. You deserve this. You're the last Dragomir. A daughter of royalty."

Lissa gave him a brief, astonished look, surprised to hear the fierceness in his voice—and that he clearly believed his words. Straightening up, she turned toward her fans, smiling and waving back, which excited them that much more. *Take this seriously*, she reminded herself. *Don't disgrace our history*.

In the end, getting through the crowd to the gate proved easier than getting time alone with Serena. The guardians were swamped and insisted on keeping Serena for screening, but my mom had a quick conversation with the guardian in charge. She reminded him of Lissa's importance and offered to stand in for Serena for a few minutes.

Serena had long since healed from the Strigoi attack. She was my age, blond-haired and pretty. She was clearly surprised to see her former charge. "Princess," she said, maintaining formalities. "How can I help you?"

Lissa pulled Serena away from the cluster of guardians speaking to the Moroi drivers lined up at the gate. "You can call me Lissa. You know that. You taught me to stab pillows, after all."

Serena gave her a small smile. "Things have changed. You might be our next queen."

Lissa grimaced. "Unlikely." *Especially since I have no clue how to solve that riddle,* she thought. "But I do need your help. You and Grant spent a lot of time together . . . did he ever mention training Moroi for Tatiana? Like, secret combat sessions?"

Serena's face gave the answer away, and she averted her eyes. "I'm not supposed to talk about that. He wasn't even supposed to tell me."

Lissa gripped the young guardian's arm in excitement, making Serena flinch. "You have to tell me what you know. Anything. Who he was training . . . how they felt about it . . . who was successful. *Anything.*"

Serena paled. "I *can't,*" she whispered. "It was done in secret. On the queen's orders."

"My aunt's dead," said Adrian bluntly. "And you said yourself you might be talking to the future queen." This earned a glare from Lissa.

Serena hesitated, then took a deep breath. "I can pull together a list of names. I might not remember all of them, though. And I have no clue how well they were doing—only that a lot resented it. Grant felt like Tatiana had purposely picked those most unwilling."

Lissa squeezed her hand. "Thank you. Thank you so much."

Serena still looked pained at giving up the secret information. *They come first* didn't always work when your loyalties were split. "I'll have to get it to you later, though. They need me here."

Serena returned to her post, bringing my mother back to Lissa. As for me, I returned to my own reality in the car, which had come to a stop. I blinked to clear my eyes and take in our surroundings. Another hotel. We should have had gold member status by now. "What's going on?"

"We're stopping," said Dimitri. "You need to rest."

"No, I don't. We need to keep going to Court. We need to get Jill there in time for the elections." Our initial goal in finding Jill had been to give Lissa voting power. It had since occurred to us that if Lissa running was mucking up the elections, the surprise appearance of her sister would likely create just as much sensation and disbelief. A genetic test would clear up any doubts and give Lissa her voting power, but the initial confusion would buy us more of the time we so badly needed to find the murderer. In spite of the random evidence my friends kept turning up, they still had no substantial theories on a culprit.

Dimitri gave me a *don't lie to me* look. "You were just with Lissa. Are the elections actually happening yet?"

"No," I admitted.

"Then you're getting some rest."

"I'm *fine*," I snapped.

But those fools wouldn't listen to me. Checking in was

complicated because none of us had a credit card, and it wasn't the hotel's policy to take a cash deposit. Sonya compelled the desk clerk into thinking it *was* their policy, and before long, we had booked two adjoining rooms.

"Let me talk to her alone," Dimitri murmured to Sonya. "I can handle it."

"Be careful," Sonya warned. "She's fragile."

"You guys, I'm right here!" I exclaimed.

Sonya took Jill's arm and guided her into one of the rooms. "Come on, let's order room service."

Dimitri opened the other door and looked at me expectantly. With a sigh, I followed and sat on the bed, my arms crossed. The room was a hundred times nicer than the one in West Virginia. "Can *we* order room service?"

He pulled up a chair and sat opposite me, only a couple feet away. "We need to talk about what happened with Victor."

"There's nothing to talk about," I said bleakly. The dark feelings I'd been shoving back during the drive suddenly fell upon me. They smothered me. I felt more claustrophobic than when I'd been in the cell. Guilt was its own prison. "I really am the murderer everyone says I am. It doesn't matter that it was Victor. I killed him in cold blood."

"That was hardly cold blood."

"The hell it wasn't!" I cried, feeling tears spring to my eyes. "The plan was to subdue him and Robert so we could free Jill. *Subdue*. Victor wasn't a threat to me. He was an old man, for God's sake."

"He seemed like a threat," said Dimitri. His calmness was

the counter to my growing hysteria, as usual. "He was using his magic."

I shook my head, burying my face in my hands. "It wasn't going to kill me. He probably couldn't have even kept it up much longer. I could have waited it out or escaped. Hell, I did escape! But instead of capturing him, I slammed him against a concrete wall! He was no match for me. An old man. I killed an *old man*. Yeah, maybe he was a scheming, corrupt old man, but I didn't want him dead. I wanted him locked up again. I wanted him to spend the rest of his life in prison, living with his crimes. *Living*, Dimitri."

It seemed strange that I'd feel this way, considering how much I hated Victor. But it was true: it hadn't been a fair fight. I'd acted without thinking. My training had always been about defense and striking out against monsters. Honor had never really come up, but suddenly, it meant a lot to me. "There was no honor in what I did to him."

"Sonya said it wasn't your fault." Dimitri's voice was still gentle, which somehow made me feel worse. I wished he'd chastise me, confirming the guilt I felt. I wanted him to be my critical instructor. "She said it was a backlash of spirit."

"It was. . . ." I paused, recalling the haze of that fight as best I could. "I never really understood what Lissa experienced in her worst moments until then. I just looked at Victor . . . and I saw everything evil in the world—an evil I had to stop. He was bad, but he didn't deserve that. He never stood a chance." *Honor*, I kept thinking. *What honor is there in that?*

"You aren't listening, Rose. It wasn't your fault. Spirit's a powerful magic we barely understand. And its dark edge . . . well, we know it's capable of terrible things. Things that can't be controlled."

I lifted my eyes to his. "I should have been stronger than it." There it was. The thought behind all my guilt, all these horrible emotions. "I should have been stronger than it. I was weak."

Dimitri's reassuring words didn't come so quickly. "You aren't invincible," he said at last. "No one expects you to be."

"*I* do. What I did . . ." I swallowed. "What I did was unforgivable."

His eyes widened in shock. "That . . . that's crazy, Rose. You can't punish yourself for something you had no power over."

"Yeah? Then why are you still—"

I stopped because I'd been about to accuse Dimitri of continuing to punish himself. Except . . . he no longer was. Did he feel guilt for what he'd done as a Strigoi? I was certain of it. Sonya had admitted as much. But somewhere in this journey, he had taken control of his life again, bit by bit. She'd told me that, but only now did I truly understand.

"When?" I asked. "When did it change? When did you realize you could keep living—even after all that guilt?"

"I'm not sure." If the question surprised him, he hid it. His eyes were locked with mine, but they weren't quite focused on me. The puzzle occupied him. "In bits, really. When Lissa and Abe first came to me about breaking you out, I was ready to do it because she asked me to. Then, the more I thought about it, the more I realized it was personal too. I couldn't stand the thought of you locked in a cell, being cut off from the world.

It wasn't right. No one should live like that, and it occurred to me that I was doing the same—by choice. I was cutting myself off from the world with guilt and self-punishment. I had a second chance to live, and I was throwing it away."

I was still in turmoil, still raging and full of grief, but his story kept me quiet and transfixed. Hearing him pour his heart out was a rare opportunity.

"You heard me talk about this before," he continued. "About my goal to appreciate life's little details. And the more we continued on our journey, the more I remembered who I was. Not just a fighter. Fighting is easy. It's *why* we fight that matters, and in the alley that night with Donovan . . ." He shuddered. "That was the moment I could have crossed over into someone who fights just to senselessly kill—but you pulled me back, Rose. That was the turning point. You saved me . . . just as Lissa saved me with the stake. I knew then that in order to leave the Strigoi part of me behind, I had to fight through to be what they *aren't*. I had to embrace what they reject: beauty, love, honor."

Right then, I was two people. One was overjoyed. Hearing him talk like that, realizing he was fighting his demons and close to victory . . . well, I nearly wept with joy. It was what I'd wanted for him for so long. At the same time, his inspiring words only reminded me how far I'd fallen. My sorrow and self-pity took over again.

"Then you should understand," I said bitterly. "You just said it: honor. It matters. We both know it does. I've lost mine. I lost it out there in the parking lot when I killed an innocent."

"And I've killed hundreds," he said flatly. "People much more innocent than Victor Dashkov."

"It's not the same! You couldn't help it!" My feelings exploded to the surface again. "Why are we repeating the same things over and over?"

"Because they aren't sinking in! *You* couldn't help it either." His patience was cracking. "Feel guilty. Mourn this. But move on. Don't let it destroy you. Forgive yourself."

I leapt to my feet, catching him by surprise. I leaned down, putting us face to face. "Forgive myself? That's what you want? *You* of all people?"

Words seemed to escape him. I think it had to do with my proximity. He managed a nod.

"Then tell me this. You say you moved past the guilt, decided to revel in life and all that. I get it. But have you, in your heart, really forgiven *yourself*? I told you a long time ago that I forgave you for everything in Siberia, but what about you? Have you done it?"

"I just said—"

"No. It's not the same. You're telling me to forgive myself and move on. But you won't do it yourself. You're a hypocrite, comrade. We're either both guilty or both innocent. Pick."

He rose as well, looking down at me from that lofty height. "It's not that simple."

I crossed my arms over my chest, refusing to be intimidated. "It *is* that simple. We're the same! Even Sonya says we are. We've always been the same, and we're both acting the same stupid way now. We hold ourselves up to a higher standard than everyone else."

Dimitri frowned. "I—Sonya? What does she have to do with any of this?"

"She said our auras match. She said we light up around each other. She says it means you still love me and that we're in sync, and . . ." I sighed and turned away, wandering across the room. "I don't know. I shouldn't have mentioned it. We shouldn't buy into this aura stuff when it comes from magic users who are already half-insane."

I reached the window and leaned my forehead against the cool glass, trying to decide what to do. *Forgive myself.* Could I? A small city sprawled before me, though I'd lost track of where we were. Cars and people moved below, souls out living their lives. I took a deep breath. The image of Victor on the asphalt was going to stay with me for a long, long time. I had done something horrible, even if my intentions were good, but everyone was right: I hadn't been myself. Did that change what had happened? Would that bring Victor back? No. And honestly, I didn't know how I would move past what I'd done, how I'd shake the bloody images in my head. I just knew I had to go on.

"If I let this stop me," I murmured, "if I do nothing . . . then that's the greater evil. I'll do more good by surviving. By continuing to fight and protect others."

"What are you saying?" asked Dimitri.

"I'm saying . . . I forgive myself. That doesn't make everything perfect, but it's a start." My fingertip traced the line of a tiny crack in the glass's surface. "Who knows? Maybe that outburst in the parking lot let out some of the darkness Sonya says is in my aura. Skeptic that I am, I have to give her some points. She was right that I was at a breaking point, that all I needed was a spark."

"She was right about something else too," Dimitri said after a long pause. My back was to him, but there was a strange quality to his voice that made me turn around.

"What's that?" I asked.

"That I do still love you."

With that one sentence, everything in the universe changed.

Time slowed to one heartbeat. The world became his eyes, his voice. This wasn't happening. It wasn't real. None of it could be real. It felt like a spirit dream. I resisted the urge to close my eyes and see if I'd wake up moments later. No. No matter how unbelievable it all seemed, this was no dream. This was real. This was life. This was flesh and blood.

"Since . . . since when?" I finally managed to ask.

"Since . . . forever." His tone implied the answer was obvious. "I denied it when I was restored. I had no room for anything in my heart except guilt. I especially felt guilty about you—what I'd done—and I pushed you away. I put up a wall to keep you safe. It worked for a while—until my heart finally started accepting other emotions. And it all came back. Everything I felt for you. It had never left; it was just hidden from me until I was ready. And again . . . that alley was the turning point. I looked at you . . . saw your goodness, your hope, and your faith. Those are what make you beautiful. So, so beautiful."

"So it wasn't my hair," I said, unsure how I was even

capable of making a joke at a time like this.

"No," he said gently. "Your hair was beautiful too. All of you. You were amazing when we first met, and somehow, inexplicably, you've come even farther. You've always been pure, raw energy, and now you control it. You're the most amazing woman I've ever met, and I'm glad to have had that love for you in my life. I regret losing it." He grew pensive. "I would give anything—anything—in the world to go back and change history. To run into your arms after Lissa brought me back. To have a life with you. It's too late, of course, but I've accepted it."

"Why . . . why is it too late?"

Dimitri's eyes grew sad. "Because of Adrian. Because you've moved on. No, listen," he said, cutting off my protests. "You were right to do that after how I treated you. And more than anything else, I want you to be happy once we clear your name and get Jill recognized. You said yourself that Adrian makes you happy. You said you love him."

"But . . . you just said you love me. That you want to be with me." My words seemed clumsy, unworthy of his eloquence.

"And I told you: I'm not going to pursue another man's girlfriend. You want to talk honor? There it is in its purest form."

I walked toward him, each step ramping up the tension around us. Dimitri kept saying the alley was his turning point. For me? It was *now*. I stood on the precipice of something that would change my life. For the last week, I'd done a very good job of detaching myself from anything romantic with Dimitri. And yet . . . had I? What *was* love, really? Flowers, chocolate, and poetry? Or was it something else? Was it being able to finish someone's jokes? Was it having absolute faith that someone was there at your back? Was it knowing someone so well that they instantly understood why you did the things you did—and shared those same beliefs?

All week, I'd claimed my love for Dimitri was fading. In reality, it had been growing more and more. I hadn't even realized it was happening. I had been re-establishing our old rapport, strengthening the connection. Reaffirming that of all the people in the world—even Lissa—Dimitri was the only one who truly *got* me.

I'd meant it: I loved Adrian. It was hard to imagine life without him, but my other words at the Mastranos' had betrayed me: *I have fun with him.* Now, you should have fun with the one you love, but that shouldn't have been what first came to mind. I should have said, *We strengthen each other.* Or, *He makes me want to be a better person.* Perhaps most importantly: *He understands me perfectly.*

But none of that was true, so I hadn't said those things. I'd sought Adrian for comfort. His familiarity and humor were an important part of my world. And if he was in danger? I'd throw my life before his, just as I would for Lissa. Yet, I didn't inspire him, not really. He was trying. He did want to be a better person, but at this moment in his life, his motivations were more about impressing others—about impressing me. It wasn't for himself. That didn't make him bad or weak, but it made me his crutch. He would get past that, I was certain. He would eventually come into his own and be an amazing man, but he wasn't at that point of self-discovery yet. I was.

I stood in front of Dimitri now, looking into those dark eyes again, the eyes I loved so much. I placed my hands on his chest, feeling his heart beating strong and steady—and maybe a bit faster than normal. Warmth spread through my fingertips. He reached up and caught hold of my wrists but didn't push me away. The lines of that gorgeous face looked strained as he fought some inner conflict, but now that I knew—now that I knew for sure—I could see his love for me. Love mingled with desire. It was so, so obvious.

"You should have told me," I said. "You should have told me this a long time ago. I love you. I've never stopped loving you. You have to know that."

His breath caught when I said *I love you*, and I could see his internal struggle for control become an all-out war. "It wouldn't have made any difference. Not with Adrian involved," he said. The fingers around my hand tightened slightly as though he really might push me away this time. He didn't. "I mean it. I won't be that guy, Rose. I won't be that man who takes someone else's woman. Now, please. Let go. Don't make this any more difficult."

I ignored the request. If he'd wanted to get away from me, he could have. I splayed my fingers, touching more of his chest, drinking in the feel of that warm contact I'd missed for so long.

"I don't belong to him," I said in a low voice, pushing close to Dimitri and tilting my head back so that I could see his face clearly. So much emotion, so much conflict as his heart tried to decide right from wrong. Being pressed against him felt like . . . completion. Sonya had said no couple could share one aura or one soul, but ours weren't meant to be apart. They fit together like a puzzle, two individuals making something greater than themselves. "I don't belong to anyone. I make my own choices."

"And you're with Adrian," said Dimitri.

"But I was meant for you."

And that did it. Any pretense of control or reason either of us possessed melted away. The walls crumbled, and everything we'd been holding back from each other came rushing out. I reached up, pulling us together for a kiss—a kiss he didn't let go this time. A kiss I didn't end by punching him. His arms encircled me as he lifted me onto the bed, one hand soon sliding along my hip and down to my leg, already half-bare, thanks to that poor tattered dress.

Every nerve in my body lit up, and I felt that desire returned in him—and then some. After a world of death, he seemed to appreciate love more. Not only that, he *needed* it. He needed life. He needed me—not just physically, but in the same way my heart and soul always cried out for him. What we did then, as our clothes came off and we brought our bodies together became more than just lust—even though there was plenty of that too.

Being with him after so long, after everything we'd endured . . . it was like coming home. Like finally being where—with whom—I belonged. My world, my heart . . . they'd shattered when I lost him. But as he looked at me, as his lips spoke my name and ran along my skin . . . I knew those pieces could come back together. And I knew, with absolute certainty, that waiting for this—for my second time having sex—had been the right thing to do. Anyone else, any other time . . . it would have been wrong.

When we finished, it was like we still couldn't get close enough. We held each other tightly, our limbs entwined, as though maybe closing the distance now would make up for the distance that had been between us for so long.

I closed my eyes, my senses flooded with him, and sighed dreamily. "I'm glad you gave in. I'm glad your self-control isn't as strong as mine."

This made him laugh, and I felt it rumble through his chest. "Roza, my self-control is ten times stronger than yours."

I opened my eyes, shifting to look into his. I brushed his hair back and smiled, certain my heart would expand and expand until there was nothing left of me. "Oh yeah? That's not the impression I just got."

"Wait until next time," he warned. "I'll do things that'll make you lose control within seconds."

That comment was just asking for a witty Rose Hathaway quip. It also made my blood burn, which was why we were both surprised when I abruptly said, "There may not be a next time."

Dimitri's hand, tracing the shape of my shoulder, froze. "What? Why?"

"We have a couple of things to do before this happens again."

"Adrian," he guessed.

I nodded. "And that's *my* problem, so put your honorable thoughts aside. I have to face him and answer for this. I will. And you . . ." I couldn't believe what I was about to say. I couldn't believe I meant it. "You still have to forgive yourself if we're going to be together."

His puzzled expression turned to pain. "Rose—"

"I'm serious." I met his eyes unflinchingly. "*You* have to forgive yourself. For real. Everyone else has. If you can't, then you can't go on either. *We* can't."

It was one of the biggest gambles of my life. Once, I would have run to him without question, ignoring our problems, overjoyed just to be with him. Now . . . after everything I'd been through, I'd changed. I loved him. I loved him so much, and I wanted him. But it was because of the strength of that love that I had to do this. If were going to be together, we had to do it the right way. Sex had been amazing, but it wasn't a magical cure for everything. Damn. Somewhere along the way, I'd picked up common sense. I still intended to confront Adrian. And if Dimitri wouldn't do what I asked, I really would walk away. I'd lose both men, but it was better to be alone with my self-respect than be in the wrong relationship.

"I don't know," Dimitri said at last. "I don't know if I can . . . if I'm ready."

"Decide soon then," I said. "You don't have to right this second, but eventually . . ."

I didn't push the topic after that. For now, I would let it go, though I knew he would hold onto it and grasp its importance. I knew I was right to stand by it too. He couldn't be happy with me if he wasn't happy with himself. It occurred to me then, as I stood up for myself and what I needed, that our old teacher-student roles were gone forever. Now we really were equals.

I rested my head on his chest and felt him relax. We'd bask in this moment, if only for a little longer. Sonya had said we needed "rest," making me think we still had some time here before the ticking clock drove us back to Court. As Dimitri and I continued to keep close to one another, I found myself actually wanting to sleep. I was exhausted from the fight—which, I realized, had taken a very unexpected turn. My guilt and despair over Victor and the explosion of spirit had taken their toll too, no matter the healing locket still around my neck. And yes, I thought with a small smile, I was simply exhausted from what Dimitri and I had just done. It was kind of nice to use my body for something that didn't result in serious injury for a change.

I fell asleep in his embrace, blackness wrapping around me as warmly as his arms. It should have been that simple. It should have been peaceful, happy rest. But as usual, I wasn't that lucky.

A spirit dream pulled me from the enveloping depths of sleep, and for half a second, I thought maybe Robert Doru had come for me to take revenge for his brother's death.

But, no. No vindictive Dashkov. Instead, I found myself staring into a pair of emerald-green eyes.

Adrian.

THIRTY

I DIDN'T RUN INTO HIS arms like I usually did. How could I? After what I'd done? No. I couldn't playact anymore. I still wasn't entirely sure what the future held for Dimitri and me, not until he answered my ultimatum. I did, however, know I had to cut Adrian loose. My feelings for him were still strong, and I wondered if it was even remotely possible for us to be friends. Regardless, I couldn't lead him on after sleeping with Dimitri. It hadn't been murder, no, but it had certainly been dishonorable.

Yet . . . I couldn't say any of that to Adrian now, I realized. I couldn't break up with him in a dream. That was almost as bad as a text breakup. Besides, I had a feeling that . . . well, I'd probably need his help. So much for honor. *Soon*, I swore. *Soon I'll tell him.*

He didn't seem to notice my lack of embrace. But he did notice something else.

"Wow."

We stood in St. Vladimir's library of all places, and I gave him a puzzled look across the study tables stretching before us. "Wow what?"

"Your . . . your aura. It's . . . amazing. It's shining. I mean, it always shines, but today . . . well, I've never seen anything like it. I didn't expect that after everything that happened."

I shifted uncomfortably. If I lit up around Dimitri normally, what on earth happened to my aura post-sex? "After what happened?" I asked, deflecting the comment.

He chuckled and approached me. His hand reached unconsciously for his cigarettes, paused, and then dropped to his side. "Oh, come on. Everyone's talking about it. How you and Belikov kidnapped Jailbait—what's up with that anyway?—and coerced that Alchemist. It's the hottest news around here. Well, aside from the elections. The last test is coming up."

"That's right . . ." I murmured. It had almost been twenty-four hours since Lissa had received the riddle. There was only a little time left, and last I knew, she had no answer.

"Why are you sleeping in the middle of the day anyway?" he asked. "I didn't really expect to catch you. Figured you'd be on a human schedule."

"It . . . it was kind of a rough night, what with escaping a legion of guardians and all."

Adrian caught hold of my hand, frowning slightly when I didn't squeeze his in return. The frown lightened quickly into his easy smile. "Well, I'd worry more about your old man than them. He is *pissed* that you didn't stay put. And that he can't get in to see the Alchemists. Believe me, he's been trying."

That almost made me laugh, except it wasn't the outcome I'd wanted either. "So he's not all-powerful after all." I sighed. "That's what we need. Sydney. Or, well, that guy who's with her. The one who allegedly knows something." I flashed back, again seeing the recognition on Ian's face. *He knows the man who attacked Lissa and bribed Joe*. "We need him."

"From what I picked up," said Adrian, "the guardians are just kind of lingering around the hotel, mostly concerned with the Alchemists leaving. But they're controlling who's getting in. They won't let any of us—or other Alchemists—get through. There are lots of other human guests, and I guess Abe tried to disguise himself—and failed."

Poor *Zmey*. "He should have had more faith in the guardians. They aren't going to let anyone but themselves get in and out." My own words brought me to a halt. "That's it . . ."

Adrian eyed me suspiciously. "Oh no. I know that look. Something crazy is about to happen."

I caught hold of his hand, now out of excitement, rather than love. "Get to Mikhail. Have him meet us . . ." I blanked. I'd seen the town the Alchemists were staying in. As the closest to Court, we often drove through it. I racked my brain, trying to think of some detail. "At that restaurant with the red sign. It's on the far side. Always advertising buffets."

"Easier said than done, little dhampir. They're using every guardian at Court to keep the elections under control. If Lissa hadn't been attacked, they wouldn't let your mom stay with her. I don't think Mikhail can get out."

"He'll find a way," I said confidently. "Tell him this is it—it's the key to the murder. The answer. He's resourceful."

Adrian looked skeptical, but it was hard for him to refuse me anything. "When?"

When indeed? It was almost noon, and I hadn't paid much attention to where we'd stopped. How long would it take us to reach Court? From what I knew about the elections, those who passed this last test would give speeches when the Moroi day started. In theory, they'd then go straight to voting—except, if our plan worked, Lissa's involvement would slow that down for days. Provided she passed.

"Midnight," I said. If I was guessing correctly, the Court would be completely wrapped up in the election drama, making it easier for Mikhail to get out. I hoped. "Will you tell him?"

"Anything for you." Adrian swept me a gallant bow. "Although, I still think it's dangerous for you to be involved directly with this."

"I have to do this myself," I said. "I can't hide."

He nodded, as though he understood. I wasn't sure he did.

"Thank you," I told him. "Thank you so much for everything. Now go."

Adrian gave me a crooked grin. "Boy, you don't waste any time kicking a guy out of bed, huh?"

I flinched, the joke hitting a little too close to home. "I want Mikhail to be prepared. And I also need to watch Lissa's last test."

This sobered Adrian. "Does she have a chance? Will she pass?"

"I don't know," I admitted. "This is a tough one."

"Okay. We'll see what we can do." He gave me a small kiss. My lips responded automatically, but my heart wasn't into it. "And Rose? I mean it. Be careful. You're going to be awfully close to Court. Not to mention a bunch of guardians who have you on their most wanted list and will probably try to kill you."

"I know," I said, choosing not to mention that there was no "probably" about it.

With that, he vanished, and I woke. Strangely, what I found in my own world seemed almost more dreamlike than what I'd experienced with Adrian. Dimitri and I were still in bed, snuggled under the covers, our bodies and limbs still wrapped around each other. He slept with that rare peaceful look of his and *almost* seemed to smile. For half a second, I considered waking him and telling him we had to hit the road. A look at the clock happily squashed that thought. We still had time, plus it was getting close to the test. I had to go to Lissa and trusted Sonya would come by if we overslept.

Sure enough, I'd gauged the testing correctly. Lissa was cutting across the Court's lawns, marching like someone going to a funeral. The sun, flowers, and birds were lost on her. Even her company did little to cheer her up: Christian, my mom, and Tasha.

"I can't do this," she said, staring ahead at the building that held her fate. "I can't do this test." The tattoo kept her from giving out any more information.

"You're smart. Brilliant." Christian's arm was around her waist, and in that moment, I loved him for his confidence in her. "You can do it."

"You don't understand," she said, with a sigh. She'd come up with no answers to the riddle, meaning the plan was at stake—and her desire to prove herself.

"For once he does," said Tasha, a slight teasing tone in her voice. "You can do it. You *have* to do it. We have so much riding on it."

Her confidence didn't make Lissa feel better. If anything, it added to the pressure. She would fail, just like in the Council dream the chalice had shown her. She'd had no answer there either.

"Lissa!"

A voice brought them to a halt, and Lissa turned to see Serena running toward them, her long athletic legs quickly covering the distance between them. "Hi Serena," said Lissa. "We can't stop. The test—"

"I know, I know." Serena was flushed, not with exertion, but with anxiety. She proffered a piece of paper. "I made your list. As many as I could remember."

"What list?" asked Tasha.

"Moroi that the queen was having trained, to see how well they could learn fighting."

Tasha's eyebrows rose in surprise. She hadn't been around when they'd discussed it last time. "Tatiana was training fighters? I never heard about anything like that." I had a feeling she would have liked to be one of the ones helping with instruction.

"Most didn't," agreed Lissa, straightening the piece of paper. "It was a big secret."

The group crowded around to read the names, listed in Serena's neat handwriting. Christian let out a low whistle. "Tatiana might have been open to the idea of defense but only for certain people."

"Yes," agreed Tasha. "This is definitely an A-list."

All the names were royal. Tatiana hadn't brought in "commoners" for her experiment. This was the elite of the elite, though as Ambrose had noted, Tatiana had gone out of her way to get a variety of ages and genders.

"Camille Conta?" asked Lissa in surprise. "Never saw that coming. She was always really bad in P.E."

"And there's another of our cousins," added Christian, pointing to *Lia Ozera*. He glanced at Tasha, who was still in disbelief. "Did you know that?"

"No. I wouldn't have guessed her either."

"Half the nominees too," mused Lissa. Rufus Tarus, Ava Drozdov, and Ellis Badica. "Too bad they—oh my God. Adrian's mother?" Sure enough: Daniella Ivashkov.

"Whoa," said Christian. That summed up my reaction too. "Pretty sure Adrian didn't know about that."

"Does she support Moroi fighting?" asked my mom, surprised as well.

Lissa shook her head. "No. From what I know about her, she is definitely in favor of leaving defense to dhampirs." Neither of us could imagine beautiful and proper Daniella Ivashkov in a fight.

"She already hated Tatiana," noted Tasha. "I'm sure this did lovely things for their relationship. Those two bickered all the time behind closed doors."

An uncomfortable silence fell.

Lissa looked at Serena. "Did these people see the queen a lot? Would they have had access to her?"

"Yes," said Serena uneasily. "According to Grant, Tatiana watched every training sessions. After he died . . . she started debriefing with the students individually, to see how well they'd learned." She paused. "I think . . . I think she might have met with some the night she died."

"Had they progressed enough to learn to use a stake?" asked Lissa.

Serena grimaced. "Yes. Some better than others."

Lissa looked back at the list, feeling ill. So much opportunity. So much motivation. Was the answer here on this piece of paper? Was the murderer right before her? Serena had said earlier that Tatiana had purposely picked people resistant to training, probably to see if the obstinate could still learn. Had she gone too far with someone? One name in particular kept scrolling across Lissa's mind.

"I hate to interrupt," said my mother. Her tone and stance indicated sleuth time was over; it was back to business. "We've got to move, or you'll be late."

Lissa realized my mom was right and shoved the piece of paper in her pocket. Being late to the test meant failure. Lissa thanked Serena, reassuring her that this had been the right thing to do. Then, my friends moved away quickly, feeling the press of time as they hurried toward the testing building.

"Damn," muttered Lissa, in a rare show of swearing. "I don't think that old lady'll tolerate any lateness."

"Old lady?" My mother laughed, surprising us all. She could move faster than everyone and was obviously restraining her pace for them. "The one running most of the tests? You don't know who she is?"

"How would I?" asked Lissa. "I figured she was just someone they recruited."

"Not just someone. That's Ekaterina Zeklos."

"*What*?" Lissa nearly stopped but still had their time crunch in mind. "She was . . . she was the queen before Tatiana, right?"

"I thought she retired to some island," said Christian, just as surprised.

"Not sure if it was an island," said Tasha, "but she did step down when she thought she was too old and went off to live in luxury—and away from politics—once Tatiana was on the throne."

Too old? That had been twenty years ago. No wonder she seemed ancient. "If she was happy to get out of politics, then why is she back?" asked Lissa.

My mother opened the door for all of them when they reached the building, after first peering inside for any threats. It was so instinctual for her that she continued the conversation without missing a beat. "Because it's custom for the last monarch to test the new one—if possible. In this case, it obviously wasn't, so Ekaterina came out of retirement to do her duty."

Lissa could barely believe that she'd been chatting casually with the Moroi's last queen, a very powerful and beloved queen. As soon as her group entered the hallway, Lissa was escorted by guardians and hurried toward the testing room. Their faces showed they hadn't thought she'd make it. Several spectators, also apparently worried, cheered at her appearance giving the usual shouts about Alexandra and the dragons. Lissa had no chance to respond or even say goodbye to her friends before she was practically pushed into the room. The guardians looked relieved.

The door shut, and Lissa found herself staring once more at Ekaterina Zeklos. Seeing the old woman had been intimidating before, but now . . . Lissa's anxiety doubled. Ekaterina gave her a crooked smile.

"I was afraid you wouldn't make it," she said. "Should have known better. You aren't the type to back down."

Lissa was still starstruck and almost felt the need to ramble out an excuse, explaining about Serena's list. But, no. Ekaterina didn't care about that right now, and one didn't make excuses to someone like her anyway, Lissa decided. If you screwed up, you apologized.

"I'm sorry," said Lissa.

"No need to be," said Ekaterina. "You made it. Do you know the answer? What must a queen possess in order to truly rule her people?"

Lissa's tongue felt thick in her mouth. She didn't know the answer. It really was just like the Council dream. Investigating Tatiana's murder had taken so much time. For a strange moment, Lissa's heart burned with sympathy for that prickly queen. She'd done what she thought best for the Moroi and had died for it. Lissa even felt bad now, staring at Ekaterina. This former queen had probably never expected to be taken away from her—island?—retirement and forced back into

Court life. Yet, she had come when needed.

And just like that, Lissa suddenly knew the answer.

"Nothing," she said softly. "A queen must possess nothing to rule because she has to give everything she has to her people. Even her life."

The widening of Ekaterina's gap-toothed grin told Lissa she'd answered correctly. "Congratulations, my dear. You've made it through to tomorrow's vote. I hope you've got a speech ready to win over the Council. You'll have to give it in the morning."

Lissa swayed slightly, not sure what to say now, let alone in a formal speech. Ekaterina seemed to sense how in shock Lissa was, and the smile that always seemed so mischievous turned gentle.

"You'll be fine. You made it this far. The speech is the easy part. Your father would be proud. All the Dragomirs before you would be."

That nearly brought tears to Lissa's eyes, and she shook her head. "I don't know about that. We all know I'm not a real candidate. This was just . . . well, kind of an act." Somehow, she didn't feel bad admitting that in front of Ekaterina. "Ariana's the one who deserves the crown."

Ekaterina's ancient eyes bored into Lissa, and that smiled faded. "You haven't heard then. No, of course you wouldn't have with how quickly this is all happening."

"Heard what?"

Sympathy washed over Ekaterina's face, and later, I'd wonder if that compassion was because of the message she delivered or because of Lissa's reaction.

"Ariana Szelsky didn't pass this test . . . she couldn't solve the riddle . . ."

"Rose, Rose."

Dimitri was shaking me, and it took several seconds for me to shift from being a shocked Lissa to a startled Rose.

"We have to—" he began.

"Oh my God," I interrupted. "You will not *believe* what I just saw."

He went rigid. "Is Lissa okay?"

"Yeah, fine, but—"

"Then we'll worry about that later. Right now, we have to leave."

I noticed then that he was fully dressed while I was still naked. "What's going on?"

"Sonya came by—don't worry." The shock that my face must have shown made him smile. "I got dressed and didn't let her come in. But she said the front desk called. They're starting to realize we had an unusual check-in. We need to get out of here."

Midnight. We had to meet Mikhail at midnight and get the last piece of the mystery that consumed us. "No problem," I said, tossing the covers off me. As I did, I saw Dimitri's eyes on me, and I was kind of surprised at the admiration and hunger I saw there. Somehow, even after sex, I'd kind of expected him to be detached and wear his guardian face—particularly considering our sudden urgency to leave.

"You see something you like?" I asked, echoing something

I'd said to him long ago, when he'd caught me in a compromising position at school.

"Lots," he said.

The emotion burning in those eyes was too much for me. I looked away, my heart pounding in my chest as I pulled my clothes on. "Don't forget," I said softly. "Don't forget . . ." I couldn't finish, but there was no need.

"I know, Roza. I haven't forgotten."

I slipped on my shoes, wishing I was weaker and would let my ultimatum slide. I couldn't, though. No matter what had passed between us verbally and physically, no matter how close we were to our fairy-tale ending . . . there was no future until he could forgive himself.

Sonya and Jill were ready and waiting when we emerged from our room, and something told me Sonya knew what had happened between Dimitri and me. Damned auras. Or maybe you didn't need magical powers to see that kind of thing. Maybe the afterglow just naturally showed on someone's face.

"I need you to make a charm," I told Sonya, once we were on the road. "And we have to stop in Greenston."

"Greenston?" asked Dimitri. "What for?"

"It's where the Alchemists are being held." I had already started slinging the pieces together. Who hated Tatiana—both because of her personality and for having Ambrose? Who resented her wanting Moroi to fight Strigoi? Who feared her endorsing spirit and its dangerous effects on people, say, like Adrian? Who wanted to see a different family on the throne to support new beliefs? And who would be happy to have me locked away and out of the picture? I took a deep breath, scarcely believing what I was about to say.

"And it's where we're going to find proof that Daniella Ivashkov murdered Tatiana."

THIRTY-ONE

I WASN'T THE ONLY ONE who had come to that startling conclusion. When the Moroi Court woke up several hours into our road trip, Lissa was also putting all the pieces together in her room as she prepared herself to give her pre-election speech. She'd thought of all the arguments I had, plus a few more—like how frantic Daniella had been that Adrian might be implicated with me, which would undoubtedly unravel a carefully laid out plan. There was also Daniella's offer of having her lawyer cousin, Damon Tarus, defend me. Would that have actually helped? Or would Damon have subtly worked to weaken my defense? Abe's uncouth involvement might have been a blessing.

Lissa's heart pounded rapidly as she twisted her hair into a chignon. She preferred it down but thought for the coming event, she should put on a more dignified look. Her dress was matte ivory silk, long-sleeved and ruched, about knee length. Some might have thought wearing that color would make her look bridal, but when I saw her in the mirror, I knew no one would make that mistake. She looked luminous. Radiant. Queenly.

"It can't be true," she said, completing the look with pearl earrings that had belonged to her mother. She had shared her theory with Christian and Janine, who were with her now, and had half hoped they'd tell her she was crazy. They hadn't.

"It makes sense," said Christian, with none of his usual snark.

"There's just no proof quite yet," my mother said, ever practical. "Lots of circumstantial stuff."

"Aunt Tasha's checking with Ethan to see if Daniella was there the night of the murder," said Christian. He made a slight face, still not happy about his aunt having a boyfriend. "Daniella wasn't on the official lists, but Aunt Tasha's worried some things might have been altered."

"That wouldn't surprise me. Even so, putting Daniella there at the right time builds the case but still isn't hard proof." My mother should have been an attorney. She and Abe could have opened a law firm together.

"It's as much proof as they've got for Rose!" exclaimed Lissa.

"Aside from the stake," Janine reminded her. "And people are more willing to believe sketchy evidence about Rose than Lady Daniella Ivashkov."

Lissa sighed, knowing it was all true. "If only Abe could talk to the Alchemists. We need what they know."

"He'll do it," said my mother confidently. "It'll just take time."

"We don't have time!" The dramatic turn of events was giving spirit a nice chance to raise its ugly head, and like always, I tried to pull the darkness from Lissa. You'd think I would have learned my lesson after Victor, but well . . . old habits died hard. *They come first.* "Marie Conta and Rufus Tarus are the only candidates left! If he wins, Daniella's going to have a lot of influence. We'll never prove Rose is innocent then."

Ariana failing the last test had come as a huge blow to everyone, smashing a future Lissa had thought was set in stone. Without Ariana, the outcome didn't look good. Marie Conta wasn't Lissa's favorite person, but Lissa felt she'd make a much better ruler than Rufus. Unfortunately, the Conta family had been quiet in politics in recent years, giving them fewer allies and friends. The numbers were leaning dangerously toward Rufus. It was frustrating. If we could get Jill there, Lissa could vote, and on a Council of twelve, even one vote would be powerful.

"We have time," my mom said calmly. "There'll be no vote today, not with the controversy you'll cause. And for every day the election is delayed, we have another chance to build our case. We're close. We can do it."

"We can't tell Adrian about this," warned Lissa, moving toward the door. It was time to go.

Christian's trademark smirk returned. "That," he said, "is something we can all agree on."

The elaborate ballroom—yet again made a Council room for size reasons—looked like a rock concert. People were fighting for spots inside. Some, realizing that was futile, had camped outside the building, picnic style. Someone had thankfully had the brilliant idea to hook up a sound system with outdoor speakers so that those who didn't make it in could still hear the proceedings. Guardians moved through the crowds, trying to contain the chaos—particularly as the candidates arrived.

Marie Conta had shown up just before Lissa, and even if she was the least-likely candidate, there were still roars and surges of excitement in the crowd. Guardians hastily—and roughly, if necessary—held the mob back so she could pass. That attention had to be scary, but Marie didn't show it. She walked proudly, smiling at supporters and non-supporters alike. Both Lissa and I recalled Christian's words: *You're a queenly nominee. Act like it. You deserve this. You're the last Dragomir. A daughter of royalty.*

And that was exactly how she behaved. It was more than Christian's urging, too. Now that she'd passed all three tests, the gravity of the ancient procedure she was entering continued to grow. Lissa walked in, her head held high. I couldn't see her whole body, but I recognized the feel of her walk: graceful, stately. The crowd loved it, and it occurred to me that this group was particularly vocal because most weren't royal. Those gathered outside were ordinary Moroi, the ones who had come to truly love her. "Alexandra's heir!" "Bring back the dragon!" For some, it was simply enough to shout her name, adding on the titles of an old Russian folktale heroine who shared the same name: "Vasilisa the brave! Vasilisa the beautiful!"

I knew no one would guess the fear she felt inside. She was that good. Christian and my mother, who had initially flanked her, fell back as one, letting Lissa walk a couple steps ahead. There was no question of Lissa's position and authority. She took each step with confidence, remembering that her grandfather had also walked this path. She tried to give the crowd a smile that was both dignified but genuine. It must have worked because they went even wilder. And when she paused to comment on a dragon banner a man had painted in support, the artist nearly passed out that someone like her would notice and compliment him.

"This is unprecedented," remarked my mom, once they'd safely made it inside. "There's never been this sort of turnout. There certainly wasn't during the last election."

"Why so great this time?" asked Lissa, who was trying to get her breathing under control.

"Because there's so much sensation, between the murder and you muddling the law. That and . . . well, the way you're winning the hearts of every non-royal out there. The dhampirs too. There's a dragon sign in one of our coffee rooms, you know. I even think some of the royals love you, though maybe it's just to spite whatever family they're feuding with. But seriously? If this were up to all of the people and not just the Council—and well, if it was a vote you were eligible for—I think you'd win."

Lissa grimaced but then reluctantly added, "Honestly? I think we *should* have popular votes for our leaders. Every Moroi should cast a vote, not just a handful of elite families."

"Careful there, princess," teased Christian, putting his arm through hers. "That's the kind of talk that'll start another revolution. One at a time, okay?"

The ballroom's crowd wasn't as crazy as the outside one had been—but was pretty close. The guardians were ready for the numbers this time and had made sure to keep strict control from the very beginning. They kept a tight count of how many were allowed in the room and stopped royal and non-royal squabbles. It was still intimidating, and Lissa reminded herself over and over that playing this role was helping me. For me, she would endure anything, even the fanfare. This time, fortunately, Lissa was swept up pretty quickly to the room's front, to where three chairs facing the crowd had been set up for the candidates. Rufus and Marie were already seated, speaking in low voices to a few select family members. Guardians stood around them. Lissa sat alone, of course, but nodded to nearby guards when Tasha approached.

Tasha crouched beside Lissa, speaking low and keeping a wary eye on Rufus as he talked to someone. "Bad news. Well, depending on how you look at it. Ethan says Daniella was there that night. She and Tatiana met alone. He didn't realize it hadn't been put on the records. Someone else wrote those up on behalf of all the guards on duty, but he swears he saw Daniella himself."

Lissa winced. Secretly, she'd been hoping—praying, even—that she'd made a mistake, that surely Adrian's mother couldn't have done this. She gave a swift nod to show she understood.

"I'm sorry," said Tasha. "I know you liked her."

"I think I'm more worried about Adrian. I don't know how he'll take it."

"Hard," said Tasha bluntly. After what she'd faced with Christian's parents, she knew better than anyone else what it was like to have family betray you. "But he'll make it through.

And as soon as we can put all this evidence forward, we'll have Dimitri and Rose back."

Those words filled Lissa with hope, strengthening her. "I miss her so much," she said. "I wish she was here already."

Tasha gave her a sympathetic smile and patted her shoulder. "Soon. They'll be back soon. Just get through this for now. You can do this. You can change everything."

Lissa wasn't so sure about that, but Tasha hurried off to join her "activist friends" and was replaced by—Daniella.

She'd come to talk to Rufus, offering support and family love. Lissa couldn't bear to look at the older woman and felt even worse when Daniella spoke to her.

"I'm not sure how you got involved with this, dear, but good luck." Daniella's smile seemed sincere, but there was no question which candidate she supported. Her kindly expression turned to concern. "Have you seen Adrian? I thought for sure he'd be here. I know the guardians would let him in."

Excellent question. Lissa hadn't seen him in the last day or so. "I haven't. Maybe he's just running late. Doing his hair or something." *Hopefully not passed out somewhere.*

Daniella sighed. "I hope so."

She left, taking a seat in the audience. Once again, Adrian's father was running the session, and after several false starts, the room quieted.

"In the last week," Nathan began, speaking into a microphone, "many worthy candidates have taken the tests required to rule our people. Before us sit the final three: Rufus Tarus, Marie Conta, and Vasilisa Dragomir." Nathan's tone sounded displeased over that last one, but thus far, the law would let her give her speech. After that, the law's inconsistency kicked in, and all hell would break loose.

"These three have shown they have the ability to rule, and as their last act, before we vote, each will speak about their plans for our people."

Rufus was up first, delivering exactly the kind of speech I'd expected. He played on Moroi fears, promising extreme forms of protection—most of which involved dhampirs but didn't get into much detail.

"Our safety must be our top priority," he proclaimed. "At all costs. Will it be difficult? Yes. Will there be sacrifices? Yes. But aren't our children worth it? Don't we care about them?" Bringing children into it was just low, I decided. At least he'd left puppies out.

He also used dirty politician tricks, slandering his rivals. Marie was mostly slammed for her family's lack of activity. Lissa, however, was a great target. He pushed her age, the danger of spirit, and the fact that her being there in the first place was a violation of the law.

Marie's speech was much more thoughtful and detailed. She laid out very explicit plans on all sorts of issues, most of which were reasonable. I didn't agree with all she said, but she was clearly competent and didn't lower herself to mocking her competition. Unfortunately, she wasn't nearly as charismatic as Rufus, and it was a sad truth that that could make a big difference. Her monotone closing summed up not only her speech but also her personality.

"Those are the reasons why I should be queen. I hope you enjoyed this talk and will vote for me when the time comes. Thank you." She abruptly sat down.

Lissa's turn came at last. Standing before her microphone, she suddenly saw the chalice's dream, where she'd faltered in front of the Council. But no, this was reality. She wouldn't fail. She would go forward.

"We're a people at war," she began, voice loud and clear. "We're constantly attacked—but not just by Strigoi. By one another. We're divided. We fight with one another. Family against family. Royal against non-royal. Moroi against dhampir. *Of course* the Strigoi are picking us off. They're at least united behind a goal: killing."

If I had been sitting there in that audience, I would have been leaning forward, mouth open. As it was, there were plenty of people there to do it for me. Her words were volatile. Shocking. And utterly captivating.

"We are one people," she continued. "Moroi and dhampir alike." Yeah, that got some gasps too. "And while it's impossible for every single person to get their way, no one will get anything done if we don't come together and find ways to meet in the middle—even if it means making hard choices."

Then, extraordinarily, she explained how it could be done. True, she didn't have the time to give fine details on every single issue in our world, but she hit a lot of the big ones. And she managed to do it in a way that didn't offend anyone *too* badly. After all, she was right in saying not everyone could get their way. Still, she spoke about how the dhampirs were our best warriors—and would be better with a stronger voice. She spoke about how non-royals needed a greater voice too—but not at the cost of losing the exalted royal lines that defined our people. Finally, in addressing the issue of training Moroi to defend themselves, she did emphasize its importance—but not as something mandatory and not as the only method needing to be explored.

Yes, she gave something to everyone and did it beautifully and charismatically. It was the kind of speech that could make people follow her anywhere. She concluded with, "We have always mixed the old with the new. We've kept magic alongside technology. We conduct these sessions with scrolls and—with these." She smiled and tapped her microphone. "That's how we have survived. We hold onto our pasts and embrace our present. We take the best of it all and grow stronger. That's how we have survived. That's how we *will* survive."

Silence met her conclusion—and then the cheers began. I actually heard the roar from outside on the lawn before it started within. People I would have sworn supported others were practically in tears, and I hadn't forgotten that most of the people I had visuals on in this room were royal. Lissa herself wanted to burst into tears but instead took her due bravely. When she finely sat down, and the crowd quieted, Nathan resumed his role.

"Well," he said. "That was a very pretty speech, one we all enjoyed. But now, the time has come for the Council to vote on our next leader, and—by law—only two candidates stand ready for that position: Rufus Tarus and Marie Conta." Two

Moroi, one each from the Tarus and Conta families, came forward to join their respective candidates. Nathan's gaze fell on Lissa who had risen like the others but stood alone. "According to the election laws—laws set down since the beginning of time—each candidate must approach the Council, escorted by someone of their bloodline in order to show family strength and unity. Do you have any such person?"

Lissa met his eyes unflinchingly. "No, Lord Ivashkov."

"Then I'm afraid your part in this game is over, Princess Dragomir." He smiled. "You may sit down now."

Yup. That's when all hell broke loose.

I'd always heard the expression, "And the crowd goes wild!" Now, I saw it in the flesh. Half the time, I couldn't even keep track of who was shouting or supporting what. People argued in clusters and one-on-one. A couple of Moroi in jeans challenged every well-dressed person they could find, operating under the irrational assumptions that anyone in nice clothes must be royal and that all royals hated Lissa. Their devotion to her was admirable. Creepy, but admirable. One group from the Tarus family stood face to face with a Conta group, looking prepared for either a gang fight or a dance-off. That was one of the most bizarre pairings of all since those two families were the only ones who should be in complete agreement on anything.

On and on it went. People fought about whether Lissa should be eligible for the vote. They fought about having a session to change the law books right at that moment. Some fought over things I'd never even heard of before. A rush of guardians to the door made me think the outside crowd was trying to break in. My mother was among that defense, and I knew she'd been right: there'd be no vote today, not with this anarchy. They'd have to close the session and try again tomorrow.

Lissa stared at the crowd, feeling numb and unable to keep up with all the activity. Her stomach twisted as something dawned on her. All this time, she'd sworn that she'd respect the dignity of the election tradition. Yet, it was because of her that things were now anything but dignified. It was all her fault. Then, her eyes fell on someone sitting in a back corner, far from the pandemonium. Ekaterina Zeklos. The old former queen caught Lissa's eye—and winked.

I faded out of that room, not needing to see any more of the arguing. I returned to the car ride, a new thought in my head. Lissa's words burned in my soul. They had stirred my heart. And even if she'd given her speech as a decoy, there had been passion in them—ardent belief. If she had been eligible to be queen, she would have stood behind those words.

And that's when I knew. She *would* be queen.

I decided then and there that I would make it happen. We wouldn't bring Jill simply to give Lissa her Council vote. Jill would give Lissa the status that would allow Moroi to vote *for her*. And Lissa would win.

Naturally, I kept these thoughts to myself.

"That's a dangerous look," said Dimitri, giving me a brief glance before returning his eyes to the road.

"What look?" I asked innocently.

"The one that says you just got some idea."

"I didn't just get an idea. I got a *great* idea."

Jokes like that used to make Jill laugh, but turning to look at her in the backseat showed me she didn't find much funny at all.

"Hey, you okay?" I asked.

Those jade eyes focused on me. "I'm not sure. A lot's kind of happened. And I don't really get what's going to happen next. I feel like . . . like some kind of object that's going to be used in someone's master plan. Like a pawn."

A bit of guilt tugged at me. Victor had always used people as part of a game. Was I any different? No. I cared about Jill. "You're not an object or a pawn," I told her. "But you're very, very important, and because of you, a lot of good things are going to happen."

"It won't be that simple though, will it?" She sounded wise beyond her years. "Things are going to get worse before they get better, aren't they?"

I couldn't lie to her. "Yeah. But then you'll get to contact your mom . . . and well, like I said, good things will happen. Guardians always say 'They come first' when we're talking about Moroi. It's not exactly the same for you, but in doing this . . . well . . ."

She gave me a smile that didn't seem very happy. "Yeah, I get it. It's for the greater good, right?"

Sonya had spent a lot of the ride working on a charm for me, using a silver bracelet we'd bought at a roadside gift shop. It was tacky-looking but made of real silver, which was what counted. When we were about a half hour from Greenston, she deemed it finished and handed it over. I slipped it on and looked at the others.

"Well?"

"I don't see anything," said Sonya, "but then, I wouldn't."

Jill squinted. "You seem a little blurry . . . like I just need to blink a few times."

"Same here," said Dimitri.

Sonya was pleased. "That's how it should look to people who know she's got a charm on. Hopefully, to the other guardians, she'll be wearing a different face." It was a variation of what Lissa had made when we'd busted Victor out of prison. Only, this required less magic because Sonya only had to slightly alter my features and didn't need to obscure my race. She was also more practiced than Lissa.

The restaurant I'd chosen in Greenston had long since closed when we rolled in at eleven thirty. The parking lot was nearly black, but I could make out a car in the back corner. Hopefully, it was Mikhail having gotten there early—and not a guardian hit squad.

But when we parked nearby, I saw that it was indeed Mikhail who got out of the car—along with Adrian.

He grinned when he saw me, pleased at the surprise. Really, I should have seen this coming when I'd told him to pass the message on to Mikhail. Adrian would have found a way to come along. My stomach rolled. No, no. Not this. I had no time to deal with my love life. Not now. I didn't even know what to say to Adrian. Fortunately, I wasn't given the chance to speak.

Mikhail had come striding toward us with guardian efficiency, ready to find out what task I had in mind. He came to a screeching halt when he saw Sonya get out of our car. So did she. They both stood frozen, eyes wider than seemed physically possible. I knew then that the rest of us had ceased to exist, as had all our intrigue, missions, and . . . well, the world. In that moment, only the two of them existed.

Sonya gave a strangled cry and then ran forward. This jolted him awake, in time to wrap her in his arms as she threw herself against him. She started crying, and I could see tears on his face too. He brushed her hair back and cupped her cheeks, staring down at her and repeating over and over, "It's you . . . it's you . . . it's you . . ."

Sonya tried to wipe her eyes, but it didn't do much good. "Mikhail—I'm sorry—I'm so sorry—"

"It doesn't matter." He kissed her and pulled back only enough to look into her eyes. "It doesn't matter. Nothing matters except that we're together again."

This made her cry harder. She buried her face against his chest, and his arms tightened more fiercely around her. The rest of us stood as frozen as the lovers had been earlier. It felt wrong witnessing this. It was too private; we shouldn't have been there. Yet . . . at the same time, I just kept thinking that this was how I'd imagined my reunion with Dimitri would be when Lissa had restored him. Love. Forgiveness. Acceptance.

Dimitri and I briefly locked eyes, and an uncanny sense told me he was recalling my words: *You have to forgive yourself. If you can't, then you can't go on either. We can't.* I glanced away from him, looking back at the happy couple so that he wouldn't see me tear up. God, I wanted what Mikhail and Sonya had. A happy ending. Forgiveness of the past. A bright future ahead.

Jill sniffled beside me, and I put an arm around her. That small sound seemed to draw Mikhail back to our world. Still holding Sonya, he looked over at me.

"Thank you. Thank you for this. Anything you need. Anything at all—"

"Stop, stop," I said, afraid I might choke up. I'd only just managed to blink away traitorous tears. "I'm glad . . . glad to have done it, and well . . . it wasn't really me at all."

"Still . . ." Mikhail looked down at Sonya who was smiling at him through her tears. "You've given me my world back."

"I'm so happy for you . . . and I want you to have this, to just enjoy this right now. But I have a favor. One more favor."

Sonya and Mikhail exchanged glances in a knowing way. You never would have guessed they'd been apart for three years. She nodded, and he returned his gaze to me. "I figured that's why he brought me here." He inclined his head toward Adrian.

"I need you to get me into the hotel where the Alchemists are staying."

The small smile on Mikhail's face dropped. "Rose . . . I can't get you into any place. You being this close to Court is dangerous enough."

I pulled the bracelet from my pocket. "I'll have a disguise. They won't know it's me. Is there a reason you'd have to see the Alchemists?"

Sonya stayed in his arms, but his eyes were dark with thought. "They'll have guardians near their rooms. We could probably pass ourselves off as relief."

Dimitri nodded in agreement. "If it's too different from their scheduled shift change, it'll raise eyebrows . . . but hopefully you'll have long enough to get in and find out what you need. The guardians are probably more worried about the Alchemists getting out than other guardians getting in."

"Absolutely," said Mikhail. "So it's you and me, Rose?"

"Yup," I said. "The fewer, the better. Just enough to question Sydney and Ian. I guess everyone else waits here."

Sonya kissed his cheek. "I'm not going anywhere."

Adrian had strolled over by now and given Jill a light, brotherly punch in the arm. "And I'm going to stay and hear how on earth you got involved with this, Jailbait."

Jill mustered a smile for him. She had a pretty hardcore crush on him, and it was a sign of her stress that she didn't blush and go all weak-kneed. They started a conversation, and Dimitri gestured for me to follow him around the car, out of sight.

"This is dangerous," he said quietly. "If that charm fails, you probably aren't going to get out of that hotel." There was an unspoken *alive* at the end of his words.

"It won't fail. Sonya's good. Besides, if we're caught, maybe they'll bring me back to Court instead of killing me. Imagine how much *that* will slow the elections."

"Rose, I'm serious."

I caught hold of his hand. "I know, I know. This'll be

easy. We should be in and out in under an hour, but if we aren't . . ." Man, I hated grim contingencies. "If we aren't, then send Adrian to Court with Jill, and you and Sonya hide out somewhere until . . . I don't know."

"Don't worry about us," he said. "You just be careful." He leaned down and pressed a kiss to my forehead.

"Little dhampir, are you—"

Adrian came strolling around the car, just in time to see that small kiss. I dropped my hand from Dimitri's. None of us said anything, but in that moment, Adrian's eyes . . . well, I saw his whole world come crashing apart. I felt sicker than if a fleet of Strigoi were around. I felt worse than a Strigoi. *Honor*, I thought. For real: the guardians should have taught it. Because I hadn't learned it.

"Let's hurry," said Mikhail, walking over, oblivious to the drama that had just exploded beside him. "Sonya says you guys have a ticking clock at Court too."

I swallowed, dragging my eyes from Adrian. My heart twisted within my chest. "Yeah . . ."

"Go," said Dimitri.

"Remember," I murmured to him. "Talking to him is my responsibility. Not yours."

I followed Mikhail to his car, slipping on the charmed bracelet. Before getting inside, I cast a quick glance back. Jill and Sonya were speaking together, Dimitri stood alone, and Adrian was taking out a cigarette, his back to them all.

"I suck," I said dismally, as Mikhail started the car. It was ineloquent but pretty much summed up my feelings.

He didn't respond, probably because it wasn't relevant to our task. Either that, or he was still too wrapped up in the renewal of his own love life. Lucky bastard.

It didn't take long to reach the hotel. There were guardians around, covertly placed so as not to draw human attention. None of them stopped us as we walked inside. One even gave Mikhail a nod of recognition. They all looked at me like . . . well, like they didn't recognize me. Which was good. With so many guardians helping at Court, new faces were to be expected, and mine didn't look like Rose Hathaway's. No one was concerned.

"Which rooms are they in?" Mikhail asked a guardian who was standing in the lobby. "We're supposed to relieve that shift." Mikhail's manner was perfectly self-assured, enough that the guardian—while a little surprised—seemed to think this must be okay.

"Only two of you? There are four up there."

I saved us on that one. "They want more back at Court. Things are getting out of hand, so just two are being assigned here now."

"Probably all we need up there," agreed the guardian. "Third floor."

"Quick thinking," Mikhail told me in the elevator.

"That was nothing. I've talked myself out of much worse."

The rooms were easy to spot because a guardian stood outside them. *The rest are inside,* I realized, wondering if that would be a problem. But, with that same authoritative attitude, Mikhail told the guy that he and the others had been recalled to Court. The guardian summoned his colleagues—one from each Alchemist's rooms, though we couldn't tell whose was whose—and they gave us a brief status report before leaving, including who was in which room.

When they were gone, Mikhail looked to me. "Sydney," I said.

We'd been given key cards and walked right into Sydney's room. She sat cross-legged on her bed, reading a book and looking miserable. She sighed when she saw us.

"Well, what is it now?"

I took off the bracelet, letting my illusion vanish.

There was no jaw dropping or raised eyebrows from Sydney. Just a knowing look. "I should have guessed. Are you here to free me?" There was a hopeful note in her voice.

"Um, not exactly." I hated that Sydney was going to get punished, but smuggling her out wasn't part of the plan now. "We need to talk to Ian, and it's probably best if you're there. He knows something important. Something we need."

That got the raised eyebrow. She pointed at the door. "They won't let us talk to each other."

"They aren't out there," I said smugly.

Sydney shook her head ruefully. "Rose, you really do scare me sometimes. Just not for the reasons I originally thought you would. Come on. He's next door, but you'll have a hard time getting him to talk."

"That's where you'll help," I said, as we walked into the hall. I slipped the bracelet back on. "He's totally into you. He'll help if you ask."

As I'd guessed, Sydney was completely oblivious to Ian's crush. "What! He does not—"

She shut her mouth as we entered Ian's room. He was watching TV but jumped up when he saw us. "Sydney! Are you okay?"

I shot her a meaningful look.

She gave me a pained one in return and then turned her attention back to Ian. "They need your help with something. Some information."

He turned his gaze on us, and it immediately went colder. "We answered your questions a hundred times."

"Not all of them," I said. "When you were at Court, you saw a picture on the table. Of a dead man. Who was it?"

Ian's lips went into a straight line. "I don't know."

"I saw—er, that is, we know you recognized him," I argued. "You reacted."

"I actually saw that too," admitted Sydney.

His tone turned pleading. "Come *on*, we don't need to help them anymore. This whole hotel-prison thing is bad enough. I'm sick of their games."

I didn't blame him, really, but we needed him too much. I glanced at Sydney beseechingly, telling her that only she could get us through this.

She turned back to Ian. "What's the deal with the guy in the picture? Is it . . . is it really horrible? Something secret?"

He shrugged. "No. I just don't want to help them anymore. It's irrelevant."

"Will you do it for me?" she asked sweetly. "Please? It

might help me get out of trouble." Sydney was no master of flirting, but I think just the fact she came close to it astonished him. He hesitated for several moments, glanced at us and then back to her. She smiled at him.

Ian caved. "I meant what I said. I don't know who he is. He was with a Moroi woman over in the St. Louis facility one day."

"Wait," I said, derailed. "Moroi come to your places?"

"Sometimes," said Sydney. "Just like we came to yours. Some meetings happen in person. We don't usually hold your people prisoner, though."

"I think this guy was like her bodyguard or something," Ian said. "She was the one there on business. He just followed and stayed quiet."

"A Moroi bodyguard?"

"Not uncommon for those that can't get guardians," said Mikhail. "Abe Mazur is proof of that. He's got his own army."

"I think of them more as a mafia." My joke aside, I was getting confused. Despite the widespread disdain about learning to fight, sometimes Moroi did have to hire Moroi security because they just couldn't obtain a guardian. Someone like Daniella Ivashkov wouldn't have that problem. In fact, I was pretty sure she'd be entitled to two guardians if she stepped outside protective borders—and she'd made it clear she didn't think Moroi should fight. Why would she travel with Moroi protection when she could have better trained guardians? It made no sense. Still . . . if you'd killed a queen, you probably did all sorts of unorthodox things. They didn't have to make sense. "Who was she?" I asked. "The woman?"

"I didn't know her either," said Ian. "I just passed them while they were on their way to something. A meeting, maybe."

"Do you remember what she looked like?" Something. We needed *something*. This was on the verge of falling apart, but if Ian could identify Daniella, we might just be set.

"Sure," he said. "She's easy to remember."

The ensuing silence irritated me. "So?" I asked. "What did she look like?"

He told me.

The description was not what I had expected.

THIRTY-TWO

SYDNEY AND HER FRIENDS weren't happy that we weren't going to take them with us.

"I would," I told her, still reeling from what I'd learned from Ian. "But getting us in and out has been hard enough! If we step outside with you, we'll all be busted. Besides, soon it won't matter. Once we tell everyone at Court what we know and clear my name, the guardians won't need you anymore."

"It's not the guardians I'm worried about," she replied. She used that blasé tone of hers, but I could see a glint of legitimate fear in her eyes—and I wondered who she was referring to. The Alchemists? Or someone else?

"Sydney," I said hesitantly, despite knowing Mikhail and I needed to get out of there. "What did Abe really do for you? There has to be more than just the transfer."

Sydney gave me a small, sad smile. "It doesn't matter, Rose. I'll deal with whatever comes. Just go now, okay? Go help your friends."

I wanted to say more . . . to find out more. But Mikhail's expression told me he agreed with her, and so, with brief farewells, he and I left. When we got back to where the others were waiting in the parking lot, I saw the situation hadn't changed much. Dimitri was pacing, no doubt restless at being out of the action. Jill still stood near Sonya, as though seeking protection from the older woman, and Adrian stayed away from all of them, barely sparing a glance when Mikhail's car pulled up.

When we told the group what we'd learned, however, *that* got a reaction from Adrian.

"Impossible. I can't believe that." He stamped out a cigarette. "Your Alchemist pals are wrong."

I could hardly believe it either, yet I had no reason to think Ian would lie. And honestly, if Adrian was having a hard time with this, there was no telling what he would have thought if we'd told him who our previous suspect was. I stared off into the night, trying to come to terms with who had murdered Tatiana and framed me. It was hard even for me to believe. Betrayal was harsh.

"The motives are there . . ." I said reluctantly. Once Ian had described whom he'd seen, a dozen reasons for the murder clicked into place. "And they *are* political. Ambrose was right."

"Ian's ID is hard evidence," said Dimitri, as shocked as the rest of us. "But there are a lot of other holes, a lot of pieces that don't fit into it."

"Yeah." One in particular had been bothering me. "Like why *I* was set up for the fall."

No one had an answer for that. "We need to get back to Court," Mikhail said at last. "Or I'm going to be missed."

I cast Jill what I hoped was an encouraging smile. "And you've got to make your debut."

"I don't know which is crazier," said Adrian. "The killer's identity or Jailbait being a Dragomir." His words to me were cold, but the look he gave her was gentle. Crazy as the news was, Adrian hadn't had that hard of a time believing Jill's parentage. He was jaded enough to believe in Eric's infidelity, and those telltale eyes sealed the deal. I think hearing what Ian had told us was hurting Adrian more than he was letting on. Finding out the person responsible for his aunt's murder was someone he knew had to intensify the pain. Finding out about me and Dimitri couldn't help matters either.

Much to Mikhail's dismay, Sonya offered to stay behind while the rest of us went to Court. We couldn't bring both cars, and his only held five. She considered herself the least useful in this endeavor. With much hugging, kissing, and tears, she promised Mikhail they'd see each other again, once this mess was sorted out. I hoped she was right.

My charm would obscure my face enough to get me through the gate. But Jill was a trickier problem. Her kidnapping was hot Moroi news, and if she was recognized by any of the gate guardians, we would be stopped then and there. We were gambling that the guards would be too harried to notice her like they would Dimitri and me. That meant Dimitri took priority for disguising—requiring Adrian's help. Adrian wasn't quite as adept with illusion as Sonya was, but he understood enough of it to make Dimitri's appearance altered to the eyes of others. It was similar to how he'd used spirit during my jail escape. The question was whether or not Adrian would actually do it for us. He hadn't said a word to anyone about what he'd seen between me and Dimitri, but the others must have felt the sudden rise in tension.

"We have to help Lissa," I told him, when he didn't respond to the request. "Time's running out. Please. Please help us." I wasn't above groveling, if that was what he needed.

Fortunately, it wasn't. Adrian took a deep breath and closed his eyes for a brief moment. I was certain he wished he had something stronger than cigarettes. At last, he nodded. "Let's go."

We left Sonya with the keys to the second car, and she stood there with shining eyes, watching as we drove off. Dimitri, Mikhail, and I spent most of the journey analyzing the our data collection. The woman Ian had described couldn't have done everything we'd been pinning on the murderer.

I was sitting in the backseat with Adrian and Jill, leaning forward and checking things off on my fingers. "Motive? Yes. Ability? Yes. Paying off Joe? Yes. Access to Tatiana's chambers . . ." I frowned, suddenly thinking of what I'd overheard while with Lissa. "Yes."

This earned me a surprised glance from Dimitri. "Really? That was one piece I couldn't figure out."

"Pretty sure I know how she did it," I said. "But the anonymous letter to Tatiana doesn't make sense. Not to mention obscuring Lissa's family—or trying to kill her." *Or trying to frame me.*

"We might be dealing with more than one person," said Dimitri.

"Like a conspiracy?" I asked, startled.

He shook his head. "No, I mean, *someone* else had a grudge against the queen. But not someone who'd go as far as to kill her. Two people, two agendas. Probably not even aware of each other. We're mixing up the evidence."

I fell silent, turning over his words. It made sense, and I picked up on the nuance that by *someone*, he meant Daniella. We'd been right about reasons she'd dislike Tatiana—the trainings, the age law not being hardcore enough, encouraging spirit . . . But that hadn't been enough for murder. An angry letter, bribery for her son's safety? Those were the kinds of actions Lady Daniella Ivashkov took. Not staking.

In the ensuing silence, I heard soft words between Jill and Adrian, who'd been having a conversation while the rest of us plotted strategy.

"What do I do?" Jill asked him in a small voice.

His answer was swift and sure. "Act like you deserve to be there. Don't let them intimidate you."

"What about Lissa? What's she going to think of me?"

Adrian hesitated only a moment. "Doesn't matter. Just act the way I told you."

My stomach sank, listening to him give her such earnest, kind advice. Rowdy, smug, and flippant . . . he was all those things. But his heart was good. The heart I'd just broken. I knew I was right about his potential. Adrian was great. He could do great things. I just hoped I hadn't set him back. At least I hadn't had to tell him his mother was a murderer . . . but still.

All of us grew quiet when we reached the gate. The line of cars was still there, and we became more and more nervous as we crept forward. A flip to Lissa's mind told me we weren't missing anything in the Council. The chaotic situation was pretty much the same as before, though the exasperated look on Nathan's face made me think he'd call a close to proceedings soon and continue tomorrow. I wasn't sure if that was good or bad.

The guardians recognized Mikhail, of course, and while still vigilant, their initial instincts didn't suspect him of nefarious deeds. He vaguely said he'd been sent to pick up some people. The guardian looking in the car scanned over Dimitri, me, and—thankfully—Jill. Adrian, a well-known figure, got us added respect. After a mandatory check of the trunk, we were sent on through.

"Oh my God. It worked," I breathed, as Mikhail drove over to the guardians' parking area.

"Now what?" asked Jill.

"Now we reestablish the Dragomir line and call out a murderer," I said.

"Oh, is that all?" Adrian's sarcasm was palpable.

"You know," remarked Mikhail, "that the instant your illusions are dropped, you two are going to be jumped by guardians and thrown back into jail. Or worse."

Dimitri and I exchanged looks. "We know," I said, trying to ignore the memories of that terrible, claustrophobic experience. "But if everything works out . . . we won't have to stay there for long. They'll use what we've found out and then eventually set us free." I sounded more optimistic than I felt.

Once parked, our party headed toward the ballroom's building, which could have been seen miles away with all the people around it. How strange. Not long ago, I'd made this same journey, with nearly the same people, hurrying *away* from Court. We'd worn spirit disguises then, too, and had been seeking escape. Now we were knowingly walking into peril. I was convinced if I could make it in undetected and deliver my news, everything would work out. Sonya's charm had worked perfectly when I saw the Alchemists. I had no reason to doubt it, but the fear still lurked in the back of my mind: what if it stopped functioning? What if the disguise failed and I was spotted before even getting into the building? Would they arrest me? Or would they simply shoot first?

The doors were barred to spectators, but guardians were allowed access, so once again Mikhail talked us in—using a sullen Adrian as the reason. The late queen's nephew could hardly be refused, and with the chaos inside, more guardians—which Dimitri and I appeared to be—were welcome. Adrian kept an arm around Jill as they entered, and the guardians let her pass.

We slipped into the ballroom, completely unnoticed. I'd seen the arguing through Lissa's eyes, but it was totally different in person. Louder. More grating. My friends and I exchanged looks. I'd braced myself for a big confrontation with the audience—hell, it wouldn't be the first time—but this was a test of even my skills.

"We need someone to get the room's attention," I said. "Someone not afraid to make a spectacle—I mean, besides me, of course."

"Mikhail? Where have you been?"

We turned and saw Abe standing before us.

"Well, speak of the devil," I said. "Exactly what we need."

Abe peered at me and frowned. Charms could be seen through when others knew one was being used. Charms were also less effective if others knew the wearer well. It was how Victor had recognized me in Tarasov. Sonya's was too strong for Abe to fully break through, but he could tell something wasn't right.

"What's going on?" he demanded.

"The usual, old man," I replied cheerily. "Danger, insane plans . . . you know, the stuff that runs in our family."

He squinted his eyes again, still unable to fully see through the charm. I was probably blurry. "Rose? Is that you? Where have you been?"

"We need the room's attention," I said. I wondered if this was what it felt like when parents busted their kids for breaking curfew. He looked very disapproving. "We've got a way to settle this whole argument."

"Well," observed Adrian dryly, "we've at least got a way to start another one."

"I trusted you at my hearing," I told Abe. "Can't you trust me now?"

Abe's expression turned wry. "You apparently didn't trust me enough to stay put in West Virginia."

"Technicalities," I said. "Please. We need this."

"And we're short on time," added Dimitri.

Abe studied him too. "Let me guess. Belikov?" There was uncertainty in my father's voice—Adrian was doing a good job in keeping the illusion over Dimitri—but Abe was clever enough to deduce who would be with me.

"Dad, we have to hurry. We've got the killer—and we've got Lissa's . . ." How did I explain it? "A chance to change Lissa's life."

Not much startled Abe, but I think my earnest use of "Dad" did. Scanning the room, his eyes landed on someone, and he gave a small jerk of his head. Several seconds later, my mother squeezed her way through to us. Great. He called; she came. They were awfully chummy lately. I hoped Lissa remained the only one with a surprise sibling.

"Who are these people?" my mother asked.

"Guess," replied Abe flatly. "Who would be foolish enough to break into Court after escaping it?"

My mom's eyes widened. "How—"

"No time," Abe said. The sharp look he got in return said she didn't like being interrupted. Maybe no siblings after all. "I have a feeling half the guardians in this room are going to be all over us soon. Are you ready for that?"

My poor, law-abiding mother looked pained, realizing what was being asked of her. "Yes."

"Me too," added Mikhail.

Abe studied us all. "I guess there are worse odds."

He headed up to where Nathan Ivashkov was leaning against his podium. He looked weary and defeated—and utterly at a loss on what to do with the mess before him. At our approach, the monarch candidates glanced over curiously, and I sensed a sudden jolt of surprise through the bond. Lissa could see right through the spirit charms. I felt her breath catch at the sight of us. Fear, shock, and relief played through her. And confusion, of course. She was so glad to see us that she forgot all about the elections and started to stand at our approach. I gave her a quick shake of my head, urging her to keep our cover, and after a moment's hesitation, she sat back down. She was worried and puzzled—but trusted me.

Nathan came to life when he saw us, particularly when Abe simply shoved him out of the way and grabbed the microphone. "Hey, what are you—"

I expected Abe to yell for everyone to shut up or something like that. Of course, Nathan had been trying that for a while with no results. So, I was quite shocked—as was everyone else—when Abe put fingers to his lips and let out the most ear-piercing whistle I had ever heard. A whistle like that through a microphone? Yeah. It hurt my ears. It had to be worse for the Moroi, and the screeching feedback in the speakers didn't help.

The room quieted enough for him to be heard. "Now that you have the sense to keep your mouths shut," said Abe, "we have . . . some things to say." He was using his confident, I-control-the-world voice, but I knew he was taking a lot on faith here. "Act fast," he muttered, extending the microphone out to us.

I took it and cleared my throat. "We're here to, uh, settle this debate once and for all." That brought grumbles, and I hurried on loudly before the room erupted again. "The laws can stay the way they are. Vasilisa Dragomir is entitled to her

Council vote—and eligible to be a full candidate for the throne. There's another member in her family. She isn't the only Dragomir left."

Murmurs and whispers broke out, though it was nothing like the roar earlier—most likely because the Moroi loved intrigue, and they had to know how this would play out. In my periphery, I could see guardians forming a very loose perimeter around us. Their concern was security, not scandal.

I beckoned Jill forward. For a moment, she froze; then I wondered if she recalled Adrian's words in the car. She stepped beside me, so pale that I worried she might pass out. I almost felt like I could too. The tension and pressure were overwhelming. No. I'd come too far.

"This is Jillian Mastrano Dragomir. She's Eric Dragomir's illegitimate daughter—but she *is* his daughter and officially part of the bloodline." I hated using *illegitimate*, but in this case, it was a necessary fact.

In the heartbeat of silence that followed, Jill hastily leaned toward me and the microphone. "I *am* a Dragomir," she said clearly, despite her trembling hands. "Our family has its quorum, and my s-sister has all her rights."

I could see another explosion building, and Abe jumped in between Jill and me, grabbing the microphone. "For those who don't believe this, a DNA test will clear up any doubts about her lineage." I had to admire Abe's audacity. He had only learned this information sixty seconds ago and was already advocating it with certainty, as though he himself had performed the necessary tests back in his home genetics lab. More faith—and an advantage he couldn't pass up. My old man loved secrets.

The news triggered the reaction I'd expected. Once the audience had processed the information, a flurry of shouted commentary began.

"Eric Dragomir didn't have any other children, illegitimate or not!"

"This is a scam!"

"Show us the proof! Where are your tests?"

"Well . . . he was kind of a flirt . . ."

"He *did* have another daughter."

That last one shut the crowd up, both because it was spoken with authority and because it came from Daniella Ivashkov. She had stood up, and even without a microphone, she had a voice that could carry in a room. She was also an important enough person in our society to draw attention. Many among the royals were practically conditioned to listen to her. In the now quiet room, Daniella continued speaking.

"Eric Dragomir had an illegitimate daughter, with a woman named Emily Mastrano—a dancer, if I recall correctly. He wanted it kept secret and needed certain things done—things he couldn't do himself—to help with that. I was one of the few who helped." An uncharacteristically bitter smile turned up her lips. "And honestly, I wouldn't have minded it staying secret either."

Pieces clicked in my head. I knew now who had broken into the Alchemists' records. And why. In the room's silence, I didn't need a microphone to respond either.

"Enough that you'd make certain papers disappear."

Daniella fixed that smile on me. "Yes."

"Because if the Dragomirs faded, spirit might too. And Adrian would be safe. Spirit was getting too much attention too fast, and you needed to get rid of any evidence about Jill to kill Vasilisa's credibility." Daniella's expression confirmed as much. I should have left it at that, but my curiosity wouldn't allow it. "Then why admit it now?"

Daniella shrugged. "Because you're right. One DNA test will show the truth." There were gasps of awe from those who took her word as gospel and wondered what this meant. Others people refused to believe and wore looks of scorn. Daniella, undoubtedly disappointed the truth had leaked, nonetheless seemed resigned and willing to accept it. But her smile soon dropped as she studied me more closely. "What I'd like to know is: who in the world are *you*?"

A good portion of the audience appeared to want to know this as well. I hesitated. Sonya's charmed disguise had gotten me pretty far at this point. We had a fragile acceptance of Jill and the Dragomir line. If we let the system run its course, and if Lissa won like I now wanted—I'd have a queenly advocate to help in the case to clear me.

But staring at the crowd—full of people I'd known and respected and who had still condemned me without question—I felt anger burn within me. Spirit-induced or not, it didn't matter. I was still outraged at how easily I'd been accused and tossed away. I didn't want to wait for this to be settled in some quiet guardian office. I wanted to face them.

I wanted them to know I was innocent—of killing the queen, at least.

And so, surpassing my own records for dangerous, reckless behavior, I ripped off Sonya's bracelet.

"I'm Rose Hathaway."

THIRTY-THREE

CRIES AND SCREAMS FROM THE audience told me my disguise was gone.

Many eyes also went to Dimitri. Adrian had dropped that illusion too, once I'd shed mine. And, as we'd been expecting, the guardians who had been gradually taking up position around us surged forward, armed with handguns. I still thought that was cheating. Fortunately, my mother and Mikhail moved quickly into place to block our attackers and deter any gunshots.

"Don't," I snapped at Dimitri, who I knew was probably about to join our two defenders. It was crucial he and I stay perfectly still, so we weren't taken as threats. I even went as far as to hold up my arms, and—reluctantly, I suspected—Dimitri did too. "Wait. Please listen to us first."

The guardian circle was tight, with no gaps. I was pretty sure my mom and Mikhail were the only thing keeping them from shooting us then and there. Guardians would always avoid fighting other guardians if possible. Two blockers were easy to take down, though, and these guardians wouldn't wait forever. Jill and Abe suddenly moved forward, taking positions next to us. More shields. I saw one of the looming guardians grimace. Civilians complicated things. Adrian had not moved, but the fact that he was enclosed in the circle at all still made him an obstacle.

"Haul us off later if you want," I said. "We won't resist. But you have to let us talk first. We know who killed the queen."

"So do we," said one of the guardians. "Now, the rest of you . . . back away before you're hurt. These are dangerous fugitives."

"They need to talk," said Abe. "They have evidence."

Again, he pushed forward with his case, acting confidently about things he had no clue about. He was staking it all on me. I was starting to like him. It was kind of unfortunate that our evidence wasn't as 100 percent solid as I'd hoped, but as I'd said earlier . . . technicalities.

"Let them talk."

It was a new voice, but a voice I knew by heart. Lissa pushed her way through two of the guardians. They held their tight position, the immediate concern being that we not escape. This allowed her to slip through—but only so one could grab her arm and stop her from reaching us.

"They've come this far. They were right about . . . Jill." Boy, that was *not* easy for her to say with a straight face, seeing as she hadn't entirely come to terms with the issue. My imminent death was probably the only thing distracting her from the earth shattering experience of learning she had a potential sibling. She too was taking a lot on faith here, confident I was telling the truth. "You've got them. They can't go anywhere. Just let them talk. I've got evidence to support their case too."

"I'd hold off on sharing that, Liss," I said in a low voice.

Lissa still believed Daniella was the killer and wasn't going to like hearing the truth. Lissa flashed me a confused look but didn't protest.

"Let's hear them," said one of the guardians—and not just any: Hans. "After an escape like they pulled, I'd really like to know what brought them back."

Hans was helping us?

"But," he continued, "I'm sure you two will understand we'll have to restrain you before you make your great reveal."

I looked at Dimitri who had already turned to me. We'd both known what we were getting ourselves into, and honestly, this was a better scenario than I'd envisioned.

"Okay," said Dimitri. He glanced at our noble protectors. "It's okay. Let them get through."

My mom and the others didn't move right away. "Do it," I said. "Don't end up as our cellmates."

I thought for sure those loveable fools wouldn't listen to me. But Mikhail backed off first, and then the others did too, practically in sync. In a flash, guardians seized them all, leading them away. Dimitri and I stayed put, and four guardians moved in, two for Dimitri and two for me. Adrian had retreated with the others, but Lissa still stood a few feet away from us, all her trust in me.

"Get on with it," said Hans. He gripped my right arm tightly.

I met Lissa's eyes, hating what I had to say. But, no. She wasn't the one I was worried about hurting the most. Looking out into the audience, I found Christian, who was understandably watching this drama with avid attention. I had to turn away and stare at the crowd as a whole, refusing to see individual faces. Just a blur.

"I didn't kill Tatiana Ivashkov," I said. Several people grumbled doubtfully. "I didn't like her. But I didn't kill her." I glanced at Hans. "You've questioned the janitor who testified about where I was during the murder, right? And he ID'd the man who attacked Lissa as the one who paid him off to lie about where I was?" I'd learned from Mikhail that Joe had eventually admitted to taking money from the mystery Moroi, once the guardians had cornered him with the picture.

Hans frowned, hesitated, and then nodded for me to continue.

"There's no record of his existence—at least not with the guardians. But the Alchemists know who he is. They saw him at one of their facilities—acting as someone's bodyguard." My eyes fell on Ethan Moore, who stood with the guardians near the door. "A bodyguard for someone who was let in to see Tatiana the night she died: Tasha Ozera."

There was no need for any uproar from the audience this time because Tasha more than made up for it on her own. She'd been sitting next to Christian and sprang up from her chair.

"What on earth are you saying, Rose?" she exclaimed. "Are you out of your mind?"

When I'd stood there defiantly, ready to face the crowd and demand justice, I'd been full of triumph and power. Now . . . now I was just sad as I stared at someone I'd always trusted, someone who was staring back at me with so much shock and hurt.

"I wish I was . . . but it's true. We both know it is. You killed Tatiana."

Tasha's disbelief grew, tinged now with a little anger, though she still seemed to be giving me the benefit of the doubt. "I never, *never* believed you killed her—and I've fought for you on that. Why are you doing this? Are you playing on the Strigoi taint in our family? I thought you were above that kind of prejudice."

I swallowed. I'd thought getting evidence would be the hard part. It was nothing compared to revealing it. "What I'm saying has nothing to do with Strigoi. I almost wish it did. You hated Tatiana for her age law and refusal to let Moroi fight." Another memory came to me, when Tasha had learned about the secret training sessions. Tasha had been aghast with what I now suspected might have been guilt at misjudging the queen.

The crowd was riveted and stunned, but one person came to life: an Ozera I didn't know but who apparently had family solidarity on his mind. He stood up, crossing his arms defiantly. "Half this Court hated Tatiana for that law. You among them."

"I didn't have my bodyguard bribe a witness or attack Lis—Princess Dragomir. And don't pretend you didn't know the guy," I warned her. "He was your bodyguard. You were seen together." Ian's description of her when she visited St. Louis had been perfectly clear: long black hair, pale blue eyes, and scarring on one side of her face.

"Rose, I can't even believe this is happening, but if James—that was his name—did whatever you're talking about, then he acted alone. He always had radical ideas. I knew that when I hired him as outside protection, but I never thought he was capable of murder." She glanced around, looking for someone in charge, and finally settled on the Council. "I've always believed Rose was innocent. If James is the one responsible for this, then I'm more than happy to tell you whatever I know to clear Rose's name."

So, so easy. The mystery Moroi—James—was almost everywhere Tasha had been. He'd also been spotted in suspicious situations where she hadn't been—like Joe's bribery and Lissa's attack. I could save Tasha and just blame it all on him. He was already dead. Tasha and I could stay friends. She'd acted on principle, right? What was wrong with that?

Christian stood up beside her, looking at me like I was a stranger. "Rose, how can you say any of this? You *know* her. You know she wouldn't do it. Stop making a scene and let us figure out how that James guy killed the queen."

So, so easy. Blame the dead man.

"James couldn't have staked Tatiana," I said. "He had an injured hand. It takes both hands for a Moroi to stake someone. I've seen it happen twice now. And I bet if you can get a straight answer out of Ethan Moore . . ." I glanced over at the guardian who had gone pale. He could probably jump into a fight and kill without hesitation. But this kind of scrutiny? And eventual interrogation by his peers? I didn't think he'd hold up. It was probably the reason Tasha had been able to manipulate him. "James wasn't there the night Tatiana died, was he? And I don't think Daniella Ivashkov was either, despite what Princess Dragomir was told earlier. But Tasha was. She was in the queen's chambers—and you didn't report it."

Ethan looked like he wanted to bolt, but his odds of escape were about as good as mine and Dimitri's. He slowly shook his head. "Tasha wouldn't kill anyone." Not exactly the confirmation of her location I wanted—but close. The guardians would get more out of him later.

"Rose!" Christian was pissed off now. Seeing him look at me with such outrage hurt even more than Tasha's expression. "Stop it!"

Lissa took a few hesitant steps forward. I could feel in her mind that she didn't want to believe what I was saying either . . . yet she still trusted me. She thought of a controversial solution. "I know it's wrong . . . but if we used compulsion on the suspects . . ."

"Don't even suggest that!" exclaimed Tasha, turning her sharp eyes on Lissa. "Stay out of this. Your future's on the line here. A future that could make you great and achieve the things our people need."

"A future you could manipulate," I realized. "Lissa believes in a lot of the reforms you do . . . and you think you could convince her of ones she doesn't. Especially if she's with your nephew. That's why you've fought so hard to change the quorum law. You wanted her to be queen."

Christian started to step forward, but Tasha laid a restraining hand on his shoulder. It didn't stop him from speaking.

"That's idiotic. If she wanted Lissa to be queen, why make that James guy attack her?"

That was a mystery for me too, one of the holes I hadn't quite figured out. But Dimitri had. Conscious of his two guards, he shifted closer to me.

"Because no one was supposed to die." Dimitri's low, resonant voice sounded wonderful with the room's acoustics. He needed no microphone as he directed his words to Tasha. "You didn't expect a guardian to be with her." He was right, I realized. Eddie had been drafted that night under weird circumstances and only barely made it back in time to see Ambrose with Lissa. "James was probably going to fake an attack and run . . . enough to generate sympathy and more support for Vasilisa. Which it certainly did—just a little more severely."

The outrage on Tasha's face transformed to something I couldn't entirely gauge right away. She'd seemed offended at my accusations, but from Dimitri—it was more. She looked legitimately hurt. Crushed. I knew that look. I'd seen it on Adrian's face a couple hours ago.

"Dimka, not you too," she said.

Through Lissa's eyes, I watched the colors of Tasha's aura shift, burn a little brighter as she gazed at Dimitri. I could see exactly what Sonya had explained to me, how the aura showed affection.

"And that's why I took the fall," I murmured softly. No one but Dimitri and our guardians heard me.

"Hmm?" Dimitri asked.

I just shook my head. All this time, Tasha had still loved

Dimitri. I knew she had last year, when she'd made him an offer to hook up and have kids—not something a lot of dhampir men had the chance to get. He'd refused, and I thought she had accepted simply being friends with him. She hadn't. She'd still loved him. When Lissa had revealed my relationship with Dimitri to Hans, Tasha had already known. But for how long? I wasn't sure. She'd obviously known about the relationship before killing Tatiana, and putting the murder on me left Tasha free and clear *and* opened back up her chances with Dimitri.

There was no point in bringing up her personal motives for blaming me. Tatiana's murder was the real issue at stake. I just looked at Hans. "You can take me into custody, I meant it. But don't you think you've got enough to take her—and Ethan—in too?"

Hans's face was unreadable. His feelings toward me had always gone back and forth, since the day we met. Sometimes I was a troublemaker without a future. Other times I had the potential to be a leader. He'd believed I was a murderer, yet he'd still allowed me to address the crowd. He didn't really like my friends either. What would he do now?

He lifted his eyes from my face and looked to where several guardians were stationed in the audience, ready for any action. He gave a curt nod. "Take Lady Ozera. And Moore. We'll question them."

Seeing as Tasha was seated amidst other people, there was a bit of fear and panic when four guardians moved toward her. They avoided injuring other audience members as much as possible, but there was still plenty of pushing and shoving.

What came as a total surprise was how fiercely Tasha fought back. She was trained, I remembered. Not in the same way guardians were, but enough to make it hard to get a hold of her. She could kick and punch—and stake queens—and even managed to knock one guardian down.

She might actually try to fight her way out of here, I realized—though I didn't believe for an instant she could. It was too crowded and chaotic. Guardians were heading toward the fray. Terrified Moroi were trying to get *away* from the fight. Everybody seemed to be getting in everyone else's way. Suddenly, a loud *crack* echoed through the room. A gunshot. Most of the Moroi dropped to the floor, though guardians kept coming. Holding a handgun she must have seized from the guardian she'd knocked over, Tasha grabbed the first Moroi she could with her free hand. So help me, it was Mia Rinaldi. She'd been sitting near Christian. I didn't think Tasha even noticed her hostage choice.

"Don't move!" Tasha yelled at the encroaching guardians. The gun was at Mia's head, and I felt my heart stop. How had things escalated to this point? I'd never foreseen this. My task was supposed to be neat and tidy. Reveal Tasha. Put her away. Done.

The guardians froze, less because of her command and more because they were sizing up how to deal with the total threat. Meanwhile, Tasha began to slowly—very slowly—make her way toward the exit, dragging Mia along. Her progress was slow and unwieldy, thanks to all the chairs and people in the way. The delay gave the guardians time to solve this ugly dilemma. *They come first*. Mia's life—a Moroi life—was on the line. The guardians didn't want Mia killed, but a gun-toting warrior Moroi also couldn't be allowed to go free.

The thing was, Tasha wasn't the only warrior Moroi in the room. She had probably picked the worst hostage possible, and I could tell by the glint in Mia's eyes that she was not going to go quietly. Lissa realized this too. One or both of them were going to get killed, and Lissa couldn't let that happen. If she could get Tasha to look at her, she could compel her into submission.

No, no, no, I thought. I didn't need another friend involved.

Both Lissa and I saw Mia tensing to break her way out of Tasha's hold. Lissa realized she had to act now. I could feel it through the bond. I could feel her thoughts, the decision, even the way her body's muscles and nerves moved forward to get Tasha's attention. I felt it all so clearly, as if we shared the same body. I knew where Lissa would move before she even did.

"Tasha, please don't—"

Lissa sprang forward, her plaintive cry interrupted as Mia kicked back at Tasha and broke away, slipping down out of the gun's reach. Tasha, startled on two fronts, still had her gun pointed out. With Mia out of her grasp and everything happening so fast, Tasha frantically fired off a couple shots at the first threat moving toward her—which wasn't the rapidly approaching guardians. It was a slim figure in white who had shouted at Tasha.

Or, well, it would have been. Like I said, I'd known exactly where Lissa would step and what she would do. And in those precious seconds before she acted, I broke out of my captors' hold and threw myself before Lissa. Someone leapt after me, but they were too late. That was when Tasha's gun had gone off. I felt a biting and burning in my chest, and then there was nothing but pain—a pain so complete and so intense it was almost beyond comprehension.

I felt myself falling, felt Lissa catching me and yelling something—maybe to me, maybe to someone else. There was so much commotion in the room that I didn't know what had happened with Tasha. There was just me and the pain that my mind was trying to block out. The world seemed to grow quieter and quieter. I saw Lissa looking down on me, shouting something I couldn't hear. She was beautiful. Brilliant. Crowned in light . . . but there was darkness closing in around her. And in that darkness, I saw the faces . . . the ghosts and spirits that always followed me. Thicker they grew, closing in. Beckoning.

A gun. I had been brought down by a gun. It was practically comical. *Cheaters*, I thought. I'd spent my life focusing on hand-to-hand combat, learning to dodge fangs and powerful hands that could snap my neck. A gun? It was so . . . well, easy. Should I be insulted? I didn't know. Did it matter? I didn't know that either. All I knew in that moment was that I was going to die, regardless.

My vision was growing dimmer, the blackness and ghosts closing in, and I swore, it was like I could hear Robert whispering in my ear: *The world of the dead won't give you up a second time.*

Just before the light completely vanished, I saw Dimitri's face join Lissa's. I wanted to smile. I decided then that if the two people I loved most were safe, I could leave this world. The dead could finally have me. And I'd fulfilled my purpose, right? To protect? I'd done it. I'd saved Lissa, just like I'd sworn I'd always do. I was dying in battle. No appointment books for me.

Lissa's face shone with tears, and I hoped that mine conveyed how much I loved her. With the last spark of life I had left, I tried to speak, tried to let Dimitri know I loved him too and that he had to protect her now. I don't think he understood, but the words of the guardian mantra were my last conscious thought.

They come first.

THIRTY-FOUR

I DIDN'T WAKE UP IN the world of the dead.

I didn't even wake up in a hospital or some other type of medical center—which, believe me, I'd done plenty of times. No, I woke up in luxury, in a huge bedroom with gilded furniture. Heaven? Probably not with my behaviors. My canopied bed had a red-and-gold velvet comforter, thick enough to be a mattress itself. Candles flickered on a small table against the far wall and filled the room with the scent of jasmine. I had no clue where I was or how I'd gotten here, but as my last memories of pain and darkness played out in my mind, I decided the fact that I was actually breathing was good enough.

"Sleeping Beauty awakens."

That voice . . . that wonderful, honey-like voice with its soft accent. It enveloped me, and with it came the impossible truth and its full impact: I was alive. I was alive. And Dimitri was here.

I couldn't see him but felt a smile come to my lips. "Are you my nurse?"

I heard him get up from a chair and walk over. Seeing him stand over me like that reminded me of just how tall he truly was. He looked down at me with a smile of his own—one of those full and rare smiles. He had cleaned up since last I'd seen him, his brown hair tied neatly back behind his neck, though he hadn't shaved for a couple days. I tried to sit up, but he tsked me back.

"No, no, you need to lie down." Soreness in my chest told me he was right. My mind might be awake, but the rest of me was exhausted. I had no idea how much time had passed, but something told me my body had been fighting a battle—not with a Strigoi or anything like one, but with itself. A battle to stay alive.

"Then come closer," I told him. "I want to see you."

He considered this a moment and then kicked off his shoes. Turning on my side—which made me wince—I managed to wiggle over a little to make room near the bed's edge. He curled up beside me. Our faces rested on the same pillow, only a couple of inches apart as we gazed at each other.

"Is this better?" he asked.

"Much."

With his long, graceful fingers, he reached out and brushed hair from my face before tracing the edge of my cheekbone. "How are you?"

"Hungry."

He laughed softly and cautiously slid his hand down to rest on my lower back, in a sort of half-embrace. "Of course you are. I think they've only managed to get broth into you so far. Well, that and IV fluids early on. You're probably in sugar withdrawal."

I cringed. I didn't like needles or tubes and was glad I

hadn't been awake to see them. (Tattoo needles were a different matter.) "How long have I been out?"

"A few days."

"A few days . . ." I shivered, and he tugged the covers higher on me, thinking I was cold. "I shouldn't be alive," I whispered. Gunshots like that . . . they were too fast, too close to my heart. Or in my heart? I put my hand to my chest. I didn't know precisely where I'd been hit. It all ached. "Oh Lord. Lissa healed me, didn't she?" It would have taken so much spirit. She shouldn't have done that. She couldn't afford to. Except . . . why would I still feel pain? If she'd healed me, she would have gone all the way.

"No, she didn't heal you."

"No?" I frowned, unable to process that. How else would I have survived? A surprising answer came to mind. "Then . . . Adrian? He'd never . . . after how I treated him . . . no. He couldn't have . . ."

"What, you think he'd let you die?"

I didn't answer. The bullets might be long gone, but thinking of Adrian still made my heart—figuratively—ache.

"No matter how he feels . . ." Dimitri hesitated. This was a delicate topic, after all. "Well, he wouldn't have let you die. He wanted to heal you. But he didn't either."

I felt bad for thinking so little of Adrian. Dimitri was right. Adrian never would have abandoned me out of spite, but I was rapidly running out of options here. "Then who? Sonya?"

"No one," he said simply. "Well, you, I suppose."

"I . . . what?"

"People can heal without magic now and then, Rose." There was amusement in his voice, though his face stayed sober. "And your wounds . . . they were bad. No one thought you'd survive. You went into surgery, and then we all just waited."

"But why . . ." I felt very arrogant, asking the next question. "Why *didn't* Adrian or Lissa heal me?"

"Oh, they wanted to, believe me. But in the aftermath, in the chaos . . . the Court went under lockdown. They were both taken away and put under heavy protection before they could act. No one would let them near you, not when they still thought you might be a murderer. They had to be certain about Tasha first, even though her own actions were pretty damning."

It took me a moment to get past the idea that modern medicine and my body's own stamina had healed me. I'd grown too used to spirit. This didn't seem possible. As I tried to wrap my mind around the concept, the rest of Dimitri's meaning hit me. "Is Tasha . . . still alive?"

His face fell even more. "Yes. They caught her right after she shot you—before anyone else got hurt. She's detained, and more evidence has been coming in."

"Calling her out was one of the hardest things I've ever done," I said. "Fighting Strigoi was easier than that."

"I know. It was hard for me to see, hard for me to believe." There was a far-off look in his eyes, reminding me that Dimitri had known her longer than he'd known me. "But she made her choices, and all the charges against you have been dropped. You're a free woman now. More than that. A hero.

Abe's bragging that it's all his doing."

That brought my smile back. "Of course he is. I'll probably get a bill from him soon." I felt dizzy with both joy and astonishment. *A free woman*. I'd been burdened with accusations and a death sentence for what felt like years, and now . . . now it had all disappeared.

Dimitri laughed, and I wanted to stay like this forever, just the two of us, sweet and unguarded. Well—maybe not exactly this. I could've done without the pain and thick bandages I felt on my chest. He and I had had so few times alone, moments when we could really relax and openly acknowledge being in love. Things had only begun to mend between us at the end there . . . and it had almost been too late. It might still be.

"So what now?" I asked.

"I'm not sure." He rested his cheek against my forehead. "I'm just so glad . . . so glad you're alive. I've been so close to losing you so many times. When I saw you on the floor, and there was so much commotion and confusion . . . I felt so helpless. I realized you were right. We waste our lives with guilt and self-loathing. When you looked at me there at the end . . . I saw it. You did love me."

"You doubted?" I meant the words jokingly, but they came out sounding offended. Maybe I was, a little. I'd told him I loved him plenty of times.

"No. I mean, I knew then that you didn't just love me. I realized you really had forgiven me."

"There was nothing to forgive, not really." I'd told him that before too.

"I've always believed there was." He pulled back and looked at me again. "And that's what was holding me back. No matter what you said, I just couldn't believe it . . . couldn't believe you would forgive all the things I did to you in Siberia and after Lissa healed me. I thought you were deluding yourself."

"Well. It wouldn't be the first time I've done that. But no, this time I wasn't."

"I know, and with that revelation . . . in that split second that I knew you forgave me and that I really had your love, I was finally able to forgive myself too. All those burdens, those ties to the past . . . they went away. It was like . . ."

"Being free? Flying?"

"Yes. Except . . . it came too late. This sounds crazy, but while I was looking down at you, having all these thoughts coming together in my head, it was like . . . like I could see death's hand reaching for you. And there was nothing I could do. I was powerless. I couldn't help."

"You did," I told him. "The last things I saw before blacking out were you and Lissa." Well, besides the skeletal faces, but mentioning that would have killed this romantic moment. "I don't know how I survived getting shot, how I beat the odds . . . but I'm pretty sure your love—both of you—gave me the strength to fight through. I had to get back to you guys. God only knows what trouble you'd get into without me."

Dimitri had no words for that and answered instead by bringing his mouth to mine. We kissed, lightly at first, and the sweetness of the moment overpowered any pain I felt. The intensity had just barely picked up when he pulled away.

"Hey, what gives?" I asked.

"You're still recovering," he chastised. "You might think you're back to normal, but you aren't."

"This *is* normal for me. And you know, I thought with all this freedom and self-discovery and expression of our love stuff that we could finally stop with the whole Zen master wisdom and practical advice crap."

This got me an outright grin. "Roza, that's not going to happen. Take it or leave it."

I pressed a kiss to his lips. "If it means getting you, I'll take it." I wanted to kiss him again and prove who really did have greater self-control, but that damned thing called reality set in. "Dimitri . . . for real, what happens to us?"

"Life," he said easily. "It goes on. We go on. We're guardians. We protect and maybe change our world."

"No pressure," I remarked. "But what's the 'we' and 'guardians' part? I was pretty sure we were out of that career path."

"Mmm." He cupped my face, and I thought he might try another kiss. I hoped he would. "Along with our pardons, we received our guardian status again."

"Even you? They believe you're not a Strigoi?" I exclaimed.

He nodded.

"Huh. Even if I got my name cleared, my ideal future was that we'd get filing jobs near each other."

Dimitri moved closer to me, his eyes sparkling with a secret. "It gets better: you're Lissa's guardian."

"What?" I almost pulled away. "That's impossible. They'd never . . ."

"They did. She'll have others, so they probably figured it was okay to let you hang around if someone else could keep you in line," he teased.

"You're not . . ." A lump formed in my stomach, a reminder of a problem that had plagued us so long ago. "You're not one of her guardians too, are you?" It had constantly been a concern, that conflict of interest. I wanted him near me. Always. But how could we watch Lissa and put her safety first if we were worried about each other? The past was returning to torment us.

"No, I have a different assignment."

"Oh." For some reason, that made me a little sad too, even though I knew it was the smarter choice.

"I'm Christian's guardian."

This time I did sit up, doctor's orders or no. Stitches tugged in my chest, but I ignored the sharp discomfort. "But that's . . . that's practically the same thing!"

Dimitri sat up too and seemed to be enjoying my shock, which was really kind of cruel, seeing as I'd almost died and everything. "A little. But they won't be together every moment, especially with her going to Lehigh. He's not going . . . but they'll keep coming back to each other. And when they do, so will we. It's a good mix. Besides . . ." He grew serious again. "I think you've proved to everyone that you're willing to put her life first."

I shook my head. "Yeah, but no one was shooting at you. Only her." I said it lightly, but it did make me wonder: what would I do if they were both in trouble? *Trust him*, a voice in my head said. *Trust him to take care of himself. He'll do the same for you.* I eyed Dimitri, recalling a shadow in my periphery back in the ballroom. "You followed when I jumped in front of Lissa, didn't you? Who were you going for? Me or her?"

He studied me for several long seconds. He could have lied. He could have given the easy answer by saying he'd intended to push both of us out of the way—if that was even possible, which I didn't recall. But Dimitri didn't lie. "I don't know, Roza. I don't know."

I sighed. "This isn't going to be easy."

"It never is," he said, pulling me into his arms. I leaned against his chest and closed my eyes. No, it wouldn't be easy, but it would be worth it. As long as we were together, it would be worth it.

We sat like that for a long time, until a discrete knock at the half-open door broke us apart. Lissa stood in the doorway.

"Sorry," she said, her face shining with joy when she saw me. "Should have put a sock on the door. Didn't realize things were getting hot and heavy."

"No avoiding it," I said lightly, clasping Dimitri's hand. "Things are always hot with him around."

Dimitri looked scandalized. He'd never held back when we were in bed together, but his private nature wouldn't let him even hint about such matters to others. It was mean, but I laughed and kissed his cheek.

"Oh, this is going to be fun," I said. "Now that everything's out in the open."

"Yeah," he said. "I got a pretty 'fun' look from your father the other day." He gave Lissa a quick, knowing glance and then stood up. Leaning down, he kissed the top of my head. "I should go and let you two talk."

"Will you be back?" I asked as he moved to the door.

He paused and smiled at me, and those dark eyes answered my questions and so much more. "Of course."

Lissa took his spot, sitting on the bed's edge. She hugged me gingerly, no doubt worried about my injuries. She then scolded me for sitting up, but I didn't care. Happiness surged through me. I was so glad she was okay, so relieved, and—

And I had no idea how she felt.

The bond was gone. And not like during the jail escape, when she'd put the wall up. There was simply nothing there between us. I was with myself, completely and utterly alone, just as I had been years ago. My eyes widened, and she laughed.

"I wondered when you'd notice," she said.

"How . . . how is this possible?" I was frozen and numb. The bond. The bond was *gone*. I felt like my arm had been amputated. "And how do you know?"

She frowned. "Part of it's instinct . . . but Adrian saw it. That our auras aren't connected anymore."

"But how? How could that happen?" I sounded crazy and desperate. The bond couldn't be gone. It couldn't.

"I'm not entirely sure," she admitted, her frown deepening. "I talked about it a lot with Sonya and, uh, Adrian. We think when I brought you back the first time, it was spirit alone that held you back from the land of the dead and that kept you tied to me. This time . . . you nearly died again. Or maybe you did for a moment. Only, you and your body fought your way back. It was *you* who got out, with no help from spirit. And once that happened . . ." She shrugged. "Like I said, we're only guessing. But Sonya thinks once your own strength broke you away, you didn't need any help being pulled back from death. You did it on your own. And when you freed yourself of spirit, you freed yourself from me. You didn't need a bond to keep you with the living."

It was crazy. Impossible. "But if . . . if you're saying I escaped the land of the dead, I'm not, like, immortal or anything, am I?"

Lissa laughed again. "No, we're certain of that. Sonya explained it, saying anything alive can die, and as long as you've got an aura, you're alive. Strigoi are immortal but not alive, so they don't have auras and—"

The world spun. "I'll take your word for it. I think maybe I do need to lie down."

"That's probably a good idea."

I gently eased myself onto my back. Desperately needing distraction from what I'd just learned—because it was still too surreal, still impossible to process—I eyed my surroundings. The lush room was bigger than I'd previously realized. It kept going and going, branching into other rooms. It was a suite. Maybe an apartment. I could just make out a living room with leather furniture and a flat screen TV. "Where are we are?"

"In palace housing," she replied.

"*Palace* housing? How'd we end up here?"

"How do you think?" she asked dryly.

"I . . ." I couldn't work my mouth for a moment. I needed no bond to realize what had happened. Another impossibility had occurred while I'd been out of it. "Crap. They had the election, didn't they? They elected you queen, once Jill was there to stand in for your family."

She shook her head and almost laughed. "My reaction was a little stronger than 'crap,' Rose. Do you have any idea what you've done?"

She looked anxious, stressed, and totally overwhelmed. I wanted to be serious and comforting for her sake . . . but I could feel a goofy grin spreading over my face. She groaned.

"You're happy."

"Liss, you were meant for this! You're better than any of the other candidates."

"Rose!" she cried. "Running for queen was supposed to be a diversion. I'm only *eighteen*."

"So was Alexandra."

Lissa shook her head in exasperation. "I'm so sick of hearing about her! She lived centuries ago, you know. I think people died when they were thirty back then. So she was practically middle-aged."

I caught hold of her hand. "You're going to be great. It doesn't matter how old you are. And it's not like you have to call meetings and analyze law books all on your own, you know. I mean, *I'm* sure not going to do any of that, but there are other smart people. Ariana Szelsky didn't make the last test, but you know she'll help if you ask her to. She's still on the Council, and there are others you can rely on. We just have to find them. I believe in you."

Lissa sighed and looked down, her hair hanging forward in a curtain. "I know. And part of me is excited, like this will restore my family's honor. I think that's what's saved me from a total breakdown. I didn't want to be queen, but if I have to . . . then I'm going to do it right. I feel like . . . like I have the world at my fingertips, like I can do so much good. But I'm so afraid of messing up too." She looked up sharply. "And I'm not giving up on the rest of my life either. I guess I'm going to be the first queen in college."

"Cool," I said. "You can IM with the Council from campus. Maybe you can command people to do your homework."

She apparently didn't think the joke was as funny as I did. "Going back to my *family*. Rose . . . how long did you know about Jill?"

Damn. I'd known this part of the conversation would eventually be coming. I averted my eyes. "Not really that long. We didn't want to stress you until we knew it was real," I added hastily.

"I can't believe . . ." She shook her head. "I just can't believe it."

I had to go on her tone, not the bond. It was so strange, like losing one of my key senses. Sight. Hearing. "Are you upset?"

"Of course I am! How can you be surprised?"

"I figured you'd be happy . . ."

"Happy to find out my dad cheated on my mom? Happy to have a sister I hardly know? I've tried to talk to her, but . . ." Lissa sighed again. "It's so weird. Almost weirder than suddenly being queen. I don't know what to do. I don't know what to think of my father. And I sure as hell don't know what to do with her."

"Love them both," I said softly. "They're your family. Jill's great, you know. Get to know her. Be excited."

"I don't know if I can. I think you're more of a sister to me than she'll ever be." Lissa stared off at nothing. "And of all people . . . I was convinced for so long that there was something going on between her and Christian."

"Well, out of all the worries in your world, that's one you can let go because it's not true." But within her comment was something dark and sad. "How *is* Christian?"

She turned back to me, her eyes full of pain. "He's having a hard time. I am too. He visits her. Tasha. He hates what she did, but . . . well, she's still his family. It hurts him, but he tries to hide it. You know how he is."

"Yeah." Christian had spent a good portion of his life masking dark feelings with snark and sarcasm. He was a pro at fooling others about how he truly felt.

"I know he'll be better in time . . . I just hope I can be there for him enough. So much is happening. College, being queen . . . and always, always, there's spirit there, pressing down on me. Smothering me."

Alarm shot through me. And panic. Panic over something far worse than not knowing what Lissa was feeling or where she was. Spirit. I was afraid of spirit—and the fact that I couldn't fight it for her. "The darkness . . . I can't absorb it anymore. What will we do?"

A twisted smile crossed her lips. "You mean, what will *I* do. It's my problem now, Rose. Like it always should have been."

"But, no . . . you can't. St. Vladimir—"

"Isn't me. And you can protect me from some things but not all."

I shook my head. "No, no. I can't let you face spirit alone."

"I'm not exactly alone. I talked to Sonya. She's really good at healing charms and thinks there's a way to keep myself in balance."

"Oksana said the same thing," I recalled, feeling hardly reassured.

"And . . . there's always the antidepressants. I don't like them, but I'm queen now. I have responsibilities. I'll do what I have to. A queen gives up everything, right?"

"I guess." I couldn't help feeling frightened. Useless. "I'm just so worried about you, and I don't know how to help you anymore."

"I told you: you don't have to. I'll protect my mind. Your job's to protect my body, right? And Dimitri will be around too. It'll all be okay."

The conversation with Dimitri came back to me. *Who were you going for? Me or her?*

I gave her the best smile I could. "Yeah. It'll all be okay."

Her hand squeezed mine. "I'm so glad you're back, Rose. You'll always be part of me, no matter what. And honestly . . . I'm kind of glad you can't see my sex life anymore."

"That makes two of us." I laughed. No bond. No magical

attachment. It was going to be so strange, but really . . . did I need it? In real life, people formed bonds of another nature. Bonds of love and loyalty. We would get through this. "I'll always be there for you, you know. Anything you need."

"I know," she said. "And actually . . . I need you for something now . . ."

"Name it," I said.

She did.

THIRTY-FIVE

I WISHED LISSA HAD "needed" me to go take out an army of Strigoi. I would have felt more comfortable with that than what she needed to do now: meet with Jill to discuss the coronation. Lissa wanted me there for support, as a kind of go-between. I wasn't able to walk that well yet, so we waited another day. Lissa seemed glad for the delay.

Jill was waiting for us in a small room I'd never expected to see again: the parlor where Tatiana had berated me for moving in on Adrian. It had been a pretty bizarre experience at the time, seeing as Adrian and I hadn't actually been involved back then. Now, after everything that had occurred between him and me, it just felt . . . strange. Confusing. I still didn't know what had happened to him since Tasha's arrest.

Walking in there, I also felt terribly . . . alone. No, not alone. Uninformed. Vulnerable. Jill sat in a chair, her hands folded in her lap. She stared straight ahead with an unreadable face. Beside me, Lissa's own features were equally blank. She felt . . . well, that was the thing. I didn't know. *I didn't know.* I mean, I could tell she was uncomfortable, but there were no thoughts in my head to tip me off. I had no specifics. Again, I reminded myself that the rest of the world worked like this. You functioned alone. You did your best to manage strange situations without the magical insight of another person. I'd never realized how much I'd taken the thoughts of even just one other person for granted.

The one thing I felt sure of was that both Lissa and Jill were freaked out by each other—but not by me. That was why I was here.

"Hey, Jill," I said, smiling. "How are you?"

She snapped out of whatever thoughts had been occupying her and jumped up from the chair. I thought that was strange, but then it made sense. Lissa. You rose when a queen entered the room.

"It's okay," said Lissa, stumbling over her words a little. "Sit." She took a seat opposite Jill. It was the biggest chair in the room—the one Tatiana had always sat in.

Jill hesitated a moment, then shifted her gaze back to me. I must have provided some encouragement because she returned to her chair. I sat in one beside Lissa, wincing as a small pain tightened in my chest. Worry for me momentarily distracted Jill from Lissa.

"How are you feeling? Are you okay? Should you even be out of bed?" The cute, rambling nature. I was glad to see it again.

"Fine," I lied. "Good as new."

"I was worried. When I saw what happened . . . I mean, there was so much blood and so much craziness and no one knew if you'd pull through . . ." Jill frowned. "I don't know. It was all so scary. I'm so glad you're okay."

I kept smiling, hoping to reassure her. Silence fell then. The room grew tense. In political situations, Lissa was the expert, always able to smooth everything over with the right words. I was the one who spoke up in uncomfortable scenarios, saying the things that shocked others. The things no one wanted to hear. This situation seemed like one that required her diplomacy, but I knew it was on me to take charge.

"Jill," I said, "we wanted to know if you'd be willing to, well, take part in the coronation ceremony."

Jill's eyes flicked briefly to Lissa—still stone-faced—and then back to me. "What does 'take part' mean, exactly? What would I have to do?"

"Nothing hard," I assured her. "It's just some formalities that are usually done by family members. Ceremonial stuff. Like you did with the vote." I hadn't witnessed that, but Jill had apparently only had to stand by Lissa's side to show family strength. Such a small thing for a law to hinge on. "Mostly, it's about being on display and putting on a good face."

"Well," mused Jill, "I've been doing that for most of this week."

"I've been doing it for most of my life," said Lissa.

Jill looked startled. Again, I felt at a loss without the bond. Lissa's tone hadn't made her meaning clear. Was it a challenge to Jill—that the girl hadn't faced nearly what Lissa had? Or was it supposed to be sympathy for Jill's lack of experience?

"You'll . . . you'll get used to it," I said. "Over time."

Jill shook her head, a small and bitter smile on her face. "I don't know about that."

I didn't either. I wasn't sure how one handled the kind of situation she'd been dropped into. My mind rapidly ran through a list of more meaningless, kind things I could say, but Lissa finally took over.

"I know how weird this is," she said. She determinedly met Jill's green eyes—the only feature the sisters shared, I decided. Jill had the makings of a future Emily. Lissa carried a mix of her parents' traits. "This is weird for me too. I don't know what to do."

"What do you want?" asked Jill quietly.

I heard the real question. Jill wanted to know if Lissa wanted *her*. Lissa had been devastated by the death of her brother . . . but a surprise illegitimate sibling was no substitute for Andre. I tried to imagine what it would be like to be in either girl's place. I tried and failed.

"I don't know," admitted Lissa. "I don't know what I want."

Jill nodded, dropping her gaze, but not before I caught sight of the emotion playing across her face. Disappointment—yet, Lissa's answer hadn't entirely been unexpected.

Jill asked the next best thing. "Do you want . . . do you *want* me to be in the ceremonies?"

The question hung in the air. It was a good one. It was the reason we'd come here, but did Lissa actually want this? Studying her, I still wasn't sure. I didn't know if she was just following protocol, trying to get Jill to play a role expected among royalty. In this case, there was no law that said Jill had to do anything. She simply had to exist.

"Yes," said Lissa at last. I heard the truth in her words, and something inside of me lightened. Lissa didn't just want Jill for the sake of image. A part of Lissa wanted Jill in her life—but managing that would be difficult. Still, it was a start, and Jill seemed to recognize that.

"Okay," she said. "Just tell me what I need to do." It occurred to me that Jill's youth and nervousness were deceptive. There were sparks of bravery and boldness within her, sparks that I felt certain would grow. She really was a Dragomir.

Lissa looked relieved, but I think it was because she'd made a tiny step of progress with her sister. It had nothing to do with the coronation. "Someone else will explain it all. I'm not really sure what you do, to be honest. But Rose is right. It won't be hard."

Jill simply nodded.

"Thank you," said Lissa. She stood up, and both Jill and I rose with her. "I . . . I really appreciate it."

That awkwardness returned as the three of us stood there. It would have been a good moment for the sisters to hug, but even though both seemed pleased at their progress, neither was ready for that. When Lissa looked at Jill, she still saw her father with another woman. When Jill looked at Lissa, she saw her life completely turned upside down—a life once shy and private now out there for the world to gawk at. I couldn't change her fate, but hugging I could do. Heedless of my stitches, I put my arms around the young girl.

"Thanks," I said, echoing Lissa. "This'll all be okay. You'll see."

Jill nodded yet again, and with no more to discuss, Lissa

and I moved toward the door. Jill's voice brought us to a halt.

"Hey . . . what happens after the coronation? To me? To us?"

I glanced at Lissa. Another good question. Lissa turned toward Jill but still wasn't making direct eye contact. "We'll . . . we'll get to know each other. Things'll get better."

The smile that appeared on Jill's face was genuine—small, but genuine. "Okay," she said. There was hope in that smile too. Hope and relief. "I'd like that."

As for me, I had to hide a frown. I apparently could function without the bond because I could tell, with absolute confidence, that Lissa wasn't exactly giving the whole truth. What wasn't she telling Jill? Lissa *did* want things to be better, I was certain, even if she wasn't sure how. But there was something . . . something small that Lissa wasn't revealing to either of us, something that made me think Lissa didn't actually believe things would improve.

Out of nowhere, a strange echo from Victor Dashkov rang through my mind about Jill. *If she has any sense, Vasilisa will send her away*.

I didn't know why I remembered that, but it sent a chill through me. The sisters were both mustering smiles, and I hastily did as well, not wanting either to know my concerns. Lissa and I left after that, heading back toward my room. My little outing had been more tiring than I expected, and as much as I hated to admit it, I couldn't wait to lie down again.

When we reached my room, I still hadn't decided if I should ask Lissa about Jill or wait to get Dimitri's opinion. The decision was taken from me when we found an unexpected visitor waiting: Adrian.

He sat on my bed, head tipped back as though he was completely consumed by studying the ceiling. I knew better. He'd known the instant we approached—or at least when Lissa approached.

We stopped in the doorway, and he finally turned toward us. He looked like he hadn't slept in a while. Dark shadows hung under his eyes, and his cute face was hardened with lines of fatigue. Whether it was mental or physical fatigue, I couldn't say. Nonetheless, his lazy smile was the same as ever.

"Your majesty," he said grandly.

"Stop," scoffed Lissa. "You should know better."

"I've never known better," he countered. "*You* should know that."

I saw Lissa start to smile; then she glanced at me and grew serious, realizing this was hardly let's-have-fun-with-Adrian time.

"Well," she said uneasily, not looking very queenly at all. "I've got some things to do." She was going to bolt, I realized. I'd gone with her for her family chat, but she was going to abandon me now. Just as well, though. This conversation with Adrian had been inevitable, and I'd brought it on myself. I had to finish this on my own, just as I'd told Dimitri.

"I'm sure you do," I said. Her face turned hesitant, as though she was suddenly reconsidering. She felt guilty. She was worried about me and wanted to stand by me. I lightly touched her arm. "It's okay, Liss. I'll be okay. Go."

She squeezed my hand in return, her eyes wishing me good luck. She told Adrian goodbye and left, closing the door behind her.

It was just him and me now.

He stayed on my bed, watching me carefully. He still wore the smile he'd given Lissa, like this was no big deal. I knew otherwise and made no attempts to hide my feelings. Standing still made me tired, so I sat down in a nearby chair, nervously wondering what to say.

"Adrian—"

"Let's start with this, little dhampir," he said cordially. "Was it going on before you left Court?"

It took me a moment to follow that abrupt Adrian conversation format. He was asking if Dimitri and I had gotten back together before my arrest. I shook my head slowly.

"No. I was with you. Just you." True, I'd been a mess of emotions, but my intentions had been firm.

"Well. That's something," he said. Some of his pleasantness was starting to slip. I smelled it then, ever so faintly: alcohol and smoke. "Better some rekindling of sparks in the heat of battle or quest or whatever than you cheating right in front of me."

I shook my head more urgently now. "No, I swear. I didn't—nothing happened then . . . not until—" I hesitated on how to phrase my next words.

"Later?" he guessed. "Which makes it okay?

"No! Of course not. I . . ."

Damn it. I'd screwed up. Just because I hadn't cheated

on Adrian at Court didn't mean that I *hadn't* cheated on him later. You could phrase it however you wanted, but let's face it: sleeping with another guy in a hotel room was pretty much cheating if you had a boyfriend. It didn't matter if that guy was the love of your life or not.

"I'm sorry," I said. It was the simplest and most appropriate thing I could say. "I'm sorry. What I did was wrong. I didn't mean for it to happen. I thought . . . I really thought he and I were done. I was with you. I wanted to be with you. And then, I realized that—"

"No, no—stop." Adrian held up a hand, his voice tight now as his cool façade continued to crumble. "I really do *not* want to hear about the great revelation you had about how you guys were always meant to be together or whatever it was."

I stayed silent because, well, that kind of had been my revelation.

Adrian ran a hand through his hair. "Really, it's my fault. It was there. A hundred times there. How often did I see it? I knew. It kept happening. Over and over, you'd say you were through with him . . . and over and over, I'd believe it . . . no matter what my eyes showed me. No matter what my heart told me. My. Fault."

It was that slightly unhinged rambling—not that nervous kind of Jill's, but the unstable kind that worried me about how close he was getting to the edge of insanity. An edge I might very well be pushing him toward. I wanted to go over to him but had the sense to stay seated.

"Adrian, I—"

"I loved you!" he yelled. He jumped up out of his chair so quickly I never saw it coming. "I loved you, and you destroyed me. You took my heart and ripped it up. You might as well have staked me!" The change in his features also caught me by surprise. His voice filled the room. So much grief, so much anger. So unlike the usual Adrian. He strode toward me, hand clasped over his chest. "I. Loved. You. And you used me the whole time."

"No, no. It's not true." I wasn't afraid of Adrian, but in the face of that emotion, I found myself cringing. "I wasn't using you. I loved you. I still do, but—"

He looked disgusted. "Rose, come *on*."

"I mean it! I do love you." Now I stood up, pain or no, trying to look him in the eye. "I always will, but we're not . . . I don't think we work as a couple."

"That's a bullshit breakup line, and you know it."

He was kind of right, but I thought back to moments with Dimitri . . . how well we worked in sync, how he always seemed to get exactly what I felt. I meant what I'd said: I did love Adrian. He was wonderful, in spite of all his flaws. Because, really, who didn't have flaws? He and I had fun together. There was affection, but we weren't matched in the way Dimitri and I were.

"I'm not . . . I'm not the one for you," I said weakly.

"Because you're with another guy?"

"No, Adrian. Because . . . I don't. I don't know. I don't . . ." I was fumbling, badly. I didn't know how to explain what I felt, how you could care about someone and love hanging out with them—but still not work as a couple. "I don't balance you like you need."

"What the hell does that mean?" he exclaimed.

My heart ached for him, and I was so sorry for what I'd done . . . but this was the truth of it all. "The fact that you have to ask says it all. When you find that person . . . you'll know." I didn't add that with his history, he'd probably have a number of false starts before finding that person. "And I know this sounds like another bullshit breakup line, but I really would like to be your friend."

He stared at me for several heavy seconds and then laughed—though there wasn't much humor in it. "You know what's great? You're *serious*. Look at your face." He gestured, as though I actually could examine myself. "You really think it's that easy, that I can sit here and watch your happy ending. That I can watch you getting everything you want as you lead your charmed life."

"Charmed!" The guilt and sympathy warring within me got a little kick of anger. "Hardly. Do you know what I've gone through in the last year?" I'd watched Mason die, fought in the St. Vladimir's attack, been captured by Strigoi in Russia, and then lived on the run as a wanted murderess. That didn't sound charmed at all.

"And yet, here you are, triumphant after it all. You survived death and freed yourself from the bond. Lissa's queen. You got the guy and your happily ever after."

I turned my back to him and stalked away. "Adrian, what do you want me to say? I can apologize forever, but there's nothing else I can do here. I never wanted to hurt you; I can't say that enough. But the rest? Do you really expect me to be sad about everything else having worked out? Should I wish I was still I was accused of murder?"

"No," he said. "I don't want you to suffer. Much. But the next time you're in bed with Belikov, stop a moment and remember that not everyone made out as well as you did."

I turned back to face him. "Adrian, I never—"

"Not just me, little dhampir," he added quietly. "There's been a lot of collateral damage along the way while you battled against the world. I was a victim, obviously. But what about Jill? What happens to her now that you've abandoned her to the royal wolves? And Eddie? Have you thought about him? And where's your Alchemist?"

Every word he slung at me was an arrow, piercing my heart more than the bullets had. The fact that he'd referred to Jill by her name instead of "Jailbait" carried an extra hurt. I was already toting plenty of guilt about her, but the others . . . well, they were a mystery. I'd heard rumors about Eddie but hadn't seen him since my return. He was clear of James's death, but killing a Moroi—when others still thought he might have been brought in alive—carried a heavy stigma. Eddie's previous insubordination—thanks to me—also damned him, even if it had all been for "the greater good." As queen, Lissa could only do so much. The guardians served the Moroi, but it was customary for the Moroi to step back and let the guardians manage their own people. Eddie wasn't being dismissed or imprisoned . . . but what assignment would they give him? Hard to say.

Sydney . . . she was an even greater mystery. *Where's your Alchemist?* The goings-on of that group were beyond me, beyond my world. I remembered her face that last time I'd seen her, back in the hotel—strong but sad. I knew she and the other Alchemists had been released since then, but her expression had said she wasn't out of trouble yet.

And Victor Dashkov? Where did he fit in? I wasn't sure. Evil or not, he was still someone who'd suffered as a result of my actions, and the events surrounding his death would stay with me forever.

Collateral damage. I'd brought down a lot of people with me, intentionally or no. But, as Adrian's words continued sinking into me, one of them suddenly gave me pause.

"Victim," I said slowly. "That's the difference between you and me."

"Huh?" He'd been watching me closely while I'd considered the fates of my friends and was caught off guard now. "What are you talking about?"

"You said you were a victim. That's why . . . that's why ultimately, you and I aren't matched for each other. In spite of everything that's happened, I've never thought of myself that way. Being a victim means you're powerless. That you won't take action. Always . . . always I've done something to fight for myself . . . for others. No matter what."

I'd never seen such outrage on Adrian's face. "That's what you think of me? That I'm lazy? Powerless?"

Not exactly. But I had a feeling that after this conversation, he would run off to the comfort of his cigarettes and alcohol and maybe whatever female company he could find.

"No," I said. "I think you're amazing. I think you're strong. But I don't think you've realized it—or learned how to use any of that." And, I wanted to add, I wasn't the person who could inspire that in him.

"This," he said, moving toward the door, "was the last thing I expected. You destroy my life and then feed me inspirational philosophy."

I felt horrible, and it was one of those moments where I wished my mouth wouldn't just blurt out the first thing on my mind. I'd learned a lot of control—but not quite enough.

"I'm just telling you the truth. You're better than this . . . better than whatever it is you're going to do now."

Adrian rested his hand on the doorknob and gave me a rueful look. "Rose, I'm an addict with no work ethic who's likely going to go insane. I'm not like you. I'm not a superhero."

"Not yet," I said.

He scoffed, shook his head, and opened the door. Just before leaving, he gave me one more backward glance. "The contract's null and void, by the way."

I felt like I'd been slapped in the face. And in one of those rare moments, Rose Hathaway was rendered speechless. I had no witty quips, no elaborate explanations, and no profound insight.

Adrian left, and I wondered if I'd ever see him again.

THIRTY-SIX

I'D OFTEN DREAMED ABOUT waking up with Dimitri, waking up in a way that was . . . ordinary. Sweet. Not because we were hastily trying to catch sleep before fighting our next foe. Not because we were recovering from sex we had to hide, sex laden with baggage and myriad complications. I just wanted to wake up together, in his arms, and have it be a good morning.

Today was that day.

"How long have you been awake?" I asked drowsily. My head was on his chest, and I was wrapped against him as best as I could manage. My wounds were healing rapidly but still had to be babied. We'd found a few creative workarounds last night. Sunlight now spilled in through the windows, filling my bedroom with gold.

He was watching me in that quiet, solemn way of his, with those dark eyes that were so easy to get lost in. "A little while," he admitted, lifting his gaze to the sunlight-filled window. "I think I'm still on a human schedule. Either that, or my body just wants to be up when the sun is. Seeing it is still amazing to me."

I stifled a yawn. "You should have gotten up."

"I didn't want to disturb you."

I ran my fingers over his chest, sighing in contentment. "This is perfection," I said. "Is every day going to be like this?"

Dimitri rested his hand on my cheek and then moved down, tipping my chin up. "Not every day but most days."

Our lips met, and the warmth and light in the room paled compared to what burned inside me. "I was wrong," I murmured when we finally broke the long, languid kiss. "*This* is perfection."

He smiled, something he was doing an awful lot of lately. I loved it. Things would probably change once we were back out in the world. Even if we were together now, Dimitri's guardian side would always be there, ready and watchful. But not right now. Not in this moment.

"What's the matter?" he asked me.

With a start, I realized I'd begun to frown. I tried to relax my face. Unbidden, Adrian's words had come back to me, that the next time I was in bed with Dimitri, I should think about others who weren't so lucky.

"Do you think I ruin lives?" I asked.

"What? Of course not." The smile changed to shock. "Where would you get that idea?"

I shrugged. "There are just a lot of people whose lives are still kind of a mess. My friends, I mean."

"True," he said. "And let me guess. You want to fix everyone's problems."

I didn't answer.

Dimitri kissed me again. "Roza," he said, "it's normal to want to help the people you love. But you can't fix everything."

"It's what I do," I countered, feeling a little petulant. "I protect people."

"I know, and that's one of the reasons I love you. But for now, you only have to worry about protecting one person: Lissa."

I stretched out against him, noticing my injuries really were constantly improving. My body would be able to do all sorts of things soon. "I suppose that means we can't stay in bed all day?" I asked hopefully.

"Afraid not," he said, lightly running his fingertips along the curve of my hip. He never seemed to get tired of studying my body. "They come first."

I brought my mouth back toward his. "But not for a little while."

"No," he agreed. His hand slid up to the back of my neck, tangling in my hair as he drew me closer. "Not for a little while."

I had never attended a royal coronation before, and honestly, I hoped I never would again. I only wanted there to be this one queen ruling in my lifetime.

Eerily, the coronation was kind of a reverse of Tatiana's funeral. What was the old saying? *The queen is dead. Long live the queen.*

Custom dictated the monarch-to-be spend the first part of the coronation day at the church, presumably to pray for guidance, strength, and all that spiritual stuff. I wasn't sure what custom did in the case of atheist monarchs. Probably they faked it. With Lissa, who was fairly devout, I knew that wasn't a problem and that she was probably legitimately praying she'd do a good job as queen.

After the vigil, Lissa and a huge procession walked back across Court to the palace building, where the crowning took place. Representatives from all the royal families joined her, along with musicians who were playing much more cheerful tunes than they had for Tatiana's procession. Lissa's guardians—she had a fleet now—walked with her. I was among them, wearing my finest black and white, including the red collar marking me as a royal guardian. Here, at least, was a notable difference from the funeral. Tatiana had been dead; her guardians were for show. Lissa was very much alive, and even if she'd won the Council's vote, she still had enemies. My colleagues and I were on high alert.

Not that you'd think we needed to be, not with the way the onlookers cheered. All those who had camped out during the trials and election had stayed for this fanfare, and more had shown up still. I wasn't sure when there'd ever been this many Moroi in one place.

After the long and winding walk, Lissa made it to the palace building and then waited in a small antechamber adjacent to what served as the Moroi throne room. The throne room was almost never used for modern business, but every once in a while—like a new queen being sworn in—the Moroi liked to pull out ancient traditions. The room was small and couldn't hold all the witnesses from outside. It couldn't even hold the entire procession. But, the Council and highest-ranking royal members were there, along with some select invitees of Lissa's.

I stood off to the side, watching the glamour unfold. Lissa hadn't made her grand entrance yet, so there was a low hum of conversation. The room was all green and gold, having been given a thorough and fast remodel in the last few days, since custom dictated the ruling family's colors dominate the throne room. The throne itself sat high against the far wall, accessible by steps. Carved of wood I could no longer identify, I knew the throne had been carried around the world by Moroi monarchs for centuries. People were lining up in carefully assigned positions, preparing for when Lissa would enter last. I was studying one of the new chandeliers, admiring how realistic the "candles" in it looked. I knew they were electric, but the craftsmen had done amazing work. Technology masked in old-world glory, just as the Moroi liked. A small nudge drew my attention away.

"Well, well, well," I said. "If it isn't the people responsible for unleashing Rose Hathaway on the world. You've got a lot to answer for."

My parents stood before me in their typical and wildly contrasting clothing. My mom wore the same guardian outfit I did, a white shirt with black slacks and jacket. Abe was . . . well, Abe. He had on a black pinstripe suite, with a black dress shirt underneath. Splashed against the darkness was a bright, lemon-yellow paisley tie. A matching handkerchief peeped out one of the jacket's pockets. Along with his gold earrings and chains, he also wore a black fedora, which was a new addition to his outlandish wardrobe. I guess he wanted to go all out for an event like this, and at least it wasn't a pirate hat.

"Don't blame us," said my mother. "We didn't blow up half of Court, steal a dozen cars, call out a murderer in the middle of a crowd, or get our teenage friend crowned queen."

"Actually," said Abe, "I *did* blow up half of Court."

My mom ignored him, her expression softening as she studied me with her guardian eyes. "Seriously . . . how are you feeling?" I'd seen them only briefly in the days since waking up, just enough for us all to check in on each other. "You're doing an awful lot of standing today. And I've already told Hans not to put you on active duty for a while."

It was one of the most motherly things I'd ever heard her say. "I . . . I'm fine. A lot better. I could go on active duty right now."

"You will do no such thing," she said, in exactly the tone she'd use giving orders to a troop of guardians.

"Stop coddling her, Janine."

"I'm not coddling her! I'm looking out for her. You're spoiling her."

I looked back and forth at them in amazement. I didn't know if I was witnessing a fight or foreplay. I wasn't thrilled about either option. "Okay, okay, just back off you guys. I survived, right? That's what counts."

"It is," said Abe. He suddenly seemed very fatherly, which weirded me out even more than my mom's behavior. "And despite the property damage and string of broken laws left in your wake, I'm proud of you." I suspected that secretly, he was proud of me *because* of those things. My cynical interior commentary was brought to a halt when my mom concurred.

"I'm proud too. Your methods were . . . not ideal, but you did a great thing. Great *things*, really. Finding both the murderer and Jill." I noticed her careful wording of "the murderer." I think it was still hard for all of us to accept the truth about Tasha. "A lot will change because of Jill."

All of us looked over at the foot of the throne. Ekaterina stood on one side, ready with the book of royal vows. The other side was where members of the monarch's family stood—but only one lone person was there. Jill. Someone had done a great job of cleaning her up. Her curly hair had been elaborately styled and pinned, and she wore a knee-length sheath dress with a wide portrait style collar, just barely showing off her shoulders. The dress's cut made the most of her lanky figure, and the dark green satin looked great with her features. She was standing straight, chin high, but there was anxiety all over her, made more obvious by her being so conspicuously alone.

I glanced back at Abe, who met my eyes expectantly. I had a lot of questions for him, and he was one of the few who might tell me the truth. The decision was: which question to ask? It was like having a genie. I'd only get so many wishes.

"What will happen to Jill?" I asked at last. "Will she just go back to school? Are they going to train her to be a princess?" Lissa couldn't be both princess and queen, so her old title went to the next-oldest member of her family.

Abe didn't answer for several moments. "Until Lissa can get the law changed—and hopefully, she will—Jill is all that allows her to keep her throne. If something happens to Jill,

Lissa will no longer be queen. So. What would you do?"

"I'd keep her safe."

"Then you have your answer."

"It's kind of a broad one," I said. "'Safe' means a lot of things."

"Ibrahim," warned my mother. "Enough. This isn't the time or place."

Abe held my gaze a bit longer and then broke into an easy smile. "Of course, of course. This is a family gathering. A celebration. And look: here's our newest member."

Dimitri had joined us and wore black and white like my mother and me. He stood beside me, conspicuously not touching. "Mr. Mazur," he said formally, nodding a greeting to both of them. "Guardian Hathaway." Dimitri was seven years older than me, but right then, facing my parents, he looked like he was sixteen and about to pick me up for a date.

"Ah, Belikov," said Abe, shaking Dimitri's hand. "I'd been hoping we'd run into each other. I'd really like to get to know you better. Maybe we can set aside some time to talk, learn more about life, love, et cetera. Do you like to hunt? You seem like a hunting man. That's what we should do sometime. I know a great spot in the woods. Far, far away. We could make a day of it. I've certainly got a lot of questions I'd like to ask you. A lot of things I'd like to tell you too."

I shot a panicked look at my mother, silently begging her to stop this. Abe had spent a good deal of time talking to Adrian when we dated, explaining in vivid and gruesome detail exactly how Abe expected his daughter to be treated. I did not want Abe taking Dimitri off alone into the wilderness, especially if firearms were involved.

"Actually," said my mom casually. "I'd like to come along. I also have a number of questions—especially about when you two were back at St. Vladimir's."

"Don't you guys have somewhere to be?" I asked hastily. "We're about to start."

That, at least, was true. Nearly everyone was in formation, and the crowd was quieting. "Of course," said Abe. To my astonishment, he brushed a kiss over my forehead before stepping away. "I'm glad you're back." Then, with a wink, he said to Dimitri: "Looking forward to our chat."

"Run," I said when they were gone. "If you slip out now, maybe they won't notice. Go back to Siberia."

"Actually," said Dimitri, "I'm pretty sure Abe *would* notice. Don't worry, Roza. I'm not afraid. I'll take whatever heat they give me over being with you. It's worth it."

"You really are the bravest man I know," I told him.

He smiled, his eyes falling on a small commotion at the room's entrance. "Looks like she's ready," he murmured.

"I hope I am," I whispered back.

In true grandiose fashion, a herald brought the room to attention. Perfect silence fell. You couldn't even hear breathing.

The herald stepped back from the door. "Princess Vasilisa Sabina Rhea Dragomir."

Lissa entered, and even though I'd seen her less than half an hour ago, I still caught my breath. She was wearing a formal gown but had once again dodged sleeves. No doubt the dressmaker had had a fit. The dress was floor-length, with a skirt of silk and chiffon layers that moved and fluttered around Lissa as she strode forward. The fabric was the same jade as her eyes, as was the dress's top, with a halter collar covered in emeralds that gave the illusion of a necklace. Matching emeralds covered the dress's belt, and bracelets completed the display. Her hair was worn long, brushed out to gleaming, platinum perfection, an aura unto itself.

Christian walked beside her, a sharp contrast with his black hair and dark suit. Customs were being modified significantly today since a family member normally would have escorted Lissa, but . . . well, she was kind of running out. Even I had to admit he looked amazing, and his pride and love for her shone on his face—no matter what troubled feelings stirred within him over Tasha. *Lord Ozera*, I remembered. I had a feeling that title would become more and more important now. He led Lissa to the base of the throne and then joined the Ozera delegation in the crowd.

Ekaterina made a small gesture to a large satin pillow on the floor in front of the steps. "Kneel."

There was the briefest hesitation on Lissa's part, one I think only I noticed. Even without the bond, I was so attuned to her mood and tiniest actions that I could pick up on these things. Her eyes had gone to Jill. Lissa's expression didn't change, and it was so strange not to know her feelings. I could make some educated guesses. Uncertainty. Confusion.

Again—the pause was only a moment long. Lissa knelt, artfully spreading her skirts around her as she did. Ekaterina had always seemed so frail and wizened in that testing room, but as she stood there with the ancient Moroi coronation book, I could sense a power still within the former queen.

The book was in Romanian, but Ekaterina translated it effortlessly as she read aloud, beginning with a speech about what was expected of a monarch and then going to the vows Lissa had to swear to.

"Will you serve?"

"Will you protect your people?"

"Will you be just?"

There were twelve in all, and Lissa had to answer "I will" three times to each one: in English, in Russian, and in Romanian. Not having the bond to confirm her feelings was still so strange, but I could see on her face that she meant every word she said. When that part finished, Ekaterina cued Jill forward. Since I'd last noticed the girl, someone had given her the crown to hold. It had been custom-made for Lissa, a masterpiece of white and yellow gold intertwined with emeralds and diamonds. It complemented her outfit beautifully, and, I noticed with a start, Jill did too.

Another tradition was that the monarch was crowned by a family member, and this was what Jill had been saved for. I could see her hands tremble as she laid the bejeweled wonder on her sister's head, and their gazes met briefly. A flash of troubled emotions swirled in Lissa's eyes once more, gone quickly as Jill stepped back and the weight of the ceremony took precedence.

Ekaterina held out her hand to Lissa. "Rise," she said. "You will never kneel to anyone again." Holding Lissa's hand, Ekaterina turned so that they both faced the rest of us in the room. With a voice startling for her small body, Ekaterina declared, "Queen Vasilisa Sabina Rhea Dragomir, first of her name."

Everyone in the room—except Ekaterina—dropped to their knees, heads bowed. Only a few seconds passed before Lissa said, "Rise." I'd been told this was at the monarch's discretion. Some new kings and queens enjoyed making others kneel for a long time.

Paperwork followed, which we all watched dutifully as well. Basically, it was Lissa signing to say she'd been made queen while Ekaterina and a couple witnesses signed that they'd seen Lissa made queen. Three copies were on the ornate paper Moroi royalty so loved. One was plain white letterhead, which would go to the Alchemists.

When the signing was done, Lissa took her place on the throne, and seeing her ascend those stairs was breathtaking, an image that would stay with me for the rest of my life. The room broke out into cheers and clapping as she settled into the ornate chair. Even the guardians, who normally stayed so deadly serious, joined in the applause and celebration. Lissa smiled at everyone, hiding whatever anxiety she felt.

She scanned the room, and her grin broadened when she saw Christian. She then sought me out. Her smile for him had been affectionate; mine was a bit humorous. I smiled back, wondering what she would say to me if she could.

"What's so funny?" asked Dimitri, looking down at me with amusement.

"I'm just thinking about what Lissa would say if we still had the bond."

In a very bad breach of guardian protocol, he caught a hold of my hand and pulled me toward him. "And?" he asked, wrapping me in an embrace.

"I think she'd ask, 'What have we gotten ourselves into?'"

"What's the answer?" His warmth was all around me, as was his love, and again, I felt that completeness. I had that missing piece of my world back. The soul that complemented mine. My match. My equal. Not only that, I had my life back—my *own* life. I would protect Lissa, I would serve, but I was finally my own person.

"I don't know," I said, leaning against his chest. "But I think it's going to be good."

First and foremost, thank you to all of the loyal and enthusiastic readers around the world who have accompanied Rose and me throughout the series. I couldn't have made this journey without you and hope you'll continue to enjoy the many Moroi and dhampir adventures to come.

Thank you also to all of the friends and family who have supported me—especially my husband, who continually amazes me with his patience, love, and ability to live with the ups and downs of a "creative type." A special shout-out also goes to Jesse McGatha for creating the forest riddle, something I could never have come up with, let alone solve.

And as always, I'm grateful to the publishing folks who work behind the scenes to make these books happen: Jim McCarthy—my agent, occasional therapist, and non-stop advocate; Lauren Abramo, who keeps finding more countries I've never heard of to send Rose to; Jessica Rothenberg and Ben Schrank, editors extraordinaire whom I'm pretty sure forego food and sleep to perfect these books; and publicist Casey McIntyre, who organizes my tours and interviews, with great care to arrange them around my hair appointments.

A final thanks to all the others who work on this series at Penguin Books, Dystel & Goderich Literary Management, and my international publishers. There are far too many of you to list, but all of you are essential in telling Rose's story. Thank you.